# STEALING
# THUNDER

# STEALING THUNDER

## ALINA BOYDEN

ACE
New York

ACE
Published by Berkley
An imprint of Penguin Random House LLC
penguinrandomhouse.com

Copyright © 2020 by Alina Boyden
Penguin Random House supports copyright. Copyright fuels creativity, encourages diverse
voices, promotes free speech, and creates a vibrant culture. Thank you for buying an authorized
edition of this book and for complying with copyright laws by not reproducing, scanning, or
distributing any part of it in any form without permission. You are supporting writers and
allowing Penguin Random House to continue to publish books for every reader.

ACE is a registered trademark and the A colophon is a trademark of
Penguin Random House LLC.

Library of Congress Cataloging-in-Publication Data

Names: Boyden, Alina, author.
Title: Stealing thunder / Alina Boyden.
Description: First edition. | New York: Ace, 2020.
Identifiers: LCCN 2019037400 (print) | LCCN 2019037401 (ebook) |
ISBN 9781984805461 (paperback) | ISBN 9781984805478 (ebook)
Subjects: GSAFD: Fantasy fiction.
Classification: LCC PS3602.O9339 S74 2020 (print) |
LCC PS3602.O9339 (ebook) | DDC 813/.6—dc23
LC record available at https://lccn.loc.gov/2019037400
LC ebook record available at https://lccn.loc.gov/2019037401

First Edition: May 2020

Printed in the United States of America
1   3   5   7   9   10   8   6   4   2

Cover art by Greg Ruth
Cover design by Adam Auerbach
Map design by Soraya Corcoran
Book design by Laura K. Corless

*This book is dedicated to the trans girl who is reading it in secret.*
*You are beautiful, you are loved, and you are not alone.*

# AUTHOR'S NOTE

*Stealing Thunder* is a product of both my own life history and my friendships with trans women in South Asia. Growing up in a conservative household in Texas, I lived with the daily fear that if anyone knew who I really was on the inside, they would abandon me. To cope, I turned to fantasy novels for company, as did many other young trans women of my generation. At that time there were no fantasy novels with trans women characters, let alone with trans women protagonists, making it impossible for me to find trans heroines and role models. So, after my transition in 2002, I set about creating some.

Over the next fifteen years I wrote more than a hundred manuscripts, and while I didn't find a publisher, I did start a new career in anthropology. At the time I wrote *Stealing Thunder*, I was pursuing a PhD in cultural anthropology, having left my PhD research in archaeology behind in order to work more closely with the Indian and Pakistani trans women I'd befriended as a fellow transgender rights activist. Learning about these women's lives was a healing experience for me. Not only was it comforting to know that other trans women in other countries shared much of my life history, and much of my understanding of the world, but these women also provided an incredible model of what a visible, unapologetic transgender community could look like. The hijra (or khwaja sira, depending on their country of origin) community, of which many of my friends are members, is a centuries-old network of individuals assigned male at birth with transfeminine gender identities who live together, both for safety and for camaraderie. This community has been a visible part of South Asian culture for much of recorded history, and my encounters with it were a source of inspiration for this novel. If you'd like to learn more about this special community of transgender persons, I highly recommend reading their own accounts of their experiences. Several autobiographies of hijras have been recently translated into English and are widely available from major booksellers.

As for my book, I never expected that *Stealing Thunder* would be read by anyone but my mom and my trans women friends in South Asia and America. By the time I wrote it I had stopped trying to interest publishers in my work. I was content with telling stories that appealed to me and to my select group of readers. But *Stealing Thunder* was different from my previous books. It ignited something in my readers that my previous novels hadn't. It thrilled the trans women who read it, both American and South Asian, and they demanded that I try to get it published. So I did. Now, I'm proud to say that *Stealing Thunder* will be the first adult fantasy novel with a trans woman main character, written by a trans woman, ever to be published by a mainstream press in the United States.

While my greatest dream as an author is to create transgender heroines to inspire the next generation of trans women, it is my sincere hope that my cisgender (non-transgender) readers will also see something of themselves in Razia and will be inspired by the story of a world-conquering transgender princess (even if she is a fictional one). For cis audiences, the trans experience is often framed as a foreign one, and when trans characters appear in film and literature, we are almost invariably glimpsed from the outside looking in. I hope that inhabiting a trans woman's mind will help to demystify us and will lead cis readers to discover that we are actually far more similar than we are different.

While *Stealing Thunder* is the first book of its kind, I know in my heart that it will not be the last. Soon, a new generation of trans girls will pick up their pens (or more likely take out their keyboards) and share their stories with the world. Until then, I hope that this book provides them some small inspiration and reminds them that they can do and be anything, that their transness is not a disability or a limitation, but a beautiful, natural, and normal part of the human condition, and one as worthy of celebration as any other.

*Alina Boyden*

KINGDOM OF RAKHA

Kunduz

DURANIA

LAHANUR
SUBAH

Rampur

KHANATE OF KHUZDAR

Lahanur

GHAZIABAD
SUBAH

SUBAH

Gelak

Ghaziabad

YANG

Surna River

Jamuna River

Lakhnauti

Shalkot

Mirpur

Indhu River

ZINDH SUBAH

Nizam

Gulf
of
Arakan

Shikarpur

Jaigarh

NINA
SUBAH

Bikampur

Kadiro

REGISTAN

Gwalipur

Rajkot

GWALIPUR SUBAH

Khambhat

MAHISAGAR
SULTANATE

VIRAJENDRA EMPIRE

Devasamudra

Kalikota

Sea
of

Daryastan

DARYASTAN

@SosayaCorcoran

Like all creatures of the desert, I had learned to sleep off the worst of the day's heat and to enjoy the cooling breezes that came with the night. All around me, the city of Bikampur was springing to a second life, invigorated by the same chill air that rippled across the surface of my own skin and threatened to snatch my dupatta from my head. My ears were filled with the sounds of men and women conversing from their canopied rooftops, their low murmurs of conversation mingling with the cries of street vendors and the rattling of their carts on the limestone-paved streets. There was nothing that stirred my heart quite like the magic of a desert night, and I followed close on the heels of our guru, Varsha, as she led us out of the courtyard's front gate.

"I heard that Govind Singh's haveli has gems embedded in the walls," Sakshi said to me, drawing me out of my thoughts. She was baiting me, fighting to keep a grin off her face.

"So?" I asked, giving her the shrug she expected, showing her just how unimpressed I was with such a paltry display of wealth.

Once upon a time, when I was young and foolish, I'd made such comments in earnest, but those days were long past, and now it was a game I played with her and no one else.

Sakshi rolled her eyes with the drama of a performer and groaned. "Well, we weren't all born in the lap of luxury like you, Razia. Who was your father again? The sultan of Nizam?"

My heart skipped a beat. Did she remember? I hadn't mentioned him in years. I swallowed the knot of fear in my throat that always rose up at the mention of my homeland and kept my voice light. "No one so famous. But my father's mahal did have gems embedded in the walls, and his throne was pure gold." I hoped the details would distract her from my father's precise identity. I trusted Sakshi with my life, but I'd never been able to make her understand the danger I was in, and I didn't want to. She wouldn't be able to sleep if she knew the truth.

"And you rode your first zahhak when you were four . . ." Sakshi heaved a wistful sigh. Her whole life, she'd always wanted to ride a zahhak, but had never got within a hundred paces of one. I relaxed a little as she stared off into the distance, no doubt imagining herself atop an azure-winged thunder zahhak. This was what she'd been after—a daydream. Sometimes I wondered if that was what she thought my past was—nothing more than a bedtime story I told myself to feel important.

"Enough of that nonsense," Varsha chided, and I knew it was for my benefit. Unlike Sakshi, she hadn't forgotten who my father was, and she was clever enough to know the dangers my identity might bring down upon our heads if anyone were to find out. "Razia, I don't care if you grew up in a royal palace or a gutter, our clients don't like arrogant girls. So you'll act impressed, even if you think Govind Singh is a camel herder with delusions of grandeur."

There was more truth to Varsha's words than she would have

openly admitted. Govind Singh was a wealthy man, to be sure, but he had made most of that fortune investing in camels, or more particularly, in camel-laden caravans, which ferried goods from the interior, across the trackless desert, to the port cities of the south and the west. It was a far cry from the ideal for a Registani nobleman; they were supposed to be ferocious warriors who enriched themselves through force of arms.

But whatever I thought about Govind Singh, my guru was right: I couldn't afford to be arrogant. I was a hijra, and while I belonged to a wealthy dera, my social standing was below even the most debased laborer. That was the bargain I had struck to live as my true self. There were times when I regretted it—nights when I missed my family, and my zahhak, Sultana, and the palace, but they were surprisingly few and far between. As difficult as life could be here, at least my life was my own, and at least I was me.

"Hot samosas! Hot jalebis!" a street vendor cried into the darkness, as he shoved his cart in the direction of the bazaar.

"Want to go to the bazaar after we're finished with Govind Singh?" Sakshi asked me, her eyes lingering over the samosa walla's cart, stories of gem-studded palaces forgotten in the wafting aromas of fried pastry dough and spiced potatoes.

"If Razia does her job well, she won't be going home tonight," Varsha reminded her—and me too. She glanced in my direction. "And you will do your job well, won't you, dear?"

"Of course, Ammi," I replied. I even managed to sound cheerful about it, though inwardly I was dreading the night to come. I didn't know much about Govind Singh, but nobody had ever told me that he was handsome. Still, he was rich, so that was something. If I did well, I might earn myself a pretty bauble or a few silver rupees. It wasn't much, but it would go toward the money I was saving up to start my own dera someday. Then, I would take on young girls like me and train them in the fine art of making men desperate for their affections. Not that there was much art to it. I found that a wiggle of my hips and an alluring glance usually sufficed.

The houses around us began to shift as we made our way into the Neelam Mandi, the wealthiest part of the city. Gone were the mud-brick buildings in which the bulk of the city's populace dwelled. Now, the gradually widening streets were lined with fine havelis of sandstone, their facades covered in intricately chiseled floral motifs. They stretched up above us, higher and higher as we walked, the tallest being five or six stories above the hustle and bustle of the street.

"When I'm a guru, I'm going to have a dera like that one," Sakshi declared, gesturing to a tall building of pink sandstone, whose ground floor was ringed all around with arched doorways. The doors stood open, letting in the night air, but each entrance was guarded by a servant in a cheap white kurta wielding a sizable club.

"With the way you spend money?" Varsha laughed. "Sakshi, you'll be lucky if you can afford a hut on the outskirts of town."

"I've just had a lot of expenses this month is all, Ammi," she replied, looking to me for support.

"Fortunately, she has a few years to save up," I said, which brought a smile to Sakshi's face, though I thought we both knew that there wasn't a chance in the world that she would ever set foot in a house as beautiful as that one without being hired by its owners to do so.

"Not that it matters," I told Sakshi, resting my arm across her shoulders. "Ammi has big plans for our dera, and a rising tide lifts all boats."

"So I do," Varsha agreed, but her tone told me not to say anything more, not out on the streets where people could hear.

I didn't need the warning. I wasn't stupid. If anyone found out that I was robbing our clients, I would be the one facing the punishment, and I wasn't in any hurry to lose my head to the executioner's sword just yet. Fortunately, I didn't have time to linger on that line of thought, as we had arrived at Govind Singh's home.

His haveli dominated one whole side of the Mahal Bazaar, its pink sandstone walls towering over those of its neighbors. The stone flowers and vines that snaked across the building's facade were so delicately wrought that but for their color one could have been forgiven for believing that they were living, growing plants. A pair of men stood guard at the doors. Their colorful silk kurtas and gleaming armor set them apart from the common servants who served as the watchmen in the houses of the lesser nobles, as did the spears and shields they carried in place of the ubiquitous wooden clubs.

For hijras like us, approaching these armed men would have been a dangerous prospect had we not been hired by Govind Singh. Even so, I noticed the way that Sakshi's eyes made a careful study of the ground at the men's feet, while she stood back and let Varsha handle matters, and I wasn't any braver. Four years of life as a hijra had stolen some of the princely confidence from my bearing, and I stood near my sister with eyes properly downcast.

Our guru showed no such trepidation. She clapped once, in the peculiar manner of our kind, and said, "I am Varsha Khan, and I have brought my girls to perform for Govind-Sahib."

The men leered at us, paying particular attention to me, as I was dressed like a dancer in a bright silk lehenga, with a dupatta that was nearly transparent. To Varsha, the more senior of the two men said, "Govind-Sahib is expecting you." At his pronouncement, the junior guard opened the gate to admit us into the courtyard, as if he were the guardian of a maharaja's fortress, and not the doorman for a vainglorious spice trader.

Govind Singh's courtyard doubled as a beautiful garden. Rose-

bushes lined the walkways, and mango trees stood proudly alongside them, their branches drooping beneath the weight of nearly
ripened fruit. A marble fountain bubbled in the center of the
courtyard, and perched atop it was the reason Varsha had chosen
me to dance tonight instead of one of my older sisters: a golden
statue of a peacock, with gemstones in place of its feathers. It was
as big as my torso and must have been far heavier. Stealing it
wasn't going to be easy, but I liked a challenge.

A eunuch came forward to greet us. Though he shared our
hairless faces and slender physiques he wasn't like us hijras in any
way that mattered. We viewed nirvan, or castration, as a gift, and
dressed as women and took alchemical medications to maintain a
properly feminine appearance, but he was one of the poor unfor-
tunates who had been sold into slavery and had been mutilated
without his consent. The difference was made manifest by the
way he wore men's clothing and a man's turban, and stood with an
exaggerated posture to emphasize his height, as if he were afraid
of being seen as small or weak. It was apparent too, from our social positions. We were hired courtesans, and he was the respectable chamberlain of a fine home.

I had found that such men typically despised us. They resented
the fact that we enjoyed the very same procedure that had ruined
their own lives, and they were infuriated by the way other men
referred to them as "hijras" to mock their emasculation. But if
this particular eunuch hated us, it wasn't plain on his face as he
bowed his head and said, "Govind-Sahib is expecting you. Please,
follow me, Varsha-Sahiba."

"Thank you, Rawal-Sahib," Varsha replied, following the eunuch toward a stairwell at the far end of the courtyard. "Are you
well?"

"Quite well, thank you," he assured her, though he didn't in-
quire as to Varsha's health. He just marched briskly ahead of us,

barely glancing over his shoulder long enough to say, "Govind-Sahib is hosting his party on the roof today. I trust that won't cause you any undue difficulties?"

"Not at all," she said. "Sometimes I think Razia is graceful enough to dance on air."

Rawal-Sahib snorted in response to that, but he was polite enough not to say anything insulting, which put him ahead of half the servitors I'd dealt with in the havelis of wealthy men.

We mounted the stairs, following him up flight after flight. Govind Singh's haveli was eight stories tall, and everyone but me was breathing hard by the time we got to the top. I had climbed buildings taller than this one without the benefit of stairs, so I was mostly just concerned about sweating off my makeup. Fortunately, the higher we climbed, the cooler the air became, and that kept my perspiration at bay. By the time we reached the top, I could scarcely believe it was a summer evening rather than a winter one. It was no wonder Govind Singh had built his house so tall.

Cushions had been laid out all around the roof in a horseshoe-shaped pattern, with the two ends pointing at the stairwell. Tall candelabras of shining silver held dozens of candles, which sent cascades of light over the pink stones. Men sat on fine silk cushions, communal hookahs placed in front of them.

My eyes had only the briefest moment to take in the scene before a stirring of movement drew the crowd's attention to the far end of the roof, where a mound of scales and feathers heaved a sigh and stopped my heart. Curled up in the corner was a zahhak. I hadn't been so close to one since I'd fled home four years before, and the sight of her flame-colored scales and wings brought back a flood of emotions that I'd fought for years to repress.

"Is that . . ." Sakshi whispered.

"A fire zahhak." Reverence filled my voice as I nodded to the thick, armor-like scales that covered the beast's beaked snout, her sinuous neck, and the flesh of her enormous, muscular shoulders. She kept her feathered wings tucked close to her body, their plumage the color of fire itself. For the moment, she was lying placidly on the warm tiles of the haveli's roof, but when she stood, those huge wings would double as front legs, lifting her shoulders a dozen feet off the ground.

"How can you tell it's a fire zahhak?" Sakshi asked, startling me out of the spell I had fallen under.

"Her coloration, to begin with," I replied, my voice dazed and distant, my mind filled with memories of the wind in my face and the world at my feet. It was hard to focus on dull description in the face of those racing thoughts, but it was safer, because my memories never came without fear.

"Fire zahhaks are creatures of the deserts of the world," I continued. "They're always colored like a Registani sunset."

"*Her* coloration? How do you know she's a female?"

"A male would be smaller," I said, and it was a struggle to keep an exasperated tone out of my voice at having to explain something so obvious. Sometimes I had to remind myself that Sakshi wasn't my real sister, that she hadn't fled with me from the palace, that four years ago, a poor village girl like her would have had her tongue torn from her skull for daring to speak to me. I shouldn't have felt so close to her, not after the way I'd been raised, but we hijras were bonded in ways outsiders could never understand.

"The males of all zahhak species are too small for serious flying," I told her, keeping my voice gentle, "but the females are just the right size."

"And how does a hijra come to know so much about zahhaks?" a man asked, drawing our attention away from the animal.

I turned my head, annoyed at having been interrupted in my lecture by some backward noble from Bikampur, and by the insulting tone with which he'd asked his question. My eyes landed on the speaker, and I forgot my irritation in a flash. He was a well-built, handsome man with a carefully trimmed beard that shone like obsidian in the candlelight. His eyes were the warm, almost liquid brown of a perfectly cooked jalebi. He wore a kurta of the finest green silk, shot through with golden threads, woven into patterns of fire-breathing zahhaks roaming the skies. On his head, in place of a turban, he wore a pair of goggles that would keep the wind from his eyes as he flew through the air. This zahhak must have belonged to him.

"Forgive me, my lord, I don't think we've been introduced," I said, bowing to him with perfect grace, unable to disguise the interest in my voice.

He stood up, and he was much taller than I'd expected, his presence more imposing than I'd been prepared for, as he came forward and addressed me properly. "My name is Arjun Agnivansha. And what is your name, my dear?"

My breath caught in my throat. Arjun Agnivansha was the prince of Bikampur, the only son of the Maharaja Udai Agnivansha. I forced a smile and said, "My name is Razia Khan, my prince."

He smiled back, his lively amber eyes taking me in from head to toe. "And how does a pretty little thing like you come to know so much about zahhaks?"

"Razia was a zahhak rider before she became a hijra, my prince," Sakshi said, as proudly as if it had been her own accomplishment.

I was mortified at the prospect of having to craft some lie to disguise my past before the prince of Bikampur himself, but fortunately a portly man with a slender mustache distracted us all from Sakshi's words with a loud guffaw. He sat at the center of the horseshoe of cushions, and he slapped his knee with mirth, bellowing, "Have you brought me a jester in place of a dancer tonight, Varsha?"

"You'll have to forgive Sakshi, Govind-Sahib," Varsha replied. "She has quite the imagination. But, I assure you, as a sitar player she has no equal in Bikampur."

"Let's put that claim to the test!" He clapped his hands and said, "Come, Prince Arjun, sit with me, and let's find out if Varsha's girls are worthy of their reputation."

Prince Arjun smiled at me and went back to his place beside Govind, which was a huge relief. Servants immediately began plying him with fine wine. If I was lucky, he'd be too drunk to remember Sakshi's words by the time the performance was over.

While the men prepared themselves, we took our places in front of them. Varsha laid out her tabla drums, and Sakshi handed me my bells before unwrapping her sitar.

"Are those zahhak bells?" Arjun asked, eyeing them intently.

I smiled at him just as sweetly and innocently as I could manage. "I wouldn't know, my prince. I don't have quite the imagination Sakshi does."

My answer seemed to please him, and it drew a bark of laughter from Govind Singh. As it happened, they were zahhak bells, small ones used for training the young beasts before they were old enough to ride. They had the benefit, however, of being very loud, and very clear, and they added a distinctive sound to my dance when I tied them around my ankles. It was a sound that reminded me of home, and of long days hiking through the hills with a young zahhak on my fist in pursuit of game, though it had been many years since my Sultana had been small enough for such things.

When I had finished tying on my bells, and Sakshi had finished arranging her sitar, she began to play. I raised an eyebrow at the song she'd chosen, and she smiled back. It was a love song, of course, but one in which the woman doing the singing compares herself to a zahhak, and the man she loves is compared to the beast's master.

With no choice but to perform the dance, I sat in the center of the roof, my knees drawn up to my chest, my gauze-thin silk dupatta draped over almost the whole of my body, mimicking a baby zahhak in her egg. As Varsha pounded out a beat on the tabla, and a cascade of notes spilled from Sakshi's sitar, I began to sing, "Before I could breathe, I knew your voice."

Slowly, as I repeated the lines again and again, I began to pull free of my dupatta, to expose first my hands, and then my arms, and then my face. Already, the men were leaning forward on their cushions eagerly. I stomped my foot on the ground, rattling my bells, in imitation of the crack of the egg finally splitting open. I stood up in a rush, like the explosive wriggle of a baby zahhak pulling herself free from her eggshell prison. The second verse of the song tumbled from my lips, the couplets expounding on the virtues of my master's face—the first thing I had glimpsed in all the world.

The technical part of the dance began then, a constant drumming of my feet and swaying of my hips. I tried to mimic the undulating motions of a flying zahhak as I made my way across the floor, straight toward Prince Arjun. My dancing mistress had taught me to focus on a single man during this dance, to make him feel like he was my master, so I fixed my eyes on Arjun and was pleased to see his fixed on mine in return. I stamped my feet, ringing my bells in time with the beats of Varsha's drums and the lively chords thrumming from Sakshi's sitar. For a long, teasing moment, I swayed before Prince Arjun, looking at him the way Sultana used to look at me in those first few days after hatching, as if there was nothing in all the world but him, and I would follow him to the ends of the earth. Then, with mincing steps, I retreated from him, my dupatta billowing in the air behind me, obscuring my face from view.

Growing up, dancing had not been an occupation fit for a young prince, but I'd always loved it. There was something about the way I moved to the music that made me feel at home in a body that had always felt like a foreign prison. Now, having been trained by the finest dancing instructors in Bikampur, it was easy to get carried away by the music and the spirit of the dance. The movements came without thinking. It was very much like the connection between a rider and his zahhak—a connection I sorely missed. Even now, after so many years away from home, Sultana haunted my dreams. I would have given my right arm for the chance to fly with her in the skies above Nizam one last time.

I channeled that sense of loss into my dancing and my voice, and I watched Prince Arjun, keenly aware of every slight movement of his head, of every flicker of his eyes. He was gnawing hungrily on his lower lip, but his untouched food and wine suggested that his appetite had nothing to do with his stomach.

The little girl in me who still loved fairy tales wondered what it would be like to be loved by a prince, but the jaded courtesan I had become knew better. If I played my cards right, I could have the wealthiest client in the whole city before the night was out, but that was all it could ever be. I would enjoy his company for a few hours, and when he finally fell asleep, I would steal the peacock Varsha wanted. Come the morrow, I would be back home in the dera, ready to do it all over again. However much I wished it were otherwise, I couldn't let myself forget that there are no fairy-tale endings for hijras.

I spun in mad circles across the floor, my skirt billowing out, revealing teasing hints of my calves, as Sakshi's playing reached its crescendo and the beats of Varsha's tablas roared in my ears. At the song's moment of climax, I threw myself to my knees before

Arjun, my body swaying from side to side in imitation of the sinuous movements of a zahhak's neck. I lowered my head and brought my dupatta back in front of my face as the last notes reverberated through the still night air.

My performance was met with cries of "Wah!" and "Mashkhuda!" but it was Prince Arjun's reaction I was waiting for. It was difficult to discern the meaning behind his smile. Was he pleased? Was he just being polite? He still hadn't remembered his wine or the men around him. That boded well.

"Come and sit with me, dear," Prince Arjun said, gesturing to the cushion beside his. "I want to hear all about your zahhak."

I frowned as I puzzled for a moment over whether he was teasing me or he had really believed Sakshi's story. Ultimately, it didn't matter; he had made a request, and my duty was to fulfill it. So I bowed my head and murmured, "Yes, my prince," moving as gracefully as I could to his side, sinking slowly to the cushion beside his own.

"You're a Nizami, aren't you?" he asked me.

My hackles went up at the question and my heart fluttered in my chest, but I managed to keep a smile plastered over my face to hide the terror the question stirred in me. "How did you know?"

"With such fair skin, and green eyes like a thunder zahhak, what else could you be?"

My cheeks burned a little, and I felt a little rush of pleasure at having been compared favorably to the most beautiful zahhaks in all the world, but mostly I was just relieved that he didn't know who I was. He couldn't know. I'd been too careful for that, but the fear always lurked just beneath the surface of my heart, and the bare mention of my homeland was always enough to send it roaring through my body once more.

Prince Arjun stared at me for quite a long time before he asked, "So, you rode a thunder zahhak, did you?"

I found his smile insufferably inscrutable. Was he mocking me? Was he serious? I was half tempted to lie, because the threat of being discovered by my father was so much worse than a prince's scorn, but I didn't think he'd really believe me anyway, so I decided to answer him honestly. "That's right. I rode with my father atop his zahhak as a child. I think from that moment forward I was never happy a moment in my life that I wasn't flying."

"Did you have a zahhak of your own?"

I still couldn't tell if this was all a joke to him or not, and part of me was waiting for him to reveal the punch line, but he just stared at me without saying anything more, leaving me with no choice but to answer him. After all, if I failed to engage him in conversation, if I failed to please him, then Varsha would be furious with me. She'd force me to do the housework and to stay home while my sisters danced and earned pretty baubles. I was in my prime earning years, so I could survive such punishments once or twice, but any more than that and I might find myself on the streets, or living as a glorified servant for my more talented sisters. I couldn't bear the thought of serving Jaskaur's smug face while she wore silks and gems. The mere prospect of it was enough to make me throw caution to the wind.

"When I was six, my father gave me an egg from the mountains of Rakha," I said, hoping that my knowledge of thunder zahhaks would intrigue Arjun, though I couldn't keep a note of wistfulness out of my voice as I recalled that day so long ago, when I'd cradled a hot egg the size of a cannonball in my lap, knowing that someday it would become a beautiful zahhak. "She hatched when I was seven, and I was riding her by the time I was ten. Her name was Sultana. Her scales were like polished sapphires, and her wings were cobalt above and molten gold below. By day, we were inseparable, and she slept at the foot of my bed each night."

As soon as the words were out of my mouth, I regretted them.

I couldn't bear the mockery that I was sure would follow. I missed Sultana so much, missed how safe she'd made me feel when I was a child. After I ran away, there wasn't a night that I didn't wake up terrified not to find my great feathered guardian watching over me. Even now, years later, there were nights when I reached my hand down to pat a familiar snout, only to snatch cold air.

"I've never heard of a zahhak rider running off to become a hijra," Arjun said, and his tone made it plain that he doubted my story.

I bristled at that, offended, though I knew it was a foolish reaction. However irritating it was to be thought of as a liar and a fraud, being believed would have been far more dangerous. And anyway, this wasn't my first night on the job. I knew better than to bare my soul to a client. I forced myself to smile, to put a lilting, teasing tone in my voice, as I asked, "My prince, are you not named for a zahhak rider who ran off to become a hijra, or have I misremembered the story of Arjun the Archer?"

His cheeks reddened a little, and he said, "That's different. If I remember that story correctly, he was cursed to become a hijra."

"So was I," I replied, with more venom in my voice than I'd intended.

"You were?" he asked, his eyes widening. "Who cursed you?"

"God," I answered, as that was the whole truth of it. How else could I explain my incurable desire to be a woman? What but a curse would have been powerful enough to convince me to run away from my father's palace, to leave behind my beloved zahhak, to trade the life of a prince for that of a beggar? It defied all rational explanation.

"And what did you do to so offend your god?" he asked.

"If I knew that, my prince, I would be back home with my father at this very moment," I declared, because even after everything that had passed between us, there was a part of me that would never stop seeking his approval.

"Why not go back now and ask for his forgiveness?"

I smiled at the naïveté of that. "My prince, if I went home now, my father would kill me, if the shame of seeing me this way didn't strike him dead first."

"Well, it pleases me to see you this way." I was surprised to hear the huskiness in his voice, the yearning. I'd thought I was making a mess of things with all this talk of lost zahhaks and regret. That wasn't normally a winning recipe in my line of work.

"On that we can agree, my prince." I took the opportunity to pick up one of the silver-wrapped sweets from the tray in front of him and held it out to him like I intended to feed him. He leaned forward and opened his mouth, and I laid the sweet on his tongue, but I'd only just placed it when he snapped his teeth shut. I jerked my hand away with a startled gasp.

He laughed around the sweet as he chewed it. "Well, she's got the reflexes of a zahhak rider," he said to Govind Singh.

The older man laughed longer and louder than the joke deserved. He gave Arjun a thump on the back. "I'm glad she pleases you, boy."

"Very much so," Arjun replied, his amber eyes lingering on my face.

I stared right back at him, but I was careful not to smile. I'd found that men didn't much care for a girl who knew how pretty she was, who understood men's desires, because that would lead them inexorably to the all-too-correct conclusion that such a girl would know how to manipulate their affections for her own gain. Still, it was hard not to let the possibilities run through my mind. If I could make the maharaja's son my client, I could rebuild the life that I'd been forced to give up to live as my true self. Wealth and power would be mine for the asking. It was a seductive idea, but a dangerous one too. Princes are like wild zahhaks—they have their pick of prey, they're difficult to trap, and they're deadly if they know they're being hunted.

"When you told me you had hired hijras to dance for us, Uncle, I envisioned a gang of bearded ruffians in lehengas," Arjun said, which hurt more than I wanted to admit. He smiled at me, faintly amused, and for an instant that made me even angrier, but as his grin widened, I realized my irritation was visible in the pout of my lips. He was teasing me deliberately, poking holes in the sensual mask I was always so careful to construct in front of the men I served.

"Varsha's girls? Ruffians?" Govind laughed and shook his head. "No, they're elegant creatures, women in all but name."

"So they are," Arjun agreed, his eyes roving over my chest, the bare flesh hidden only by the diaphanous silk of my dupatta. I stretched my pout into a smile on hearing that, like I was totally unaware of the game he was playing, and I thought I caught a twinkling in his amber eyes in response.

"I'd never bring low-class dancers into my home, hijra or otherwise. I'm a cautious man in whom I hire to serve me," Govind continued. "I have to be these days, what with the rash of thefts sweeping the city."

My ears perked up at the mention of thefts, though I was careful to look disinterested. Still, the thought that they were talking about my handiwork right in front of me quickened my heart. If they ever found out that I was the thief, I would die a terrible death, but judging from the looks they were sending my way, I thought they hadn't the slightest clue. I didn't particularly care for stealing, but I relished the feeling of outsmarting a group of men who were so certain that they were better than me—especially Prince Arjun Agnivansha, who was still looking smug over his triumph in our earlier exchange.

"I heard about that," said another man. "Just last week, the necklace Suresh Satav bought for his wife was stolen."

"Probably a light-fingered servant," Prince Arjun muttered as I refilled his wine cup for him.

"Perhaps," Govind allowed, "though if it was one of Suresh's servants, he's been a very busy man. Two weeks before that, a rare statue was stolen from Narendra Chadakar's altar."

I smiled a little. That job had been particularly tough. I'd had to scale the walls of his home, then take the stairs all the way back down to the first floor without being spotted. And then I'd had to take the idol and do the whole thing over again. Of course, that little escapade was nothing compared to what it would take to get the peacock. Tonight's work would be a real test of my skills.

"Have there been more such thefts?" Arjun asked.

"Many more," said Govind.

"And no one's been caught?"

"No one even knows who to blame."

"Well, I'll catch him, then," Arjun declared, and it was very hard to keep a smug look off my own face. The poor boy hadn't the slightest clue who he had sitting beside him. Ruffian in a lehenga indeed.

"You?" Govind asked. "And how do you propose to do that?"

"I'll make nightly patrols with Padmini, of course," he said, gesturing to his zahhak. "If the thief is out there, we'll find him."

He sounded so confident that I pitied him a little, but even if he didn't have much chance of catching me, his declaration brought the same stirring in the pit of my stomach that I always got before a really dangerous theft. It was a feeling I treasured, a feeling that reminded me I was alive. It would be a thrill to match wits with a handsome prince, though I didn't much care for his chances.

"I'll drink to that," Govind declared, raising his wine goblet in salute. Both men downed their cups, and I rushed to refill them.

Arjun noticed, and his arm fell over my shoulders. His grin was a little lopsided. He'd had quite a bit of wine—all part of the plan. "Boy, you're in no condition to fly back to the palace," Govind informed him. "I would be honored if you would stay the night here. I'm sure Razia wouldn't mind helping you with all that you require."

"It would be my honor, my prince," I told him, my voice breathy, my tone promising help of all kinds.

Arjun's grin widened. He stood up abruptly, pulling me to my feet alongside him. "In that case, Razia-Sahiba, allow me to honor you," he said, as the pair of us walked arm in arm toward the stairs.

# CHAPTER 2

Arjun's body was warm against mine, but his breathing had slowed to the steady rhythm of a deep sleep. It was now or never. He was still embracing me, but fortunately it was just the one arm, and I could wriggle free of that easily enough. I slipped my shoulders through first, and then my head, and then I was sitting up in bed.

I waited, watching the rising and falling of his chest, staring hard at his eyelids, holding my breath to better listen to the sounds of his breathing. It was slow and steady, totally unchanged. I hadn't woken him up.

I should have gotten up right then and got to work, but I lingered, staring at him. Even in sleep, his belly was marked by the muscles lying beneath his flesh, giving him a firmness that I had felt when he had wrapped me up in his arms and laid me on the bed to begin with. I could still feel their strength around me somehow, and I wanted for all the world to go back to bed, to crawl back into his embrace.

But I couldn't. Ammi had her plans, and I had my own. I couldn't live like this forever. Ammi made that clear enough. She was too old to attract rich clients who preferred younger women. Someday, I'd be too old too. When that day came, if I didn't have enough saved away to start my own dera, I'd find myself begging on street corners and being beaten like a dog.

No. I wasn't going to live that way. I dressed quickly and then crept out of the room, my slippers scarcely making a sound on the polished sandstone floors. I found myself standing in the narrow corridor that wrapped around the perimeter of the haveli's court-yard. Six floors below me, the fountain still bubbled, and the golden peacock still glinted in the moonlight. I had to get down there, get the peacock out of the house, and then get back into bed before Arjun was any the wiser. It was a tall order, but I thought if anyone could do it, I could. After all, it wasn't just dancing that I'd been practicing these last four years.

The house was as silent as a graveyard as I made my way down the stairs, but I kept my ears pricked for noise.

The risk of being spotted made my pulse pound, but I had certain advantages. To begin with, everyone had been drunk when I'd left them. Govind Singh would have given his servants the leftovers of his feast, and the combination of an unusually heavy meal and the dregs of the wine would probably put them all in a deep sleep. My second advantage was waiting for me in the court-yard. I could see it resting there, tucked behind one of the mango trees, just where Ammi had promised it would be.

It was nothing more than a long, sturdy dupatta, made of thickly woven cotton. To anyone else's eyes, it might have been left there by accident—perhaps a woman had taken it off during the heat of the day while strolling the gardens and had forgotten it. But to me, that scarf was the key to the whole plan. Without it, I had no chance at all of getting Govind Singh's gaudy peacock out of this house.

I crept through the gardens on my tiptoes, trying to look innocent, though that wouldn't necessarily save me. A courtesan who snooped around a nobleman's estate was risking a beating at best, and possibly far worse.

I crouched down behind the mango tree, picked up the dupatta, and took a deep breath. This was the really dangerous part. My heart was already hammering away in my chest—it was my body's attempt to dissuade me from doing something so stupidly, fatally dangerous. But my body had never been particularly successful in arguing with me, and tonight was no different.

I stepped toward the fountain, moving quickly but not too quickly. I didn't want to raise any alarms if anybody actually was watching me. I reached the fountain and sat down on its edge, like I had just come to admire the way the water sparkled in the moonlight. As I sat, I surveyed the whole of the haveli, from top to bottom. There was nobody standing at the railings, no faces peering out at me from windows. But there were so many rooms, so many floors. God, if just one of them had even a single person who was awake, I was done for.

I fought down a rising sense of panic. I'd done dangerous jobs before, but none like this, none in such a big home, none with such a large and obvious target. As soon as I laid my hands on the peacock, my theft would be obvious to anyone who so much as glanced in my direction. Maybe this was a mistake.

My hands shook as two halves of my mind argued against each other. I could do it. I'd stolen lots of things before. But this was crazy.

If Ammi hadn't begged me to do it, I'd have stayed in bed with Prince Arjun. But she'd told me over and over again how the dera needed money, how expensive it was to train little Lakshmi, how the nobles were increasingly tight-fisted, with so many other dancing girls proliferating throughout the city.

I didn't know if I really believed that or not, but Ammi had taken me in when I'd had nothing, when my clothes had become little more than rags, when I'd been so hungry I could scarcely breathe. She had brought me into her dera, adopted me as her daughter, clothed me, fed me, trained me. How could I say no when she asked me to help her make the wealth that would support my new little sister and see my adoptive mother through her declining years? What kind of daughter would I be if I refused her now?

But what about me? I'd won Arjun over tonight, or at least had begun the process. He would want to see me again, and as stupid as it was, I wanted to see him again. To have the prince as my lover . . . I shook my head. It was worth a hundred of these stupid peacocks.

Maybe if she were here, I might have convinced her of that fact, but she'd left with Sakshi, and she was expecting me to follow her orders. Those were the rules of the dera. She paid for our training, our clothes, our food, she raised us, and in exchange, we obeyed her orders. A hijra who made a habit of refusing her guru found herself living on the streets before long.

That, more than anything, settled the matter in my mind. I wasn't going back to living on the streets.

I took a deep breath, summoned my courage, and moved. I scampered up the fountain and started wrapping the dupatta around the statue, before tying it tightly to myself. I tried not to let my mind do any thinking at all. It was too late for thinking. I just had to do it and be done with it.

God, but the statue was heavy! It must have been solid gold, to say nothing of the gems. The weight made my joints ache and made it hard to move. I had to climb clumsily down from the fountain, my pace agonizingly slow, as I took one step at a time to keep from falling flat on my back. All the while, the same thoughts kept running through my head. *This is so stupid. I'm going to get caught. I have to move faster.*

My feet landed on the grass, and I ran hunched over toward the stairs, the peacock bouncing against my back, the gems scratching my flesh, the heavy weight of the thing leaving behind bruises. I ignored them. I could worry about them later. I had to get this statue out of the house. I started climbing the stairs, taking them as quickly as I could without making noise, but there were hundreds of them, stretching up eight stories. God, I was never going to make it. What had I been thinking?

I felt panic rising in my chest as I realized what a fool's errand this really was, but it was too late now. I couldn't risk putting it back. Going down the stairs was just as dangerous as going up them, and if I was caught putting the statue back, then I'd not only be executed, but it would have all been for nothing.

My breath came in ragged gasps, and my legs burned like fire. The statue weighed half as much as I did. What had Ammi been thinking about, wanting to steal this thing?

Money. The answer came easily enough. It was worth a fortune, and she had a buyer lined up to fence it for us, otherwise she'd never have ordered me to take it. It wouldn't be someone in Bikampur; that was too dangerous. No, it would be a noble from another city, someone with an ax to grind with Govind Singh. A jilted lover? A business associate he had cheated? It hardly mattered. If they would pay even a fraction of its worth, Ammi would take the money. She had plans for our dera, plans to live her old age in comfort, and I was the donkey she would ride to reach those dreams.

No, that wasn't fair. She loved me. I was a daughter to her. But I felt just like a donkey, as I clawed my way to the roof, the heavy statue straining my back. And I had all the sense of a donkey, trying to steal this statue in the middle of a crowded home. After this, I would tell Ammi no more—not for a while anyway. It just wasn't worth the risk, not when I was in the prime of my career and money came fast enough from legitimate work. She would understand that. She wanted what was best for me too.

I reached the roof, scarcely believing my good fortune. No one had spotted me, and the roof was deserted. I just had to get the statue down and out of the compound, and then it would all be over. I'd be safe again. I started to walk toward the far railing, when something rustled in the roof's far corner.

I gasped and jumped, turning to see who had spotted me, only to find myself staring into the golden eyes of a fire zahhak. She was still resting where her master had left her, but her head was up now, her eyes watching me closely, her pupils widening to take in the light. Zahhaks were smart, but not smart enough to understand theft. They were more like dogs, though thankfully they weren't prone to barking.

"Good evening, Padmini," I whispered, keeping my voice gentle. She responded as most zahhaks would to being soothed by a stranger—she turned away and put her head back down on the stones. Good. I didn't need her interfering. Though, in truth, if I could have ridden her, my mission would have been accomplished even more swiftly. But that was too much to risk. Perhaps she was tame enough to let a stranger ride her, but I rather doubted it. More likely, as soon as I climbed onto her back, she would screech and bite in a mad panic.

I turned away from her and walked swiftly to the wall. There was no sense prolonging this, not now, not when I was so close to being safe. I reached the railing and stared down at the alley far, far below. It looked deserted, though I knew that Ammi was hiding in the shadows somewhere down there. If I'd had eighty feet of rope, I might have been able to get the statue down then and there, but I had no such luck. I was going to have to carry it down myself.

I'd only agreed to this job because of the decorative stonework on the building. Those pretty designs that Govind Singh had had carved all over the walls of his home were to be his undoing. They made for perfect handholds and footholds. Without them, what I was about to do would have been suicidal. With them, it wasn't safe, but I thought I could do it.

I swung myself over the railing and started to climb down, my feet feeling the stones through the thin leather of my slippers, my toes curling to get a good grip before I moved my hands. One foot, then one arm. Always three points of contact. The basic rules I'd been taught by a climbing instructor from the Rakha mountains rang in my ears as I descended. The fear was gone. I should have been scared of falling, or of being seen, but I wasn't. I was too busy choosing my route, feeling for footholds, making sure that the stonework could hold my weight and the weight of the statue. There was no room in those calculations for panic.

I was amazed by how smoothly it went. I'd been so sure something horrible would happen, but the weight of the peacock wasn't so bad. It made my fingers hurt a little, but if I kept most of my weight on my feet, that was all right. And I'd been right about the stonework: It was dead easy to climb—practically a ladder compared to some of the buildings I had scaled over the years.

My feet hit the paving stones, and I could scarcely believe my luck.

No. Not luck. Talent. I was so good at this. I was grinning as I untied the statue, lowering it slowly to the dirt of the alley. Mission accomplished.

"Mashkhuda, darling," Ammi told me as she stepped out of the shadows. She came forward and took my cheeks in both hands and gave me a kiss on the forehead. "Now run along back to bed, dear, before Prince Arjun notices you've gone."

"Yes, Ammi," I agreed. As Varsha hefted the statue, I scampered back up the wall, moving much faster now that I wasn't burdened by half my own weight in gold and gems.

I reached the top of the wall without any trouble. I pulled myself up, dusted off my hands and my clothes, and started walking toward the stairwell. I'd only taken five or six steps, before someone came up them—Arjun.

I froze in place. My heart stopped. All the air went out of my lungs. I couldn't think, couldn't breathe. What would I say? He'd know I'd left our room. Now he could say that I hadn't been in my room when the statue was taken. I was done for.

"There you are," he whispered, smiling and stepping closer. "What are you doing up here, Razia? Stealing my zahhak?"

"No!" I exclaimed, relieved that he hadn't mentioned the peacock but terrified that his mind had run so quickly to my being a thief. And then I realized he'd given me the perfect solution. "No, my prince, I only came to look at her. I miss seeing them every day." I hung my head. "I'm sorry if I woke you, but sometimes it's hard for me to sleep . . ."

His big hands fell onto my shoulders, pulling me close to him, and I let my body melt against his. I breathed deeply of his scent while he reached up and stroked my hair. "You didn't wake me, Razia. Sometimes it's hard for me to sleep too."

"Does my prince have a great many worries keeping him up at night?" I teased. I couldn't imagine that a pampered prince like him really understood the meaning of worry. I hadn't—not until I'd fled my home and been forced to live on the streets of a foreign city. Next to that, even the terror of committing robberies in powerful men's homes wasn't so bad.

"Not so many as my father, but I have my own responsibilities," he said. "I suppose now that includes catching this thief that the men were complaining about."

I breathed a little easier then. That was why his mind had run to theft. It had nothing to do with me at all, and everything to do with the conversation he'd had with Govind Singh.

"I'm sure when he finds out that you're chasing him, he'll be shaking with fear, my prince," I replied, unable to keep the corners of my lips from twisting upward in a smirk.

"Are you mocking me?" he asked, his voice deep and languid, as he caressed my body, his hands lingering on the bare flesh of my midriff.

"Never," I replied, standing on my tiptoes and kissing him on his neck, and then moving up to his jaw. "I pity the thief who finds himself staring down Padmini's gaping maw."

"She's not so scary once you get to know her," he said. He pulled away from me suddenly, and I frowned.

"Would you like to?" he asked.

"Would I like to what, my prince?" I wondered.

"Go for a ride," he replied, nodding toward his zahhak.

My eyes widened, and my heart skipped a beat. This was the answer to my prayers; if we both spent some time out of the house, we could well claim that we knew nothing whatsoever about the theft, that the peacock had been there when we'd left. After all, if Arjun had noticed it was missing, he'd have said something already.

"Could we?" I asked, my voice breathier than I was expecting, but I couldn't help it. Ulterior motives aside, I hadn't flown on a zahhak's back in four years, and I missed it terribly.

"Of course," he said, and he nodded then to his zahhak, calling softly, "Padmini, come."

The great beast stirred from her place with an agility that startled me. She was up in an instant, and she took only a single bound with her clawed wings to reach us.

I found myself falling back against Arjun's chest from the suddenness of her movement, from the violence of it. I'd forgotten how big zahhaks were, how enormous those wing claws looked when they were coming toward you. Arjun wrapped his arms around me, resting his chin on top of my head. "You're not afraid of them, are you? I thought you were a great prince."

"She's not my zahhak, my prince," I said. "She doesn't obey my commands. And she's different from my Sultana. She's so much bigger, and she has those armored scales, and that ferocious beak."

"Well, don't you worry about any of that. I won't let her hurt you," he promised. "Come here." He led me toward her, and then took my hand in his. He stretched both our hands out, and Padmini pressed her beak against my palm in response.

She felt totally different from Sultana. Where my thunder zahhak's scales had been smooth and sleek, Padmini's were thick, keeled plates of keratin that protected her from the heat of her own flames. I was careful as I rubbed my hand from her nostrils to her crown, mindful not to stroke in the other direction, as the scales were pointed sharply enough to cut human flesh without difficulty. Padmini made a sort of rumbling noise in response to my petting, which I hoped meant that she was contented.

Arjun mounted up, climbing into the saddle on her back. It was positioned carefully, directly atop her shoulder joint, so that our weight would fall in the middle of her wings. The straps holding the saddle in place were looped around her chest and the roots of her wings, so that they wouldn't bother her or interfere with her flying. Arjun settled himself in his seat, using thick leather belts with steel buckles to strap himself in place. One strap went around his midsection, and two more across his shoulders, pressing him against the saddle's tall back. With his harness secured, he could hold himself steady no matter how violently his zahhak maneuvered through the sky.

He reached down, and I took his hand. He hauled me up with just the one arm, his strength taking me by surprise. I'd never possessed the strength of a grown man—my nirvan had come long before that, and the essential salts the alchemists gave me had given me the physique of a woman. Even so, I was weaker now than I had been before, and Arjun's thickly muscled arms were a reminder of what I had given up.

I set about strapping myself to the saddle, using a set of belts designed for a passenger. Our saddles in Nizam hadn't possessed them, because our zahhaks were smaller, faster, and more maneuverable. I thought that made them better in an aerial battle, but a fire zahhak was a formidable creature, and anyway, I was grateful for the opportunity to go for an evening flight. It had been so very long since my last one.

"You *have* done this before," he said, watching me as I cinched the waist strap around my middle so tightly that the leather dug into my flesh.

"Not recently, my prince," I replied, as I searched for the shoulder straps.

Arjun took hold of a second leather belt, wrapping it tightly around me and him both, pinning me against him. "I don't have shoulder straps for you," he whispered, his chin resting on my shoulder, "so you have to stay close to me."

I wondered, as I found myself nestling closer to his body, if the missing shoulder straps were a deliberate design choice. How many other young courtesans had he enthralled with rides like this one? A few, I guessed, as I placed my arms on either side of his thighs, bracing myself against him, and he smiled in response.

He took up the reins and said, "Padmini, up!"

The zahhak bounded forward, shaking me like a rag doll as I clung to Arjun for dear life. She leapt over the roof's railing, beating her flame-colored orange and yellow wings hard on either side of us. They were so beautiful when they were stretched out, so much longer than they looked when they were folded. They were broader than my Sultana's had been, less pointed, meant for soaring rather than high-speed dives. She flapped them five or six times, and then she stopped and held them steady. We were flying.

Everything was so still up there—so unbelievably quiet and peaceful and wonderful. The wind rustled through my hair and against my clothes, but we were flying at such a sedate pace that it felt like a gentle evening breeze. The violence of takeoff was over, and now Padmini flapped once every few seconds to keep aloft, but mostly glided in lazy circles. That was different from Sultana too; her slender, pointed wings could never stop beating, not for any length of time, so riding her felt like being strapped to a bucking stallion.

The city was stretched out below us, already beginning to look like a child's toy from this height. Whenever I'd seen a city from the air as a child, I'd always imagined it as an enormous collection of dollhouses gathered together by some wealthy princess. It was so hard to believe that the havelis down there were the same ones that towered over me on the streets, hard to imagine that the thick walls ringing the city could keep anything out. And the higher we rose, the more of the world I could see. There were the sand dunes of the desert, and there the oasis that had brought the first caravans to Bikampur. And beyond that was the distant horizon, so many miles away that they were beyond the counting.

"I'd forgotten how beautiful it all is," I said, my voice catching in my throat as memories came flooding back. I'd have fled my childhood home sooner if not for Sultana. She had been the only good thing in my life. Flying with her had been my escape from the beatings and the insults, from my father's snide words about what a pathetic woman his firstborn son had turned out to be. So many unhappy memories, so many nights spent crying into my pillows so that my servants wouldn't overhear and tell my father. They all flashed before my eyes then. I'd been so desperately unhappy but for Sultana. She was the only thing I had ever done right as a boy. I had trained her well. I had ridden her well, and I had fought with her well. The only time I'd ever resembled the prince everyone had wanted me to be had been when I was strapped to her saddle.

Tears spilled down my cheeks in rivulets. Until that moment, with Bikampur's torches glittering beneath me, I'd forgotten how much I missed this, how much it had meant to me, how much it had sustained me in those dark years. Until that moment, I had forgotten how much I had given up when I had run off to be a hijra in a faraway city.

"Razia?" Arjun sounded alarmed. His arms tightened around my waist, pulling me closer to him. "Are you frightened? Do you want me to land?"

"No, please don't!" I exclaimed. I didn't want to land. I wanted this flight to last forever, because who knew when I would ever get another chance to ride a zahhak?

"Then what is it?" he asked. "What's the matter?"

"I just didn't realize how much I missed this," I said, and I leaned my head back against his chest, taking comfort in the warmth of his body pressed up against mine.

"If you really were a prince," he said, making it plain that he still didn't fully believe me, "then why in the names of all the gods did you leave?"

"I don't think I could explain it in a way that you would understand."

"Try," he whispered.

I sighed. How do you explain your soul to another person? How do you give them a glimpse of it? He wouldn't understand. Nobody ever had before, nobody except my adopted family in the dera. But they were like me, so of course they understood. Arjun was the big, strong, confident prince I was meant to be. What would he know about failing to meet all the expectations that had been placed before him? I doubted very much if he'd ever failed at anything.

"Did you have any sisters growing up, my prince?" I asked, because that was the only sure way I'd ever found to get a man to consider a woman's perspective on the world.

"Two of them, actually," he said. "And somehow we haven't strangled each other yet."

I smiled at that. "Well, imagine for a moment that your father had no sons, and that he needed an heir. What do you think would have happened had he chosen one of your sisters and raised her as a man?"

"Well," he said, pausing to consider it, "I know my sisters always wanted to ride zahhaks of their own. It would have pleased them to have been permitted to do it."

I nodded, as I thought he was on the right track, but I wanted him to work things out for himself.

"And I think my younger sister would have greatly enjoyed learning to fight with katars."

That too had been one of the happier memories of my childhood. Training in the martial arts had been a bit like dancing or flying. It had made me feel alive and free in a way I usually didn't.

"But I think it would have been more difficult for her the older she got," Arjun said, his voice growing pensive. "The poor thing is crazy for a husband. And my older sister wanted children so badly. And they both would have killed me if I'd tried to part them from their clothes and their jewelry and their fancy slippers."

"That's exactly how it was for me, my prince," I said, running my hand over his arm. "No matter what I did, I couldn't act like a man. It wasn't something I wanted to do, wasn't something I knew how to do. I could fight. I could fly. I could ride a horse and shoot a toradar, but all the rest of it was so confusing. And the idea of marrying a woman was repulsive to me." I shuddered, just imagining the horror of having a man's body, of having to take a woman to bed. It made bile rise up in the back of my throat.

He grunted, and I didn't know if that was agreement, or judgment, or what, but I pressed on nonetheless. "I tried my best to be the person they wanted me to be, I really did, but eventually I couldn't take it anymore, and not even my zahhak was enough to hold me there. There isn't a day that passes that I don't miss her, but as strange as it must sound to you, I'm happier here, living with my own kind, finally being myself."

"It's not so hard to understand," he said.

"It isn't?" I asked.

"No," he said, pulling me tightly to him. He leaned down and whispered into my ear, "A girl as pretty as you was wasted as a prince anyway."

That brought a smile to my lips. "My prince is too kind."

"So," he said, steering Padmini in a lazy circle, "who was your father?"

"I would happily tell you, my prince, but I fear he still has agents looking for me," I replied. It was a lie, not the part about the agents, but the part about happily telling him. I kept it a closely guarded secret. If anyone found out . . . I pushed that thought from my mind before it panicked me.

"I won't tell anyone," he promised, and I wanted desperately to believe him, to believe I'd found a man I could trust, a man to whom I could pour out the dark secrets that had so long burdened my heart.

For a moment, I considered telling him the truth. I was tired of being looked upon as some dancing girl whose past life was a carefully concocted story to make her sound richer and better placed than she was. And what harm would it do if he knew my secret? If he knew who I really was, wouldn't he find me all the more alluring?

But what if he didn't keep that secret? What if he chose to tell someone? The consequences filled my mind in the form of dark shadows creeping through my bedchamber, and of long, wicked blades of poisoned daggers glinting in the moonlight. To anyone else, such nightmares would have been flights of fancy, but I knew my father. I knew what he would do to me if he ever found me.

And Arjun was a prince, I couldn't let myself forget that. His loyalty was to his city, to his family, to his dynasty. What if there was a political advantage in giving me back? It wasn't unheard of. Or what if there was a political advantage in keeping me hostage? That seemed all too likely. I didn't think Arjun would do that to me, but how well did I really know him? And it didn't have to be him who made that decision. His father might. Or an ambitious vizier. And then I would be a helpless prisoner, waiting for my father to pay them for the honor of executing me.

And even if Arjun kept my secret, my presence at a royal court would be a deadly risk. My father had agents and ambassadors everywhere, some of whom were my cousins, who might still recognize me. They had coveted the throne my whole childhood and had viewed me as a disgrace to the family even before I'd run away to be a hijra. They would send assassins if they knew I was still alive. I was too much of a threat to the succession for them to do otherwise, even if I wasn't a boy any longer.

"Forgive me, my prince, but it's not safe for people to know— for me or for them." I knew full well as soon as the words passed my lips that Arjun would take them for a lie, that he would think I was just some courtesan spinning stories to attract better clients, but that was probably for the best.

"You think your father's agents could reach us here?" He laughed. "Nizam is strong, but so is Bikampur, and no Nizami subahdar could threaten me without provoking the wrath of all the maharajas of Registan. I would think a Nizami nobleman would know that much at least."

I couldn't have missed the challenge in that last comment, but I ignored it. It would be better for both of us if he thought me a lying commoner.

"I'm sure you're right, my prince," I told him. It hurt. Maybe I was acting like a stupid little girl, but I wanted him to think well of me; I wanted him to believe me. But the risk was far too great. Bikampur was powerful, but it was just one city-state—nothing compared to the power my father wielded. The only reason Registan wasn't a conquered province of his empire was that the individual maharajas, divided among themselves in times of peace, were bound by bonds of blood and kinship and came together when any one of them was confronted by outsiders. It was a loose confederation, one that was powerful enough in defense but which lacked the unity to conquer new territories outside of its desert domain. But that unity wouldn't extend to a young prince keeping a hijra away from the sultan of Nizam. I'd be given up in an instant.

We flew on in silence for a time, and I could sense Arjun's irritation. He didn't like me lying about my past. A part of him had believed that I really was a runaway prince from Nizam, and he'd liked that. Now the mystery was gone, and I was just another street rat looking to earn a meal with her looks.

I sighed with disappointment, but I kept silent. It was better this way. Having a prince for a client was just begging for trouble. I looked up at him. "My prince?"

He was scowling. "What?"

"Would you be willing to return me to my dera? It's late, and I should be getting home."

He opened his mouth to reply, and then closed it again, his eyes flickering as if in deep thought. The scorn was gone, the irritation was gone, and I realized I'd made a terrible mistake. No liar would have asked to be separated from him, not when she'd be desperate to make him believe her so that he would be her client. The only reason I would have for wanting to go home would be if my story was true, and it really was as dangerous as I said it was.

God, I was a fool. A prince like him would know Nizam, would know the princes there, and would know who had gone missing just a few years ago. He would know the stories of the royal family of Nizam, and of the fabulous green eyes they all possessed, eyes he'd already remarked upon once.

Arjun looked down at me and uttered the two words I'd been dreading since I'd run away from home. "Salim Mirza."

If I'd been smarter, I'd have denied it with a smile on my face, but I flinched in spite of myself, and I had to take a gasping breath because it felt like my chest was going to explode from the tension in it.

His eyes widened as he realized he'd guessed right.

"Please don't tell anyone!" I begged, not caring how pathetic it made me sound. "They'll come for me, and they'll kill me." I couldn't stop my limbs from shaking as I imagined my father's assassins finding me, their knives tearing through my flesh as they sawed off trophies to bring back to him.

It was so stupid of me to react the way I had. I should have kept quiet, should have kept my fear under control. Now I'd ruined everything. Tears spilled from my eyes and poured down my cheeks as I realized that I might have to run away again, that I might have lost my second family in four years, that everything I'd worked so hard for might be taken from me. And that was if I was lucky and Arjun let me go rather than selling me back to my father for my weight in gold and jewels.

"It's all right, Razia," he whispered, hugging me close to him, his chin resting on my shoulder, his voice soft in my ear. "I'm not going to hurt you, and I'm not going to tell anyone—I promise."

I batted at tears with the loose end of my dupatta and fought to get myself back under some semblance of control, but it was impossible now that that awful jinn had been let out of its bottle. I was going to have to run south, maybe to Mahisagar. I'd have to change my name. I'd take what money I could and start a dera in a tiny trading post, somewhere nobody would think to look.

"Razia?" Arjun sounded concerned, like he'd been talking to me and I'd been ignoring him in my blind panic.

"Please . . ." I didn't even know what I was begging him for— not to tell anyone? To help me escape? To drop me off in some godforsaken patch of desert and leave me there so I could disappear into the wilderness?

"You're really the heir to the throne of Nizam," he murmured, and I thought the dire implications of that fact had finally got through to him.

I gripped his arm with a strength born of wild terror. "You can't tell anyone! You don't know my father, you don't know what he's capable of!"

"I won't tell anyone," he whispered, embracing me with the one arm that I wasn't clinging to like a drowning sailor.

I barely heard him. "If my father finds out, he'll send men to kill me. He despises me. And it's not just him—my cousin Tariq is desperate for the throne; he needs me dead. His father, my uncle Shahrukh, has been scheming to get rid of me the whole of my life. They have spies everywhere, and their assassins have killed kings in their fortresses, surrounded by their bodyguards."

"Razia, there are no spies up here." Arjun swept his arm through the air around us. "Nobody is listening but Padmini, and she's not telling anyone—are you, girl?"

The zahhak gave no response, and for whatever reason that helped to calm me down. He was right. There was nobody else here. Nobody else was listening. No spies were flying high above the city with us. If he didn't tell anyone, nobody else would know. But what if he told?

I took a few deep breaths to quell the frantic beating of my heart. I finally managed to stanch the tears, and the panic began to fade. I leaned back against him, resting my head against his chest, trying to convince myself that it would be all right, but in my heart, I knew it wouldn't be.

"They would pay you well for my head . . ." I whispered, not sure why I was telling him that, but I couldn't stop myself. "As much gold and silver as you could want, gems the size of your fist. They—"

"I'm not going to sell you," Arjun told me, his voice so strong and forceful that I found myself believing him. "I have gold and gems enough, and we Registanis have no love lost for the sultan of Nizam. I see no reason to make his life any easier, and to deprive myself of such a beautiful girl in the process. So let us speak no more of this matter."

I nodded, but my mind was still frantically plotting my escape. "If you would be so kind as to drop me at the dera, your highness, I'll make my own way after that."

"Make your own way where?" he asked.

"Best if you don't know."

"Razia." His voice was so sharp that it drew my attention away from my escape plans and back to reality. I looked up at him and found his honey-colored eyes staring straight into mine.

"Listen to me," he said, his voice slow and clear and direct. "I am not going to tell anyone who you are. This is my city, and I want you in it, so I give you my word that I will protect you. No one is coming for you. No one will know. No one will hurt you. I promise."

"Why?" I asked. I couldn't figure it out, because for all my beauty, and all my skill at dancing, I knew full well that I was more trouble than I was worth. I'd been lucky that Ammi had kept me safe for all these years, that she hadn't sold me herself.

"Because I like you," Arjun answered, brushing one of my tears from my cheek with the back of a finger. "And I've never met a courtesan who outranked me before."

He was teasing, and all my training was screaming at me to respond with something sultry, something flirtatious, but the only thing I could muster up the courage to do was hug his arm tightly to my chest, clinging to it for dear life.

"The sun's coming up," Arjun observed, nodding his head toward the eastern horizon. "I suppose we should get back to Govind Singh's before he thinks we've abandoned him."

The relaxed, casual way he said it helped to calm me down more than anything. I managed to say, "Of course, my prince," and then I set about wiping my face clean of tears, hoping it wouldn't be too obvious to those on the ground that I'd been crying.

He pulled the reins sharply to the left and twisted his weight in that direction. Padmini responded instantly with a hard bank, beating her wings through the turn. I felt pressure pushing me down into the saddle and back against Arjun's chest as we whipped through the turn. The fear fled, replaced with jubilation. This was the feeling that I'd missed for so long, my one source of strength in a life that had been filled with terror and doubt.

"Faster," I ordered.

He laughed and Padmini dipped her head and we began to pick up speed. She tucked her wings closer to her body, and the wind roared past us, threatening to tear my clothes from my body and making my eyes water. There, at least now I had an excuse for my red and puffy eyes.

Govind Singh's haveli grew and grew in my vision, but it wasn't the same quiet place we'd left a few hours before. Now the roof-top was crowded with people, and they seemed agitated.

# CHAPTER 3

My fingers fumbled with the straps as I tried to extricate myself from the saddle. Already, Govind Singh was striding toward us, flanked by his eunuch servitor and followed by half a dozen men who had slept over after having enjoyed his festivities. I'd barely managed to free myself and climb down from Padmini's back before they were upon us.

"Is she the one?" Govind Singh demanded, jabbing his finger at me. "Did you catch her?" He stepped toward me then, along with half of his servants, and I fell back until I was pressed tightly against Padmini's feathers.

Catch me? My mind ran back to my conversation with Arjun, and I was suddenly terrified. How did he know? How could he have guessed my identity? He couldn't have heard us, not flying high in the sky.

Arjun slid down from the saddle and stepped in front of me before they could tear me limb from limb. He looked worried too;

the same thoughts must have been flooding his own mind. "What's this about, Uncle?"

"What do you mean, what is this about? That's why you were flying, isn't it? To bring the girl back to face justice?"

"To face justice?" He looked at me and frowned, and I hung my head and waited for the ax to fall. "What has she done?"

"Stolen my peacock statue, of course!" Govind Singh exclaimed.

It was so stupid, but I actually breathed a sigh of relief on hearing that accusation. I'd forgotten all about the statue, I'd been so much more terrified of my father's wrath. But the relief only lasted for an instant, as I reminded myself that I *had* been the one who had stolen the statue. But I was more puzzled than afraid. I'd been so careful. Who could have seen me? Why hadn't they sounded the alarm? Why wait until morning to make their accusations, when I might well have already made good my escape?

"Peacock . . ." Arjun murmured, like he didn't have the faintest notion what Govind was going on about. "The one on top of the fountain, you mean? The golden one?"

"The very same!" he declared. "I take it you caught her in the act?"

"When did this happen, Uncle?" Arjun asked, and I realized that my life was hanging in the balance. If Arjun had any idea how long I had been absent from his bedchamber, he might well provide the very evidence these men needed to see me arrested and executed. Then again, it was plain that he was still more worried about protecting my secret than dealing with some silly statue.

"Last night," Govind said. "It was taken last night. Someone plucked it right off the fountain, and now it's nowhere to be found."

"Uncle, in the first place, I can assure you that Razia was with me the whole night. We didn't even know the statue had been stolen. And anyway"—he gestured to my slender physique—"that statue must weigh as much as she does. There's no way she could have lifted the thing."

"So you weren't out looking for the thief?" Govind asked, and he seemed terribly put out by that.

"No, Uncle. We just went for a flight, because the weather was so perfect for one," Arjun said. "I promise you, whoever stole your statue, it wasn't Razia. I was with her the whole night."

Govind Singh sighed and glanced at me with disappointment in his eyes, but he didn't apologize. Why would he? I was a hijra, and he was a nobleman. I'd have been angry about it, but convenient scapegoat or not, he wasn't wrong—I had stolen the statue. And anyway, after the terror of having my identity discovered, I was only too happy to be ignored.

"Are you sure it wasn't one of your servants who took it?" Arjun asked.

"No, no," he said, shaking his head. "I've checked their rooms— we've checked everywhere. And the men I had guarding the gate were not mere servants; they were professional soldiers, and they assured me that the gate remained closed for the entire night and was not opened once after the guests left for the evening."

Arjun frowned. "Then how did the thief get the statue out of the house? Through one of the windows, perhaps?"

"I can think of no other explanation," Govind said.

"Well, we should start with the first-floor rooms, then. Are they all occupied?"

Govind frowned. "They are."

"Then the likely culprit is someone who lives in a first-floor chamber—unless you believe someone scaled the walls of the haveli while holding the statue in his arms." He shook his head to show how likely he thought that was. I fought down a smirk.

"That's logical enough . . ." Govind Singh allowed.

"Unless someone sneaked in, my lord," said Rawal. "If the

statue could be removed from a first-floor window, certainly someone could enter in such a fashion."

"But the first-floor windows are still ten feet above the level of
the street," someone else said. "It's an awfully long distance to
jump while holding a heavy golden statue."

"Certainly not something a girl could have managed," said Arjun, and I thought he was still worried that I was going to be
blamed. He was rubbing my back in gentle circles, and I prayed
that his fingers didn't find the scrapes and bruises that I bore from
having carried the statue on my back. Though, I supposed I could
just claim I'd had a rough client the night before last. That was a
believable-enough lie for a young woman in my line of work.

"No, I suppose not," Govind agreed, and he seemed to regard
me with a little less suspicion. "But I don't believe it was one of my
servants. They would have had many opportunities to take it.
Why do it tonight of all nights?"

"Perhaps it was one of the other guests, Uncle, or one of their
agents," Arjun suggested. "A man of your standing has enemies.
Maybe they hired someone to steal your statue."

The idea of a conspiracy by his political enemies seemed to appeal to Govind Singh's vanity. He stroked his mustache, nodding.
"Yes, yes, that makes sense. But which enemy, is the question."

"Do you have any ideas?" Arjun asked.

"None so concrete that I would wish to make public accusations," he replied.

I clenched my jaw against making a smart reply to that. He
certainly hadn't seemed reluctant to sling accusations at me, had
he? Sometimes I had to remind myself that I wasn't a prince any
longer, that nobody really gave a damn what I thought or what my
feelings were. And Arjun's discovery of my identity had been a
pointed reminder of why I was so willing to put up with being
treated like a cheap dancing girl. There were far worse alternatives.

"I have an idea," Arjun said. "Since we suspect that it must have been someone outside your household, perhaps even one of your enemies, we must begin by looking for suspects."

"Sensible, your highness," Govind agreed, though he didn't sound like he really believed this line of reasoning would get him anywhere.

"So, let us begin by looking into your guests," Arjun said. "I want you to prepare a list of all the guests you've invited to your home since you purchased the statue. And then I will seek out similar lists from the other victims, and I will limit my suspects to those who appear on all three lists."

The older man's face brightened considerably. "That's a very clever idea, your highness." He turned to his chief eunuch. "Rawal, you will write up the list for his highness."

"I would be happy to do so, my lord," Rawal replied. "And I will send requests to the other victims to send their own lists to his highness. I'm sure they will be very grateful to you for garnering his highness's support in this matter, my lord."

Govind grinned, quick to see the advantage of the prince's request going through him. It would enhance his prestige and leave the other lords indebted to him for advancing their interests. To Arjun, he said, "We will arrange everything and have the lists sent directly to you."

"Excellent," Arjun replied. "I promise you that I will find the man responsible for stealing from you, Uncle, and that he will face the maharaja's justice."

"You're too kind, your highness," Govind replied, bowing deeply. He gestured back to the cushions in the middle of the roof. "Would you do me the honor of joining me for breakfast?"

"Yes, of course," Arjun said. And then he seemed to remember that I was still standing beside him, and he asked, "Do you mind if Razia eats with us? I don't think the poor thing has had a bite to eat since before she arrived."

"Oh, no, my prince, I should be returning to my dera," I said, not liking the scowl Govind Singh had given me on the mention of my name. If he'd accepted that I wasn't to blame for stealing his dumb statue, why was he still angry with me? I'd performed above and beyond all reasonable expectations, hadn't I? Not that it mattered. If he was angry with me, then he was as likely as not to poison me, and I didn't want to take that risk.

"You will eat with us, and then I will fly you back to your dera," Arjun replied.

It was an order, not a request. I heard the difference in his tone, and for a moment I was irked. He was a prince of a single city of Registan. I was the crown prince of all Nizam, or once had been, and it piqued my pride to be treated like I was some servant. But after a moment's reflection, I found myself smiling. He was treating me just like any other courtesan, like he hadn't the slightest idea who I really was. He was keeping his promise to protect me.

"Of course, my prince." I bowed my head then and followed along with him, as meekly and mildly as was expected of a low-class dancing girl like myself, but I was secretly smiling. Maybe he really did like me. And maybe there was more to him than just another rich client.

I noted that Govind Singh's reaction was to look mollified. After all, the role of polite, submissive servant girl was what he expected of me. But Arjun's reaction was quite different; his lips were twitching with the same thinly suppressed amusement as my own. We shared a secret now. And it couldn't have been lost on him that I was the crown prince of the sultanate of Nizam, perhaps the fiercest enemy the maharajas of Registan had ever faced, and I was playing the role of courtesan for him. While it was al-

ways difficult for me to truly fathom the minds of men, I thought
that perhaps I'd have been equally amused if the great rival I had
been warned about my whole life had served me sweets and ca-
tered to my every whim.

That worried me a little. He'd said he liked me, but in what
way? Did he just want me as a trophy to bolster his ego? Did it
simply amuse him to see an enemy prince acting like a woman? It
was a depressing thought, but I didn't linger on it as I took my
place on the cushion beside Arjun's own.

Servants came with nimbu pani and early-season mangoes, as
well as onion kachori, rotis, and acchar. I tore off a piece of roti,
wrapped it around a sweet mango acchar, and offered it to Arjun,
who happily ate it straight from my hand.

"The girl seems to please you," Govind observed, nodding to
me with a good deal less disdain than he'd shown before. Perhaps
his anger at the theft had worn off somewhat, or perhaps I'd
merely reminded him that my presence was helping him to win
the favor of the prince.

"Yes, she's not like any courtesan I've ever met," Arjun agreed.
"You have my thanks for introducing us, Uncle."

"Your happiness is always gratitude enough for me, boy," Govind replied, giving him a friendly pat on the shoulder, before going
back to his food.

I fed Arjun some mango and one of the onion kachoris. My
stomach was growling, but I knew better than to put my needs
before the needs of my clients. I'd eat when I got back to the dera.
Ammi always said that men didn't like watching women eat anyway, and I thought there was probably some truth to that.

"More?" I asked, once he'd eaten his fill straight from my fingertips.

"My turn," he replied, and he picked up a piece of mango and
offered it to me.

I raised an eyebrow but leaned forward and opened my mouth, letting him place the mango on my tongue. I closed my lips around his finger and pulled back. His eyes widened, and I smiled and swallowed.

He tore off a piece of roti next, and I ate that in just the same fashion, moving slowly, languidly, really stretching out the process in spite of the hunger pangs in my stomach. With each new piece of food, Arjun's interest seemed to grow. It didn't do much to answer my doubts regarding his motives, but the interest itself was well worth my investment, whatever its source. Not only could a rich client like him make my fortune, but now that he knew my secret, I found myself even more desperate to please him. And maybe that was why he was willing to keep it for the time being— at least until some other girl caught his eye, and maybe one who hadn't been born a boy.

Although, I wondered if being a hijra wasn't to my advantage on that score. There would be no chance of my birthing any bastards, no chance of complicating the royal succession. Still, I had to be careful. If I took his interest for granted, I would surely lose it, and I had no intention of doing that. It wasn't just because a relationship with Prince Arjun was my ticket to a different life, or even because he knew my secret. The kindness he had shown me on our flight had felt more genuine than anything I'd experienced at a man's hands in the whole of my life, and the part of me that had been dreaming of winning the heart of a prince since I was a child was daring to hope again.

But I was getting ahead of myself. This was just the first step. I couldn't rush things. I couldn't put too many expectations on him. Not yet. For now, I had to make myself the most pleasant company I could, and judging from the grin on his face, I was managing it.

He offered me an onion kachori, but I held up my hand to stop him. I was still hungry, and onion kachoris were my favorite, but I didn't think my good-bye kiss would be worth very much if I had onion on my breath. So I took a sip of the nimbu pani to cleanse my palate instead and resolved that I'd eat properly once I got home.

"Full already?" he asked, and his smile told me that Ammi was right about men appreciating women who didn't eat.

"A girl has to mind her figure, my prince," I replied.

He seemed to remember that figure then, and his arm went around me, his hand running over the curve of my hip. "Now that I'm here, I'll mind your figure for you," he promised.

"My prince's assistance is most welcome," I told him, my tone slightly mocking, but my eyes downcast in the perfect picture of innocence. Most men found that combination irresistible.

Arjun said, "I think I should take you home, before I decide to keep you."

"Yes," I agreed, not wanting to seem too clingy on our first meeting. "My ammi is probably worried that I've been abducted."

He smiled at that and turned back to Govind Singh. "Thank you for everything, Uncle, and don't worry about your statue. I'll see the thief caught and the peacock returned to you."

"I know you will," Govind agreed, and he hugged Arjun like a real uncle. "You're a credit to your father."

It was silly, but hearing that, I felt a jab of pain in my heart. Arjun was a credit to his father, a noble prince, everything he was meant to be. And what was I? A thief and a whore. It was no wonder nobody had ever said those words about me. How could they have when I was always such a disgrace?

"Razia?"

I looked up, startled, and realized that I'd been lost in my own thoughts. Arjun was holding out his hand to me, and I took it. "Forgive me, my prince. I don't know where my mind went."

"I have a few ideas," he replied, earning a chortle from Govind, and loud laughs from his compatriots.

I managed a weak smile, but was grateful that I wasn't being called upon for more than that, as it was hard to push the dark thoughts from my mind. Being so close to a prince like Arjun was the strongest reminder of my past that I'd had in years. He was the yardstick by which I had always measured myself growing up, and I'd always fallen short of the mark.

Arjun took me by the arm and led me back toward Padmini. We said nothing to each other as we climbed into the saddle and strapped ourselves in. I couldn't stop my mind from drifting back to the thoughts I'd had before—did he enjoy me because I was such a miserable failure of a prince? I had a hard time believing it was because he was enamored of me, not after just one night's passion.

He picked up the reins and gave them a snap, and Padmini leapt into the air, beating her wings hard for altitude. My cares vanished then, lost in the rush of the wind. All I could think about was how wonderful it was to slip free of the bonds of the earth, to soar high above the cares of ordinary people, to see the city in the same way that God himself must have seen it.

"I don't know the way," Arjun said.

"My prince?" I asked, wondering if I'd been so caught up in flying that I'd missed something.

He chuckled. "I don't know the way to your dera. You'll have to point me in the right direction."

"I'd rather make you fly in circles all day," I said, leaning over and looking down at the city below us, filled with people scurrying to and fro, with donkeys pulling little carts and camels pulling bigger ones, with dark alleys and bright markets. It was all so magical from the air.

"Now there's an idea," he murmured, and he pressed the reins into my hands, crossing his arms over his chest to show that I had full control over Padmini. "Why don't you show me how princes fly in Nizam?"

"How about I show you how princesses fly in Nizam?" I suggested.

"I can't wait," he replied.

The well-oiled leather of the reins felt reassuringly familiar in my hands, though it had been years since I'd commanded a zahhak in the skies. Still, it wasn't the sort of thing you could forget, and my fingers twisted the reins into the proper position with practiced ease. All zahhaks were flown with two separate sets of reins, a left and a right, held such that the thumb and forefinger of each hand controlled the top reins, and the rest of the fingers curled tightly around the lower ones.

Arjun was eyeing my posture carefully, his lips curved into a crooked grin. "You must have had a good riding instructor."

"The best in the world," I agreed, snapping both sets of reins as hard as I dared, not sure if Padmini would respond to a foreign rider, but she immediately began beating her wings faster and faster until they were blurs on either side of us. The wind rushed up so hard that it made my eyes sting and burn without goggles to protect them. I suddenly threw my weight to the right, pulling back on the right set of reins, my pinky finger yanking down hard at the same time.

Padmini rolled to the right in a flash, diving as she went. The wind howled in my ears as she tucked her wings tight to her body, sending us plummeting toward the ground like a stone dropped from the heavens. I had to blink constantly to keep from being blinded by the force of air blowing past us, but I kept my eyes fixed on the Rose Fort, the royal palace of Bikampur, its pink sandstone walls blocking it off from the rest of the city. There was a great gate in its southern wall that stood atop a hill. The zigzag path leading down from it passed through three more massive gates before opening onto Bikampur's main boulevard—a wide street that cut all the way through the city itself. It was the perfect place to show off my skills.

I aimed Padmini's snout for the southern gate of the palace, the slight slack in the reins telling her not to slow down as she dove. She was an obedient beast; she didn't balk. She had courage. She may have been a fire zahhak, but she was a good girl, a perfect mount for a prince like Arjun.

"You wouldn't dare!" Arjun shouted in my ear to be heard above the roar of the slipstream. He'd finally figured out what I was after.

"Do you forbid it, my prince?" I asked, prepared to pull hard on the top reins and bring Padmini up short, but if he wanted me to pull out, he was running out of time to order it.

"No . . ." he said, like he couldn't quite believe he was letting me do this.

That was all the permission I needed. I waited until the last possible second and then pulled back on the reins with my thumbs and forefingers, bringing Padmini out of her dive just feet above the ground. Her belly scales were practically skimming the stones of the palace courtyard. Her snout was aimed squarely at the southern gate, and she seemed as eager as I was to take it on, flapping her wings for still more speed in the bare seconds it took us to reach it.

She tucked her wings in to either side of her, and we roared through the gate, a donkey cart passing by just a foot beneath us. And then I rolled my body hard to the right, yanking on the reins for all I was worth. Padmini responded by turning in a sharp bank, the violence of the maneuver making it feel like a crushing weight had been placed atop my head and shoulders.

The second gate was just ahead of us. Men were diving for cover, desperate to get out of our way, though they needn't have bothered. We had plenty of room, and Padmini darted through with all the grace of a falcon. I threw myself left then, and we made a hairpin turn, racing for another gate. By now, I was confident, sure that she would do whatever I asked of her, certain that I could handle whatever was coming. So I snapped the reins again and she fluttered her wings in a frenzy, the next gate whipping past us so quickly that I scarcely even saw it.

A hard turn to the right saw us lined up on the final gate, the largest of the four, the one that opened up onto Bikampur's tree-lined boulevard. People were standing in the road, shouting and pointing. Men were scrambling to herd their camels away from the onrushing zahhak, but there was little they could do. We were moving far too quickly for them to escape.

Padmini tucked her wings in as she passed through the final gate, and her tail feathers spread wide to keep us from falling. As soon as our momentum carried us clear of the gate, Padmini's wings shot out to either side of her, and I pulled back on the top reins. The leather straps pulled on the metal toggles of her bridle, lifting her snout to the heavens. Soon we were climbing skyward, almost straight up, our speed dropping slower and slower the longer I held the climb. I waited until Padmini was on the point of falling, and then I leaned my body to the left and pulled hard on the right set of reins. Her response was a perfect reversal. She flipped in midair, like an acrobat doing a cartwheel, and in an instant her snout was pointing toward the ground, as she began another death-defying dive.

We picked up speed, but I pulled out before we got too close to the ground, contenting myself with skimming the city's canopied rooftops, causing children who had been sitting down to breakfast to leap up and point excitedly at our passage. I waved back, remembering with a bittersweet feeling in my heart what it had been like to do this every morning back home in Nizam.

"I think I'll be taking these back now," Arjun said, pulling the reins from my hands.

"I'm sorry, my prince," I said, unable to keep a mischievous tone out of my voice. "It wasn't too much for you, was it?"

He laughed and rested his chin on my shoulder, his beard scratching at my neck and my ear. "You're not the demure little girl you pretend to be, are you?"

"Whatever do you mean, my prince?" I asked, endeavoring to sound properly horrified at the notion that I was anything other than a perfectly well-behaved maiden.

He rolled his eyes and said, "My father is holding a wrestling contest the day after tomorrow. You will join me in attending."

"As my prince wishes," I replied, unable to keep from smiling. He really wanted to see me again. Maybe he didn't think I was an embarrassment after all.

"Now," he said, "where is this dera of yours?"

"It's just there," I said, pointing out the building, which seemed like a dirty little hovel from the air, particularly when set beside the lavish havelis of the Neelam Mandi.

If Arjun thought it was beneath him, he said nothing about it. Instead, he flew Padmini straight to the courtyard, landing in the shade of our mango trees, her wings kicking up a cloud of dust.

As I worked to loosen the straps tying me to the saddle, Ammi and the other girls rushed out of the house to see what had happened. They were all pulling their dupattas around themselves in feigned modesty, but their eyes were as big as saucers. Sakshi was leading them, practically jumping up and down with excitement.

"He let you ride his zahhak?" she gasped.

"Is that all he let her ride?" Disha, one of my older sisters, asked, drawing giggles from the girls. I ignored the jibe.

"His highness has been very kind to me," I said as I dismounted. I turned back to look at Arjun, who had kept his seat.

He stretched out his hand, and I reached up and took it with my own. He brought it to his lips and kissed it.

"You will come to the palace the day after tomorrow at the third bell."

"Yes, my prince," I agreed, bowing my head.

He let my hand go, but his eyes lingered so long that I wondered if he was going to change his mind about leaving. But eventually he took up the reins and gave them a snap. Padmini raced across the courtyard, leaping onto our courtyard wall, using it as a springboard to propel herself still higher into the air, her wingbeats at last carrying her aloft. I stared after her as she circled for altitude, her orange and yellow feathers blazing above me like the noonday sun.

"Mashkhuda, dear," Ammi said, her voice and her embrace stirring me from my fixation on Arjun and his mount. "You've done very well for yourself. Did I hear rightly that he wants you to attend to him at the palace?"

"Yes, Ammi," I said.

"Wonderful." She was grinning from ear to ear. She gave my cheek a gentle pat. "Come on, I have some sweets inside waiting for you, and you won't have to do any chores today."

Not having to do chores after the exhausting night I'd had was a welcome relief, and one that brought a smile to my face. "Thank you, Ammi."

"It's nothing, dear," she assured me, and she ushered me into the house to ply me with sweets and cool drinks, but my mind was on Arjun, on the feeling of his body pressed against mine as we soared through the sky, and on the promise he had made to protect me.

# CHAPTER 4

My fingers ran over the silky smooth surface of my sandalwood box as my nostrils drank in the sweet aroma. The box smelled just like it had the day it was presented to me. I'd never forget that day. Sikander, my father's master-at-arms, had ordered me to fight six of my young guards-in-training. I'd been quick as lightning that day, more graceful than a dancer and stronger than an elephant. I had done everything right, and one by one, I had defeated all six of them. My father had been watching from the balcony above the courtyard, and when I had beaten the sixth boy, I looked up to him, and I saw on his face a look of pride that I had never seen before and would never see again.

That evening, after dinner, my father had come to me in the harem. He never did that, except to beat me or yell at me for being too effeminate. But that night was different. That night, he brought a sandalwood box with him, and he handed it to me, and he gave me a pat on the shoulder, and he said, "Son, today you fought like a zahhak. So it is only fitting that you should have a zahhak's claws."

I remembered opening that box and seeing what lay within— the most beautiful pair of katars I had ever laid eyes on. They were made of wootz steel, the blades decorated with lightning bolts of gold koftgari. The base of each blade seemed to grow organically out of the steel head of a thunder zahhak, the scales intricately carved into the metal, the lines left by the sculptor's chisel filled with beaten gold wire.

I looked inside the box now, at the katars resting in their velvet cushions. They were just as brilliant as they had been that day, when my father had been proud to have me as his son. I reached down and took them in my hands, remembering how familiar they had once been.

How strange they looked in my hands now. My arms seemed too slender by half, and my golden bangles rattled whenever I moved them. The delicate patterns of mehendi on my hands were so feminine, so graceful, so unlike the deadly sharp steel that projected from my fists.

I didn't know why I kept them. On the road from Nizam, they'd been my only protection. I'd had to use them twice to ward off bandits. But after I'd come to the dera, when I'd been penniless, why had I not traded them away or sold them? Why had I kept them in this box, unused, for so long?

Proof.

They were the only proof I possessed that I had once been the crown prince of Nizam. That life seemed so far away now. My clothes were the clothes of a courtesan. My body was the body of a courtesan. My movements, my speech, my posture, they all belonged to a courtesan, honed for years under the watchful eyes of Varsha and the tutors she had hired. They had beaten all traces of that prince out of me in a perverse analogue of the way my father and his men had tried to beat the girl out of me back home.

I didn't know why I wanted to remember. I'd been so miserable in Nizam, so desperate to be anyplace else. I'd hated myself and hated my life. Why did I want proof of all that? That question wasn't so easy to answer.

I tucked the katars back in their box, careful to wipe them down first with a clean silk cloth so that they wouldn't rust. I closed the lid, then tucked the sandalwood box back in its spot on the shelf in Varsha's storeroom. Here, in the very center of the house, she kept all her jewelry, all her treasures, everything of value in the dera. Stealing from it was punishable by exile. I knew they would be safe here, as they had been these last four years. Maybe in four more years, I'd come back and gaze upon them again.

"Razia, what are you doing in here?" Varsha was standing in the doorway, watching me, though I didn't know how long she'd been there.

"I was looking at my katars, Ammi," I replied, color rushing to my cheeks. She probably thought I was an idiot for keeping them around.

She frowned and came to me and put her arms around me, pulling me close to her, just like she had on that first night, when I'd been dirty and starving and scared and all alone in the world. "Did the prince make you homesick?"

I rested my head against her and sighed. She saw it more clearly than I did. "It's not that I'm unhappy here, Ammi . . ."

"It's all right," she said. "We all get homesick sometimes. Even me. And I didn't have to give up being a prince when I ran away from home."

"I didn't like being a prince," I said. "I just liked riding zahhaks. And fighting. Fighting always made me feel graceful—like I was a dancer. But I was miserable as a prince."

"It's good that you were a prince," she told me. "Most of the other girls can't read or write half so well as you can. They can't recite poetry like you can. They don't know history the way you do. That's why Arjun likes you so much; you're just like him."

"I'm not *just* like him," I protested, for more reasons than Varsha could ever know. I wasn't a man like he was. I wasn't a prince like he was. I could never be like him, no matter how hard I tried. And whenever I looked at him, a part of me was reminded of all those failures.

"You are," she insisted. "And that's a good thing too. You'll see. There's nothing a prince will find quite so intriguing as a beautiful young woman who can fly a zahhak like a king and dance like a courtesan. He's not going to be able to resist you."

"I don't know about that, Ammi," I murmured, but I wanted to believe it.

"Well, I do," she replied. "Now come along. You have to get ready. You can't be late to the palace, and I want you looking your most beautiful."

"All right," I agreed. I walked hand in hand with her out of the storeroom, into the courtyard. We got about halfway across it when somebody pulled the bell at the gate. We exchanged confused glances, and I asked, "Shall I see who it is, Ammi?"

"No, I'll see to it." She let go of my hand and went to the gate, opening a small window in it to see who was there. Our neighborhood wasn't the best, and though thieves rarely came out in the morning, one couldn't be too careful. Whoever it was, though, they must not have been thieves, because Ammi opened the gate right away, and a pair of men came in.

I could tell that they were eunuchs from their beardless faces and tall, slender frames, but they weren't hijras like us. They wore turbans and men's kurtas, and khandas swung from their hips. Each man carried a sandalwood box, one wide and flat, and the other shorter but deeper. The man holding the wide, flat box asked in his effeminate voice, "Is Razia Khan here?"

"I'm Razia Khan," I said, coming forward. My sisters were peering out from the doorways and windows around the courtyard, trying to discern what was going on. I myself couldn't quite work it out. Were these eunuchs from Govind Singh? Was it something to do with the statue I'd stolen?

"His Royal Highness, Prince Arjun Agnivansha, son of the Maharaja Udai Agnivansha, wishes for you to be properly attired for today's festivities. We have come to prepare you to his highness's desire."

I looked to Ammi, who was nodding decisively, and then turned back to the eunuchs. "Of course. My chambers are just this way." I led them through the courtyard, keenly aware of the watchful eyes of my sisters, particularly Sakshi's excited ones and Jaskaur's jealous ones. I was grateful to leave them behind, to enter the little sanctuary that was my bedchamber. It was small, little more than a closet with a bed and a desk and a chair, but it was my own, and it was private, which was more than most hijras could have ever dreamed of possessing.

The eunuchs shut the door, laid their boxes down on my bed, and looked me over carefully. It made me a bit nervous, having two strangers in my bedchamber.

I asked them, "What are your names, sirs?"

"I am called Jai," said the one who had been holding the wide, flat box. He was the taller of the two, and slightly older, I thought. He'd been cut later too, as his jaw was heavier and more masculine and his voice was a touch deeper. His skin was paler, though— maybe he came from somewhere to the north like I did.

"My name is Shiv, my lady," said the shorter, darker-skinned one. I thought he was the more beautiful of the two. He'd have made a perfect hijra, though I supposed if he'd wanted that he wouldn't have been wearing a turban.

"She's a hijra, not a lady," Jai grumbled.

"His highness likes her," Shiv said.

"So he does." Jai sighed. He looked me over, glanced around my room, and said, "I don't suppose you have a hairbrush and any makeup?"

I bristled at that. "Of course I do." I took them out of my desk, along with coconut oil for my hair, a couple of perfumes Ammi had given me, and a bottle of rose water.

"Good," he said. "Now take your clothes off."

I gasped at his abruptness. "Be nice," Shiv chided. When Jai met his suggestion with a glare, Shiv added, "Or I'll tell his highness that you were mean to her."

Jai sighed heavily and looked back to me. "Please undress, my lady, so that we can get to work."

"We often help prepare the ladies at the palace," Shiv said, smiling at me. "We're not going to hurt you."

"Right," I agreed, not wanting to play the role of the timid damsel anyway. I pulled my bangles off my wrists and took off my clothes, then stood there completely naked in front of them, my eyes fixed on Jai's so he would know I felt no shame at who I was.

Shiv got to work straightaway, rubbing my body down with rose water and running coconut oil through my hair. As he worked, Jai opened the flat box, and I saw that it was filled with beautiful silks.

"How did you manage such a womanly figure, my lady?" Shiv asked.

"Essential salts," I answered. "The alchemist sells them to us. He says they come from a distillation of something related to pregnant mares. I don't know the details."

"Well, they work wonders," Shiv observed.

"They do that," I agreed.

When Shiv was finished rubbing all manner of scented oils over me, Jai approached with a satin skirt, stiffened by means of petticoats of netted fabric, giving it a wide silhouette. It was a brilliant shade of saffron, embroidered everywhere with golden zahhaks that twisted and turned over the fabric, flames of red silk issuing forth from their mouths. Once I'd stepped into it, he brought out a short-sleeved blouse of the same material, with more golden zahhaks and crimson flames dancing across the fabric. Lastly, he removed a dupatta from the box. It was diaphanous cinnabar silk, with a border of saffron fire.

I'd never seen clothes like those before, not even back home in Nizam. They'd have been considered far too decorative for any man. I thought I looked like a proper princess in my new clothes, but the two eunuchs weren't finished with me yet. Shiv made me sit still for my makeup, and when that was finished, he braided my hair with fresh flowers like I was a bride.

Jai opened the second box then and began removing pieces of jewelry that made my jaw drop. He shoved half a dozen bangles onto my arms. They were all identical—two zahhak heads growing out of a single scaled body, with feathery wings pressed close around them like the wings of a bird, holding rubies in their open mouths, with just the tiniest gap between the perfect scarlet spheres. The motif was repeated on the earrings, which were the heads of zahhaks holding rubies in their mouths, and in the necklace, which was a collar of zahhaks connected feathered wingtip to feathered wingtip, each one clutching rubies in its hind talons. Last of all came the nose ring, which was a zahhak eating its own plumed tail, exquisitely rendered in gold.

Shiv pressed beautiful cinnabar slippers onto my feet, covered in golden embroidery, and then he smiled. "You look radiant, my lady."

"Let's get her into the palanquin and get her back to the palace before we're late," said Jai, sounding a good deal less impressed. He led the way out of my room, and Shiv gestured for me to go next, so I did, leaving him to bring up the rear.

Sakshi squealed with delight as I came out of my room. I felt my cheeks burning, and there was a twinge of guilt there too. She deserved to be dressed like this more than I did; I'd had my turn, being a prince. She'd come from a very poor family. Someday, I hoped, I'd have the money to buy her clothes as fine as these, as she had always been a true sister to me. Maybe if I pleased Arjun, that day would be coming sooner than I'd ever dreamed.

"Mashkhuda, Razia!" she exclaimed, running up to me, but too afraid of messing up the eunuchs' careful work to embrace me. "You look like the maharani herself!"

"You look wonderful," Ammi told me. "Mashkhuda. You're going to make Prince Arjun so happy."

I smiled and opened my mouth to reply when Jai growled from the gate, "Come on, girl, we haven't got all day."

"Coming, sir!" I exclaimed. I said to Sakshi, "I'll tell you about everything when I get back," and then I rushed to the gate to follow Jai, who was already standing out in the street, beside a golden palanquin supported by four porters.

For a moment, I could do nothing but stare at the palanquin in slack-jawed wonderment. Its roof was domed like a palace's garden pavilion, but its innumerable golden panels were pierced and cut, producing writhing vines and blooming flowers that gleamed in the light of the sun. Its walls were made of dozens of panes of glass, set into a golden frame and shaded by red velvet curtains, held back by golden rope pulls. Inside was a plush mattress with a red velvet pillow to support my back, and two more to support my arms, lest any part of me be forced to touch an unyielding surface.

"Let me help you, my lady," Shiv offered, holding my hand to steady me as I held back my long, bouffant skirt on the way up the palanquin's step. Jai could have taken my arm to help me, as he was already standing beside the door, but he stood back with his arms crossed over his chest. That was all right; I'd scaled more difficult things in similar clothes, and I soon found myself seated among the velvet cushions in the dappled shade of the palanquin's golden roof.

Shiv kept his place just on the other side of the door, in case I should need anything, and the palanquin set off down the street, following the twists and turns of the middle-class mohalla in which I lived. I felt like a prince again. No. Better than a prince. A princess. Just like Sakshi had said.

I couldn't believe my good fortune. When I'd left home four years before, I'd been wearing a servant girl's clothes and carrying my katars, some food and water, and nothing else save a little bit of money. That money hadn't lasted me long, and neither had the food and water. When I'd arrived on Varsha's doorstep, I'd been little better than a beggar, my stolen clothes soiled and frayed, my body filthy, my hair matted. I'd never felt so far from home as I had at that moment, waiting with desperation in my heart to hear if I would be taken in off the street and cared for or sent back out into the alley to die.

Varsha had chosen to spare me, but life in the dera wasn't like life in the palace. I'd been forced to do chores for the first time in my life. I'd been forced to serve others for the first time in my life. I'd been forced to treat the older girls with the respect due an older sister. I think, if not for the fact that I could be myself in the dera, I'd have killed myself from despair at being forced to live such an alien life.

But I would never forget my ammi's kindness, not as long as I lived. She had treated me like a daughter, and Sakshi had treated me like a sister. The dera had become my family in a way that my real family had never been. Oh, there were politics in the dera too, just like in the court of Nizam. There were intrigues and jealousies, as each of us girls jockeyed to win the best clients for ourselves, but in the dera I had found the acceptance I'd never found anywhere else. There, I didn't have to constantly defend my womanhood. I didn't have to explain myself to anyone. Everyone just understood.

So it had been worth it, giving up my wealth and privilege for love and acceptance. And all this time in the dera, I'd never once imagined that I could have it all, that I might someday have the wealth and power of royalty, but without having to live as a man. Now, riding in that palanquin, I wondered for the first time if it was truly possible. Was that to be my fate? Was God so kind as to shower so many blessings upon me? I prayed fervently that it was so.

"His highness told us that you were once a prince, my lady," Shiv said, as he walked alongside my velvet throne. "Is that true?"

"He told you that?" I gasped, my heart pounding. He'd told common eunuchs my secret? What had he told his father? Did they all know who I was? God, if they knew, I was a dead woman. Was that what this was—a trap? Was I being led into the life of a hostage, or the short life of a political bargaining chip?

"Just that you were a minor member of a royal house," said Shiv, his brow furrowing a little, as he realized how alarmed I was.

"Oh, yes," I agreed, taking a deep, steadying breath to get my fears under control. Of course Arjun wouldn't have told everyone the truth. If he'd meant to betray me, he'd have kept it from me until I was in his grasp, and if he truly did like me, then he knew how dangerous it would be for others to discover my identity.

"Who *was* your father?" Shiv asked, and I saw then the concern, the alarm, and the curiosity. I'd given him cause for suspicion, and I cursed my own stupidity.

"No one famous," I replied, trying to keep my voice light and easy. "But we did have a beautiful haveli, and I flew my very own zahhak. Her name was Sultana."

"No wonder you've caught his highness's fancy," Shiv replied.

"Oh?" I asked, realizing then that these eunuchs must know the prince well. Maybe they could give me advice on how to best seduce him. I felt a little bit guilty for thinking that. The truth was, there was a part of me that quite liked him, and I was very much attracted to him, but it was hard not to see him as a means to an end: a way to reclaim all that I had lost. But that was dangerous. Men could tell if you were being too mercenary. Oh, some couldn't—the drunk ones, the ones who thought too highly of themselves—but after a while even the densest men could sense the cold calculation behind your bright smile. Part of our training was to find something in every man that we genuinely liked. We focused on that, to keep them from realizing that we mostly just wanted their money. With Arjun, that wasn't so hard. There was a lot of him to like, not least the way he had sworn to protect me.

"Well, I'm not privy to much, my lady," Shiv said. "But if you ask me, I think his highness was bored with the usual courtesans and dancing girls. He hungers for someone who can keep up with him. Someone who can understand him."

"That's enough, Shiv," Jai growled, from his place beside the other eunuch. "You shouldn't be helping that creature get its hooks into his highness."

"I don't have any hooks to put in him," I snapped. "I was paid to entertain the men at Govind Singh's home. I did my job well. Should I not be rewarded for good service as you would be?"

"So long as you don't forget your place," Jai said with disgust on his face. "You're not a princess, and you never will be. I don't know what you were before you did that to yourself, but now you're a whore."

"Jai!" Shiv exclaimed.

"What?" Jai demanded, as my cheeks burned and my anger rose. "Don't you remember how much it hurt? How humiliating it was? To be cut like that, to have a part of your body torn away . . ." He shook his head. "These ones do it to themselves. They volunteer for it. It's disgusting!"

"The way you felt after you were cut is the way I felt before I was cut," I told him through clenched teeth. "It's not my fault God gave me a woman's soul."

He sneered at my reference to the one true God, who wasn't commonly worshipped in Registan. "Mumins . . ."

"She's right, Jai," said Shiv. "Our gods have stories of hijras too."

Jai crossed his arms over his chest and didn't look at either of us. That suited me just fine. It gave me a chance to calm down. I didn't want to meet Arjun when I was angry. Not after all the gifts he'd given me.

I looked down at my bangles then, at the rubies sparkling in the sunlight. They were so delicately wrought, and perfectly resembled the fire zahhaks that the maharajas of Registan rode into battle. I never wanted to take those bangles off again. Were they gifts? Did Arjun intend for me to keep them? I couldn't believe that. They must have been so expensive. They were probably worth two years' earnings or more. He would want them back after today.

Or would he? I'd been a prince once. I remembered when money had been no object. When I'd left the palace, I hadn't even really understood what it was. I'd known that you gave coins to people in exchange for things, but I'd never done it myself. I'd just had to ask for something and it had appeared. Was that how things were for Arjun? I didn't think the prince of Bikampur was nearly as wealthy as I had been, but what did these baubles really mean to him? Not as much as they meant to me, I could say that with certainty.

The bangles made me feel like I was important to Arjun, like he really cared for me. It was foolish; I felt like an idiot girl for thinking it after we'd known each other for just a single evening, but I couldn't help myself. When I looked at those zahhaks encircling my wrists, when I saw how precious they were, it made me think that maybe I was important to someone again. Maybe somebody really could forgive me for what I'd done to myself, forgive me for what I was. I'd never imagined that anyone could.

The palanquin reached the first gate of the Rose Fort, and it was waved through by the guards. We started ascending the twisting road that led up the hill, and I was amazed by how much steeper it seemed from the ground than it had from the back of a racing zahhak. It took the poor porters quite a lot of effort to lug the palanquin through all the gates, to finally crest the top of the hill and reach the great entrance of the fortress palace of the maharaja of Bikampur.

We passed through the pink sandstone gate, guarded on either side by half a dozen men in cuirasses of mail and plates, shining helmets with feather plumes on their heads, wearing swords on their hips and carrying shields on their arms. Above us, on the ramparts, visible between the arched merlons, were men in silk kurtas, holding gleaming toradars. The matchlock muskets were slow to reload, but they outranged any bow, and the maharajas of Registan were the most fabled musketeers on the whole continent of Daryastan. Even my father employed troops of Registani musketeers when he could. I wouldn't have wanted to try to take this fort on foot.

We entered the courtyard, and I was startled to see that it was ringed by musketeers. My heart leapt into my throat. Why would they have so many guards? Did they know about the theft? No, it couldn't be, that didn't make any sense. Arjun wouldn't dress me like this to kill me. Unless he was giving me back to my father. That possibility settled like a lead weight in my stomach.

I glanced to the center of the courtyard and saw my destination—
an exquisite marble pavilion. The maharaja was seated on a velvet
cushion atop a golden platform. Beneath the platform were other
men, dignitaries in fine silk clothes with absurdly large turbans.
And there was Arjun, sitting on a cushion of his own, wearing a
kurta and trousers that were a perfect match for my lehenga. His
kurta was the same gorgeous saffron silk, but it lacked the delicate
embroidery of my own clothes. Instead, subtler, darker orange im-
ages of zahhaks could be seen winding their way across the fabric. If
he was dressed like me, that meant he wasn't giving me back to my
father, didn't it?

That was when I saw the wrestlers, all gathered together in a
knot in the courtyard, and I breathed a sigh of relief. It was a
wrestling match after all. The musketeers were just a show of the
maharaja's strength. My father had done that from time to time
too. It shouldn't have alarmed me so much, but I'd been away
from palaces for years, and my sudden return to them had brought
back old fears long forgotten.

Shiv helped me down from the palanquin and led me across
the courtyard toward the pavilion. I heard men whispering as I
approached, but I was careful not to smile, not to look too full of
myself. Instead, I kept my gaze downcast and my dupatta close
around me, like a properly brought up young princess. I thought
Arjun might like that.

I stopped as we reached the steps that led up to the pavilion
and bowed low to the maharaja, as was proper. Shiv touched my
shoulder a moment later, and I stood up once more. That was
when the maharaja addressed me.

Udai Agnivansha reminded me too much of my father. He was
a fierce-looking man, with scars on his face from battles won and
lost. He was strong still, burly almost, his power plain in his big,
callused hands and in the breadth of his shoulders. His full beard

was streaked throughout with gray, as were his eyebrows, which were bushy and slanted, making him look angry. I couldn't see his mouth to know whether he was smiling or not, so I imagined that he wasn't, that he was scowling, that he was disgusted with me and angry at his son for bringing me here.

"So you're the little hijra who can ride a zahhak, are you?" His voice was deep and rumbling, but it didn't sound angry—more bemused if anything.

"Yes, your majesty," I replied, keeping my eyes downcast.

"What's your name?" he demanded.

"Razia Khan, your majesty," I said.

"Not that name," he snapped, like I was wasting his time. "Your name. The name your father gave you."

My eyes flickered to Arjun, who gave a very small shake of his head. He hadn't told him. That was something. So I used the name I always used when I had to lie to protect myself. "Junaid Karrani."

"You were the son of the subahdar of Vanga?" he asked, sounding intrigued by that.

"Yes, your majesty," I said, hearing my voice as a pathetic squeak. My father had mocked me for it my whole life. *Speak like a man*, he'd said. *No one on the battlefield is going to listen to your shrill shrieking.*

"And how long have you been living here like this?" he asked, gesturing to me in much the same way that Jai had, his disdain apparent.

"Four years, your majesty," I replied. "I was taken in by Varsha Khan. She runs a dera here in the city for ones like ourselves."

"And how do I know that you're really a hijra, and not secretly an assassin posing as one to get close to me and my son?" he asked.

"Well, your majesty," I replied, a smirk creasing my face, "considering what I let your son do to me the night before last, if I am an assassin, I'm a very committed one."

The men chuckled knowingly at that, looking very much amused. One reached over and gave Arjun a slap on the back. Udai Agnivansha looked somewhat less entertained.

"If you were my son, I would track you down and kill you to erase the stain to my honor," he growled.

"If my father knew where I was, I think I would be more in danger of assassins than you or your son, your majesty," I said, my voice tight with emotion. It hurt so much to admit that my father would rather see me dead than happy, but he was a lot like Udai Agnivansha. I was beginning to regret taking Arjun up on his offer. As much as I liked him, his father reminded me of my own so strongly that it turned my insides to mush.

Not that what I wanted mattered. It hadn't been an offer. More like an order. And who was I to refuse the order of a prince? Nobody. Absolutely nobody. So there I stood, enduring the glare of the most powerful man in Bikampur, because I had no choice.

"Your majesty, I was dressed and brought here by your servants at your son's command. If you do not wish me to be here, I beg that you let me return home to my dera and permit me to remain here in your city. I've lived here for four years without causing anyone the least harm—"

He cut me off with a gesture, and I hung my head. He looked annoyed. Maybe pleading with him had been a mistake. "You act like a little girl," he said, his tone accusatory. "Did your father raise you to be this way?"

"No, your majesty," I said. "I was raised to fight and to fly zahhaks and to command men in battle, but God gave me a woman's soul and I was powerless to change it."

He gestured to Arjun then. "Go and attend to my son, girl."

"Yes, your majesty," I agreed, unable to keep the relief from my voice. It made some of the guards standing around the pavilion scowl. The men resting on the cushions seemed less hostile. Most of them had hired our dera, or another like ours, for dances in the past. So they couldn't look down their noses at Arjun for desiring me. Such things were fairly normal, even at my father's court.

I climbed the stairs and came to sit on the cushion beside Arjun's, showing as much grace as I possessed just to spite the old king. I kept my eyes downcast and said, "Good day, my prince." I even managed not to sound upset, though my emotions were roiling inside of me—anger, frustration, shame, disgust, and I think sadness most of all. It was the sadness that came with knowing that whatever I did, however hard I worked, I would never be the person I was meant to be.

Arjun's arm came around my shoulders, and he whispered into my ear, "Don't mind my father. He's a miserable old bastard, but if he really didn't like you, he'd never have let you stay."

I wasn't sure if that was true or not, but I wanted it to be. I whispered back, "Thank you for inviting me, my prince, and for . . ." I didn't even know where to begin thanking him for the jewels and the clothes. I still didn't quite believe that I was meant to keep them, and I didn't want to imply that I was keeping them if he didn't want me to. So I lamely finished the sentence with, "everything."

"It was nothing," he assured me. I knew he'd said it to make me feel better, but it just made me feel worse. If the jewels weren't important to him, then I probably wasn't either.

## CHAPTER 5

"Have you ever watched a wrestling competition before?"
Arjun asked me as I poured him chilled wine.

"No, my prince," I replied, careful to keep my voice
neutral, to fight down the amused smirk that kept trying to
stretch my lips.

"You haven't?" he asked, and he looked puzzled, like that
wasn't the answer he'd expected. He must have known how crazy
my father had been for wrestling competitions as a source of en-
tertainment.

"No, my prince," I answered. "My father always forced me to
compete. Watching is for women and slaves, he would say."

The maharaja must have heard us, because he grumbled, "Is
that why you lopped off your manhood, then? To avoid wrestling
competitions?"

The question annoyed me, but I wasn't going to show it. Instead, I took Arjun's cheeks between my palms, caressing them

gently, and said, "No, your majesty. I simply wanted to indulge in a more interesting sort of wrestling competition."

Arjun smiled at me and placed his hands over my own, slowly lowering them from his face. "Later," he promised. "For now, we should give the competitors our respectful attention."

"Of course, my prince," I agreed, folding my hands in my lap and turning my attention toward the courtyard in front of us. My cheeks were burning. I wasn't usually so forward, and I wondered if it had embarrassed him. Of course, I wouldn't have said anything if not for his father. Why did the man take my existence so personally? Probably the same reason my father had. There was something about big, burly, hairy men that made them despise anyone who wasn't cut from the same cloth as themselves.

"Welcome, competitors!" Udai roared to a group of men who had come to stand before him wearing nothing but loincloths. They were all tough men like the maharaja himself, heavily muscled, with cauliflower ears. They had shaved the hair from their bodies to avoid giving their opponents an easy handhold, and they looked ready to kill.

"The rules are simple," the maharaja continued. "The man who lands on his back first loses. No kicking, no punching, and no biting allowed. Fight well, and may the fire god Agni look on you with favor!"

"Thank you, your majesty!" they chorused in response.

Though I wouldn't have admitted it to the other girls in the dera, as they'd have mocked me for being too masculine, I liked wrestling competitions. I hadn't particularly cared for competing in them growing up, but watching them was another matter. Most of the girls I knew found such events obscenely boring, but I had two very good reasons for liking them. In the first place, I knew all the techniques, and when you know the techniques and their counters, you know what the men are thinking. Knowing that makes the competition exciting. And as for the second reason, well, the men were answering that now as they stood there nearly naked, their bronzed flesh flashing in the sun. Yes, there were much less enjoyable ways to spend a day.

The first pair of men moved to their respective places in the courtyard and faced off, waiting for the order to begin. I already had a favorite. I thought the shorter man moved better. He was a little quicker on his feet; he seemed a little more coordinated. I looked to Arjun and asked, "Would you care to place a wager, my prince?"

"With you?" He seemed surprised that I'd make such an offer. When I nodded, he asked, "What are the terms?"

"If I win, you serve me today," I said.

"And if I win?" he asked.

"Whatever you like," I answered, feeling fairly confident in my choice.

"Whatever I like?" He grinned. "All right. Who are you choosing?"

"The short one," I said.

Men laughed all around me. The maharaja gave a derisive snort. Arjun put his arm around me and said, "Razia . . . the taller one is Mohan Gaur."

"Is that supposed to mean something?" I asked, which drew even more laughter from the men.

Arjun stroked my hair and said in a gentle tone, "He's a very famous wrestler. The other man, Ramamurthy, I think his name is, has never wrestled at court before. He's from the south— Virajendra, I believe. But he's never fought here before."

"I still want to pick the shorter one," I said, and I noted the way the men around me sniggered into their wine goblets and shook their heads in response.

One said, "I'd take that bet if I were you, your highness."

"Anything I want?" he asked me, his voice husky.

"Anything you want, my prince," I replied. Maybe I would lose the bet, but I still didn't think I would. I liked the looks of the shorter man. He seemed like he would do well. And anyway, what did it matter? I had to give Arjun whatever he pleased regardless of the outcome of our silly bet.

"Well, I'd be a fool to refuse a bet like that," he said.

I poured him a little more wine, and some nimbu pani for myself, and held up my glass in salute. "We shall see, my prince."

"I suppose we shall," he agreed.

"Begin!" the maharaja shouted.

The men started toward each other at once, moving around in cautious circles, swiping with their hands, searching for an opening. Like most wrestling matches, it started slow as they felt each other out. They locked hands, and then slipped free of each other several times. As they moved, I smiled. This Ramamurthy impressed me. He was strong, he was short, which typically conferred some advantage in such contests, and he was smart. Every time Mohan went in for a technique, he would slide free and evade it.

After a few moments of searching each other out, the real action began without warning. Mohan stepped forward and grabbed for Ramamurthy's arms, but the shorter man dropped low and grabbed one of Mohan's legs, screaming as he lifted up to throw him. For his part, Mohan grabbed Ramamurthy in a headlock and tried to sink his weight down to keep from being lifted up.

Ramamurthy's muscles bulged beneath his dark skin, the veins becoming visible as he tensed with every ounce of his strength. This was the moment of truth. If he made the throw, the match would be over, but if he didn't, he'd be too tired to fend off Mohan's counterattacks. Had I bet wrong? Had I mistaken Ramamurthy's youth for talent?

Mohan Gaur toppled over onto his back, his bare flesh hitting the stones of the courtyard with a loud slap. Ramamurthy slipped out of the other man's headlock, pounded his chest, and screamed to the heavens in triumph. For his part, Mohan sat in stunned silence, just like the men around me, who had thought he would be the victor.

I took a swig of my nimbu pani and then held out the cup to Arjun and cleared my throat.

"How did you know he would win?" he asked, like he still couldn't believe it had happened.

"It was obvious," I said, and then I shook my empty cup a second time.

"Oh, forgive me, my princess," he said, rolling his eyes and taking the hint, but he did fill my cup.

"You're forgiven," I replied, sipping the sweet and salty liquid, which tasted almost as good as victory. The men all around didn't think I was so stupid now—nor did the maharaja.

"The winner is Ramamurthy," he announced, his voice somewhat dazed as his eyes were still fixed on me. "The next competitors are Karanbahadur of Rakhastan and Mahmood Bhatti of Nizam."

"Care to give me a chance to reclaim my dignity?" Arjun asked.

I eyed the competitors as they approached. Mahmood Bhatti was a burly man, but so was this Karanbahadur fellow. Karanbahadur was slightly shorter and definitely older. He had a wild black beard that might have worked for a handhold, but otherwise it was hard to see which might have the advantage over the other. I was leaning toward Mahmood for the sake of patriotism, but there was something about the Rakhan that made me think he would win.

"My bet is for the Rakhan, my prince," I said.

He smirked. "Done. If I win, you go back to serving me."

"And if I win, you have to let me fly Padmini again," I replied.

He pulled me close to him and said, "I'd have let you do that anyway. I saw how much it pleased you."

"Those are my terms, my prince."

"We're agreed, then," he said.

I rested my head on his shoulder as his father gave the order for the wrestlers to start fighting. This day was going better than I'd expected. I'd learned in my training that making bets with men was a good way to keep their interest, especially if you could keep up a winning streak. It made them eager to beat you, and all the more interested if they couldn't figure out how you kept winning. But you never asked for anything from a man that he didn't want to give you anyway. Otherwise, he would grow annoyed with losing. But if he wanted to lose as much as he wanted to win . . . well, that was the trick.

"I'm hungry," I complained, as the wrestlers circled each other, batting at each other's hands in an attempt to get a grip they could use to their advantage.

Arjun reached down and picked up a piece of mango and placed it in my mouth. I sucked on one of his fingers for a long second, drawing a contented sigh from his lips before I pulled away.

Mahmood got a grip on Karanbahadur's arm, and Arjun pumped his fist. He grinned at me and said, "You're going to be back to serving me in a second."

"Oh?" I asked, feigning complete diffidence. Of course, I was eagerly praying to God that he would see fit to give Karanbahadur the strength to win this fight. As it was, the Rakhan was being manhandled by Mahmood, who had both hands on him and was twisting and jerking him this way and that in an attempt to upset his balance.

There it was! Mahmood gave a shove, and then swept his leg to trip Karanbahadur, but the Rakhan pulled his foot back and kicked out and swept Mahmood instead. The Nizami man dropped like a stone, landing flat on his back.

Arjun turned to look at me slack-jawed, and he wasn't the only one. All the nobles were staring. Even the maharaja himself was glancing at me suspiciously. But it was Arjun who demanded, "How do you keep doing that?"

"It was just luck, my prince," I said, wrapping my arms around one of his and placing my head back on his shoulder.

"The winner is Karanbahadur of Rakhastan!" the maharaja declared. "Now, Karanbahadur and Ramamurthy will fight to determine the winner of this group!"

"I think Ramamurthy will win this," said Arjun. "What do you say to another wager?"

I looked at the two competitors and shook my head. "No, my prince, I agree with you. Ramamurthy will win the match."

"You're not going to let me win back my dignity?" he asked in mock horror.

"Never," I replied, and I shook my empty glass for emphasis.

He poured the nimbu pani for me and said, "You know, I get the feeling you're going to cause me nothing but trouble."

"You wouldn't be the first to say such things, my prince," I confessed.

Ramamurthy and Karanbahadur squared off then, providing a momentary distraction—momentary being the key word. They met in the center of the courtyard and clutched each other, and Ramamurthy hurled Karanbahadur to the ground with a scream of effort. It was the fastest of the matches by far. Hardly a contest at all. He slapped his chest and held up his arms in victory, shouting to the gods in whatever stream of syllables passed for a language in the Virajendra empire.

"Ramamurthy is the victor!" the maharaja declared. Gifts were brought out to him—fine clothes and gems and a magnificent khanda, a kind of straight, double-edged sword preferred by the maharajas of Registan.

When Ramamurthy had received his acclamations, the maharaja turned to us and said, "Well, we've got a few minutes before the next round of matches begins. Shall we have an impromptu competition to keep things interesting?"

"A fine idea, your majesty," said Jai from his place behind the throne. "Perhaps we eunuchs could wrestle one another for your amusement?"

"Got something to prove, Jai?" the maharaja quipped.

"Perhaps, your majesty," he allowed, and his smile was positively wicked. I didn't envy the palace eunuch who would be facing off against him.

"And what would the rules of this contest be?" Udai asked.

"Simple, your majesty," Jai replied. "The rules would be the same as for the ordinary competition. The only difference is any eunuch can challenge any other he likes, and that one has to fight."

"No refusals?" The maharaja stroked his bushy black beard with a smirk on his face. "Yes, I like that. Very well, then, Jai, issue your challenge."

"Yes, your majesty," Jai said. This would be interesting. Would he challenge Shiv? If he did, I'd definitely be placing bets on the taller man to win the fight.

"I challenge Razia Khan," he announced, his angry eyes focused squarely on me.

I scowled. "I'm not a eunuch."

"You're a hijra," said the maharaja, as if that counted.

"It's not the same thing, your majesty," I told him, trying to keep the hurt from showing on my face.

"It is to me," the maharaja replied. "Besides, you seemed plenty eager to show off your understanding of the sport. You must be itching for the chance to show us how it's done."

I looked at Jai with an expression of pure loathing. He was one of those eunuchs who thought it was somehow my fault that he'd been cut. How was I to blame for that? So what if I'd sought it out? So what if I was happier this way? Who was he to blame me for it?

"I don't want to ruin my clothes, your majesty. They were a gift from your son," I said, grasping at straws to avoid the humiliation of being made to stand before the entire court and grapple with a sweaty man like some low-class comic acrobat.

"If they're ruined, they'll be replaced," the maharaja replied. "Now stop stalling and get out there." He gestured to the courtyard.

"It's hardly fair, your majesty," said Shiv. "The hijras aren't like us. They have women's physiques."

"Who wants to see the hijra fight?" the maharaja asked, ignoring Shiv.

The question was met with a roar of approval, and I knew that I wasn't getting out of it. I sighed and stripped off my bangles and my earrings and my necklace and my nose ring, placing them all on the cushion beside Arjun. I took off my dupatta too, and then checked myself over to make sure that I was free of anything that might give Jai too great a handhold.

For his part, Jai had stripped off his kurta and now stood bare chested before us all. He wasn't rippling with muscle the way that Ramamurthy had been, but he was a lot more muscular than I was. He had every advantage really, save one. He didn't know that I could wrestle, didn't really believe it. It was plain that none of them did. Well, I could use that to win the match, I thought. I just had to play my cards right.

Arjun stood up, put his hands on my shoulders, and leaned in close. He said, loudly enough that everyone could hear, "If he hurts you, I'll make him wish he'd never been born. You have my word."

"Have no fear, your highness, I'll put her in her place gently," Jai promised. He walked out to the courtyard then, head up, an irritating smirk plastered across his face.

I embraced Arjun and then entered the arena like a condemned criminal on her way to the executioner. I shuffled down the steps, head down, shoulders slumped. I stood where the other competitors had, but I was careful to shift from foot to foot like I was afraid, and to keep my eyes downcast, like I was being utterly humiliated. The response from the men was immediate. Both Jai and the maharaja were grinning. Some of the other men laughed. Arjun gave me an apologetic frown, and then he glared in Jai's direction, his eyes promising vengeance.

Jai stood across from me, sneering at me, like he fully intended to go back on his promise not to hurt me. I bowed my head. "I'm sorry if I offended you today, my lord, I . . ."

"Shut up," he snapped.

"No talking among the competitors," growled the maharaja.

I glanced uncertainly from the spectators to the guards all around us to Jai, and huddled before him like I didn't know anything at all about wrestling or how to defend myself. The more helpless and pathetic I looked, the better it would be.

"Fight!" the maharaja ordered.

Jai wasted no time in coming straight at me, as I'd known he would. He wasn't even in a wrestler's crouch, he was just walking toward me with complete confidence. I wanted to encourage that, so I backed away, looking around like I was trying to find somewhere safe to hide. It just made his sneer grow.

He cut me off from the path I was taking away from him, and

he lunged forward. I backpedaled frantically, nearly tripping over the hem of my satin skirt in the process. The men on the stage were laughing long and loud, especially the maharaja himself. He was chortling at how pathetic I was.

Jai lunged at me again, and this time I twisted away, backing now toward the pavilion where the men were watching. I wanted to be close to them when I did it. I wanted them to see it. I wanted it to happen right in front of the maharaja's ugly face.

Jai grabbed for me, and I could have avoided him, but I didn't. I let him grip my arm, let him throw his other arm over my shoulder, grabbing the fabric of my blouse in the middle of my back. He twisted toward me, intent on throwing me over his hip, but just as he jerked me toward him, I grabbed the hair at the base of his neck and threw my right foot across the front of his legs, springing off with my left, helping him throw me. With my hand clutching his hair, the force of his throw pulled him forward right along with me, and my outstretched leg tripped him.

My move was the perfect counter. The force he'd put into his throw had been doubled by the leap I'd taken, flinging Jai over my body and slamming him flat on his back with more than twice the force I could have managed just trying to throw him on my own.

He lay there in a daze, having hit his head pretty hard. I stood up, dusted my skirt off, and walked back to my place beside Arjun without another word.

Silence reigned in that courtyard. Not one of the men said a single word. They just stared at me, slack-jawed, and then looked to Jai, who was still sitting on the ground, wondering how he'd come to be there. It was Arjun who finally broke the silence. He pulled me close to him, kissed me on the top of my head, and said, "I told you she was special, Father."

The maharaja looked at me and demanded, "If you knew how to wrestle, why act the part of the coward?"

"He's bigger than me, your majesty. He's stronger than me, and I haven't wrestled in four years," I said. "If we fought the rest of the afternoon, I don't think I'd win another match. But all I needed to do was beat him once, and I knew the only way I could do that would be if he was overconfident, if he thought I knew nothing. Then, he wouldn't defend himself properly, he wouldn't guard himself against potential counters. Battles are won in the mind before victory or defeat is decided on the field."

"And who taught you that?" the maharaja asked, sounding impressed for the first time since I'd met him.

"My father," I replied.

He scowled at me. "Mustafa Karrani never fought a battle in his life."

He was right. How could I have been so stupid? I'd forgotten that the whole reason I'd pretended to be Mustafa Karrani's son was because he was a worthless coward of a subahdar who wouldn't be considered a serious enemy by anyone.

"I don't permit liars in my house, girl," Udai Agnivansha growled. "You'll tell me your real name, or I'll have your head struck from your shoulders."

I fought to come up with a different name, one that would make sense, one that wouldn't get me killed outright, but which might explain why I would be reluctant to admit it, but before I could say anything, Arjun spoke, and I knew I was a dead woman.

"Her father is the subahdar of Zindh, Javed Khorasani," Arjun said. "She told me the day I met her, but made me promise not to tell anyone. She was afraid we would hurt her."

I didn't know if I wanted to kiss Arjun or slap him. The lie he'd chosen was an awfully dangerous one. Zindh was a province just across the desert to the west, one of the most important in my father's empire. Javed Khorasani was a brave and fierce warrior, one of my father's most trusted generals, the defender of Nizam's western border, and an ever-present thorn in the sides of the maharajas of Registan. Worse, he had inflicted on Maharaja Udai of Bikampur a stinging defeat just five years prior. If the maharaja wanted revenge . . .

"You swore you wouldn't tell anyone!" I exclaimed, knowing that I had to sell things properly to keep my true identity a secret. I let my whole body tremble, which wasn't hard. Even if I wasn't the child of Javed Khorasani, the suggestion was fatal enough.

"No one is going to hurt you, Razia," Arjun promised me. He held me tightly to him and stroked my hair. "It's all right. My father isn't going to kill you for who your father is."

Udai Agnivansha was chortling. He was laughing so hard it was practically choking him. He pounded his fist into his own thigh again and again as he laughed. The men around him were too stunned to join in. They just stared at the pair of us in abject horror.

When he'd finally calmed himself, the maharaja of Bikampur said, "Fuck her good, boy. This is the fire god's own justice and nothing else. Javed Khorasani is a pain in my ass. It's only fitting that my son should be a pain in his son's ass." And then he started laughing again, and this time his men joined in, having got the joke.

This was what I'd been afraid of all along, that Arjun would see me as some hilarious conquest, a way of sticking it to the sultan of Nizam, of feeling superior.

But if Arjun had felt that way, he'd have told his father the truth, and he hadn't. He'd protected me. I clung to him and rested my head against his chest, my heart still beating like a startled gazelle's.

"You know, she did best Jai in the match, your majesty," Shiv said. "Perhaps some reward is in order?"

I knew he was trying to be helpful, but I silently prayed that Shiv would choke to death on his own tongue. I didn't want the maharaja's attention, let alone to go begging him for rewards.

"Reward?" the maharaja grumbled, clearly not liking the sound of giving a reward to his rival's son.

"Being permitted to live in your city is reward enough, your majesty," I assured him.

"There, you see, she's been rewarded," he said, giving a dismissive wave in Shiv's direction.

"I'll give you a proper reward later," Arjun whispered into my ear, as he pulled me back down to the cushions.

"My prince is too kind." I poured a fresh glass of wine and served it to him.

"I thought that was my job now," he teased.

I managed a weak smile, but I was too rattled to muster much more than that. "I think I'll lay off the betting for a little while, if it pleases my prince," I told him, as that was how all this nonsense had got started.

"Understandable," he replied.

They called up the next group of wrestlers, and I was careful to keep my mouth shut and my predictions to myself for the rest of the afternoon. I contented myself with serving food and drinks to Arjun, congratulating him when his chosen wrestler won and consoling him when he lost. It was much safer than making a big show of how good I was at predicting the outcome. I didn't think I'd ever do that again. I was lucky the lesson hadn't cost me more than a wrestling match and a little mockery.

When the wrestling matches finally ended and the victors had been rewarded, Arjun stood up, then helped me to my feet. My legs were cramped from having sat so long in one place, but I was just thankful that nothing worse had happened. Arjun's father was glancing at me out of the corners of his eyes, and he was scowling. I knew he was thinking about Javed Khorasani and the victory he had won in their last battle.

"Care to go for a flight?" Arjun asked.

"I would like that very much, my prince," I replied, eager to get away from his father, and from Jai, and from the other men. It was a relief that nobody stopped us from walking off in the direction of the zahhak stables. I waited until we were out of the courtyard, away from prying eyes and keen ears, and then I stopped, stood on my tiptoes, and kissed Arjun on the cheek, saying, "Thank you for protecting me, my prince."

He pulled me close to him, his strong arms holding me tightly. "I wouldn't let anyone hurt you, Razia. Not even my father."

"It was risky, telling him that I was Javed Khorasani's child," I murmured.

"It would have been riskier telling him the truth," he pointed out.

"Oh, I know, my prince," I rushed to say, worried he might take it the wrong way and get angry with me. "You did everything perfectly. I was just afraid of how he might react."

"He would have reacted differently had you been a eunuch like Jai, or simply a man whose tastes ran toward other men. But you're not a threat to anyone, so killing you would be unnecessarily cruel. My father isn't the easiest man to get along with, but I've never known him to hurt anyone without cause. Besides, I think he likes you."

"Likes me?" I gasped, wondering if Arjun had even been paying attention all day. "Did you hear the things he said to me?"

"You just confused him is all. He doesn't have much use for women, but you impressed him twice—first with your knowledge of wrestling, and then when you bested Jai. It's not often that a woman impresses him, much less a hijra. I think he views you as worse than women, because at least women didn't choose their lot in life."

"Neither did I, my prince," I said, unable to keep the irritation out of my voice. I was tired of people accusing me of having chosen my path in life, like my soul was something I had picked out in the bazaar and not something I'd been born with. "Nobody would be this way if it was something as simple as a choice."

"Well, I hope I don't offend you by saying this, Razia," he said, "but however it happened, I'm glad you are the way you are."

I quirked an eyebrow at that. "You are?"

"Sure," he said. "I don't think I'd have enjoyed kissing Salim Mirza nearly so much."

"Definitely not," I agreed, reaching up and wrapping my arms around his neck. "Salim Mirza was a total bore."

"He did have that reputation," Arjun agreed.

"What?" I squawked. Was that true? Had I had a reputation when I was a boy?

"You didn't know?" He smirked as he ran his hands through my hair, his lips just out of reach of my own. "Everyone said that Prince Salim was a spoiled brat who wouldn't even look you in the eyes when he talked to you."

"Is that so?" I asked, my eyes looking straight into Arjun's.

"So I was told." He leaned a little closer. "But I've heard his sister is another matter altogether."

"Oh?"

"Mm-hmm." He planted his lips on mine, and we kissed for a long time before we both had to come up for air.

"Well," I said, kissing his neck and working my way up to his jaw, "I heard that Prince Arjun Agnivansha was a handsome, dashing zahhak rider, unbeatable with khanda or katars, and exceedingly good company."

He grinned as my kisses edged closer to his lips. "Is that so?"

"Oh, yes," I said, and I kissed him on the mouth then. "My father would never stop talking about you, telling me how great you were, and how worthless I was. 'You'll be the death of the dynasty,' he would say. 'The maharajas will slaughter us when the time comes for you to face their prince on the field of battle.'"

Arjun pulled away from me sharply. "He really said all that to you? To his own son?"

I shrugged. "Look at you, and look at me."

"So why don't you hate me, then?" he asked.

"Hate you?" I puzzled over that for a moment. I supposed it was a fair question. Shouldn't I have hated him for being the ideal I could never attain? I shook my head. "It wasn't just you, my prince. It was Prince Suraj of Virajendra and Prince Karim of Mahisagar. It was all the subahdars' sons who liked girls and who acted like men. My father compared me unfavorably to every man in Daryastan."

"I would despise them all if my father had compared me to them like that," Arjun said.

I shrugged. "Whenever my father would say those things, I would just tell him that they sounded awfully handsome, and that always shut him right up. In truth, my prince—" I cut myself off, my cheeks heating. Maybe this wasn't the right time to be so honest.

"In truth what?" he asked.

"Nothing, my prince," I said, my blush growing until it engulfed me from my neck to my ears.

"Tell me," he said, trying and failing to sound imperious. But then he added, "Or I won't take you flying."

"You lost a bet," I reminded him.

"And you called it off," he replied. "Now, what was it you were going to say?"

"It's silly, my prince," I said.

"Then there's no harm in my hearing it."

I sighed, realizing that it was just going to sound more ridiculous the more I resisted him. "Well, I heard a lot about you in the palace growing up. They talked about how you fought against Javed Khorasani with your father when you were just fourteen, and how even though your father lost, you knocked down two thunder zahhaks atop Padmini's back, and laid waste to Lord Khorasani's right flank with her fire. If not for the artillery, you might have won the day for your father."

"You heard about that?" he asked, endeavoring to sound humble and not coming anywhere near the mark.

I rolled my eyes and kissed him on the cheek. "I heard nothing else for six whole months. My father made me practice flying five hours a day, every day, just so I could reach the standards set by the amazing Prince Arjun of Bikampur."

"And?" he pressed, knowing that this wasn't the part that had made my whole face flush crimson.

"And . . . I . . ." I took a deep breath and let it out slowly. "And I used to have dreams about you."

His eyes widened, and a big grin creased his face. He leaned close to me, until his breath was warm on my face. "Dreams? What sort of dreams?"

"Good dreams," I said, smiling in spite of myself.

"Just good dreams?" he teased. "Not great dreams?"

"Very good dreams, my prince," I said. "I always wanted to meet you. I'd hoped for years that I might someday be asked to perform for you."

"So this is all your doing, then?" he asked.

"Oh, yes," I told him. "I've been plotting ceaselessly all these years to make those dreams come true."

"And have they?" he asked.

"Nearly," I replied.

"In that case," he said, "I suppose I have some work of my own to do."

"Yes," I agreed, "you do."

# CHAPTER 6

You told him that you had dreams about him?" Sakshi gasped as we worked together on kneading the dough for the rotis. "What did he say?"

I shrugged, unable to suppress a smile. "It wasn't what he said so much . . ."

Her eyes widened. "What did he *do*?"

"Well, we never did make it to the stables," I murmured, knowing what reaction that would cause in her.

She giggled and sighed. "Gods, you're so lucky, Razia. I wish I'd been born a prince."

"Being born a prince wasn't so great," I told her, as I started taking flattened raw rotis and packing the inside of the tandoor with them.

"Of course it was," she said. "You got to learn to read and write and fly zahhaks and fight with swords." She swung a kitchen spoon through the air in a fairly feeble impression of swordplay. "All I learned growing up was how to help my mother in the kitchen and how to hide when my father found me wearing my sister's clothes."

"You're right, I was lucky to learn all those things," I allowed. "But it wasn't so much fun for me either. My father would beat me if I didn't act like a man. And so did his master-at-arms. And so did some of the servants. And my father's harem had mahaldars, eunuchs and women whose job it was to spy on everything. They always watched me to see if I would wear girls' clothes, and if I did, they'd report it to my father. It felt like living in a prison."

"Still," Sakshi said, wagging a doughy finger at me, "Prince Arjun wouldn't want anything to do with you if you were born in a poor farming village like me."

"I don't know about that," I said. "The way you play the sitar, I think you're bound to find a really good patron sooner or later."

"I hope it's sooner," she muttered.

"Me too," I told her. I wanted to share my joy with her at having finally found a patron of my own, but it was hard when she didn't have anyone, when she was always the one playing the sitar and never the one dancing. It was hard to earn money that way, however good she was with her instrument. And I didn't want to let on how much Arjun was paying both me and Varsha so that I would be exclusively his. It was the kind of money that Sakshi had dreamed about her whole life but had never seen.

But it was hard not to share with her how wonderful it felt to be wanted as my true self. The last time I'd felt that was when Varsha had taken me in off her doorstep and said, "You're our own kind, and we know how to treat our own kind."

"I'm just lucky Ammi took me in," I murmured, as the memories of that moment washed over me.

"We all are," said Sakshi. "If not for her, I wouldn't have survived another week."

"I don't think I'd have survived another day."

"No," she agreed. "You wouldn't have. I remember when Ammi brought you in, all dirty and skinny and with this lost look in your eyes. And you were clutching that sandalwood box like a drowning man clutching a log."

"I guess I was."

"I was glad she took you in," she said. "I'd always wanted a sister my age."

"You didn't leave my bedside for a whole week," I recalled.

"Well, you were sick," she said, with a shrug of her shoulders, like anyone would have done exactly the same thing. But, in truth, I didn't know many fourteen-year-olds who would have had the compassion to spend seven sleepless nights in the service of some girl they didn't even know.

"Thank you for taking care of me," I said.

She frowned, like that was a strange thing to say. "Razia, that was four years ago."

"I know," I said. "But I'll never forget it."

Sakshi laughed and gave her head a rueful shake. "Gods, this prince has your mind running in such strange places."

"It has nothing to do with him," I protested.

"Oh, no?" she asked. "He hasn't got you talking about your childhood for the first time in years? Or running down to the storeroom to look at those katars of yours? Or talking about zahhaks again?" She ticked each point off on her fingers as she went.

"You like when I talk about zahhaks," I reminded her, hoping to deflect her attention from just what a lovesick girl I must have sounded like.

"You know I'm right," she said.

"You usually are," I agreed, which put a very smug smile on her face, though it also got her to stop talking about my love life for a minute, which was really the point.

"How are the rotis coming, girls?" Varsha asked, sticking her head into the kitchen.

"Nearly finished putting them into the oven, Ammi," I replied.

"Good," she said. "Sakshi, you finish up. I need your sister for something."

"Okay, Ammi," Sakshi agreed. To me, she asked, "Off to fly through the skies with your dashing prince?"

"Not today," I said. I wiped my hands on a towel and then turned and joined Varsha as she led me away from the kitchens. I wondered what this was all about. She'd been given her share of the payment to secure my exclusivity with Arjun. It had been far more generous than either of us could have dared hope. So what did she want with me now?

She led me to the storeroom, which was never a good sign. That was where she liked to go when she was plotting a theft. But I kept my mouth shut until I knew for certain what it was she was after. She was my mother, or the closest thing I would ever have to one anyway, so it was my duty to listen respectfully and to do what was asked of me. I owed her that much at least for saving my life and bringing me up and letting me be myself. If not for her, I'd never have had the chance to meet Arjun, let alone to spend my evenings with him. And we both knew I'd never be able to repay her for that.

We sat on the floor together, and I waited patiently for her to get down to business. It didn't take long. She put her hand on my knee and said, "Disha was dancing at Vikram Sharma's house the night before last. She says he has just come into possession of a magnificent khanda, with a hilt of solid gold, encrusted with diamonds. I have a buyer who is interested. You will take it tonight."

"But, Ammi, what about all the money that Arjun just gave us?" I asked, fidgeting in my seat. I didn't want to refuse her, but it seemed an insane risk to take when we didn't need the money.

Oh, my burglaries were always exciting, I couldn't deny that, and
I never took anything from a man who couldn't afford to replace
it, so it wasn't the morality of it that really bothered me. It was
the risk. Every time I went out and stole, there was a chance I
would be caught and executed. And maybe that risk had made
sense last year or the year before, but I was the chosen courtesan
of the prince now. How could I chance all that on stealing some
bauble? How could Ammi ask me to risk so much when I was
already bringing in more money than either of us had ever
dreamed of?

"The dera has expenses, Razia. You're not the only one living
here," Varsha replied. "I want this thing done, and you will do as
you are told. It is every girl's duty to help the dera to the very best
of her ability. Or do you think that your precious prince would be
so interested in you if I hadn't taken you in and trained you at my
own expense these last four years? Do you think he would want
anything to do with you if I hadn't paid for your nirvan, for your
essential salts?"

"No, of course not, Ammi," I said, hoping to calm some of the
irritation I had aroused. "But Arjun is looking for the thief who
has been stealing things from the havelis. He swore he would
catch me."

"And how close is he to discovering you?" she scoffed. "Not
very if he's sleeping with you."

She was right about that. I hadn't even seen him lift a finger on
this investigation. It was looking more and more like it had just
been an idle promise. Even so, that wasn't really the point.

"Arjun aside, Ammi, it's not worth the risk. I'm bringing in
good money now, aren't I?"

"Not so good that we can stop now." She leaned forward, taking my hands in hers. "I know you don't like taking things from
people, Razia, but we're so close now. Soon, the dera will want for

nothing, and you'll never have to take anything from anyone ever again. All right?"

She was lying. I knew it without even having to think about it. I'd been with her for four years, long enough to know when she was deceiving someone. And in that moment I realized a fundamental truth that I'd been either unable or unwilling to see before—it would never stop. I was too good at stealing.

And Ammi was too greedy. There would never be a last time, not until I got caught, or I left the dera behind. But I wanted to believe her, I wanted to lie to myself, so that I could stay here with my adoptive family. So I asked, "How much longer will it be, Ammi?"

"Not much longer," she said, like she always did. She gave me a pat on the cheek. "You're a good girl. You're making such big sacrifices for me. I won't forget your loyalty when the time comes for you to start your own dera."

The threat couldn't have been clearer. I needed my guru's permission to start a dera, or I would be outside the protection of hijra society, which stretched across the whole of the continent. Ammi had her own guru, the nayak of Bikampur, who had to agree to the creation of any new deras, and their dancing territories had to be carefully carved out, with the agreement of all deras in the lineage. Without that permission, I could never take celas of my own, and Ammi had made sure to hammer into our heads the fact that the time would come when we would be too old to be desirable to wealthy men, when we would have no way of making a living. If I stood outside of our society at that stage in my life, I would die poor and alone and miserable.

While it seemed far away, it wasn't so far away as all that. I had perhaps ten good years of earning in me. Fifteen if I was very exceptional. That was all. After that, I would have to rely on my own celas, and I would have to have Varsha's approval to recruit them. And that meant that I had to do whatever she told me, no matter how much I hated it.

I wished our relationship was simple—just mother and daughter, like it had been that first year when I'd come to the dera. She'd doted on me, fed me, clothed me, given me nirvan and essential salts, and trained me in the arts of a courtesan and a thief. I hadn't realized then that the reason for her kindness had been that I had a pretty face that would have been ruined by masculinity. That was why I'd been given nirvan before some of the girls who had been in the dera longer. It had all been an investment. An investment that was now paying off.

Was that all I was to her? A means to an end? I didn't want to believe that. She had kissed me good night for all those years. She had told me how pretty I was—something no one in the palace had ever said to me. She'd accepted me for who I was. I had to mean something to her beyond money.

I sighed. "All right, Ammi. Where is this sword?"

She smiled at me and gave me a pat on the cheek. "You're a very good girl, Razia. Now, the khanda is being kept by Vikram Sharma in his bedchamber. That's on the fourth floor of his haveli, on the southeastern corner, facing the Mahal Bazaar."

"So anyone in the bazaar will be able to see me come and go through that window?" I shook my head. That was madness. A surefire way to get caught.

"Obviously, you'll have to enter a different window, move through the house to his bedchamber, and then make your way back," said Varsha.

I frowned. That was no easy task. Moving through an unfamiliar house at night was difficult enough, but I would have to avoid servants and night watchmen, and Vikram Sharma himself. If I were caught, I knew what the consequences would be, and my relationship with Arjun, such that it was, wouldn't be enough to save me.

Still . . . I thought I could do it. The golden peacock had been harder. At least a sword was meant to be carried.

"You want me to do this tonight, Ammi?" I asked, more to remind myself and give myself a moment to prepare than to actually hear her say it again.

"That's right," she said. "Vikram Sharma is having a party this evening. The men will be very drunk, which should put them all in a deep sleep. You will take the khanda, and then in the morning, he will presume it was stolen by one of his guests."

"All right, Ammi, I'll go get ready," I said. I stood up from the floor and walked out of the storeroom, my mind still mulling over how exactly I was going to get that khanda out of Vikram Sharma's haveli. I was annoyed that she'd asked it of me today of all days. We'd just received a huge sum of money from Prince Arjun. It was enough to pay for the dera's expenses for the next year, and maybe more than that. What did she need with this stupid sword?

I didn't know where all the money went, that was what bothered me so much. I knew the essential salts we took to feminize our bodies were expensive. I knew our nirvan operations were expensive. I knew our clothes were expensive, and our tutors were expensive. But we brought in money too. Every time I danced, a rich man handed Ammi a purse bursting with rupees. And now Arjun had given her even more than that, to say nothing of the money he had given me personally. And he'd let me keep the jewels and the clothes, which were more valuable than a stupid sword.

And I wasn't her only daughter. My sisters had their own expenses, but most of them earned more than they spent. But I was the best. That was why she'd been so kind to me growing up, why she'd growled at some of my other sisters but always stroked my hair and called me her daughter. I had a pretty face, and a prince's education, and I was a natural athlete who took to climbing like a duck takes to water. This had been her plan all along.

I wasn't sure what that meant for us and didn't want to think about it just then. It would distract me from the job at hand, and stealing things from rich havelis was risky enough that I couldn't afford distractions.

I took my clothes off, trading them for my black shalwar kameez and a black dupatta. They were comfortable, cozy, and easy to climb in, and they made me hard to see. As I dressed, I tried to push thoughts of Ammi from my mind, but I couldn't help myself. My thoughts kept spinning in circles, and the more I thought about it, the clearer it became that she was using me to enrich herself, and that she had no plans to stop.

But it didn't matter.

That was the other thought that I kept coming back to. She was my mother. She had taken me in when I was sick and starving and alone in the world, and she had given me medicine and comfort and care. She was the only adult I had ever met in my whole life who had been willing to accept me for me. She was my savior.

I left my room and went to join my sisters for dinner on the roof of our home. It was always cooler up there, and the breezes were a little stronger. Most nights, we slept up there too, all gathered around on our mats made of old clothes, with the stars above us. This evening, with the sun having nearly set, the cool breezes were beginning to stir, and they rustled my hair and my dupatta as I mounted the steps to the roof.

My sisters were already gathered around the platters of food and the steaming piles of fresh rotis. Disha, the eldest, sat on Ammi's right. She was five or six years older than I was, but still quite popular with the men. She had been like a second mother to me growing up. It had been Disha who had showed me how to put on my makeup, how to oil my hair, and how to braid it.

Jaskaur, as the next oldest, sat beside her. She had never been as kind to me. I think because I was too much younger than her to be seen as an equal, but not so much younger that I was seen as a child. That had strained our relations growing up, and they seemed even more strained since Arjun had taken an interest in me. It would have been one thing had I gone to Govind Singh's haveli and simply committed the theft we'd planned, but now that I'd ensnared the prince as my patron, she was furious at having been passed over. I didn't dare tell her that she wasn't Arjun's type, though part of me wanted to. But it wasn't worth the fight.

Sakshi, as the third oldest, sat on Ammi's left, and my place was beside her. I had been the youngest until this year, when Lakshmi had arrived. She was just eleven and had run away from her family—a wealthy noble house in the Virajendra empire far to the south. She spoke our language with an accent, and her dark skin wasn't popular here, but I thought she was beautiful.

She sat opposite Ammi, in the lowest-ranking position, which happened to be on my left. That suited me just fine. Lakshmi was cute and carefree, and still young enough that our line of work hadn't left its marks on her. I prayed some days that I would be able to steal enough so that it never would, but I knew better.

"That pink lehenga suits you, Lakshmi," I told her, taking my seat beside her.

"Thank you, Akka!" she exclaimed. I'd come to learn that "akka" meant "older sister" in her language. She turned her beautiful dark eyes to my clothes and asked, "Are you really going out again tonight?"

"Going out" was the code we used for stealing things. It always worried Lakshmi terribly when I went out, but I didn't want her to be afraid, so I smiled and said, "Yes, it's just a small thing." I gave her a pat on the shoulder, but I could see the worry in her eyes.

"I'll pray for your safe return," she said.

I smiled at her by way of thanks. Lakshmi and I had more in common with each other than we did with the others in the dera. We both came from wealthy, powerful families. While she hadn't been the crown prince of Nizam, she'd been the child of a governor in Virajendra. Like me, she'd been trained from birth to read and write, to recite poetry, to rule, and to lead. Her father had raised acid zahhaks after the fashion of the south, and she had been raising hers when she'd run away. Whenever she got homesick for her family, I was the one whose lap she crawled into until she cried herself to sleep.

Lakshmi picked up my plate before I could and placed rotis and korma on it, along with some daal. I smiled at her. "You don't have to do that, little sister."

"I want to," she replied, and she placed the plate in front of me with all the deference of a palace servant.

I gave her a gentle pat, and then set about eating. I was hungry, and it was going to be a very late night, so I needed to fill up. But I couldn't eat too much. I didn't want to be heavy and sluggish when the time came to scale the wall of Vikram Sharma's haveli.

"What's the prince like?" Lakshmi asked, while she pushed her food around her plate with her fingers, more interested in my stories than her daal.

"Oh, so that's why you're serving me my food, you want me to tell you stories about handsome princes," I teased, wagging a finger at her.

She blushed, her dark skin flushing, especially at the apples of her cheeks. She cast her gaze downward in the perfect approximation of a delicate and chaste young princess and said, "I was just curious, Akka."

I glanced at my other sisters, who were all leaning forward eagerly, all except for Jaskaur, who kept her eyes focused on her food. I didn't want to make her angry by talking about it, but I couldn't live in fear of her either. And anyway, I wanted to make Lakshmi happy more than I wanted to salve Jaskaur's wounded pride.

"He's tall and strong and handsome, and very kind," I told Lakshmi, trying to make it sound like one of the romantic stories we'd both grown up with as children. My whole life, I'd heard tales of dashing princes and beautiful princesses and soaring zahhaks and exciting swordfights. I'd always wanted life to be like that, always believed that someday it would be. I wanted Lakshmi to believe in that a little bit longer.

"And he rides a beautiful fire zahhak named Padmini, whose scales and feathers are all the colors of the desert sunset. He lets me ride her with him, and we fly up so high that the whole city looks like it's nothing more than a bunch of dollhouses made for a rich princess. And at night, all the torches and candles glitter like the stars, and you feel like you're flying through the heavens themselves."

Sakshi gave a wistful sigh. Lakshmi imitated her at once, drawing a snort of laughter from Disha and a dramatic eye roll from Jaskaur. But it was Ammi who spoke, saying to Lakshmi, "If you work hard, you can achieve all the things Razia has. You're from a good family, and the noblemen will like that once you're of a proper age."

"I'll work very hard, Ammi!" she exclaimed.

"If you're good and do all your chores, maybe you can meet Prince Arjun," I told her.

"Really?" she gasped.

"Really," I said. I gave her a pat on the back and then went back to my food, feeling well pleased with myself. Bringing a smile to her face always brought a smile to mine. I think it was because of how scared she'd been when she'd come to us. We all were, but she was the first one I'd ever seen arrive the way I had—all dirty from the road and hungry and weak and terrified. I had taken care of her, just like Sakshi had taken care of me. To see her smiling now, happy, with hopes and dreams and a place in the world, it made me willing to do anything at all to help her—even risking my life stealing useless trinkets.

"When will he be coming next?" Lakshmi asked.

"I don't know, little sister," I said. "He'll send for me when he wants me."

"I hope it's soon . . ." she murmured.

"Me too," I replied, heaving a wistful sigh of my own. When I was with Arjun, I felt . . . well . . . I felt more like myself than I ever had before, if that made sense. He saw me for the woman I was, but he saw me for my regal upbringing too. He treated me like I was a foreign princess, not like I was some dancing girl from the slums. He didn't have to do that. He could have bought my time and I wouldn't have been able to refuse him. But he wasn't like that. He really seemed to care about me. I hoped it was true, that it wasn't just my own desperate desires transferring themselves onto him, but it was hard to know for sure. Not that it really mattered. I was a hijra. It wasn't like I could marry him—or anybody else for that matter. I had to just enjoy what I could while I could. Lasting happiness didn't exist for girls like us.

As if to prove it, Ammi nodded to me and said, "You should get moving, Razia."

I nodded, cleaned my right hand off on a towel, and then stood up. Lakshmi leapt up from her place and wrapped both arms around me tightly. "Be careful, Akka!"

"I'll be careful," I promised, hugging her back.

I was surprised when Sakshi hugged the both of us together. To me, she said, "Don't take any risks, Razia. If it's too dangerous, just come home safe. You've already done enough for the dera."

"I'll be okay," I said, though I wasn't at all certain of it. I gave

Lakshmi a kiss on the top of her head and Sakshi a tight embrace. Then I pulled away from the both of them, gave them a wave good-bye, and headed down the stairs to the courtyard.

I knew they were watching me, so I tried to look confident as I left through the courtyard gate, careful to close it behind me. Once I was out on the streets, though, out of sight, I let my shoulders slump a little. I didn't want to do this—not tonight, not when things were going so well with Arjun, not when he had given us so much money. For the first time in a long time, I felt like I actually had something to lose.

It was such a strange feeling, but I was truly happy, maybe for the first time in my whole life. I had sisters I loved. I had a man who liked me, and whether or not we loved each other, we made each other happy. I had nice clothes, I had a good life, and I was accepted as my true self. Why would I risk any of that for some stupid sword? I supposed it was precisely because I would be risking all those things if I didn't take it that I plodded along the streets toward the Mahal Bazaar and a theft I wasn't eager to perform.

## CHAPTER 7

I kept to the labyrinth of dark, dusty alleys that paralleled Bikampur's main thoroughfares as I made my way toward the Mahal Bazaar. I immediately regretted not bringing my katars with me, as men smoking hashish were lying on piles of rags pressed up against the buildings, and their glassy eyes were roving over every inch of my body with lascivious intent. Though those men made my skin shiver, they weren't the dangerous ones. The dangerous ones were the ones standing in the doorways of broken-down hovels, the ones lurking even deeper inside the narrowest alleys, visible only by the glint of their blades in the moonlight. I heard men fighting off to my right, and I darted to my left, taking three adjoining alleys to move myself around any potential trouble.

It was the grace and confidence with which I moved that kept me safe most nights. A woman alone at night garnered far too much attention—even a hijra. But when I moved with purpose, when I showed no fear, it tended to keep some of them at bay. But not all of them. Never all of them.

As if to prove it, a pair of rough-looking men in dirty kurtas moved to stand in front of me. They didn't have weapons, but they were taller than I was by the breadth of a hand, and much broader through the shoulders. I might still be able to win a fight. I knew how to use my fists and my feet to best advantage, and I knew a thing or two about wrestling. But who knew if these men had knives? And anyway, this was their neighborhood. They would have friends who would take their side if it came to blows.

For most women, the best defense would have been attracting attention to herself by screaming in the hopes of publicly shaming her assailants into backing off. But that might not work here—even a well-bred lady should have known better than to go out at night alone. Most women wouldn't walk these alleys in the daytime. Crying out might do little more than draw an unsympathetic crowd to cheer on the abuse. Not that it mattered; I couldn't attract attention. That was the last thing I wanted, and these men probably knew it. A pretty girl like me, dressed all in black, could only have been a prostitute looking to escape notice. So I took the only avenue that was available to me—I walked straight toward them, like I wasn't aware of their intentions.

At the last second, just as one of them opened his mouth full of rotten teeth to growl something at me, I darted down an alley to my right, running as fast as I could. I turned left as the men shouted behind me in surprise, and then back right, and then left again, zigzagging my way toward the bazaar. I kept going, running past opium eaters lying in their blissful stupors and brushing past unsavory men who were stepping out of their houses to see what the commotion was all about. I ran until I was sure I wasn't being followed, and then I ran a little farther still.

By the time I stopped, I could hear the voices coming from the Mahal Bazaar. It was late into the evening, but the weather was cool now and the moon was half-full. It was the perfect time to eat samosas and pakoras and wander the stalls of Bikampur's largest market. It was heartening to know that I was nearing my destination, and I thought I was getting close enough to the havelis of the well-to-do that the risk of being attacked had lessened considerably.

I wondered how I was going to get the khanda back to the dera, and then I remembered that it was a khanda; if anyone bothered me, I'd just cut them down. I didn't think a little blood would lower the price, and the threat of it would be enough to keep all but the most desperate from trying their luck. But I was getting ahead of myself. I was going to have to steal it first.

The alleys gradually widened as I walked. The houses got bigger. This was the middle-class neighborhood that served as a buffer between the truly rich and the truly poor. I was safe here, or as safe as a woman alone in Bikampur at night could be. The men here were more respectable, more likely to shoo me away than try to have their way with me. They too would know what a lone woman wandering the alleys was, and they would want no part of me, especially since I wasn't dressed with all the jewels and accoutrements of a proper courtesan. No, at the moment, I looked to most people's eyes like the kind of whore who could be had in any alley in the city for two paise or a couple of samosas, whichever was ready to hand.

I kept moving, not wanting to make myself too obvious to anyone, not wanting to force anyone to try to yell at me to get me away from his neighborhood. I saw the dirty looks from some of the men, and the come-hither looks from some of the others. One even waved a roti at me, like I would fall all over him for his gracious offer. But with my body covered beneath my loose, flowing clothes, they couldn't know that I wasn't emaciated like most of the girls forced to make a living in Bikampur's back alleys.

I swung around the western side of the bazaar at long last.

Through the narrow alleys, I could see glimpses of it, still well lit and roiling with crowds of men, but I didn't want to get too close. Well-bred women didn't prowl the bazaar at night without escorts, and the wealthiest set didn't leave their homes at all. As a hijra, I should have had more freedom than most women, but Ammi had given us our nirvan young, and paid for our essential salts, so short of taking my clothes off, I didn't think I could convince anyone that I actually was a hijra. Not that it mattered. Even the poor hijras with mannish bodies would have attracted far too much male attention. That was why we always traveled in groups big enough to cause trouble of our own.

There it was. Vikram Sharma's haveli. It was just five stories tall, but the walls weren't as well decorated as Govind Singh's. It would make climbing a little tougher, but I didn't have to bring a giant peacock back down, so there was something to be said for that. The real trouble, though, would be prowling through the haveli without being spotted by the night watchmen, or by servants up late, cleaning after the party.

First things first, I pressed myself up against the wall and listened for sounds of carousing. If the party was still going on, I would have to wait until it ended. It was fairly late, as I'd had a long walk and I'd set out after sundown, but I heard the sounds of music up above me, of laughter and cries for wine. So I settled down against the wall, hugging my knees to my chest until I was nothing more than a pool of black cloth pressed into the shadows. A man would have stumbled over me before he saw me.

I waited. And waited. And waited. It was stressful, just sitting there, waiting for the moment when I would begin my climb to the top of the haveli. My heart was hammering, and my stomach was churning. I just wanted to get it over with. But trying to sneak through the house when I knew people were awake was stupid.

Better to be patient, to wait until I was certain everyone had gone to bed. Then I could get in and get out quickly without anyone being the wiser.

It occurred to me that I could just get up and go home. I wanted to. I wanted to go home and sit with Lakshmi and sing songs to her while Sakshi played her sitar. I wanted to go to bed at a reasonable hour and feel safe and warm and cozy piled onto the rooftop mats with my sisters. I wanted to be able to look Arjun in the eye the next time he came to see me, without the guilt of being Bikampur's most notorious thief hanging over me. And though I wasn't the most religious sort of girl, I knew what God thought of thieves.

The music petered out, and gradually the conversation did too. I waited until the haveli was silent, and then I waited a good deal longer than that. When I thought everyone would be sound asleep, I stood up and started searching for my first handholds and footholds. It was so automatic that thoughts of going home without the khanda fled my mind entirely. Varsha had trained me well.

I had to jump up for my first handhold—a windowsill. I pulled myself up it, grabbing the top of the shrouded window, and then hoisting myself beyond it. My mind went blank as I climbed. It was like a sort of prayer really. I just did what needed to be done, moving one hand, one foot, and repeating the sequence until I got to where I was going. There were enough cracks in the stonework to help me get from window box to window box. But it wasn't easy, not like climbing the side of Govind Singh's ornate haveli had been. And going down was always harder. There was always a desire to rush it, and rushing always presaged disaster.

In spite of my difficulty finding good handholds, it was an uneventful climb. I reached the roof and peeked between the balusters of its railing, searching for any signs of movement. It was quiet up there; quiet and still. The cushions were laid out, but the guests had gone. The goblets of wine had been gathered up, the trays of food taken away. The carousers were nowhere to be found, and their servants had all gone to bed.

I waited a moment anyway, taking slow, steady breaths, watching the stairs, checking the edges of the rooftop for any signs of movement, from a couple who had pressed themselves into the shadows for privacy or from a drunk who had fallen asleep on the way to his bedchamber. I was listening too, listening so intently that it made my ears buzz for want of noise. Everything was quiet. The silence beckoned me onward. I climbed over the railing, keeping low as I made my way across the rooftop, until I reached the stairwell that headed down to the lower floors. I paused there, crouching behind the railing, my eyes flickering from floor to floor, taking in every inch of the haveli and its courtyard far below.

There were the night watchmen, two of them standing guard near the gate. Another was patrolling the courtyard with a lantern in hand. The candle within bathed the man in a shallow puddle of warm orange light and cast flickering shadows all around him. He walked along, blissfully unaware of my presence fifty feet above, and I watched and waited for my opportunity to move.

The man with the lantern turned his back to me, continuing his patrol. I got up and crept down the stairs. The air was so still that I could hear the footfalls of the watchman patrolling the courtyard below. The creaking of the lantern as it swung on its handle was loud in my ears. How did they not hear me when I heard them so clearly? How did they not see my dark clothes against the white marble of the staircase?

It didn't matter. My feet hit the polished stone of the fourth-floor balcony, and I followed it toward the haveli's southeastern corner. It was positioned roughly on the same side of the house as the main gate, which was dangerous. If the watchmen chanced to look up, they might spot me. I walked doubled over, scurrying like a rat, pausing in the shadows of columns to check and make sure no one was watching. My eyes flicked frantically from the court-yard to each of the floors in turn, but still the watchmen didn't notice me, and still no servants stirred.

Ahead of me was a diaphanous curtain separating a large chamber from the open courtyard. That must have been Vikram Sharma's bedchamber. I wondered how many girls he had in his room with him. I wondered if any of them were awake.

I ducked my head in the curtain, low near the floor, where peo-ple might not think to look. There, highlighted by the pale moon-light, was the sleeping form of the nobleman, stark naked, his clothes strewn about the room. Two girls lay on either side of him, naked both. He was snoring softly, and their breathing was slow and steady.

I crept into the room, keeping to the shadows at its edge. My heart was pounding now, and it was hard not to take loud, gasping breaths to calm myself. My palms were sweating. This was the moment of truth. Where was that damned khanda? If I could just get my hands on it, and get out, everything would be all right. I could go home, go back to my life, and maybe not steal anything again for a good long while.

It was the same lie I always told myself, but it was a comfort-ing lie, so I told it again. Once I got the khanda, I would stop stealing things. It would be enough. We would have all the money we would need. I just had to do this one last thing.

My eyes finally landed on the sword. It was sitting on a wooden stand not so far from where I was kneeling. I crept over to it, my skin tingling with the certainty that someone was watching, that I would soon be caught, that the alarm would be shouted and this would be the end of me. I took one last look around, and then took the sword and buckled the belt around my waist so that it hung naturally from my left hip, just like my talwar had back home in Nizam.

I had what I came for, now I just had to get away with it.

I left the way I'd come in, first sticking my head out of the curtain, paying attention to the men in the courtyard and keeping an eye out for any wandering servants. It was clear. I crouched low and moved to the stairwell as quickly as I dared. I darted up the stairs, ran across the roof, and threw myself over the side, clinging to the railings as my toes found purchase in the cracks of the wall.

I heaved a sigh of relief. I'd done it again. I'd got the sword, and now the hard part was over. I just had to get down and walk back home. But the danger had passed. There were no servants to see me, no night watchmen, no Vikram Sharma himself. It was just me and God, and he had always seen fit to keep my secrets.

"So that's how you did it."

The voice rumbled out of the darkness. I was so startled that I lost my grip on the wall and started to fall. I managed to grab hold of a decorative carving at the last moment, and that saved me. But then I glanced over my shoulder, and my heart leapt into my throat.

Prince Arjun was sitting atop Padmini, who was standing on the roof of the next haveli over. She was stretching her neck out, like she meant to eat me, the nares at the base of her beak flaring as she took in great whiffs of my scent.

It was over. Everything was over. My new life. My relationship with the prince. Gone. All the things I held dear would be taken from me. I would be executed as a petty thief. All because Ammi had wanted one more trinket to sell.

I waited for Padmini to finish me, for her beak to open, for the flames to issue forth, but the fire didn't come. And that was when I realized why. She couldn't burn me without burning down the haveli and half the neighborhood with it. Hundreds would die. Arjun couldn't risk that. So that meant there was still a chance.

I started climbing down as quickly as I could, racing toward the bottom. From his place on Padmini's back, Arjun cried out, "What do you think you're doing?"

I didn't trust my voice. He might recognize it. So I didn't say anything, I just kept going. He yelled, "Stop!" but I didn't stop. I jumped. I leapt the last dozen or so feet to the ground, tucking and rolling and popping back up. And then I ran for all I was worth.

"Damn it!" Arjun swore. I heard the great flaps of Padmini's wings as she took to the skies. I didn't care. I had to get away. I had to get back home. I had to make sure Arjun never knew what I'd done. I ducked down one alley, and then another, and then a third. I kept changing direction, kept burying myself deeper into the maze of streets south of the Mahal Bazaar.

But Padmini was flying above me. I saw her as a dark silhouette against the pale half-moon. She was looking straight at me, and that was when I remembered my training as a child. Fire zahhaks could see heat the way ordinary people saw light. It made them unparalleled trackers, especially at night. How in God's name was I going to lose a beast that could track me by the heat of my own body?

"If you surrender now, I'll be lenient!" Arjun called from where he sat on Padmini's back.

I ignored him and cut down another alley, hoping that the houses were close enough together that they would block Padmini's view of me. They certainly blocked my view of her—not that I could risk running with my head twisted skyward. There was too much chance of running headlong into a wall.

I turned left quite suddenly, squeezing into a narrow gap between two houses. It was a tight space—if I'd been any broader through the shoulders, I'd have had to turn myself sideways to get through. But it did the trick. There was no sign of Padmini. Maybe I'd lost her.

The shadow of a man appeared at the far end of the alley, and I stopped dead in my tracks. I turned around to run back the other way, but a bigger shadow was lurking there now—Padmini.

"If you give up now, it will go easier for you, boy," Arjun told me. "I don't want to have to kill you. I'm sure you're not alone in this operation. You must have masters ordering you to do it."

Boy? It must have been too dark to make out my clothes. That meant if I got away, he'd be looking for a boy and not a girl. I looked around for a way out, and I saw it at once. The crumbling wall of the building on my right was made for climbing. I grabbed hold of the first handhold and started scampering up. Arjun shouted, "Stop!" and he began to run toward me. Now it was a race. Was he going to reach me before I could climb high enough to escape him?

I broke all the rules of climbing then, jumping for a handhold, stretching for all I was worth, hanging all my hopes on it being firm, on my fingers holding my weight. I shoved them into a crack in the wall, and I hung firm for an instant, before the plaster started to crumble and give way.

I scrambled with my feet, desperately trying to get a toehold, but there was nothing. And that was when I remembered the building behind me. As my handhold gave way, I kicked one leg out, pressing it up against the building behind me, while the other leg was pushing against the building in front of me. The muscles in my groin burned from doing the splits with the whole of my body weight pressing down on me. But I stayed up, and the wall didn't collapse. Of course, Arjun was still after me.

I glanced down and saw him standing below me, about ten feet down—just far enough that he couldn't reach me. I started using my legs to climb the walls, finding it was much easier than searching for cracks to use as finger- and toeholds.

Below me, Arjun started imitating me, trying to climb up behind me, but he was slow. I'd outdistance him easily enough. I was nearing the top. Another second and I'd be safe. I smiled, but at that moment, he cried, "Padmini! Roof!" And he pointed to the spot above me.

My heart seized. The zahhak leapt up from the alley, landing on the roof of a building at its far end. She was big enough that she could just take the gaps between them in leaps and bounds, and she was coming on like a charging elephant.

I reached the rooftop and ran for all I was worth. The sound of Padmini's talons scraping on the stones of the rooftops behind me sent shivers down my spine. I ran to the edge of a roof, and then leapt to the next one, knowing that she was right behind me, that she was going to catch me and eat me. I had to get off the rooftops if I wanted to survive.

I threw myself over the railing of the rooftop I was on, noting the narrow alley that opened up below me. It was small enough that Padmini would have a hard time squeezing herself through, I thought. I started scrabbling down, but at that moment, she was on me. Her jaws snapped, her razor-sharp teeth and her wickedly curved beak clacking together just inches above my head. I hunched down, barely out of her reach, her breath hot on my face. She roared at me and snarled and scraped at the walls as she tried to push herself farther into the space between the buildings, her long, slender neck giving her far too much reach for comfort.

I raced down the building so quickly that I wasn't sure how I'd done it. But I was down, and she was still on the roof. I took off running then, desperate to get away, to get some distance between us. I used the alleys to my advantage, putting buildings between myself and Padmini. I was breathing hard, sweat was covering my body, and my arms and legs burned from exertion. If I didn't get away now, I didn't think that I ever would.

I cut down a narrow alley, sprinting for all I was worth. I hit a bigger street, raced right across it, jumped over some opium eater curled up in my path, and then entered the next alley. I ducked through a narrow, winding passage between two buildings that was covered with the contents of emptied chamber pots, and then I burst out the other side, into a narrow road. I ran along it for a few feet until I found another alley, and then I slipped inside that one and stopped, trying to catch my breath as my heart pounded in my ears.

I couldn't hear anyone, couldn't see anyone. The streets were deserted at this hour. Arjun wasn't shouting for me. I couldn't make out Padmini's talons scraping on the paving stones or the muffled sounds of her wingbeats in the night air. I was alone.

I looked around to get my bearings and found that I knew where I was. It wasn't such a long walk back to the dera, but it would be longer sticking to the alleys. I was too cautious to do anything else. Being spotted from the air would be the death of me. I was too tired to climb, too tired to run. I just plodded along, twisting through the narrow alleys until I came out on the street in front of my dera.

I rushed to the gate and rang the bell, huddling there in the gateway, pressing my body against the stones of the wall to try to make myself harder to see. I heard footsteps inside, and then the gate swung open, and I darted in, still breathing hard, my whole body shaking.

"Razia?" Ammi gasped, like she was shocked to see me there. And then her eyes fell on the glittering hilt of the khanda swinging from my hip, and her eyes widened. "You got it?" She sounded surprised by that too. Had she expected me to fail? Was that why Arjun had been there? Had she betrayed me?

I shook my head. That was nonsense. I was her top earner. She would have no reason to get rid of me. I was just scared and angry and it was making me think stupid things. I unbuckled the khanda from my waist and handed it over to her. I never wanted to look at it again.

"Razia? Are you all right?" Sakshi asked. She rushed over to me, her concern plain on her face. She embraced me, and it was only then that I realized I was shaking all over.

I dropped to my knees in the courtyard, and Sakshi pulled my head into her lap and stroked my hair. She didn't say a word; she just let me lie there and shiver against the cold sweat soaking my clothes and the fear that was still driving the frantic beats of my heart.

"Akka?" Lakshmi asked, having been awakened by the commotion. She ran over to me and knelt beside me, taking my hand in her smaller ones, holding it in her lap. "What's wrong? Is she sick?"

I forced myself to smile then. "No, little sister. I'm just tired."

"Did anyone spot you?" Varsha asked, and I realized that she was still standing there, holding her ill-gotten gains, having made no effort to comfort me whatsoever.

"Arjun was there," I said, testing the waters, fishing for her reaction.

Ammi pursed her lips, her eyes flickering from side to side. It was a look not of concern but of cold calculation. "Did he recognize you?"

I shook my head. "It was too dark. He thought I was a boy. I managed to lose him in the alleys."

"Good work," she said, coming forward and stroking my hair

then, but the gesture felt stiff and wooden. "You just get some rest. Tonight, you can sleep as much as you like. And don't worry about your chores tomorrow."

"Yes, Ammi," I agreed, too exhausted to be properly angry with her. I closed my eyes and fell asleep right there in the courtyard, my sisters holding me close to them.

## CHAPTER 8

"Akka!"

"Huh?" My eyes flickered open, and my vision was filled with a smiling face shoving a plateful of food right beneath my nose.

"I brought you breakfast in bed!" Lakshmi exclaimed, laying the metal plate down on the floor beside my head.

"Oh . . ." I blinked a few times and groaned once and tried to remember where I was.

"Lakshmi!" Sakshi hissed from the doorway. "I told you to let her sleep!"

"I thought she would want breakfast in bed," Lakshmi replied. "Halwa poori is her favorite."

I propped myself up on an elbow, my hair spilling around me in wild tangles. Lakshmi noticed, and she immediately crawled over to me, taking a seat on my little mattress. She took hold of my tangled hair and began brushing and braiding it.

I sighed and flopped back down on my side, resting my cheek

on one of Lakshmi's bony knees as her little fingers worked. It was comforting, relaxing, the perfect way to spend a lazy morning—if it was even still morning. The sun was pretty high in the sky. That was why I'd chosen to sleep in my private chamber and not with my sisters on the roof.

"Sorry. I kept her out as long as I could," Sakshi told me, as she came to sit beside me.

I moved my head from Lakshmi's bony knee to Sakshi's softer thigh and sighed. "You make a good pillow."

"Why, thank you, your highness. I live to serve," she replied with a roll of her mahogany eyes.

"Can you feed me?" I whimpered. "I think I'm too weak to move my arms."

Sakshi tore a piece of poori, scooped some halwa, and placed the bite in my mouth. I sighed with pleasure, chewed, and swallowed. While I ate, she asked, "What happened last night?"

"Didn't I tell you?" I asked, only vaguely remembering my return to the dera.

"Why do you think Arjun was waiting for you, I mean?" she asked.

"Did he recognize you?" Lakshmi asked, sounding worried. "He's not going to hurt you, is he?"

"No, little sister, he's not going to hurt me," I assured her. "He doesn't know it was me."

"I wish you didn't have to steal things . . ." she murmured.

"Me too," I said. "I was hoping that I was bringing in enough money that Ammi wouldn't make me do it anymore, but . . ."

"But nothing," Sakshi said. "We have enough money. You just focus on making Arjun happy, and let me worry about Ammi."

"I don't want you getting in trouble," I told her.

"I won't," she promised. And then she shoved a little more

halwa poori into my mouth. "You just leave everything to me, little sister, and focus on making your prince happy."

"That sounds like a brilliant idea."

I looked up to the doorway and saw Arjun leaning against the doorframe, grinning down at me. "Light of the Fire God, is this how your sisters treat you? It's no wonder you gave up being a prince."

"Your highness!" Sakshi exclaimed, her face going pale as she bowed low to him.

I scrambled to do the same thing, wondering if he'd overheard our conversation, if he knew what I'd done. "When did you get here, my prince?"

"Just now," he said, and he went to me and lifted me up, guiding me to my feet. He looked me over in my simple white shalwar kameez. Sakshi must have changed my clothes while I was sleeping, and I couldn't have been more grateful for it.

"Your highness!" Ammi had arrived on the scene, but I could tell from the sound of her voice that she was as surprised as the rest of us. "What are you doing here? How did you get in?"

"I flew," he said, and then he glanced at her. "Forgive me, I didn't mean to be rude, but the terms we negotiated stipulated that Razia was mine to do with as I pleased when it pleased me, didn't they?"

"They did, your highness," Ammi agreed. "I just . . . wasn't expecting you is all. She's not dressed, not prepared. If we'd known you were coming—"

Arjun raised a hand to stop her. "I don't mind seeing her without her makeup and her finest clothes." He looked to me then. "And you don't mind, do you, Razia?"

"Of course not, my prince," I said, putting my arms around his neck to draw him closer to me. I'd have said it whether I believed it or not, but frankly I was relieved to see him. He was here to see me; he wasn't angry with me. He didn't know what I'd done. My days of thieving were behind me. From this moment forward I'd never do it again. I had too much to lose.

"And who is this lovely lady?" he asked me, nodding to Lakshmi.

"This is my little sister, Lakshmi," I replied, unable to keep the tone of a proud mother from my voice. After all, I'd been the one to take care of her from the moment she'd arrived in the dera, and I tutored her even more extensively than the men and women Varsha hired.

Arjun let go of me and turned his attention to Lakshmi, bending down to get at her eye level. "And how old are you, dear?"

"Eleven, your highness," she replied, her Virajendran accent plain to hear, but she looked like a proper little princess with her clasped hands and downcast eyes, with the easy way she wore her dupatta and the fine silk of her pink lehenga.

The smile fled Arjun's face as a realization dawned on him. "You're eleven years old and you ran away from your home to come here?"

"Yes, your highness," she said, and for a brief moment, there was a crack in her usually happy facade. But it was gone an instant later, and she added, "My family beat me for acting like a girl, and for not being a proper man. So I ran away, and this is where I ended up."

"Are you happy here?" he asked.

"Oh, yes, your highness," she said. "I get to wear pretty clothes, and I get to have a girl's name, and my sisters take very good care of me. Especially Akka, I mean, Razia." She smiled up at me like I was her hero, and it made my heart melt.

"Well, I'm very glad to hear that," he said, giving her a gentle pat on the cheek. "If your big sister is ever mean to you, you just come to me and I'll take care of everything."

"She's never mean," Lakshmi assured him.

"I believe you," he said, and he stood up then and draped his arm across my back, pulling me closer to him, as if her words had reminded him of my presence. To Lakshmi, he asked, "You came from Virajendra?"

Lakshmi glanced at me nervously. We'd had talks about telling people who she was. Virajendra was the greatest empire on the continent besides Nizam. The emperor there ruled the southern jungles with an iron fist and commanded a fleet that traded across the far east. He rivaled my father in power, and the war between our peoples was one of religion and of culture as much as it was of politics. But this was not Nizam, and Arjun was not my father, so I nodded to show her that it was safe to talk about such things with him. She said, "My father is Vidarth, the zamorin of Kolikota."

"Your father is the ruler of Kolikota, the City of Spices?" Arjun gasped. He glanced at me for confirmation, and when I nodded, he said, "Is everyone in your dera a princess?"

"Just the pair of us," I said, taking Lakshmi's hand and pulling her close to me.

"It seems quite the coincidence," he remarked.

I shrugged. "Bikampur is on the caravan routes, and Varsha's dera is well-known, even in the outlying towns." I didn't tell him the whole truth, that Varsha paid good money to merchants and traders plying the caravan routes to direct pretty young runaways to her doorstep. That was how I'd ended up here. I'd been running to Safavia, hoping to escape the reach of my father and his generals and assassins, but the desert had sapped the life from me, and kindly merchants had recognized me for what I was and had dropped me off outside Varsha's dera.

"Did you have a zahhak too?" Arjun asked Lakshmi, having accepted my explanation without comment.

Her face fell, and she gave a weak nod. In a small voice, she said, "Her name was Mohini. She was an acid zahhak. She had such pretty green scales, like emeralds, and bright blue feathers like a kingfisher's."

"It's okay," I told her, hugging her close to me and stroking her hair. "I miss my Sultana too. But it won't always hurt so much." That last was a lie. I didn't think I'd ever get over leaving my zahhak behind. There was something about the connection between a zahhak and her rider that had made it the subject of poets' imaginations. People always compared it to love, but it wasn't quite love, not exactly. It was . . . loyalty? That didn't quite encapsulate it either, but it was a feeling that came from raising a zahhak from an egg, from seeing her eyes when she hatched, from hunting with her every day. It was a bond of sorts, an unbreakable, eternal bond. But I didn't want to tell Lakshmi that. Maybe she'd been too young when she'd left home. Maybe the bond had been too new. Maybe she wouldn't spend her whole life feeling the emptiness inside of her that I felt whenever I thought about Sultana.

"I have an idea," Arjun said. "How about before I steal your sister for the rest of the day, I take you up for a flight on Padmini. Would you like that?"

"Really?" Lakshmi gasped. She glanced to Varsha. "Can I?"

"If it's all right with his highness," she said. "But you have to be back in time for your dancing lessons."

"I will, Ammi," she promised.

I gave Arjun a smile that promised him a substantial reward for this act of kindness, and he smiled back, as if to say that it was nothing at all. He took Lakshmi by the hand and led her out to the courtyard. I followed along behind them, realizing only as my eyes landed on Padmini that she could smell far better than a human. Would she remember me as the thief from last night? Would she attack me for it?

If the zahhak saw me as a thief, she gave no signs of it. She raised her head at her master's approach and kept her eyes focused on him, looking for his commands. She only briefly glanced at Lakshmi, probably wondering if she was a bite-size morsel ready for the eating, but the rest of us might as well have been made of stone for all the interest we aroused in her.

"Is she nice?" Lakshmi asked, clinging to Arjun's arm as she took in Padmini's enormous hooked beak and even larger wing claws.

"She's very sweet to my friends," Arjun assured her, "and you're my friend. Watch." He took her hand the way he had mine that first night, and he helped her to stroke Padmini's beak.

Lakshmi's eyes lit up. She was grinning so much that it made my heart ache. And then Arjun lifted her into the saddle, and helped with the straps, and the expression of sheer joy on her face brought tears to my eyes. Why couldn't I give her this? Why couldn't people like us have the lives other people had?

I vowed then and there that Lakshmi wouldn't have to sell herself to men the way I had. She wouldn't have to have them choke her or beat her or rape her. She wouldn't have to let them put their hands all over her body whether she wanted it or not. She wouldn't have to dance and smile while they stared at her with such naked lust that she felt like sobbing. Life was going to be different for her. I was going to find a way to make enough money to protect her if it was the last thing I ever did.

Arjun climbed into the saddle behind her, and the pair of them took off into the skies. I heard Lakshmi's cries of joy over the beating of Padmini's wings. She was so excited to be riding a zahhak again. It was like she'd never been forced to flee her family, like her father had never threatened to murder her at the tender age of ten for wearing a sari, like she hadn't trekked across half the continent alone and scared until she had come to our doorstep.

"Razia?" Sakshi's hand fell to my shoulder, and I realized then that I had tears streaming down my cheeks. I didn't know if it was because of what had happened to Lakshmi or because of what had happened to me. Maybe it was both. Maybe it was the fact that having lived this life, I knew what was going to happen to that bright-eyed little girl who just wanted to be herself without anyone hurting her, and I wanted to make it stop because nobody had made it stop for me.

"Sorry." I wiped my eyes on the corner of my dupatta.

"Never be sorry for caring," Sakshi told me, and she put her arm around me and pulled me close to her.

"I want to protect her," I whispered, at a volume that Ammi couldn't hear. "I don't want her to have to live like us. She deserves better."

"So did you," Sakshi said.

I shrugged. "Maybe if I keep Arjun happy, we'll have enough money so that Lakshmi doesn't have to do it."

"She'll want to do it. She wants to be grown up like us. She wants boys to like her."

I had nothing to say to that. Sakshi wasn't wrong. There was probably nothing I could do. Lakshmi was being groomed for this line of work. She was training hard so that she would please wealthy men when her time came. Maybe I was already too late to save her.

My eyes had dried by the time Padmini landed in the courtyard once more. Arjun hopped out of the saddle and helped Lakshmi down. She wrapped her arms around his neck, and he carried her over to where we were standing, supporting her weight with one arm.

"Did you have fun?" I asked her.

Her response was to leap from Arjun's arms, hug me tightly, and exclaim, "It was amazing, Akka! The city is so beautiful from the air, and it's much cooler, and there's such a nice breeze. And Padmini is very sweet. And his highness let me fly her a little bit. I got to make her climb and dive and do a loop and everything! It was just like my father taught me."

"She's a natural flier," Arjun said, ruffling her hair. "A little bit of training and she could hang with the best of them."

"My prince should hire us all as zahhak riders," I teased.

"Yes, because nothing strikes fear into the hearts of our enemies like pretty girls," Arjun quipped, placing his hands on my hips.

"Anything is scary if it's riding a zahhak," I replied.

"Shall we go and terrorize the countryside, then?" he asked me, nodding to Padmini.

"I'd like nothing better, my prince," I assured him. I pulled away for an instant to give Lakshmi a good-bye hug and a kiss on her forehead, and then I waved to Sakshi, who put her arms around our littlest sister.

"Have fun, Razia," Sakshi told me, without the barest hint of jealousy in her voice. It still gave me a pang of guilt in my heart. She deserved this more than I did. She'd never lived in a palace, never ridden a zahhak, never been waited upon hand and foot. She'd been born poor, had suffered hunger and cold and beatings her whole childhood, and somehow she was still the sweetest person I'd ever known in my whole life. If I lived to be a thousand, I didn't think I'd ever be able to adequately repay her for the way she'd cared for me upon my arrival in the dera.

"I will," I promised her, and I hoped for the moment that was enough.

I turned my attention back to Arjun, stood on my tiptoes, and planted a kiss on the bristly whiskers of his bearded cheek. "Thank you, my prince."

"For what?" he asked. His big hands took hold of my waist, and he hoisted me up into Padmini's saddle without so much as a grunt of effort.

"For being so nice to my sister," I replied.

"She's very sweet . . ." he said, and there was something unsaid there, some lingering sadness or confusion.

"What is it?"

"It's nothing," he said, and he turned his attention to his straps.

I strapped myself in but wasn't quite ready to let the matter drop. "Forgive me, my prince, but it sounded like something."

"I'm just confused is all," he said. He kissed me on the cheek and then took up the reins and called for Padmini to take to the air. The zahhak was quick to respond, and in a matter of seconds, we were soaring above the city's rooftops, a cooling breeze blowing past us from the speed of our flight.

"Confused?" I pressed.

"Lakshmi is a very sweet little girl. She reminds me of one of my half sisters," he said.

"And?" I asked.

"And her family beat her and threw her away like she was nothing . . ." He shook his head. "How could they do something like that?"

"She was their son," I answered. "What do you think your father would have done to you if he'd caught you wearing girls' clothes at that age?"

"Worse than beatings . . ." he murmured.

I took one of his hands in both of mine, pulling it into my lap so that his arm was snaked around my waist. "Thank you for being so kind to her. She means more to me than anything in the world."

"I could see that. You'd have made a good mother."

I flinched, and I knew he felt it, but I couldn't help it. He'd meant it as a compliment, but it was like a dagger to the heart. I'd always wanted that growing up. I'd dreamed of marrying a handsome prince and having children of my own to raise. I'd always liked children. I'd helped to take care of them in the harem until my father had forbidden it. It wasn't appropriate for a young man to take such interest in babies, after all.

"Did I upset you?" he asked.

I realized only then that I was wringing his hand between both of mine. I stopped at once, my cheeks burning. "Forgive me, my prince. I was just thinking of something is all."

He was kind enough not to ask what it was. He just said, "We're going to be spending our afternoon in the palace today. My father is hosting the prince of Mahisagar. My servants will see that you're properly dressed."

"Prince Karim is going to be here?" I gasped, horrified at the prospect.

"Have you met before?" Arjun asked.

"Once," I said, shuddering as I remembered it. "Six years ago. I was eleven. He came to Nizam on a diplomatic mission. He made a comment about how pretty I was. And then he did more than comment. My father beat me bloody that night."

"More than comment?" Arjun asked, his voice taking on a dangerous edge.

I sucked in a deep breath and let it out slowly. It helped to calm my racing heart, to unravel the knot in the pit of my stomach. I forced the memories away, shoved them back down into that dark place in my heart where all my secrets lurked. "Forgive me, my prince, but I'd rather not talk about it."

He held me close to him and rested his chin on my shoulder, and my breathing eased. It was so easy to feel safe with his strong arms wrapped around me. He'd sworn that he would protect me, and he'd done that. I wanted so badly to give him my whole heart, but I was afraid he would crush it in the end. After all, what future can a hijra have with a prince, even a kind one like Arjun?

"Do you think Karim would recognize you?" he asked.

I shook my head. "No, my prince. It's been six years, and I was dressed like a boy then. And the essential salts and the nirvan have changed my body tremendously."

"Good," he said. "You will attend to me then. And you have my word that no one is going to lay a finger on you."

"Not even Jai?" I asked, not at all excited to be seeing the eunuch again.

"Shiv will attend to you alone," Arjun promised me.

"My prince is very good to me," I told him, leaning back against his chest and craning my head up so I could kiss him on his chin.

He grinned and twisted his head so that my kiss landed on his lips instead. He had to pull away sooner than I would have liked so that he could guide Padmini down for a landing in one of the palace's inner courtyards where the zahhak pens were located. There were three other fire zahhaks, which was quite a force for a city the size of Bikampur, but what really attracted my attention were the emerald scales and iridescent turquoise feathers of an acid zahhak resting in the shade of an awning.

"That would be Prince Karim's mount—Amira," I muttered. I made her name sound like a curse, though I knew it wasn't really the zahhak's fault who owned her.

"She is," Arjun agreed, as he settled Padmini down to the paving stones. "She's a beautiful beast, but nothing you can't handle, right, darling?" He gave Padmini fond pats on her neck, and she made a rumbling noise of pleasure by way of response.

"She is gorgeous," I allowed, looking at the acid zahhak's fabulous coloration. In some ways, she reminded me more of my Sultana than Padmini did. All zahhaks had feathered wings and tails, and scales covering their long, sinuous necks, muscular shoulders, and rear legs, but they differed in size and shape. My Sultana had been a thunder zahhak, a sapphire-scaled wonder of a creature, with swept wings for speed and a long, narrow tail to help her maneuver. Padmini had a blunter tail, to help her soar better, along with wider, blunt-ended wings for the same purpose. But this acid zahhak, she had a tail like Sultana's and a size to match. It was just her short, rounded wings that set her apart from a thunder zahhak. She was built for short bursts of acceleration and for agility at slower speeds. She would fly circles around Padmini, given anything like an even chance.

Arjun unstrapped himself from the saddle, and I did the same. He climbed down first, and then took hold of me around my waist and set me down beside him. I could have managed it easily enough, but I liked the way he doted on me, and I liked the feeling of his strong hands around my waist.

Servants appeared seemingly out of nowhere. An older man took Padmini's reins and guided her toward one of the covered stalls. A eunuch came toward us, and I recognized him at once as Shiv.

"Good day, your highness, Lady Razia," he said, bowing first to his prince and then dipping his head politely to me.

I smiled. "It's good to see you again, Shiv."

"I'm honored to serve, my lady," he replied. He held out his hand. "Shall we?"

I glanced to Arjun, who said, "Yes, I'll see you shortly." He kissed me once on the lips, and then pulled away, walking toward the palace, leaving me to take Shiv's hand and follow him toward a different courtyard.

"Where are we going?" I asked.

"The zenana," he replied, referring to the space reserved for the maharaja's wives and children. "His highness has set aside an apartment for you."

"An apartment?" I gasped. Did he want me to move into the palace? On the one hand, that sounded wonderful, but on the other, I would lose my sisters. The idea of not seeing them again tugged at my heartstrings. "Does he mean for me to stay here?"

"When it pleases him, my lady," Shiv said. "Besides, this way we can more easily manage your wardrobe."

"Shiv, I haven't got a wardrobe," I told him with a laugh. "In fact," I added ruefully, "I've left my zahhak jewelry and the clothes his highness gave me at home."

"I think we'll manage all the same, my lady," said Shiv, and the smile on his face made me hopeful, though I couldn't imagine anything more beautiful than what Arjun had already given me.

I wondered at that smile of his. He was so helpful, and Jai had been so cruel. I was used to cruelty, I understood that; it was kindness I didn't understand. "Why are you so kind to me, Shiv?"

"Because you don't offend me, my lady," he said, as we passed through a heavily guarded gateway, into the halls of the harem proper. "I don't think I'll ever understand why people react the way they do to your kind. You can't help how you were born any more than anyone else can."

"You don't think we're weird for having sought out the operation that ruined your life?" I asked.

"It didn't ruin my life, my lady," he replied. "I didn't enjoy it, and I would undo it if I could, but my life is still one that brings me pleasure. And as to your question, no, I'm not confused as to why a woman would want a woman's body. That seems like a fairly obvious impulse."

I smiled at that and said, "I like you very much, Shiv."

He smiled back. "I'm glad I please you, my lady."

He led me to a room facing an exquisite courtyard with beautiful fountains and half a dozen huge mango trees. The room itself was quite large, perched on the third floor of the palace, with curtains providing privacy but allowing airflow. There was a beautiful bed in the room, and a wardrobe of finely carved sandalwood, and I saw that I had a balcony overlooking another courtyard on the other side of the room.

"This is my apartment?" I marveled.

"It is, my lady," Shiv affirmed. He led me to an adjoining room, and I saw that it was a bathroom, complete with fresh running water entering a pool in the floor through long channels of cut stone, fed by pipes in the walls. The whole room was covered in beautifully enameled tiles, and it reminded me so strongly of my bathroom in the palace back home in Nizam that it made my stomach twist into knots.

"If you would remove your clothes, please, my lady, we will wash you and perfume you so that you are pleasing to his highness," Shiv said.

"Of course," I agreed. I was eager to get into that tub, and Shiv put me at ease in a way few other men would have. The fact that he was a eunuch was part of it, but the way he just accepted me accounted for more. I stripped my clothes off and climbed into the tub, and Shiv helped to wash me and to cover me in rose water and perfumes and to run coconut oil through my hair. By the time he was finished, I smelled better than any flower in the palace gardens.

He led me back into my bedchamber and opened the wardrobe, removing some clothes for me. The skirt he offered was the brilliant green color of a finely polished emerald. The delicate silk fabric was embroidered all over with the thread-like feathers of a kingfisher, creating iridescent turquoise patterns of sinuous zahhaks. With it, I wore a new blouse of the same emerald silk, thick with gold and turquoise embroidery depicting a pair of zahhak wings that wrapped around my chest, shaped so that they seemed to be clutching my breasts in their feathers. A diaphanous turquoise dupatta with a jewel-encrusted golden border completed the outfit, providing the flimsiest screen between a man's roving eyes and my scandalous blouse.

I loved the color choice, as my new lehenga made me look for all the world like an acid zahhak myself. I wished Lakshmi could see me dressed this way. I was sure I was the spitting image of her precious Mohini.

Shiv removed bangles from a sandalwood box that were crafted to look exactly like zahhaks chasing their own tails. They were the finest cloisonné I'd ever seen, using perfectly cut and polished emeralds to match the scales on the zahhaks' heads, necks, and tails. Blue topaz had been cut to mimic their feathers.

My earrings were made in just the same fashion, representing zahhaks with wings spread wide, their tails curling through my ears, their necks stretched out, their beaks open. Their teeth were glittering diamonds, and drops of emerald acid issued forth from their mouths, suspended on golden chains. My nose ring was a long, slender zahhak eating her own tail. My necklace was perhaps the most beautiful of all, two zahhaks breathing emerald acid at each other, each emerald droplet as big as my thumbnail, connected to all the others with little rings of gold. The zahhaks themselves were so thoroughly encrusted in topaz and emeralds that it strained my neck to hold them up.

Shiv attended to my makeup last of all, and when he was finished, he directed me to a large mirror to study the effect. I couldn't believe what I was seeing. I looked like all the wealthy princesses from the storybooks. It was a bittersweet sight. I finally looked like the princess of Nizam I'd always dreamed of being, but I'd never been farther from home.

I smiled at Shiv to cover the sudden pang that realization brought. "Thank you, Shiv. I've never felt more beautiful."

"You're welcome, my lady," he replied. "Now, shall we go and see what his highness thinks?"

"Yes, I can't wait," I agreed, and I walked arm in arm with him out of the harem, eager to see the look on Arjun's face when he caught sight of me.

# CHAPTER 9

Arjun was waiting for me just outside the zenana's gate, and the look on his face didn't disappoint me. His eyes widened, and a smug smirk creased his face. He held out his hand to me, and I went to him at once.

"Do you like your new clothes?" he asked me, as I snaked my arms around his neck.

"They're the most beautiful things I've ever seen, my prince," I replied. "If I didn't know better, I'd think you were trying to make Prince Karim jealous."

He grinned. "I thought you might distract him from his official duties."

"Is that why you've brought me here?" I asked. "To unsettle your opponents?"

"That's *one* of the reasons," he said, and then he leaned forward and kissed me on the lips to show me the other reason.

"Your highness, your father is expecting you . . ." Shiv said gently.

"So he is," Arjun agreed, and he sounded terribly disappointed not to be able to ravish me right then and there. I was disappointed too, and I wasn't at all interested in seeing Karim again, not after what he'd done to me. I did wonder if he'd changed much in the last six years. And I wondered too what he would make of me. Probably nothing good, if our last meeting was anything to go by.

Arjun headed off in the direction of his father's court, with me on his arm. We passed through a very heavily guarded gate, with men holding toradars standing watch from the parapets and men with mail and plate armor, carrying naked khandas and wearing shields on their arms, standing on either side of the gate. The next courtyard was paved with marble, interspersed with fine flower gardens and rivers of flowing water. A covered dais stood in the courtyard's center. Its marble columns held up a roof of red sandstone, providing a pleasing contrast that reminded me of some of Padmini's prettier feathers.

Beneath the sandstone roof, reclining in the shade, were Udai Agnivansha and his court. They sat on fine satin cushions, with the maharaja's placed on a marble throne. Servants with fans were keeping everyone cool, and more were handing out nimbu pani or chilled wine in silver goblets.

I felt terror before my mind registered what my eyes were seeing. My fingers dug into the flesh of Arjun's forearm, clinging to him for dear life as I sucked in a great gasp of air, my heart thundering in my ears. Prince Karim was seated a little apart from the members of Bikampur's court. He was even bigger than I remembered him, tall and lean and ferocious, with dark, soulless eyes. I could still see those eyes looking down his narrow nose at me, still feel his hands pressing against my shoulders until my bones cried out from the way they were being crushed against the marble tiles of my bedchamber's floor.

"Razia?" Arjun whispered, alarmed at the sudden change in my demeanor. "What's the matter?"

His voice, the feeling of his warm palm against my back, brought me back to myself. I took a deep breath and let it out slowly. I couldn't show fear. Fear would give me away. I had to keep Karim from discovering my identity at all costs.

I swallowed hard. "I'm fine, my prince." The lie came easily to my lips. I'd been trained to set aside my own feelings in the service of pleasing wealthy men. This was no different, just more extreme.

I forced myself to look at Prince Karim the way a stranger might. I noted his white silk dhoti, embroidered at the edges of the cloth with very fine gold thread. His kurta was a little more adventurous—kingfisher blue that matched my dupatta, embroidered with a pair of magnificent zahhaks. His turban was worn in the Mahisagari style, a twisted and layered emerald cloth, with a golden zahhak pin holding it together. Thinking about fashion helped to calm me down, to remind me that what he had done to me was six years in the past.

But his face had changed remarkably little in six years, and the sight of it made my insides clench. He was still a handsome young man, with a close-razored beard and mustache, and skin that was several shades too dark to be fashionable back home in Nizam. His eyes were extraordinarily dark, the nearly black ideal among ladies of the Nizami court, though to me they would forever be the eyes of a devil.

I forced myself to look away from those eyes before I panicked, but then my gaze landed on the sword he wore, thrust through a heavily embroidered sash, and I shuddered in spite of myself. It was a firangi, a kind of sword unique to Mahisagar. It combined a curved, slashing blade taken from the Firangi foreigners with the heavy hilt of a Registani's khanda. It was the same blade that I'd found pressed against my throat that night, the edge burning my skin raw.

"God . . ." Karim breathed, his dark eyes roving over me in a way that sent chills down my spine. "Arjun, where did you find such an exquisite creature?"

"This is Razia Khan," he said, gesturing to me by way of introduction.

My mouth went dry as I realized that I was going to have to speak to him, that I was going to have to bury my fear and my disgust deep down where he couldn't see it. Fortunately, behaving like a demure young lady helped. I lowered my gaze, letting my dupatta partly shield the expression of horror on my face, and said, "It's an honor to meet you, your highness."

He grinned, paying more attention to my body and the clothes that adorned it than to my face. "You're dressed like an acid zahhak? Have you ever seen a real one, dear?"

Hearing the desire in his voice, feeling his breath on me as he leaned in close, made me forget caution and carefully laid plans and just blurt out the first thing that came to mind. "Yes, I saw Amira in the stables."

He raised an eyebrow. "And how did you know her name?"

I froze, my heart in my throat. How could I have been so stupid as to say something like that to Prince Karim? The man had hurt me once, when I was just a child. What would he do to me now? There would be so much advantage in telling my father where I was, so much money to be made, and the Mahisagaris were known for their love of making a quick rupee.

"A servant told me, your highness," I murmured, hoping that simple explanation would be enough for him.

It seemed to suffice. He turned to Arjun. "And where was it you found Lady Razia, Arjun?"

"Why?" Arjun asked. "Looking for one of your own?"

Prince Karim shrugged. "If they all look like her, I could do worse."

The maharaja laughed. "Be careful what you wish for, boy. That 'girl' is a hijra. She was once Javed Khorasani's son."

I wanted to strangle the old bastard for saying that. I'd smoothed things over, I'd saved myself, and now he was throwing me right back into the fire.

Karim was frowning, and I knew that nothing good was going to come from this conversation. Sure enough, he asked, "Which son?"

I realized then that I had a problem. Lying to the maharaja had kept me safe, but I had no way of knowing where Karim had been recently and where he hadn't. What if he'd just visited Javed Khorasani? The Mahisagaris shared a religion with us, had allied with us in the past. That was why Prince Karim had spent so much time at my father's court. It stood to reason that he'd spent time at Lord Khorasani's court too. What if he knew the man's sons well? I couldn't take that risk. I couldn't be discovered now, not when everything was going so well. I decided to answer without answering. "My name is Razia Khan now; nothing else matters."

"It matters to me," the maharaja growled. "You never did tell me your real name."

"Razia Khan *is* my real name, your majesty," I protested, with more heat in my voice than I would have dared use with him if I weren't so scared of being found out.

He narrowed his eyes, and my heart skipped a beat. Maybe I'd pushed things too far. "Don't play games with me, girl."

I stood there, frozen in terror, my mouth painfully dry, with no idea what to say. I had to think of something to get me out of this, some new lie I could spin, but nothing was coming to mind.

Arjun leaned down and whispered into my ear, "I don't think he'll sell you to your father."

"Which one?" I hissed, not trusting Udai as far as I could throw him, and trusting Karim even less.

"Either of them," he answered. "I know Karim a little. I don't think he'd want to see you killed in cold blood."

I knew Karim a little too, and I was far less certain.

My silence must have spoken volumes, because Arjun gave my shoulders a squeeze with his strong arm and whispered, "I'll protect you. I promise."

"But if my father finds out I'm here, if anyone at all speaks of it . . ." I couldn't bring myself to finish the sentence. I would die. There was no question that assassins would come for me, and they would catch me eventually. And that was if I was lucky. I thought it far more likely that Udai or Karim would just sell me to my father for the fortune he would offer them. Once I was back home, in my father's clutches . . . I shuddered and fought down the urge to scream.

"You lied to me, boy," Udai said to Arjun, understanding at once what the whispers between the pair of us meant. There was an edge to his voice that made my blood run cold.

Karim noticed, and he grinned. "Well, isn't this interesting . . ." He looked me over. "If I were you, I'd tell his majesty the truth. He's not known for his patience."

As terrifying as Udai was, my father was worse. I was half tempted to just say nothing, to let his torturers try to pry the answer from my lips, because at least they would leave me alive. More than anything, I wanted to run, but there were guards everywhere. I wouldn't make it three steps before they dragged me kicking and screaming right back here.

"This is your last chance, girl," Udai warned. "The truth. Now."

It was over. It was all over. I had to tell them the truth. If I were caught in another lie, Udai would destroy me for it. But maybe, just maybe, I could use their curiosity against them.

"Forgive me for the deception, your majesty," I choked out through a throat that was nearly closed off from fear, "but I was frightened and your son agreed to protect me. My father has assassins everywhere, and if my fate were to become known to him, I think he would stop at nothing to have me killed."

Udai and Karim leaned forward with interest, which was a good sign. I wanted them to be desperate enough to hear my name that they would give oaths to obtain it. "I need your words of honor that you will tell no one. Both of you." I looked to Karim, to show him that I meant him too, though what good was the word of honor of a man who possessed none?

"Don't try to extract promises from me, girl," Udai growled. "Tell me your name, and I'll decide what to do with you then."

All my hope went out of me in a rush. If not for Arjun's strong arm around me, I probably would have collapsed to the floor in a heap. My legs felt unsteady, my body was swaying, and my heart was thumping against the walls of my chest like the drummers in one of the festivals for the southern gods.

I was going to die. I knew it with a sick certainty that permeated the whole of my being. I hung my head, swallowed hard against the lump of emotion in my throat, and summoned the courage to say it. "The name my father gave me was Salim. Salim Mirza."

Karim burst out laughing. "I should have seen it! But you've changed so much, your highness." He leaned forward, leering at me. "You're prettier than you were six years ago—the breasts are a nice touch. Tell me, did you have your nirvan?"

I was disgusted, enraged, terrified. I wanted to tell him to burn in hell, but I knew if I said it that there would be no going back, that he would sell me to my father, that he would watch while I was led away in chains by Nizami soldiers. I looked desperately to Udai, but he was sitting on his marble throne, his arms crossed over his chest, watching and waiting.

Not that it mattered. There were dozens of courtiers and servants within earshot. They'd all heard it. They all knew. There was nothing that would keep me safe from my father's wrath now.

So I answered Karim's question with as much courage and dignity as I possessed. "Yes. Four years ago."

He grinned, enjoying my terror, which must have been plain on my face and in my posture. "And do you remember my last visit to the court of Nizam? Do you remember the time we shared together?"

"I remember," I growled, my hands balling up into fists. Now that I knew I was going to die, I had less reason to tolerate his insults. I may not have been as big or as strong as he was, but with a sword in my hand, I was willing to take my chances. "I remember what a filthy, disgusting animal you were, and I can see nothing has changed."

He clucked his tongue, the smile never leaving his face. "Still angry, dear? Come now, you can't blame me for putting my hands on you. You were quite a pretty little thing even then, and I knew you wanted it. Of course, your father beat you terribly for it, didn't he?"

"That's enough, Karim!" Arjun snapped, his hand falling to the hilt of his khanda, the threat of the gesture totally unmistakable.

"Stop it, both of you," the maharaja ordered, before a fight could break out. He was still staring at me wide-eyed, scrutinizing every inch of me. "This is the missing crown prince of Nizam?" he asked, his disbelief plain in his voice.

"Oh, I didn't recognize him at first, your majesty, but there can be no doubt. Those emerald eyes haven't changed a bit," said Karim. "And her face was pretty even then."

I gritted my teeth but said nothing. For once in my life, I couldn't find the right words. What do you say to the men who are going to sell you to your executioner?

"I worked it out the night we met, Father, but I worried for her safety," Arjun said.

"You needn't have feared that," Udai replied. "There's no profit for me in antagonizing Nizam by advertising the girl's past. She's right, if Sultan Humayun got wind of her presence here, he'd send more than assassins. We'd have an army marching to our gates to reclaim her."

I looked up at the maharaja in shock. "You're not going to sell me to him?" My hands were shaking as hope stirred within my heart. I'd been so sure he'd do it.

"What about him?" Arjun asked, nodding his head toward Karim and his delegation.

"Oh, don't fret, Arjun," Karim said in soothing tones. "Seeing her this way is far more fun than seeing her dead." To me, he added, "I knew you liked it when a man touched you, even then."

"I was eleven," I snarled. "I still don't know why my father let you keep your hands."

"Careful now," he warned. "So long as you're fun, I'll keep your precious secret, but if you take that tone with me, perhaps I'll have to tell your dear daddy just where you've been hiding all these years."

The threat made my blood run cold and took all the fight out of me in a rush.

A triumphant smirk crossed Karim's face. "As to why I kept my hands, it's because I told your father how you swished your hips, how you asked me to kiss you, and he believed every word. Besides, he had a war with Virajendra to wage, and he couldn't risk us attacking him in his vulnerable flank, couldn't risk us joining our ships to the Virajendrans' already considerable fleet. I was too valuable to punish. Curious that you were not, *my lady*." He said that last with such scorn that it made me squeeze my hands into fists.

My anger only made him laugh. "Oh, did I offend you, *girl*? What are you going to do about it?"

"Nothing," I replied, through clenched teeth. That was the sad, bitter truth of it. There was nothing I could do, just like that night six years ago.

"You should call me 'your highness,'" Karim chided. "If you don't play the part of the courtesan and address me as I deserve, I might get offended, and you wouldn't want that, would you?"

"Forgive me, your highness," I whispered.

He found that absurdly funny and chuckled to himself, swilling wine in between bouts of laughter.

I noticed Udai Agnivansha staring at me, but I didn't want to meet his gaze either. I felt strangely naked, my identity having been revealed to everyone. I'd kept my past so closely guarded all this time, but I couldn't very well be a presence at the court here without being honest. If I claimed to be someone I wasn't, and it came out that I was lying, it might offend other princes, lead to wars, or any number of other things that would result in my head being put up on a spike. Of course now, despite Udai's and Karim's guarantees of silence, it was an open secret, which is to say no kind of secret at all. I gave it a week before I woke to a dagger piercing my heart.

Arjun sat, dragging me down beside him. He put his arm around me and pulled my head against his chest, his hand reaching up and stroking my hair gently. I expected Karim to laugh again, but strangely he didn't. He just stared at me, and what I saw on his face shocked me—hunger. He wanted me. I'd seen that look on his face when I was eleven, when he'd found me in the corridors of the palace and had cornered me. He'd told me then how pretty I was, what beautiful lips I had . . . I closed my eyes against the force of the memory.

But as horrible as that look was, it gave me hope. If he lusted after me, then he wouldn't want me dead. It didn't offer much security, but I supposed it was the only hope I had left.

"Prince Karim, your father honors me with your presence," Udai said, finally taking the scrutiny off of me. I'd have been relieved if I'd believed for an instant that the others in the room would be as willing to forget about me. But I knew better, and I had to struggle not to cry in front of everyone.

"You honor the both of us by granting us this audience, your majesty," Karim replied, his mirth fleeing his face. He was all business now. My father had liked that about him. How serious he was. How stoic. How unlike me. That was probably why he'd beaten me until my insides hurt, until I couldn't lift my head, but hadn't punished him at all.

"It is my firm belief that the peace between our peoples has served us both well," said the maharaja. "To what do we owe the pleasure of your visit today?"

"As it happens, your majesty, you have already mentioned the name which has brought me to your court," said Karim. "Javed Khorasani."

The maharaja leaned forward on his cushion, a look of interest plain on his face. He wanted revenge for the defeat he had suffered at Khorasani's hands five years before. Bikampur was the closest Registani city to the province of Zindh, a part of my father's grand empire. As a result, Javed Khorasani, Zindh's governor, was constantly struggling for power against Udai. Each side fought to command the most lucrative trading posts lying along the caravan routes, and the last contest had gone to Khorasani and Nizam. The maharaja couldn't let that stand, for reasons of honor as much as politics. "You have my attention, young man."

"My father believes that Khorasani is paying the Firangis to make raids along our shores," said Karim.

"Wretched foreigners," one of the viziers grumbled, and I couldn't help but agree. The stinking Firangis with their hideous woolen clothes had visited my father's court once, desperate for a handful of peppercorns to take back to the frozen wasteland they called home.

"Further," Karim continued, "there has been an increased presence of Nizami forces along our northern border. We think that Khorasani is planning to invade, perhaps to steal Rajkot fortress from us. He has coveted it for years, and it commands the best harbor in northern Mahisagar. If Khorasani takes it, he will take the northern third of our kingdom with it, and in so doing, he will also command the trading port to which almost all of your goods flow, your majesty."

"To say nothing of having command of the road running right to our doorstep," Arjun growled, not liking the sound of that one bit. "And it would give the Nizamis a port to our south, which would let them squeeze us from both sides."

"Though it seems strange that my father would authorize such a foolish attack," I murmured, drawing more attention than I really wanted, but I couldn't help but speak my mind. "After all, the Mahisagaris share a religion with Nizam. It makes them natural allies."

"Religious affiliation has never stopped Nizam from taking what it wants, when it wants it," Karim replied, and I couldn't argue with him, as it was the simple truth.

"So, you've come for our support against Khorasani?" Udai asked.

"Just so, your majesty," said Karim. "But we don't seek to go to war with him. Defeating a Nizami subahdar like Khorasani in open battle would be an invitation to Sultan Humayun for war—a war we couldn't possibly win."

Much as I hated Karim, I found myself nodding along as he spoke. My father, Sultan Humayun, had bigger worries than the petty squabbles his vassal Khorasani was engaging in out here on the fringes of the continent. But he couldn't risk letting a defeat in battle go unavenged, not when the Registanis were always probing the western borders for signs of weakness. So if the Mahisagaris took the fight to Khorasani, they would be inviting my father's swift vengeance.

Udai had been listening intently, and he was nodding just as I was. "I presume you have a solution to this problem?"

"Of a sort," Karim replied. "The fact of the matter is that Khorasani won't risk attacking us without a fleet to support him. Rajkot's walls are practically impregnable, and without a naval blockade, its harbor would allow it to withstand a siege for all eternity."

"Which is why the Firangis have been making their raids," Arjun reasoned.

"Precisely," said Karim. "The Nizamis need a navy, and since they haven't got one, they're relying on Firangi mercenaries to do their dirty work for them."

"So, destroy the Firangi fleet, and you save Rajkot and avoid a war with my father that you can't hope to win," I concluded, seeing the logic of that.

Karim smirked at me, reminding me of the danger I was in, though he seemed more bemused than angry. "That's it exactly. If we win the sea, Khorasani won't send his armies south to attack a fortress he has no hope of capturing. He'll stay in Zindh where he belongs, and there will be no provocation worthy of stirring Sultan Humayun from his capital."

"If that's the case, then why come to us?" asked Arjun. "The Firangis keep to the sea. You know we have no ships, no sailors, no knowledge of how to fight on water. And if Khorasani won't risk drawn-out battles on land, what have we to offer you?"

"You have fire zahhaks," Karim said. "With your zahhaks, we could burn the Firangi fleet to the waterline."

"They haven't got zahhaks of their own to protect from such an attack?" Udai asked, sounding surprised by that.

"They have," I said, not willing to let Karim mislead them, no matter what threats he leveled at me. If Bikampur went to war with its zahhaks, then Arjun would be leading the attack, and I wasn't going to let him fly blindly into an ambush. "They fly ice zahhaks."

"Ice zahhaks . . ." Arjun murmured, scrunching up his face, clearly trying to remember everything he'd read about them, because they were never seen in desert lands like Registan.

"They're colored like snow and stone, and they breathe a strange gas that freezes everything it touches," I told him.

"And how many of them do the Firangis have?" the maharaja asked me.

I shrugged. "I don't know, your majesty."

"Three," said Karim. "We've scouted them from the air, and we know they've brought three on their ships. My father can muster four acid zahhaks. With two or three fire zahhaks we could overwhelm them with ease."

"These ice zahhaks, what are they like? How do they fly?" Udai asked.

"They . . . well . . . they haven't actually engaged us, your majesty," Karim admitted. "So we haven't seen them fight. They hold them in reserve, to protect them. But with your fire zahhaks on our side, we could outnumber them two to one or more."

"But you've seen them?" Udai pressed.

"Yes, your majesty," he said.

"So you must know how big they are, what their wings look like, how they fly."

Karim smiled to hide his discomfiture. "We've never been close enough that I would feel comfortable answering those questions, your majesty. As I say, the Firangis keep them in reserve to protect them."

No one said a word to that. I waited for one of the maharaja's advisers to talk about the ice zahhaks the Firangis flew, but none of them spoke up. It occurred to me, in that moment, that I might be the only one in the whole room who knew what they were like. Knowledge was valuable, and knowledge about zahhaks was rarer and more valuable still. Maybe that knowledge would make me valuable enough to protect from the assassins I was sure would be coming for me.

"They're smaller than fire zahhaks, but larger than acid zahhaks," I announced. "Their wings and tails lie between the two in shape, making them faster and more maneuverable than fire zahhaks, but less so than acid zahhaks. Their breath weapons are devastatingly effective against flying opponents, because they immediately coat their enemies' wings with ice, robbing them of the ability to keep aloft, sending them tumbling down like stones."

"How do you know this, girl?" Udai demanded.

"I've flown one many times, your majesty," I replied, sitting up a little straighter, that fact reminding me who I was. "I spent three years at the Safavian court while my father fought a civil war. There, I spent a great deal of time with the crown prince of Safavia's cousin, Tamara, crown princess of Lazistan. Her personal mount was an ice zahhak, and she taught me everything there is to know about them. It's been seven years since I flew one, but ice zahhaks are faster and more agile than fire zahhaks, and their beaks are stronger, made for biting through frozen prey. While their breath is less effective against ships and buildings than a fire zahhak's, in the air they're every bit as deadly."

The maharaja stroked his beard and looked back to Karim. "And you say they have three of them?"

"Yes, your majesty," Karim said. "We know it's only three. They can't support any more aboard their ships, and our scouts have been watching them from a distance."

"And you have four acid zahhaks with which to fight them?"

"Yes, your majesty," he agreed. "As I said, if you were to join us with two or three fire zahhaks, we would have them thoroughly outnumbered. We could sweep their beasts from the skies and then sink their ships. Without the Firangis raiding our shores, Javed Khorasani would be forced to change his plans."

"Razia?"

I sat up a little straighter. The maharaja had never called me by my name before. He hated me. Why was he trying to be nice all of a sudden?

"Yes, your majesty?" I asked.

"How do these ice zahhaks compare to acid zahhaks?" he asked me.

"I've never flown the one against the other, your majesty, but from what I remember, I would say that the acid zahhaks will be faster and more agile. However, an ice zahhak's breath is easier to aim, and it's more immediately devastating against an enemy. If they met on even terms, I would expect the acid zahhak to prevail, but if an ice zahhak had the advantage in altitude, I think that would determine the contest."

He grunted at that and looked to Karim. "It seems that even if we outnumber the Firangis, it would be no certain battle. What would you offer us that would compel us to risk all our zahhaks in a single battle against people who have never threatened us?"

"Your majesty, I don't think we should be putting too much stock in the opinions of a hijra on matters of warfare," Karim said, and his narrowed eyes promised vengeance if he didn't get the help his father had sent him to find.

"My son says that she flies a zahhak as well as he does," Udai replied. Was he defending me? "And you've said yourself that you've never been close enough to one of these creatures to observe it. She's flown one."

"So she says . . ." Karim murmured, but I thought he saw that denigrating me was a losing argument. "At any rate, your majesty, my father is prepared to offer you one lakh rupees for your help in this matter."

"One lakh will buy you the services of two of my zahhaks," said Udai. "Two lakhs will buy all four."

"Two lakhs it is, then, your majesty," said Karim without the slightest hesitation, and without the customary haggling for which Mahisagaris were justifiably famous, as natural merchants and smugglers. His father must have been truly desperate to be rid of these Firangis.

"And when will we be flying out to attack these ships?" Arjun asked.

"Immediately," Karim replied. "We know where the Firangis are, and we want to hit them before they hit us again, and before Khorasani can mass any more of his forces along our border."

"And the two lakh rupees?" Udai asked.

Karim nodded to his men, who brought forward an enormous chest that was so heavy it took two burly soldiers to carry it. They laid it in front of Udai and opened the lid, revealing a mass of silver coins inside. My eyes widened. That chest would have set anyone up for life. If it really contained two hundred thousand rupees, then those coins could have let me live better than Govind Singh from that day until the day I died, and I would have had some left over for Lakshmi and Sakshi too.

Udai grinned. "You have your zahhaks, Prince Karim. We will leave tomorrow morning for Rajkot. Tonight, we celebrate." He gestured for his servants to bring around fresh goblets of wine.

"Your majesty is too kind," Karim replied.

Udai raised his glass and said, "To our peoples' continued cooperation."

"To cooperation," said Karim loudly.

I was given a goblet, and I drank with all the rest, though I didn't much care for any toast that involved Karim. What he'd done to me that night in Nizam . . . what my father had done afterward . . . I didn't want to think about it ever again, but I could think about nothing else when I looked at him. And I had other reasons not to be in a celebratory mood. I reasoned my father would probably pay any man who found me something on the order of one lakh rupees for information on my whereabouts. That was enough money to challenge the loyalty of any man in the world, and not one of the men in this room had any loyalty at all to me. I was a dead woman. My only hope now was that Arjun really could protect me the way he'd promised.

The maharaja stood up from his throne, which prompted everyone else to stand, myself included. He said, "I will have the banquet hall prepared, Prince Karim. Now, if you'll excuse me, I have zahhaks to tend to."

"Of course, your majesty," Karim replied, favoring Udai with a courtly bow.

The older man gestured to his son. "Arjun, come with me."

"Of course, Father," he said.

I started to walk with him, not sure if that was what either of them wanted, but I really didn't want to be left alone with Karim, and after everything that had happened, I didn't want to be so much as a single step away from Arjun. I kept my head down, like that somehow made me invisible, which was stupid, but it seemed to work, because nobody stopped me. I followed Arjun and his father through a guarded gate, into one of the inner chambers of the palace.

It was a private room, one set aside for the maharaja's relaxation, I thought. There was a bubbling fountain inside, and there were many fine cushions, and it seemed like the perfect place for quiet contemplation. It made me wonder if I'd been meant to come with them or not.

Udai sat on one of the cushions and gestured for his son to sit on another next to him. I sat down beside Arjun, still not sure if I was intruding, but so long as I kept my head down and my hands folded in my lap, the maharaja seemed content to let me stay.

"You confound me, girl," Udai declared.

It wasn't what I'd expected him to say. I hadn't expected him to address me at all. In a different tone of voice, what he'd said would have worried me, but he didn't sound angry, more bemused than anything.

"Your majesty?" I asked, unable to keep my voice from sounding like an anxious squeak.

"That," he said, gesturing to me in annoyance. "If you have such knowledge of strategy, if you're such a good zahhak rider, if you can wrestle and fight with swords and katars, what are you doing living like that?"

"The one has nothing to do with the other, your highness," I replied.

"How's that?" he demanded.

"Well, women can be good strategists and commanders in battle," I said. "My great-grandmother Razia Khanum was the sultana of Nizam, and she led her troops into battle herself. And she flew the fastest thunder zahhak and was never defeated."

"So that's where your name comes from," Arjun murmured, and he was grinning. It seemed to appeal to him.

"If you're a skilled strategist, why choose to live as a woman where it's unlikely to be of any use?" Udai asked, still not quite getting the point.

I shrugged. "I have a woman's soul, your majesty. I can't help it. None of us chooses how we were born."

He seemed to mull that over for some time, though what he thought of it, I couldn't have said with any confidence. He didn't seem to despise me as much as he had before at any rate. He just stared at me, stroking his bushy beard in thought, and I was content to keep quiet and not disturb him. At length, he said, "You will be coming with us to Rajkot in case we have need of your expertise regarding these ice zahhaks."

I sat up a little straighter. He wanted me to come with them? As a sort of adviser? Was this the chance to remake my life, to be something more than a dancing girl and a whore? I nodded eagerly. "I would be greatly honored, your majesty."

"Good."

I hesitated, not wanting to infuriate him when we were finally getting along, but I couldn't stop myself from asking, "Your majesty?"

"What?" he demanded. He didn't sound angry exactly, but it wasn't friendly either.

"About my father . . . I . . ." I didn't have words to express the terror I was feeling, the grim certainty that I was going to die soon at my father's hand.

"You have value to me and to my son," Udai replied. "So long as that is the case, no harm will come to you. I may not be the sultan of Nizam, but I have guards and they will protect you."

"Your majesty is very kind," I replied, allowing myself a little sigh of relief. I wasn't sure if Udai's guards would be enough to save me, but I was glad I wouldn't be facing my father's assassins alone.

Udai glanced at Arjun. "What have you paid for the girl?"

"I paid her a hundred rupees and her guru a thousand to have exclusive use of her," Arjun replied.

My cheeks flushed, and I hung my head. It shouldn't have bothered me, but hearing my price spoken of so openly felt like a punch to the stomach. A hundred rupees. That was what Arjun had given me. Four months' pay for an ordinary soldier. Three and a half years' worth of a soldier's pay he had given my guru. But when set beside the wealth of a prince, it was nothing at all.

It wasn't so much the price itself that bothered me. I was cheap, true enough, but the fact that I had a price at all was what rankled. It made me feel like a piece of livestock more than a person.

Udai snorted. "The clothes and the jewelry she's wearing are worth ten times that."

"Yes, they are," Arjun agreed. He frowned and put his arm around me. "Is there a problem, Father? She makes me happy, and I think she's more than just a pretty face. She proved her worth today, didn't she?"

"We'll see," he murmured. To me, he said, "You will come with us to Rajkot, girl. If we all survive to make it home again, I will give you a thousand rupees as a token of my appreciation for your counsel."

A thousand rupees? My eyes widened. It was a pittance by the standards of a prince, but I was no prince and hadn't been one for a long time. A thousand rupees would change my life—and Lakshmi's and Sakshi's. It wasn't enough to set up the three of us for the rest of our lives, but it was something that we could use to build a different kind of life—if I survived long enough to spend it.

"Your majesty is very kind," I said, knowing that I sounded far too desperately earnest, but not caring.

He waved away my gratitude. "Thank me when we all come back."

"I will, your majesty," I promised him.

# CHAPTER 10

Rajkot fort sat atop a rocky cliff overlooking a narrow inlet that separated Rajkot harbor from the Ratnakara Ocean. The fort was accessible only by means of a narrow, rocky spit of land that connected it to the mainland. That, or by air.

From Padmini's back, I could see beyond the fortress's yellow stone walls, to its numerous lush courtyards, filled with fruit trees and rosebushes and marble fountains. This was the home of the Sultan Ahmed Shah, ruler of all Mahisagar.

"Look at all the cannons," said Arjun, pointing out their black muzzles visible through holes in the walls and in between the merlons on the parapets. "Do they really think the Firangis could get through *that?*"

"One zahhak could destroy the whole fort," I said.

"But they've got three of their own down there," he replied, gesturing to the ones in their stable pens, visible from the air. And then he nodded to Karim, who was flying a fourth animal alongside us. Much as I hated to admit it, his acid zahhak was absolutely stunning. Her turquoise feathers fairly glittered in the bright midday sun, her emerald scales gleamed, and my heart ached.

"Sultana . . ." I breathed, the longing hitting me harder with each passing day. It had been easier before Arjun had come into my life, before I had found myself on the back of a zahhak every day, before I'd been brought back into palace life. Now, she filled my dreams and increasingly visited me in my waking hours. The bond between human and zahhak is a strange one, that even after four long years the loss could feel as fresh as it had the first day.

I must have said her name louder than I'd intended, because Arjun's hand fell over my shoulder and massaged it gently. "I'm sorry you had to give up your whole life, Razia, but I'm glad you came to Bikampur."

"Me too, my prince," I replied, reaching up to rest my hand atop his, though my own feelings weren't as unmuddied as his seemed to be. The truth was, being with Arjun made me miss my old life in ways I hadn't thought possible, but it had also brought the fear and the pain roaring back. I was glad we were flying to Mahisagar, glad to be away from Bikampur for a few days, but I was dreading what I would find when I returned. My father's assassins, most likely.

Of course, Arjun had promised to protect me, and that meant more to me than I could have possibly expressed. "You've been very kind to me. And your father has too, after his own fashion."

He chuckled at that. "If you call his treatment of you 'kind,' then you're a more forgiving soul than I am."

"I'm a hijra, my prince," I said. "I have to be."

"You're my princess," he corrected, brushing a few loose strands of hair back behind my ear.

I forced a smile to hide the pain that rippled through me. "You'll marry a real princess someday, and she will give you children, my prince. I can never do that, no matter how much we wish it might be otherwise."

"We'll discuss it later," he said, and he steered Padmini into a descending spiral with the other zahhaks—three fire and one acid. Karim was in the lead, with Udai trailing behind him on a magnificent animal whose scales had a purplish tinge to them that was more vibrant than any fire zahhak I'd ever laid eyes on. The other two fire zahhaks were ridden by the maharaja's trusted men. I hoped the men knew what they were doing, because I'd heard that the Firangis could be fierce warriors, and Arjun's life would be at stake.

The coming battle was worrying me more than anything. I wanted to climb onto Sultana's back and follow Arjun into the fight, just so I could keep him safe, but I had no zahhak, and I wasn't foolish enough to believe that any raja would ever give one to a hijra. So I would be helpless, today and all the days to come, forced to sit in the palace and pray to God to bring Arjun back to me.

Padmini landed in the courtyard that housed the sultan's stables. Already, the sultan himself was marching out to greet us, flanked by a dozen of his finest warriors. They looked more like pirates than soldiers, in their loose dhotis and their colorful kurtas, with their firangis swinging from their hips. They didn't wear armor, as it would have slowed them down aboard ship and dragged them to the bottom of the ocean if they fell into the water. But if Prince Karim was any indication, that didn't make them any less lethal.

"Welcome home, my son," Ahmed said, embracing Karim and pounding him heartily on the back. "I see you were successful, as I knew you would be."

It was stupid, but watching that exchange made me feel a twinge of anger and jealousy that was hard to control. Karim was such a miserable bastard, but his father loved him anyway. His father was proud of him.

"Father, allow me to introduce his royal majesty, the maharaja of Bikampur, Udai Agnivansha, and his son, Prince Arjun," said Karim, sweeping his hand in their direction.

"You honor me with your presence," Ahmed said, greeting them. "Thank you for coming to our aid in our hour of need."

"It was our pleasure," Udai replied. "The Firangis should be put in their place, and it's about time someone spat acid in Javed Khorasani's eye."

"I couldn't agree more," said Ahmed. He seemed to notice me then, and his eyes went wide. He smiled at me. "And who is this charming creature? Your daughter?"

"Prince Arjun's pet hijra, Father," Karim said, grinning at me.

"Hijra?" Ahmed asked, wrinkling his nose and giving me another look, clearly trying to find some part of me that looked male enough to justify that label. Well, I knew from long experience that he wasn't going to find it, but it vexed me that he tried so hard all the same.

"My name is Razia Khan, your majesty," I said, bowing my head to him gracefully.

"And you'll never guess what her name was before they cut her," said Karim, his thin smirk showing me just how much he was enjoying the threat that he knew my name would bring.

"You swore!" I growled, but Karim wasn't listening to me, and neither was his father.

"Who is she, then?" Ahmed demanded, and my heart sank. I didn't know why it bothered me so much, not when half of the noblemen of Bikampur had already been told, along with Karim's whole delegation, but the simple fact was that the more people who knew my secret, the more likely it was that the rumor would spread and my father would feel the need to snuff me out.

I took hold of Arjun's sleeve and hissed, "Say something!"

But it was too late. Karim was already saying, "Salim Mirza."

The name made my ears burn from humiliation as much as it made my insides twist from fear. Every time I heard it uttered, it served as a reminder that I could never truly escape my past, that all the running and hiding I'd done for four long years was for nothing. I wanted desperately to snatch the words from the air before they could reach Ahmed's ears, to shove them back down Karim's hateful throat until he choked on them, but all I could do was stand there helplessly and pray that the sultan of Mahisagar wouldn't use me as a bargaining chip to solve his problems with Nizam.

"God!" Ahmed exclaimed, so overwhelmed that he suffered a coughing fit. He looked from his son to Arjun to me and demanded, "Is this true?"

I wanted to scream that it wasn't, but Arjun said, "It is, your majesty," before I could stop him. "My father has brought her as an adviser, as she's the only one of us who has flown an ice zahhak."

"Has she?" Ahmed murmured, looking at me with narrowed eyes. I could tell from the way his lips were making his gray mustache twitch that he thought involving me in all this was a waste of time.

"I have, your majesty," I told him, which seemed to startle him, like he'd forgotten that hijras could talk.

When he recovered, he looked me up and down and asked, "Does your father know what you've done to yourself?"

"If he did, I'd already be dead, your majesty," I replied.

"And he'd be right to do it," Ahmed grumbled, which sent a jolt of fear running through me.

"Well, it won't be long now, your majesty," I murmured, fighting to speak even though my mouth was dry from terror. "Now that my secret is spoken of so openly, my father's agents will find me and kill me." I couldn't help but send a withering glare in Karim's direction.

Arjun stepped in and placed his arm around me, telling Ahmed, "Your majesty, she is valuable to me, and she serves me loyally, which is a rare enough thing. Moreover, my father ordered her to come so that she could help us defeat the Firangis. As such, any attack on her would be seen as an attack on our household. And given her father's disposition, I would view the spreading of rumors regarding her identity as just such an attack."

"My son is right." My jaw dropped. Those were not the words I'd expected from Udai Agnivansha. "Whoever she was before, she is my son's servant girl now, and therefore she is his property, which makes her my property too. I will not look kindly upon those who attack my property—directly or indirectly."

"I have no interest in selling the girl to her enemies," said Ahmed in a much more conciliatory tone than he had used with me. I found myself believing him, and that helped to loosen some of the tension from my insides.

"Good," said Udai. "Now, enough about the hijra. I think we have a battle to prepare for, my friend."

"We do," Ahmed agreed. "If you'll come with me, I have re-freshments prepared. While you dine, we can discuss the finer details of the coming engagement."

"Can't wait. I'm famished," Karim said, patting his stomach with both hands.

We followed Ahmed through a gateway into a second court-yard, which had been made into a gorgeous garden of fruit trees. The shade provide a welcome respite from the relentless heat of the summer sun. Water was flowing through marble-lined canals, feeding fountains and providing life for the rosebushes and the fruit trees. Ripe mangoes were drooping from their branches, begging to be plucked, but I didn't dare, however much I wanted one. I thought that Ahmed Shah would probably take a pretty dim view of anything I did here. Better if I kept my mouth shut and looked like a proper servant girl until this was over and we could get back to Bikampur. I wasn't sure if that would save me, even with Arjun's and Udai's vows to protect me, but I wasn't going to tempt fate either.

I really didn't see why Udai had insisted on bringing me to Rajkot, and that feeling only intensified as we settled onto silk cushions beneath a pavilion of yellow sandstone. It wasn't the opulence of the place, though every inch of the pavilion was carved with floral motifs and geometric shapes. And it wasn't the presence of the servants who waited upon us, delivering trays of freshly sliced mangoes, and proper Mahisagari thalis—huge steel plates with bowls of different chutneys and curries, bhakhri and khichdi. We had those things in abundance in Bikampur, and I was comfortable enough in the rhythms of palace life. No, what made me feel out of place was the company—a pair of warrior princes, and their fathers who had likely fought twenty battles between them. What was I going to add to this conversation, when I'd spent more of my life shopping for lehengas than fighting in wars?

Arjun was staring at his thali like he didn't know what to do with it. I knew it was an invitation, but I didn't think it was appropriate to feed him just then, not in the midst of a discussion of the coming battle, and even less with Karim watching. The way the Mahisagari prince stared at me made me uncomfortable. I ate a piece of mango, ignored the wine, and tried my best to stay out of the way of the men.

"I can't tell you how much it pleases me that you accepted my offer," Ahmed said to Udai, all smiles now that I was shunted away from the center of things. "With our four zahhaks, we simply couldn't have risked an open battle against the Firangis, but with your four joining ours, I don't think they stand a chance."

Udai nodded his agreement. "And you know where these Firangis can be found?"

"Their fleet is at anchor not twenty miles up the coast. They have three zahhaks with them at all times, eight large sailing vessels, and ten smaller galleys. Their ships have very good cannons, so attacking them from the sea is futile—they'd shoot us to pieces before we got close. But an attack from the air eliminates this advantage."

"So what's the plan?" Arjun asked.

"The plan is quite simple. We'll approach low, where they won't be able to see us silhouetted against the sky until it's too late. We'll hit their ships, destroy them, and leave before they're any the wiser," Ahmed said.

The men were nodding, but I didn't much care for that plan. It would put them in the path of the Firangi cannons. It would put them near the water where the fire zahhaks wouldn't blend in as easily against the waves. It would put them on even terms with the ice zahhaks, which would be waiting to leap from the decks of the ships to defend them. At anything like even altitude, an ice zahhak would outfly and out-turn a fire zahhak in short order. The men of Bikampur would be putting themselves in grave danger.

"I don't think that's a very good idea . . ." The words escaped my lips before I could stop them.

The room went dead silent. Again, I hadn't realized how much my own voice carried. The servants were staring at me in abject horror. Ahmed looked furious. Udai looked angry too. Arjun was mortified. Karim had a smug smile plastered across his face like he was going to very much enjoy what was coming.

Before Ahmed could say anything, Udai preempted him. He growled, "Forgive me, your majesty, my servant girl doesn't seem to know her place. I assure you, I will deal with the matter when all this is over."

Ahmed opened his mouth to thank him, but I couldn't let that stand. I may not have meant to say it, but it had needed saying. "I'm very sorry, but I thought you told me that you wanted me here to help you with strategy, your majesty," I said.

"She's got you there, Father," said Arjun, his tone jocular, I think in an attempt to defuse the tension in the room.

It didn't work. Udai just narrowed his eyes and said through clenched teeth, "If you have some brilliant insight into this battle plan, then by all means, let us hear it, girl."

He wanted insight? Fine, I would give it to him. I turned to Ahmed and said, "Your majesty is quite right. You should approach low to the water, hit the ships, and kill the ice zahhaks either before they can take off or when they're still low to the water. Your acid zahhaks will blend in with the waves, their speed will put them on top of the Firangi ships before anyone is the wiser, and if the ice zahhaks do take to the skies, you'll be faster and more agile and will be able to outmaneuver them low to the waves."

The men looked annoyed. That was just me restating Ahmed's plan. The bit they were missing came next. "But a fire zahhak is not an acid zahhak, your majesty. They're not as fast as acid zahhaks are. If they follow you low, they won't be able to keep up with you. They're red and gold, not blue and green, so they'll be obvious against the water, which means the Firangi cannons will be able to take shots at them from a mile out. And they're not as agile as acid zahhaks, so they'll have a hard time turning with the ice zahhaks down low."

Arjun was fighting down a smile, but the other men were staring at me in shock. Well, I wasn't finished yet. "A better plan would be to send the acid zahhaks in low and fast, ahead of the fire zahhaks. The Firangis don't know you've made a deal with the maharaja of Bikampur. They don't know you have four more zahhaks ready to fight. So they'll be focused entirely on you. They'll attack you with everything they've got, and that's when the fire zahhaks will arrive at higher altitude, where they can dive in and use their speed to hit either the ships or the other zahhaks from a position of advantage."

"The timing will be difficult," Udai warned me, speaking to me like an adviser to whom he was batting around ideas, rather than to a virtual slave. "If we're too far back, we risk losing the acid zahhaks before we can help them."

"And if we come too quickly, they'll spot us high in the sky and be alerted," Arjun added. "We'll have to keep the acid zahhaks just at the very edge of our vision if we're going to make it work. That way, by the time the ships can see us, the attack will already be under way."

"But you can't be so far back that you take too long to get into the fight," Karim murmured. "How fast does a fire zahhak fly?"

"Thirty or forty miles to the hour if they're not exhausting themselves," Arjun said. "They can hit almost seventy in level flight, and double that in the dive."

"So, if you come in with some altitude, not too much, you'll be able to keep us on the horizon and still make it into the fight in a minute or two," Karim reasoned.

"That sounds about right to me," Arjun agreed.

"Which would get us into the fight in plenty of time to help, without ruining the element of surprise," Udai concluded.

The men all turned to stare at me then, and I sat there silently with my hands folded in my lap, my eyes downcast, like I was embarrassed to have interrupted them. I always found that worked better with men than gloating. They hated being wrong, hated being corrected, and were angrier about all of it if a woman or a hijra was involved in any of it. So I made myself seem as uninvolved as I could, even if I couldn't erase the fact that it had been my idea. Though sometimes I found that men were quick enough to forget that sort of thing too.

"It's a good plan," Ahmed admitted, which was more than I expected from him. "We'll make the attack tomorrow."

"What time?" asked Arjun.

"We'll take off at first light and head straight for the enemy," he replied.

I waited for somebody to tell him that he was wrong, not wanting to have to do it for the second time, but nobody spoke up. So I said, "Perhaps it might be better to leave a touch before first light, your majesty?"

"Oh?" he asked, and he sounded slightly less annoyed than he had a moment before, but it was plain he didn't much care for my interruptions.

"If you leave before first light, you can fly north and position yourselves directly east of the enemy ships. They won't be expecting you to come from that direction, and then you can use the rising sun at your back to hide you. With the sun low on the horizon, they'll probably never see you."

"Salim," Karim said, clapping his hands, "I don't remember you having such a head for strategy before. Did cutting your balls off make you smarter?"

"It tends to," I replied. "You should try it. I know a very skilled surgeon in Bikampur."

He grinned and shook his head. "I'd rather be stupid and keep my balls."

"You should be well pleased with yourself on both counts, then, your highness." I was annoyed at him for having called me by my old name and eager to get in a dig of my own.

Ahmed scowled, but Karim laughed and slapped his thigh. "I can see why you like her, Arjun. She wasn't this feisty back in Nizam."

Arjun responded by pulling me closer to him and kissing me on the top of my head. "I was lucky to have found her."

"So it would seem," Udai murmured, though he sounded a little more dubious about it. He turned his attention back to Ahmed. "Is there anything else?"

"No, I think that we have things well in hand for tomorrow," the sultan of Mahisagar replied. "I suggest you rest for the evening so that you're prepared to move out before dawn."

"A fine suggestion, Father," Karim said. He nodded to Arjun. "Care to join me for a little wine and a little fun prior to tomorrow's festivities?"

"Sure," Arjun said, much to my disappointment. He stood up, and I stood with him, noting the smirk that Karim tossed my way. He knew I didn't want to be in the same room with him, but he knew too that I didn't have a choice. I think he liked that as much now as he had when I was eleven years old. The crown prince of Nizam being used like a woman, yes, that was what had appealed to him then and what appealed to him now. It was exactly the attitude I'd feared from Arjun when we'd first met.

But I followed along with Arjun anyway. Pleasing him was the only thing that mattered. He was my only possible way out of the life I was in, my only source of protection from my father's wrath. He must have known that, though I wondered if he knew how desperate I was to escape the dera. Sometimes, I didn't even think I knew—not until I thought about Lakshmi and realized how much I wanted to spare her the life I was living. She was the closest thing I would ever have to a younger sibling, probably the closest thing I would ever have to a daughter. I couldn't let her do the things I had done. It just wasn't right. But if I was going to stop it, I needed money, and the only way to get it was to keep doing exactly what I'd been doing. It was a vicious trap, like a pit that you had to try to escape by digging deeper. Arjun was like a rope thrown down to pull me out.

Except he wasn't. Not really. Not yet. He had paid for me. We'd known each other only for a week or so. He liked me, but I didn't think he wanted to keep me permanently. If he'd wanted that, he could have offered me a place in the palace as a concubine, if not a lawful wife. He hadn't done that. I had to be realistic about what that meant for him, for me, and for Lakshmi.

But it was hard to always view him with such a calculating eye. I couldn't forget the night we'd met, the way he'd sworn to protect my secret and to safeguard my life. And he'd done it. He'd been telling the truth from the moment we'd met. I couldn't remember another man about whom I could say the same. And the longer we were together, the more adventures we shared like this one, the more I wanted to turn off the part of my mind that had been trained to scheme, to play men for maximum profit, the part that saw him as a means to an end. But how could I do that when he had all the power, when he could toss me aside like trash whenever he wanted, when at his whim I could be cast right back into the dera, right back into the life I increasingly despised, a life of theft, and of pleasuring men who pleased me not at all? Was I supposed to just trust him, like an unthinking goat trusting her owners right up until the moment she was slaughtered?

I wasn't being fair. I did trust Arjun. I trusted him more than anyone except for my sisters. But it wasn't a blind trust, it was a scheming trust, a trust that understood just how tenuous my status in life was, just how easy it would be for everything I had built in Bikampur to be snatched away. When the risks were so high, how could I give myself over to something as vague and shifting as love? After all, the one lesson I had learned best back home in Nizam was that love is always conditional.

Karim led us to a room with high ceilings supported by thick yellow sandstone columns. A refreshing breeze was blowing in off the sea, and the view of its glittering blue waters took my breath away. We were standing in what was, effectively, an enormous covered balcony, with cushions laid out at the room's center, so we could recline and let the sea breeze wash over us, and take in the dazzling sight of the open water beating against the cliffs.

Karim clapped his hands, and servants appeared with wine and sweets. A girl appeared too, dressed in garments that were so thin as to be almost translucent, revealing teasing hints of brown flesh through the fabric.

The girl went to Karim, who pulled her down into his lap, burying his face in her breasts in a way that made me curl in on myself in disgust. I'd seen men like him before. I'd had men like him put their hands on me before, but seeing him doing it was so much worse after what he'd done to me as a child. I pressed myself against Arjun, taking comfort in his warmth. He, at least, would never use me like that.

The girl was giggling like she enjoyed it, and I wondered if that laugh was a lie or the truth. My instincts told me it was a lie, that she despised him as much as I did, but my rational mind knew better. It knew how desperate she might have been before he'd taken her into his company. It knew how much his presence had improved her station in life, even if he was a boor. It knew that sometimes feelings developed with clients simply from repeated association, from listening to their problems, from being the source of their pleasure and the reservoir for their emotions. And I knew how validating it could be for a powerful man to love you, to want you, to desire you so much that he would pay huge sums of money for you, that he would shower you with pretty baubles and beautiful clothes. You just had to look at my relationship with Arjun to see those principles in action.

But I knew how conflicted she probably felt, how disgusted

with herself. I knew that when tonight was over, she would lie back and stare up at the ceiling and wonder what sequence of events had brought her to her present state. I knew that she wanted a way out as desperately as I did. And I knew from personal experience that Karim would never be that way out, and unless the girl was a fool, she likely knew it too.

The servants plied us with wine and sweets. I took a rava laddu both to be polite and because I quite favored them, but Arjun surprised me by bending his head down and snatching it from me with his teeth. I let out a little squawk of surprise and distress, which only made him grin all the more broadly.

"Here," he said, his mouth still full, and he took another from the servant's tray and held it out to me. I opened my mouth to take it, and he reached forward with his fingers, pressed the laddu up to my lips, and then suddenly snatched it back and put that one in his mouth too.

I tried to look offended, but it was hard when his cheeks were bulging with laddus and he was grinning so much besides. He swallowed hard and managed to get the sweets down, and then he said, "Okay, here." And he picked up a third laddu, but I shook my head and looked away, crossing my arms over my chest like I didn't want it.

He pressed it to my lips, but when I didn't take it right away, he murmured, "I have an idea." And instead, he took hold of it with his teeth, and he leaned forward and pressed it against my lips that way.

I opened my mouth and took the sweet, but we held our lips against each other's for quite a while. When he finally pulled away, I chewed on the laddu, feeling well pleased with myself. Whatever I thought of my place in the world, it wasn't all so dark and hopeless. There were good things too, times like this that were more wonderful than I'd imagined possible when I'd been living as a boy in the royal palace of Nizam.

"Do you know who that is?" Karim asked the woman in his lap.

She glanced over at us, giving me a knowing smile before turning her kohl-darkened eyes to Arjun. "Isn't that Prince Arjun Agnivansha of Bikampur, your highness?"

"Not him," Karim said. "Her." He pointed to me, and then he whispered into his servant girl's ear, "Do you know who she is?"

She shrugged. "His lover?"

"That," Karim said, "is Salim Mirza, the crown prince of Nizam." The young woman cocked her head like she didn't quite understand, and I seized on her uncertainty. "My name is Razia Khan."

"Before that, her name was Salim Mirza," Karim said, and he was grinning at me, though I couldn't figure out why he took such pleasure in telling everyone my identity. Did he just want me dead? That seemed the likeliest explanation.

Arjun must have thought so too, because he said, "It's dangerous for her identity to be spoken of so freely, Karim."

"Dangerous for her," he agreed.

"Dangerous for you too," said Arjun, much to my surprise, and Karim's amusement.

The older prince laughed. "You're smitten." He clucked his tongue. "For shame, little brother, she's only a hijra. A man should have some perspective. She's beautiful now, I'll grant you, but there are crores of beautiful women in this world, and they've all got slits instead of scars. Soon enough, one of those will strike your fancy, and you'll wonder what you found so charming in this one that you favored her so."

Hearing my deepest fears spoken of so openly hurt. I thought I managed to keep from showing it on my face, but I could tell that it had hurt the other girl too. She saw herself in Karim's description, and her eyes fell to the floor before flickering up to meet my own. There was recognition there. Whoever I was before, whatever I'd been, I was like her now—a young woman without a family making her way in the world the only way the world permitted. But as I looked into those eyes, I knew that we both saw how precarious our situations were, how capricious the desires of men could be, and how uncertain were our fortunes.

"You're jealous," Arjun said, pulling me close to him and grinning in Karim's direction.

I was shocked when Karim's face betrayed irritation for an instant. God, he was jealous! That was why he kept focusing his attention on me, why he kept calling me by my old name to irritate me, why he brought up my past with everyone. He wanted me for himself. But why? What was I to him?

"It's not jealousy exactly," Karim said. "I just haven't had her since she was eleven, and I want to see if she's improved at all." His eyes flickered to me, and the smirk returned to his face. "Have you improved, dear? Did that guru of yours teach you any new tricks?"

"Hundreds of them," I replied, in my sultriest voice, though it was hard to sound alluring when I so desperately wanted to strangle him. "But you'll never find out." I turned then and began kissing Arjun's neck passionately, working my way up toward his lips.

"You think not?" Karim asked, an edge to his voice. To Arjun, he said, "I'll give you five hundred rupees to let me have her for the night."

"She's not for sale," Arjun replied, without a moment's hesitation.

"Yes, she is," Karim declared. "She's a whore. Whores are always for sale. You think she wouldn't go with any man who offered her more money?"

"I don't think she would," said Arjun, and I smiled up at him, grateful that he recognized how much I was beginning to care for him.

"Oh, no?" Karim snorted at that and said, "Razia, I'll give you two thousand rupees to lie with me tonight."

I smiled. This was a moment I had long waited for. Six years ago, he had . . . well . . . it didn't matter what he'd done. What mattered now was that I had the power to refuse him. I said to him, "I wouldn't lie with you for all the jewels in my father's treasury."

He laughed at that. "You're a whore. You'd abandon your prince for less than that. All whores have a price, what's yours?"

"I'm a whore," I agreed, because there was no sense splitting hairs about it. "But I get to choose my clients, and I chose Prince Arjun."

"For his money, and the pretty baubles he gives you to wear," Karim taunted, and that dagger found its mark, but it didn't have the effect he'd intended. In that moment, I felt profoundly ashamed at the mercenary attitude I held toward a man who had offered me nothing but kindness and protection and love.

"He must make you feel like that princess you always wanted to be in Nizam," Karim continued, and that too undermined his own argument. Arjun did make me feel like the princess I had always dreamed of becoming. He made me feel wanted as my true self for the first time in my whole life. I didn't know how that had gotten so muddied in my mind, but the simple truth was that Arjun had treated me like a foreign princess from the first moment we met. He'd never broken a promise, never used me like a servant, never belittled me or shown me anything but the utmost respect. God, how had I missed all that?

"I chose Arjun because he has something you'll never have," I told Karim.

"And what's that?" he asked.

"Kindness," I replied, and I gave Arjun a tender peck on the cheek then. It was far more chaste than I'd been the whole rest of the evening, but I could see the impression that it left on him all the same. I wondered if he could see the impression Karim's words had left on me.

He held me close to him, and he turned to Karim and said, "Enough, Karim. She belongs to me, and I'll hear no more about her."

"As you like it, your highness," Karim said, and he picked up his wine goblet and took a long pull from it. The red liquid coated his black mustache, but I mostly saw his eyes, and the hunger in them, a hunger that was focused squarely on me.

# CHAPTER 11

I couldn't sleep. I lay in bed with my head resting against Arjun's chest, listening to the slow, steady beats of his heart, and I wondered if he would live through the day. And for the first time, I didn't wonder what would become of me if he didn't. Oh, without him, I would go back to the dera, back to pleasing men like Govind Singh, back to dancing in a different haveli every night, hoping to attract the attention of a rich patron; I knew that, but after all the things Karim said, none of that really mattered. What frightened me most about the fate that awaited me if Arjun died was that I would have to spend the rest of my life without him.

I curled my body a little closer to his and tried to take comfort in the warmth of his arm around my shoulders, the strength of his muscles, even when relaxed by the deepest sleep. God help me, I didn't want to lose him. I'd spent years being trained not to let thoughts like that one enter my mind. They were a luxury that a courtesan could ill afford, but now that I'd thought it, now that I'd felt that fear of loss in my heart, it was all I could think about.

When had Arjun Agnivansha become my whole life? I felt like
I'd been tricked somehow, drugged maybe. I'd always been so
good at my job, because I had a calculating mind, a head for strategy, I was always playing the long game. A month ago, I'd have
laughed at the thought of losing sleep over a man. I could tell myself it was because Arjun was a rich and important client, but I
knew that wasn't it. Self-interest never made a person's heart ache
the way mine was.

I was being stupid. Ammi would have told me that I was acting like a little girl, not a grown woman, and that I needed to get
my head on straight and think about my priorities. But when I did
that, the only priority that I felt was somehow helping Arjun to
survive the coming battle. Ammi would have scolded me for that
too, would have reminded me that as a hijra I would never be a
princess, I would never marry a prince, I would never even be permitted to live in a palace except as the lowest servant. And all that
was probably true, but it did nothing to lift the feeling of heavi-
ness from my heart.

A part of me hated being so dependent on a man. I'd always
been dependent on my clients for money, for clothes, for jewels, for
affection, but that was a kind of contract with clear payments to be
rendered and services to be provided, and there was almost always
a fixed end point. This, whatever it was, felt different. It felt like
something more, but I tried to push that thought aside, because if
there was one thing I had learned in the last four years, it was that
every chance I'd had at living an independent life had died the moment I'd run away from home and made myself into a woman.

The strangest thing was that I didn't regret it. Not for an instant.

It would be dawn soon. And Arjun would go. He would fly out
into the darkness atop Padmini's back, following through on the
plan I had helped to make the previous day. And he might live or

he might die. I thought the plan was good, I thought we had the advantage in zahhaks, but war was always risky. I'd seen it with my own eyes when favored cousins or uncles had left for the battle-field and never come back. There was more than a passing chance that Arjun would die today, and that made me want to cling to him and beg him not to go. It was only the certain knowledge that he had to go, that there was nothing I could say to dissuade him, that prevented me from trying.

I tried instead to imagine the moment of his return, imagine the feeling of seeing him safe and sound. I tried to picture our return to Bikampur, jubilant and victorious. I remembered then that the maharaja had promised me a thousand rupees if everyone came back alive. If only he'd known just how stupidly attached I was to his son, he'd have realized that he didn't need to pay me at all. But my feelings aside, a thousand rupees would give me some kind of insurance, something to set aside for the future—or more likely for Lakshmi. And what if there was more where that came from? What if I became a trusted military adviser?

The thought of it almost made me laugh at myself. Me? A mil-itary adviser? If you'd asked my father when I was still living at home what he thought my least likely occupation in all the world would be, it was military adviser. And anyway, it was one thing for the maharaja to give me a thousand rupees for helping him with a specific issue to which no one else was privy; it was quite another to have a man like him make me his adviser. The ridicule it would have invited from other lords precluded such a thing from ever being made manifest.

But maybe there was something there anyway. Maybe I couldn't be an adviser, but that didn't mean he couldn't pay me under the table for advice given in confidence. Men could assume it was for other services rendered. They wouldn't have to know that I was concocting stratagems for the army. Of course, I was getting ahead of myself. If today's plan failed, and Arjun and his father lived through it, I would be facing the consequences, and even though I trusted Arjun to protect me, I didn't think the aftermath would be pretty.

A figure slipped into our bedchamber, passing through the gauze-thin silk curtains. I sat bolt upright, moving to put myself between Arjun and the intruder. He was tall and burly, and he wore armor, but I could make out nothing else of him in the darkness. He was just an imposing shadow. I was wearing nothing but a long white silk kameez, and I had no weapons, but I would die first and give Arjun a chance to escape if this was an assassination attempt.

"My prince, someone is here," I said, standing between the two of them.

The figure chuckled. He wasn't Karim. I could hear that much from his laugh, and Mahisagaris didn't usually wear armor. He said, "Prostitute, general, and now bodyguard? You've got a great many hidden talents, my lady."

"It's all right, Razia," Arjun said, getting out of bed and putting his arm around me. "It's just Arvind." He nodded to the shadow. "Father sent you?"

"He did, your highness," the shadowy figure answered. I knew who he was now—Arvind Singh, eldest son of Govind Singh. He was the most prominent young man in Bikampur's court, Arjun excepted. He was one of the zahhak riders who had accompanied us. I'd just failed to recognize him in the darkness.

"Well, I suppose I shouldn't keep him waiting." Arjun gave me a pat on the behind. "Go light some candles for me, Razia, so I can get dressed."

"Of course, my prince," I agreed. I rushed off to the one candle still burning in the room, and I used it to light a dozen others set inside the decorative lanterns that hung from the ceiling and between the columns separating the bedchamber from the balcony.

In the flickering candlelight, I could see Arvind Singh more clearly. He was a handsome young man, though he shared his father's affinity for a well-waxed mustache. He wore armor made from the viper-like scales of a fire zahhak's neck and back. It was beautiful, and as strong as steel, but much lighter—a perfect combination for a zahhak rider who needed to keep his weight to an absolute minimum.

Arjun busied himself dressing, and I did the same, putting on my clothes and jewels from the day before. I noted the way that Arvind watched me dress, but I didn't pay him much attention. Life as a hijra had cured me of any bashfulness I'd had surrounding being seen by a man in various states of undress. It was a quality men seemed to appreciate, and Arvind was no exception.

"The gods have a strange sense of humor . . ." he murmured.

"How's that?" Arjun asked, as he put on his own zahhak-scale armor.

"To have made that exquisite creature a boy," Arvind replied, still staring at me.

"If it was humor, I didn't find it very funny," I said, rather annoyed that he would consider my life a joke.

He surprised me by bowing low to me, like I was royalty. "Forgive me, my lady, I meant no offense. I just meant that it's strange to think anyone could have seen you any other way—mortal or god alike."

I felt a twinge of guilt at that and I offered him a conciliatory smile and a bow in return. "Of course, forgive me, my lord. I'm more accustomed to insults than compliments regarding the circumstances of my birth, as I'm sure you'll understand."

"The gods are difficult to comprehend," Arjun agreed. Now

fully dressed, he placed his katars in his sash. They were absolutely gorgeous, with blades that were wavy like flames issuing forth from the golden heads of fire zahhaks. They were so like my katars that I wondered if the same man hadn't made both sets.

"Oh?" I asked, wondering what Arjun's thoughts on his multiple gods were.

"Well, that party where we met, at Govind Singh's haveli, that was thrown in Arvind's honor, but he was delayed coming home. Had he arrived on time, your duty would have been entertaining him instead of me, and we would never have met."

Arvind laughed. "You're just trying to make me jealous."

I glanced at his face, studying the genuine smile that lifted up the corners of his eyes as well as his mouth. There was not an ounce of deceit to be seen from him. He wasn't mocking me. He really thought I was something worthy of producing jealousy. I decided then and there that I liked him.

"I'm glad we found each other, my prince," I told Arjun. I reached up and took his cheeks in both hands and planted a kiss on his lips.

He kissed me back—hard. But only for a moment. Too soon, he broke away and said, "Well, I guess we should get moving if we want the sun to be in our favor."

"Yes," I agreed. That was crucial. He needed every advantage I could give him. I wanted him to come back to me so much that my stomach hurt. It was a tightness that crept into my chest and made it hard to breathe, but I tried not to show it as I walked with him out of the bedchamber, toward the courtyard where the zahhaks were being kept.

Karim was waiting, wearing armor made from an acid zahhak's emerald scales. It looked out of place on him, and from the way he was shifting uncomfortably, I could tell he wasn't used to it, that it was more a badge of rank than anything else. Sultan Ahmed Shah was standing beside his son, similarly attired, along with two of their retainers. Udai and his retainer, a man called Ram, were standing with them. We were the last to arrive, though it was still quite dark outside, the only light coming from pierced-brass lanterns hanging all around the courtyard.

"Are you ready, boy?" Udai asked his son.

"Ready, Father," Arjun replied. He sounded eager, happy, like this was some lark and not serious business. It made the tightness in my guts increase. Maybe I'd have been excited too, had I been going, but being left behind like some helpless damsel went against every instinct I possessed. If I'd had Sultana, I could have made a difference in this fight. I could have been there to help them. Instead, I was standing there uselessly as stable hands brought the zahhaks out so the men could mount up.

Padmini was approaching, and I took the last chance I had to throw my arms around Arjun's neck. I kissed him on the lips and whispered, "Please, be careful, my prince. Keep your altitude, don't try to turn with them down low, make the smart passes, and don't let them sucker you into range of their toradars."

He laughed at the strange combination of a woman's worry and the sound tactical advice of an experienced zahhak rider. He held me close to him and kissed me on the top of my head. "I'll be back before you know it, Razia."

"I'll pray for you, my prince," I told him. And then I glanced to Arvind, who was standing beside us, and added, "And you too, my lord."

"Why, thank you, my lady," he replied, with a smart bow. He mounted his zahhak then, and Arjun did the same with his. They marched them to the far end of the courtyard, so they would have room to take off.

It was quite a sight to witness—eight zahhaks all together in that courtyard, their riders arrayed in the finest scale armor. It was rare to see so many zahhaks in one place. I'd only seen so many back home in Nizam, and that was the most powerful empire on the continent. These eight zahhaks could have conquered other cities with their strength alone, but equally the loss of them would cripple Mahisagar and Bikampur both. They were proud animals, standing taller than a man on their wing joints and their hind legs, their feathered tails bobbing in eager anticipation of the order to fly.

The order came from Ahmed's lips. The zahhaks charged forward and leapt into the air as one, beating their wings for altitude. Already, the acid zahhaks were faster, more agile. Their shorter, rounder wings could beat faster than the fire zahhaks' longer ones. They gained altitude more quickly and left the slower fire zahhaks behind. I missed Sultana. She was swifter even than the acid zahhaks. I'd have flown circles around Karim if I'd still possessed her. But I didn't. I had to stand there helplessly and watch as the zahhaks vanished into the dark predawn sky.

I stood there staring into the blackness for a long time thereafter, my thoughts running back to the ones I had tried to leave behind in the bedchamber. My stomach was tying itself in knots, and my heart ached. He was going to fight a battle against dangerous foreigners with cannons and muskets and zahhaks, and there was nothing I could do to help him, nothing I could do but sit and wait. I'd never felt so useless, standing there in my pretty lehenga and my fine jewelry, my eyes scouring an empty sky.

"My lady?"

I was startled out of my worries by a man coming up behind me. He was older, probably a generation older than Udai Agnivansha, though maybe even a bit older than that. He had a white mustache that was carefully trimmed on his upper lip and kept his white hair cropped close to his head. Though he wore a fine turban of golden silk, a white dhoti with gold trim, and a blue silk kurta, all in the Mahisagari style, I thought his dark skin hinted

at origins farther south—perhaps in Virajendra? Was he a nobleman of some sort? An adviser to Ahmed Shah? It was hard to
know.

"Sir?" I asked, uncertain as to who he was, and even more, as
to what he knew about me. Did he think me a princess, a whore,
or a deviant? If it was one of the latter, he certainly hid it well, as
his smile seemed kindly enough.

"The battle will take some hours," he said to me. "Would you
care to sit somewhere more comfortable and have a little something to eat?"

"I'm not hungry," I murmured, my arms crossing over my roiling stomach. Just the thought of food made me want to vomit.
And it wasn't just the nausea. My heart was pounding. My limbs
were tingling. I didn't want to sit; I wanted to run, or to fight, or to
do anything but wait.

He put his hand on my shoulder, in a grandfatherly sort of
way. "The strategy you devised was a good one, but now you have
to let the men carry it out. A woman's burden is harder than a
man's, though few men have the wisdom to see it. All your hopes
and dreams for the future are in the hands of another, and you
can do nothing but wait and pray."

I looked up at him, wide-eyed, my shock written plainly on my
face. How on earth did he know something like that? How did he
understand what I'd spent the whole morning dwelling on? How
could he know without having been in this position himself?

When I asked him as much, he said, "Come with me, and we
can sit somewhere cool and quiet, and I can tell you all about it."

I nodded my assent and started walking with him, only thinking to ask after a half dozen steps, "Who are you, my lord?"

"My name is Viputeshwar," he said, proving me right about his
origins in Virajendra. "But everyone in the palace calls me Grandfather, and I welcome you to do the same, my lady."

"Razia," I corrected. "There is no need for such formality with me, Grandfather. I'm sure you know what I am."

"Let's not worry about that today, dear," he said. "You have worries enough as it is."

He wasn't wrong, but his kindness made me uneasy. Why was he so willing to help me? He couldn't have been sent by Karim or his father; they had made it clear what they thought of me. So who had sent him? What was he doing here?

I arrived in a comfortable room before my mind could conjure any answers to those questions. It had a stunning view of the ocean, and a cooling breeze was wafting in off the water, stirring the silk curtains. There were cushions laid out, and silver platters of southern breakfast fare—dosas, along with little silver bowls of sambar and various chutneys. Grandfather guided me to one of the platters and sat me down in front of it, taking the place beside mine.

He put his hand on my shoulder again and said, "At least have something to drink, dear." He picked up a glass of sweet lassi and pressed it into my hands.

I took a sip, mostly to satisfy him, but I found that the sugar made me feel a little better, and the yogurt helped to calm my stomach. I felt an absurdly strong surge of gratitude toward the man for being kind to me, so much so that I felt tears threatening at the corners of my eyes. I wondered what had provoked such a stupid reaction, if it was the result of having missed my essential salts that morning, or if it was just the foolish attachment I had for Arjun being made manifest in other ways.

After a moment, though, the answer came to me. I felt so alone. I was in a foreign palace, surrounded by foreign people, led by a ruler who didn't much care for me, and my only link to the life I had created for myself had flown off to battle. If I lost him, I would lose everything—my wealth and prestige, of course, but far more importantly the love of a man who treated me like a queen. And I had no control over any of it. And this man, of all people, had seen how upset I was, had known without being told, and had been kind to me.

"Thank you," I told him, so earnestly that I think it took him somewhat by surprise.

"I almost forgot," he said, and he reached into a purse held in his sash and removed a small tablet made of pressed white crystals, like sugar or salt. I recognized it at once as being the same sort of tablet I took every morning. He handed it to me. "I took the liberty of procuring it from a friend. I thought you might want it."

I took it at once. While my nirvan had ensured that I would never develop like a man, I wasn't about to take any chances. And anyway, I'd heard that hijras sometimes got brittle bones or got sick if they didn't take them. Mostly, though, I did it because it comforted me and reminded me of home.

"Who are you?" I asked him again. "Nobody has ever been so courteous to me."

"My sister is one of your kind," he said. "I followed her north when she ran away from home, as she had been the only one who stood between me and my abusive father. She hadn't wanted to leave me there with him, but he'd beaten her so badly when he'd caught her wearing a sari that she'd had no choice but to run. When I came to Rajkot, I had nothing, but she took me into the dera, used her earnings to pay for my education, and eventually got me a position here in the palace. I soon became one of Sultan Qutub Shah's most trusted men. I helped raise his son, Ahmed, and then, when the time came, I helped raise Ahmed's son too. My place here has given me a good income, and a good life, but I owe it all to my sister, who cared for me when I needed it most."

That did bring tears to my eyes, as I wondered what it would be like to have a brother who valued me and loved me, to have any family left at all. I batted at a tear that spilled down my cheek and tried to sniff the other ones back into my skull, but they didn't seem to want to listen to me. "That's a very beautiful story, Grandfather," I told him, trying to disguise the emotion in my voice and not doing a very good job of that either.

"You remind me of my sister," he said. "She was smart and courageous, and beautiful, and I always admired her so much growing up. I could never understand why so many others mocked her. To me, she was the one who tucked me in at night and told me stories and protected me from bullies and from my own father. She was the one who made sure I got enough to eat and who helped me with my lessons. Without her, I'd be nothing at all. But others don't see in her what I see. They just see her as a hijra, a deviant, a whore. They don't know what she's suffered or what she's sacrificed, and they can't see the good in her heart."

His arm fell around my shoulders, and he said, "Forgive an old man for rambling, dear."

"It's all right," I said. "She sounds wonderful."

"She was," he agreed.

"I'm sorry," I murmured. I should have realized she was dead from the way he'd spoken of her with such longing.

"One of her clients beat her to death," he said, the muscles of his body tensing beside mine, and I was shocked to feel how strong he was at such an advanced age. "The man was a local noble, very powerful, but I had him butchered like a goat all the same. Not that it mattered. It didn't bring my sister back. I should have been there for her when she needed me, but I was so wrapped up in my work in the palace that I hadn't visited her in more than a month."

I saw the tears spilling down his cheeks then, saw the guilt in the hard lines of wrinkles that were etched so deeply across his face. I reached up and brushed his tears away with a corner of my dupatta.

My touch startled him enough that he recoiled away from me. I hung my head, wondering if I'd offended him. "Forgive me, sir, I—"

"No, it's all right," he said, taking my hands in his bigger, gnarled ones. He gave them a gentle pat. "You'll have to forgive me for getting so emotional, it's just that I don't often see hijras, and the wisdom you shared with the sultan, the way you put Karim in his place with your sharp tongue, the care you showed for Prince Arjun, they all reminded me so strongly of my sister that it brought a flood of memories I thought I'd forgotten."

The mention of Prince Arjun sent my thoughts back to the battle. "Do you think they're on their way back yet?"

"No, dear, not yet," he said, giving my hands another pat. "Why don't you try a little more lassi, and we can sit together and wait for his return?"

"I'd like that, Grandfather," I said.

So I sat with him and drank sweet lassi and listened to stories of his sister, Vidya. I was finally starting to calm down a little when I heard a sentry shouting. I knew at once that it was the return of the zahhaks.

I leapt up so fast that Grandfather couldn't have kept up if he'd wanted to. I raced through the palace, heedless of the armed men guarding the gates, sprinting until I reached the courtyard with the zahhak stables. I turned my eyes skyward, shading them against the force of the noonday sun with both hands, scouring the cloudless blue heavens for the slightest sign of Prince Arjun and Padmini.

I saw a dot flying in from the ocean. And then a second. And a third. But they were so far away. Were they acid zahhaks or fire zahhaks? Where were the other five? Had they been killed? My heart started to pound so hard that I could hear my blood roaring in my ears. I was dimly aware of Grandfather coming up beside me, putting his hand on my shoulder, but all my attention was focused on the sky, on finding those other five zahhaks.

There was a fourth. But no more. Where were the others? And then a sick sense of dread washed over me. What if this had been a trick? What if Karim and Ahmed had intended to double-cross the maharaja all along? What if this was their way of destroying the zahhaks of Bikampur and paving the way for conquest? I cursed myself for not thinking of it sooner. And as the four zahhaks drew nearer, and I saw their turquoise feathers and green scales, the possibility seemed all the more plausible.

I looked to Grandfather, who still seemed so sympathetic, and asked, "Was this a trick?"

He saw the tears spilling from my eyes and pulled me close to him. "No, dear, of course not. We were earnest in asking for help. But you mustn't give up hope yet. You said yourself that fire zahhaks are slower. It's too soon to worry so."

The first acid zahhak was coming in for a landing. The beast's blue wings beat back the air, kicking up a storm of dust in the courtyard, before she settled down on her hind legs and her clawed wing joints. She galumphed over to me, as clumsy on the ground as she was graceful in the air, and I saw that Karim was perched in the saddle, looking proud of himself. He glanced down at me, caught my tear-streaked face and the way Grandfather was holding me, and he laughed.

"God, aren't you just the perfect little woman?" he sneered. He slid off the back of his zahhak as stableboys took the animal and led it away. He strode over to me, and I realized then just how big he really was. He dwarfed me the way that Arjun did. His size, and his closeness, reminded me too of what had happened six years before, and I suddenly found it hard to breathe. If Arjun was dead, then there would be no one to protect me.

"What happened, your highness?" I asked him, as he must have known, and I couldn't stand the suspense another second. "Is everyone all right?"

"Do you mean is your precious prince alive or dead?" he taunted, seeming to enjoy how much it hurt me to not know the answer.

He was just reaching toward me when Grandfather shouted, "Look, my lady!"

The old man was pointing toward the west, toward the ocean, and I saw then what he was showing me. Four zahhaks in perfect formation, visible only as dots on the far horizon.

I breathed a huge sigh of relief, knowing now that my life wasn't over, that Arjun wasn't gone forever, and with the relief came a flash of anger. I glared at Karim. "You might have told me!"

He grabbed my face, his big fingers squeezing my cheeks and yanking me so that I was looking up at him. "You will address me properly, *Razia*."

"Yes, your highness," I managed, my voice muffled from the way he was holding me.

He let me go then with a sniff of disdain and walked off to meet with his father, who had just landed his own zahhak. When he was out of earshot, I rubbed my cheeks and asked Grandfather, "You helped raise him?"

"Not one of my prouder accomplishments, I'm sorry to say, my lady," he replied, and he stroked my back in gentle circles. "If he hurt you, I have potions for the pain."

"I'm all right," I said. I was better than all right. Arjun wasn't dead. His zahhak was finally coming in for a landing. I'd have recognized Padmini anywhere. The moment she got her feet under her, I was running to her. I got there just as Arjun slid from the saddle, and I threw myself at him, wrapping my arms around his neck, pressing myself up against the hard scales of his armor, heedless of the way they dug into my skin.

"I'm so glad you're all right," I told him, with a kind of earnest desperation that I hadn't really intended for him to see.

He gave me a baffled look, and then took in my eyes, which were red and puffy, and he saw the red marks on my cheeks, and his eyes narrowed. "Did someone hurt you?"

"No, I'm all right, my prince," I said. I buried my face in his neck, where the armor wouldn't hurt me, and I breathed in deeply through my nose, taking in his scent.

"What's wrong?" he asked, pushing me away a little so he could look me over.

"Nothing, my prince," I said, embarrassed that I was acting like such a lovesick child. "I'm just glad you're safe."

"I'm better than safe," he said. "I got two of them."

"Two of what?" I asked.

"Ice zahhaks! What else?" He laughed, and gave a rueful shake of his head like he couldn't believe how strangely I was behaving. "Padmini and I shot down two ice zahhaks with her fire. Sultan Ahmed got the third. And then we burned the ships with fire and acid. They didn't have a chance."

"I'm very happy for you, my prince," I said, though in truth I couldn't have cared less. How stupid was it to focus on the number of zahhaks he'd knocked down? All that mattered was whether he'd lived or died. But men his age were supposed to chase glory, to garner reputations for themselves, and killing two ice zahhaks and burning the Firangi fleet would cement Arjun's reputation as a first-class warrior. I just wished he didn't have to risk his life to do it.

"Your plan was perfect, Razia," he said, leaning down and kissing me on the cheek. "I think Father is going to be very pleased with you from now on."

"I'm very happy to have served you both well, my prince," I replied, but my mind was still more focused on his survival than the status I had gained in his father's eyes. I wasn't going to be trapped in Mahisagar alone, beholden to Karim's every whim. I wasn't going to have to go back to Bikampur with a maharaja who had lost a son, or a son who had lost a father. I wasn't going to have to go back to thieving, or to sleeping with every man who asked for me. So long as Arjun was there, it was all going to be all right.

# CHAPTER 12

W e hit them from above. They never saw us coming. It was beautiful. You should have been there. I got behind one of the ice zahhaks as it turned against one of the Mahisagari men, and Padmini flamed her before she even knew we were there. They tumbled into the sea, and then I pulled up and we raced skyward. At the top of the climb, I used that maneuver you showed me, flipped Padmini inside her own tail, and we were back on top of the ice zahhaks before they could blink."

I leaned my head against Arjun's chest and snuggled my body closer to him, though it caused me to twist awkwardly in Padmini's saddle. I'd heard the story at least ten times since Arjun had come back to me the day before, but I asked, "And then what happened, my prince?" all the same. It made him happy to tell it, and I had to admit to being a little jealous that I hadn't been there. Now that I knew he'd handled himself well, that he'd defeated his enemies easily, it made me feel silly for how worried I'd been before. This was the man who had taken down two thunder zah-haks at the age of fourteen, after all.

"And then I spotted a second ice zahhak, turning to get on my father's tail," Arjun continued, sounding as excited as if he still were fourteen. "I aimed Padmini's snout in the space behind the white zahhak, and then jerked her through the hardest turn I could manage. She got her beak right on the Firangi animal, just before she could breathe her ice on my father. Padmini roared, and flames burst forth from her mouth, and the ice zahhak disappeared into their midst. Her charred remnants scattered across the water an instant later."

"It's sad," I murmured, as I imagined it in my mind's eye.

"Sad?" he asked, shocked by that response. "You wanted it to kill my father?" There was hurt in his voice.

"No, my prince!" I exclaimed, horrified that he would think such things of me. "It's just that . . ." I fell silent. It sounded silly now.

"Just that what?" he asked.

"Just that I spent years hunting and flying with Natia, Princess Tamara's ice zahhak, and she was very beautiful and had a very sweet disposition. It's not the zahhak's fault who owns her. It's sad that the Firangi animal had to die in such an awful way."

He laughed at that and stroked my hair and said, "I think you made the right choice becoming a hijra, Razia. There's no room for sentiments like that in war."

"I'd like to think I helped a little with matters of war, my prince," I replied, somewhat testily. There had been celebrations all afternoon and into the evening, but no one had mentioned the fact that I'd been the one to devise the successful plan. I wondered if it would be conveniently forgotten, along with the thousand rupees the maharaja had offered me. But I was afraid to ask, afraid to sound greedy, afraid to seem like the whore Karim had accused me of being. And anyway, I trusted that Arjun would take care of me, even if there was a part of me that still thought I was stupid for putting so much faith in a man.

"You were wonderful," he assured me. "Your strategy saved us. The ice zahhaks were tangling with the acid zahhaks down low, like you said they would, putting up a brilliant fight. They had scrambled from their ships quickly, and the Firangis were starting to shoot their toradars. If we hadn't come in with the advantage of altitude, they might have shot us all to death."

"I'm just glad you weren't hurt, my prince," I told him, planting a kiss on his lips.

"I'll try not to worry you like that ever again," he said.

"We both know that's a promise you can't keep," I replied, though the knowledge of it didn't do much to stop me worrying. "Men have to fight. Especially princes. My father taught me that, if nothing else."

"I think he taught you quite a lot. Those stratagems of yours didn't come out of nowhere. You were trained very well."

"I was," I agreed. "And though my father despised me, he always said I had a head for battle tactics."

"Did you ever fight in a real battle?" he asked.

"No, my prince," I replied. "I was only thirteen when I ran away from home, not yet old enough for such things. And while my father trusted me in matters of strategy, he didn't trust me to fight. He thought I was a coward."

Arjun frowned. "I don't think you're a coward at all, Razia."

"Thank you, my prince, but for my father, being a woman and being a coward were one and the same. He knew what I was, though he would never say it out loud, not even when he beat me. He would just say, 'You know why.' Over and over again—'You know why.'"

Prince Arjun held me tightly to him, and I rested my head on his chest, pressing my cheek against his skin, feeling his warmth, hearing the beating of his heart over the roar of the slipstream. There was something so comforting about it, something that drove away all the bad memories, something that gave me hope.

"No one is ever going to hurt you like that again—that's a promise I can keep."

"Thank you, my prince," I told him, and I closed my eyes and let out a contented sigh. "I think I could fly up here with you forever."

"You wouldn't feel sorry for poor Padmini?" he teased.

I opened my eyes and leaned my face up to his. "Not a bit."

"You're terrible," he said, planting a peck of a kiss on my lips.

"My prince, you have no idea," I replied, and I kissed him back harder.

"Gods, your highness," Arvind called from his zahhak, flying about a dozen paces off Padmini's right wing. "Now I see why you've got that extra seat on your saddle!"

"You should get one of your own, Arvind! I'm sure your father could afford it!" he shouted back.

"A saddle or a girl?" Arvind joked.

"I prefer having one of each!" Arjun declared.

"I'd rather have two of each," Karim quipped, to much laughter from the men. He'd come along back to Bikampur as a gesture of goodwill from his father, to help maintain our alliance, and to give us an extra zahhak in case Javed Khorasani tried to strike at us in revenge. Personally, I just thought he was following me. He never stopped leering at me, and it made my skin crawl.

"Well, I'm sure a young prince like you can afford as many hijras as he likes," Udai told him. "Or real girls, if you prefer."

I caught the tone in his voice, and it sent familiar waves of shame washing over me. The maharaja's slight, and the memories it evoked, made me turn my head away from Arjun, made me hunch my shoulders, made me remember the beatings I'd received back home, and the harsh words that had accompanied them.

"Don't listen to him," Arjun whispered, his arms tightening around my waist. "I know who you are, Razia, and you put every other girl in Daryastan to shame." He kissed my cheek, and then rested his chin on my shoulder, his eyes flicking toward the horizon, and the growing city of Bikampur nestled among the desert dunes.

His embrace made me feel a little better, but not much. If anything, I felt more insecure now than I ever had before, because I cared about him, and I knew how devastated I would be if I lost his affections, and I knew how likely that outcome was. Hijras didn't get to live happily ever after with princes. That fate was reserved in the fairy tales for the real girls that Udai was so sure I wasn't.

"What do you want to do when you get home?" Arjun asked, probably to distract me from my sulking.

"I want to see my sisters . . ." I murmured.

"Right away?" He sounded disappointed.

I shook my head. "First I want to go to the bazaar and buy them gifts. Especially Lakshmi. She'll be disappointed if I flew all the way to Rajkot and back without thinking to get her a souvenir anywhere."

"Well, you'll have the money for it. I'll make sure my father makes good on his promise."

"My prince is very kind," I told him, pressing my cheek up against his.

"My lady deserves it," he replied, and I cracked a smile then. He'd never called me his lady before. He seemed to realize it too, because he said, "Do you remember what we spoke of before we arrived at Rajkot palace?"

I thought I knew precisely what he was referring to, but I

didn't want to guess wrong and reveal my desires. So I said, "Refresh my memory, my prince?"

"I called you my princess, and you said you could never be that to me. Do you remember?"

"Yes, my prince," I agreed. "I remember." In truth, I remembered it all too well. He'd said we would speak of it. I hadn't quite believed him. Was this the time for that conversation? Was this the place? What if his father overheard?

"I want you to be my concubine," he said.

For a moment, I was too stunned to speak. A concubine wasn't a wife in the eyes of the law, but it was still a legal relationship, and one that was far less easily dissolved than that between a man and a courtesan. My father's concubines had all enjoyed lavish apartments, fine clothing and jewels, and monthly allowances that far exceeded the money brought in by all the girls in my dera. And a concubine was often permitted to keep all that money, all those possessions, even if she was asked to leave the sultan's service. Of course, being asked to leave was rare, reserved for those women who schemed to produce royal heirs who could claim the throne, and that was certainly no concern of mine.

If I accepted Arjun's offer, I would live in the palace, I would have all the money I would ever need, but I would legally belong to him. I would be his property in a way that I wasn't as a courtesan. Now, if I chose to leave him and find another client, there was nothing stopping me, but if I agreed to this offer, I would no longer have any say in the matter.

But even if I wanted it, it scarcely mattered. It was unheard of to make a hijra a concubine. Most men would have laughed at the very idea of it.

"That sounds wonderful, my prince, but I'm a hijra," I reminded him.

Arjun gasped in mock surprise. "You're a hijra? Gods, I had no idea!" He shouted over to Arvind, "Arvind, did you know Razia was a hijra?"

"Little brother, if you haven't figured that out yet, then I think you may need to be more careful with where you put your cock in the future!" Karim cut in, to much laughter from the other men.

Arjun returned his attention to me. "I know who you are and what you are, Razia, and I want you to be my concubine. You would live in the palace; you would never have to dance for anyone but me. You would never have to be with any man but me. And as my first concubine, you would forever be showered with the choicest gifts. And I would give you a generous allowance to dispense with as you pleased."

"And your father would approve of this?" I asked, knowing that everything flowed through him—especially where money was concerned.

"It would be a trifle for him," Arjun assured me.

I felt hope mingling with fear and guilt. If I accepted this, I would have a place in the world far better than the one I currently occupied, but I would also be wholly beholden to Arjun. If I displeased him, he could cast me out, and my life would be utterly ruined. And, lingering in the back of my mind, there was the fear that he would discover that I was the thief he'd been chasing. I felt the sudden urge to confess it to him right then and there, but I was terrified that it would ruin everything.

And anyway, why did I need to tell him? I would never have to do it again. Not once. Without Ammi forcing me to do it, I'd be good. I'd keep my hands off other people's property. He'd never catch me because I'd never take such an insane risk again.

But I wasn't the only one who knew what I had done. Ammi knew. Jaskaur knew. She was a jealous sister, and she'd be more jealous still if I became Arjun's concubine. She would definitely tell him. And accepting this position would anger Ammi tremendously. I was her best earner, and she wasn't going to let her best earner abandon the dera so easily. She would tell him too. Or, more likely, find some way to frame me.

And if I left my dera and stopped paying Ammi my earnings, I'd be ostracized from the hijra community forever. That didn't bother me as much as it probably should have. And anyway, I supposed I could always pay a big fine to the nayak. In fact, the more I thought about it, the more I thought that the community wouldn't be able to afford to ostracize me. As Arjun's concubine, I would be far more powerful than any of the city's gurus.

But Ammi could ruin me. All she would have to do would be to tell Prince Arjun that I was the thief. She could produce evidence. I was sure she had kept evidence with her over the years. I wanted to believe that she wouldn't do it, but I knew better. I'd known better for a long time now. Maybe she loved me as a daughter and maybe she didn't, but she loved money better. No mother would have sent her daughter on the kinds of missions Ammi had sent me on. No mother would risk her child's future on a few baubles, not when she was already making an income far beyond her station in life.

My heart ached as I came to the inevitable conclusion I'd been trying to avoid for weeks now. Ammi loved money more than me. More than any of us. I didn't know if it was because she had been so poor for so long, having to scrape by to make something of herself, if her greed was driven by the fear I too felt in my heart of being cast aside and left alone in the world with nothing and no one. It was an understandable fear, one I had lived with for years now. Our lives were so uncertain without families to look after us, and though the dera was a surrogate family of a sort, it sometimes lacked the hard bonds of the real thing. Every day, I was aware of the fact that everything I was, everything I possessed, was temporary, because love for me had always been a temporary thing, a gift given and taken in accordance with my behavior. It was as coldly transactional as money in the marketplace.

I'd been careful to never show that kind of love to my sisters, but I knew with painful certainty that it was the kind of love Ammi had for me. I couldn't blame her; it was the only love she herself had ever been shown. I was luckier. I'd had Sakshi watching over me, caring for me with all her heart. And I had Lakshmi now too, and I tried so hard to pass that unconditional, lasting love on to her. And now there was Arjun, and in the deepest, most vulnerable place in my heart, I was starting to believe that his love was like that too.

But Ammi had never been given those gifts. She understood loyalty, but she wouldn't understand letting a loved one go, letting her succeed where you had failed. She wouldn't let me go. She wouldn't be bought off, at least not permanently. No, she would agree to Arjun's terms, and then blackmail me, over and over again, for as long as she lived.

The only way out was to trust that Arjun's love really was the unconditional kind, the kind that so often in my life I'd been so certain didn't exist. I had to confess everything to him. I had to believe that he would love me anyway, that he would look past it, that he would understand. But I was terrified that I was wrong.

"Razia?" Arjun asked, sounding a little anxious that I'd been so quiet for so long without giving him a firm answer.

"I have something horrible to confess to you, my prince," I said, my voice becoming a squeak as my throat tried to close itself off to prevent me from ruining my own life with what I was about to say.

"What is it?" he asked, his concern plain on his face.

There was no stopping it now. I had to tell him. But I was terrified at what it might mean. Would he cast me out? Would he abandon me? Would he execute me? Execution would be easier to bear than abandonment. I didn't want to live knowing that no-body could love me the way other people were loved. Better to kill me and end it quickly.

It took me a second to work up the nerve to actually say any-thing, and when I did, all I could gasp out was, "Do you remem-ber those thefts from all the havelis?"

"What about them?" he asked. He was confused. He didn't have the slightest idea. But he was worried because I was having a hard time taking steady breaths.

"I'm the thief," I whispered. And once I said that, I couldn't stop myself from saying more. "My guru trained me as a thief. She makes me take things so that she can sell them to support the dera. I didn't want to take the sword last time, because I care for you so much and I didn't want to ruin everything, but she didn't give me any choice."

I looked up at him, at the hurt and confusion on his face, and my heart broke. I felt the tears spilling from my eyes, and I felt guilty for shedding them. It seemed so manipulative, but in truth I was just so sorry for what I'd done. Not for the thefts, those had been harmless enough—fancy baubles taken from fancy men who had unlimited wealth. No, I was sorry because I had broken Arjun's trust, because I'd let this secret lie between us when he had shown me nothing but love and affection. I covered my face with my hands and said, "I'm so sorry, my prince. I swear I didn't want to do it."

"You're the thief?" he asked, and he sounded so shocked that I knew I'd ruined everything. So I was surprised when I felt his arms come around me and I heard him whisper in my ear, "That was you I chased on the rooftops?"

"Yes, my prince," I admitted, my throat tight, my heart pound-ing. I was so sure he was going to throw me out of his service that I couldn't quite work out why he was embracing me.

He laughed, which stunned me. "Gods, Razia, do you have any other hidden talents I should know about? You're not a wizard, are you?"

"No, my prince," I gasped, like it was a serious accusation, but I was so worried I couldn't help myself. I glanced up at him, expecting to see fury reflected on his face, but all I found was a smile. "You're not angry with me?"

"Mostly, I'm impressed, but let's save this conversation for when we get home, shall we?" he said.

"Yes, my prince," I agreed, but my heart was pounding. I had to know. "Are you going to abandon me?"

"Are you going to keep stealing once you're my concubine?" he asked.

"No, my prince! I swear I won't! I really didn't want to do any of it, but—"

He held up a hand to calm me down. "It's all right. We can talk about it when we get home. But I'm not going to abandon you, so long as those days are behind you."

"They are, my prince," I promised.

"Good," he said. And then he turned his attention to landing in the palace's courtyard, skillfully managing Padmini's reins, guiding her down to a perfect landing near the stables.

I was quick to untie the straps holding me in the saddle, and to slide down to the ground. I wanted to speak with Arjun in private. I wanted to know if he still wanted me or if he'd just been avoiding a scene where others might have overheard. I needed to know if I was right or wrong about him.

"Something wrong, Salim?" Karim asked, his eyes fixed on my red and puffy ones.

"You know her name, Karim." Arjun's voice had an edge to it as he dropped down from the saddle. He put his arm around me, but he was looking at the older prince with an intensity that gave me chills. It was a challenge. I'd seen that look from men growing up, and I knew it usually presaged a fight.

"I do," Karim agreed, and his hand started to drift toward the hilt of his firangi, but I think he realized then where he was and who else was around. Already, Arvind had stepped to his prince's defense, and Ram, Udai's retainer, was starting to look uneasy.

"Forgive me, Razia, I've known you so long my tongue slips," Karim said to me. It was a bald-faced lie, but I accepted it readily because it avoided bloodshed and let everyone save face, and I had far more important worries than Prince Karim and his petty jealousies.

"It's all right, your highness, I understand," I replied, bowing my head to him. I looked back to Arjun then and asked, "Could we have that talk now, my prince?"

"Yes, I think that would be best," he agreed. He gave Karim one last glare, and then he led me out of the courtyard, toward the harem and its private chambers. As a member of the household, he still had access to it, though he was a grown man now, so I didn't know how much longer that would last. At any rate, he brought me to a splendid apartment, well separated from the others. I knew from the bejeweled weapons hanging on the walls that this room must have been his.

"Sit down," he offered, gesturing to a pile of comfortable cushions placed around an open spot for dining. I sat on one of the cushions, and he sat beside me a moment later, putting his arm around me to hold me close.

My heart was hammering in my chest. "I'm so sorry, my prince . . ." I didn't know what else I could say. I wished I could take back everything I'd done, but I couldn't.

"It's all right," he said, and he stroked my hair, brushing a few loose strands back behind my ear, unsettling my dupatta in the process. "Just tell me everything. Let's start there. How long have you been stealing for your guru?"

"Since I was fourteen. Varsha saw that I was athletic, trained to fight, and I took to dancing easily, so she gave me climbing instructors, and she had men teach me to pick locks and to hide myself." The memories washed over me. They weren't bad memories, but I didn't know if I could make Arjun understand that. I'd been proud to help my new ammi, proud that I was so clever and so skilled. And I'd been bitter too. I'd wanted to take things from rich men like my father. Each theft had felt like justice in my heart.

"My first jobs were easy enough—stealing small baubles that were easy to carry and easy for my marks to miss. But gradually the jobs got bigger and more dangerous. Eventually, I was breaking into havelis and taking whatever Varsha wanted."

"Did you steal Govind Singh's peacock?" he asked.

I bowed my head, my cheeks burning from the shame. "Yes, my prince. You almost caught me. I had just climbed back up the wall after carrying it down."

"You climbed down the wall of his haveli with that peacock in your arms?" he asked, his skepticism plain in his voice.

"Tied to my back with a sturdy scarf, my prince," I corrected. "It was hard, but it wasn't impossible. His house has many decorations that provide good hand- and footholds. It makes for easy climbing."

"And what became of all these objects you stole?" he asked.

I shrugged. "I don't know, my prince. I gave them to Ammi, and she sold them, I suppose. I never saw any of the money, except for a few rupees here and there as a reward for doing well."

"And what did she do with the money?" he asked.

I shrugged again. "She said that she used it to pay for our lessons and to feed us and to keep up the dera, but I don't know for certain. For all I know, she might have it hidden away somewhere. But it would be an awful lot of money by now."

"And the last thing you stole was the sword?" he asked.

"Yes, my prince," I answered, and I fought back tears. "I'm so sorry, I swear I didn't want to do it, but—" He held up a hand to forestall the explanation, and I fell silent and stared at the floor in front of us, trying to focus on the delicate paisley patterns in the carpet to keep from sobbing.

"If I take you as my concubine, what will your guru do?" he asked.

In my mind, I imagined Ammi hearing the news and squealing with delight. I imagined her hugging me and congratulating me and looking so proud. I imagined her visiting me in the palace as an honored guest, acting the part of the mother of a real princess. But I knew better now. Those were the lies I'd always told myself to feel better. The truth was a different animal.

"She'll demand my allowance as her right," I said. That was definitely the first thing. "She'll threaten to blackmail me, to reveal me as a thief, if I don't give her the money she wants, when she wants it. So will my sister Jaskaur. She'll blackmail me too."

"I'll deal with them," he promised.

"You won't hurt them?" I asked, worried for their safety in spite of everything else. I couldn't help it; they were my family. And maybe Ammi didn't love the way that Arjun did, but she'd saved my life and raised me when no one else would.

"No, I'm not going to hurt them." He pulled me close to him and kissed the top of my head. "I promise. I'm just going to protect you from them. You do want to be my concubine, don't you?"

"Yes, my prince," I replied, because it was my most fervent wish in all the world. I knew that Karim would mock me for it if he ever found out, that men would view such a pathetic desire with undisguised scorn, but I didn't care. This was my chance to have a life with a man who really loved me, a chance to save my sisters from everything I had suffered, my chance to trust another person to keep me safe as no one ever had before.

"Good," he said. "Then I'll arrange things with your dera."

I felt nervous, because I had questions, but I was afraid to offend him by asking them. I didn't want him to think that I didn't trust him, because I did. I didn't want him to believe that I viewed this as nothing more than a business relationship, because that was the furthest thing from the truth. Then again, he hadn't minded my being a thief, and if I really trusted him, then maybe it was time I started acting like it. "I have some questions about the arrangement, my prince."

"Well, I might have some answers," he replied. "Ask."

"Will I be confined to the harem like the other ladies of the court?" I asked. I didn't particularly care for purdah. I knew it was part and parcel of being a woman, and I supposed if he forced me to submit to it that I would, but I rather liked my freedom to come and go as I pleased.

"No," he said. "You'll have an apartment in the harem, of course, but you will be allowed to leave the harem, or the palace, as you see fit. You're a hijra, so we don't have to worry about you giving birth to another man's children, do we?"

"No, my prince," I agreed, feeling shame rising like bile in the back of my throat. I would have traded my freedom for the ability to have children like other women could, but I knew that no amount of bargaining would grant me that gift.

"Do you have any other questions?" he asked.

There was one other thing, and I knew I would have to say it and deal with his reaction one way or the other. "It's not a question so much as a request, my prince."

He smiled. "And what request might that be?"

"Well," I said, encouraged by his smile, "if I'm to be your concubine, I will be a lady of the court, won't I?"

"You will," he agreed.

"So I'll need handmaidens to help me dress and to accompany me on outings," I said.

His grin broadened. "I suppose you will."

"I think two would suffice, my prince."

"Let me guess," he said, taking my hands in his. "Sakshi and Lakshmi?"

"I can't leave them there with Ammi, my prince, especially not Lakshmi. Ammi will make her into a thief like me. And she'd be heartbroken if I left her behind. And so would I."

"You have nothing to worry about," he assured me. "I knew you wouldn't be able to leave them behind, and I think they'll make very fine handmaidens for you. I'll see that everything is arranged, and that your guru and your remaining sisters never trouble you or your sisters again."

I clung to him with shaking arms, pressing my forehead into his shoulder. I couldn't believe it. He'd given me everything I'd ever wanted, even though he knew that I was a thief and a hijra. He'd followed through on his promises—every single one of them. I'd always thought that God had cursed me, but maybe I was wrong.

"Thank you," I whispered.

"You're welcome," he said.

We sat together in that room for a long time, because I was pouring tears into the silk fabric of his kurta, and he was kind enough to just sit with me while my mind fought to adjust itself to a view of the world that I had always held in suspicion, a world where love was lasting and people didn't abandon one another for things they couldn't control.

# CHAPTER 13

What's all this about, boy?" Udai asked, as the pair of us came to kneel before his throne.

"I've come to ask your permission to take Razia as my concubine, Father," Arjun said.

Karim laughed as I'd known he would. I'd prepared myself for it, but preparing yourself for something and actually hearing it are two different things, and I felt my cheeks burn as his laugh boomed out across the courtyard. Some of the men joined him in chuckling, Jai the eunuch among them.

For his part, the Maharaja Udai didn't laugh. He looked annoyed, but not amused. He looked from me to his son and asked, "You want me to make that thing a lady of the court?"

"Razia is not a thing, Father," Arjun replied, and I heard a flash of anger in his voice. "She was responsible for our victory yesterday. She knows zahhaks as well as anyone, she has a good head for tactics—"

"And she's good at giving head too," Karim cut in. "I can vouch for that, your majesty." More laughs rippled through the hall.

My hands clenched into fists of their own volition. I tried not to show any emotion beyond that. I didn't understand why I was still so sensitive. Shouldn't I have been immune to humiliation after having been exposed to so much of it throughout the course of my life? Shouldn't those emotions have long since become dulled through overuse?

"Is she to be your military adviser or your concubine, boy?" Udai asked.

"As my concubine, she will serve me in whatever capacity I desire, Father," he replied.

"She can't give you children," Udai remarked, though from the tone of his voice I didn't think that fact particularly bothered him.

"That's what wives are for," Arjun replied.

Udai had to concede the point with a nod of his head. Wealthy men in Bikampur rarely viewed their wives as sources of true companionship. It was usually some beautiful courtesan who claimed a man's heart—or, if they were very, very good, some hijra.

"And what do you think of this, girl?" the maharaja asked me.

"Me? I am honored to serve my prince in whatever capacity he desires, your majesty," I answered, maybe a little too fervently, but I couldn't help myself.

Not even Karim had anything to say to that. They all knew it was true. I had obeyed Arjun's every command, followed his every whim, and I'd done it enthusiastically. I loved him. I didn't say it, because I knew they would scoff at it, but it was true. And I knew that whatever else he said, Udai was interested in my military talents. I'd shown him a spark that might prove useful in future campaigns, but for that, he would have to keep me around.

"All right, boy," he said after due deliberation. "She can be your first concubine. No one can tell she's a hijra by looking at her anyway, so I suppose there's no shame in it."

"Thank you, Father!" Arjun exclaimed.

"Thank you, your majesty, your highness," I said, bowing properly to each of them in turn. My heart was swelling. It was ridiculous. I'd been raised a prince, raised to hold women in low esteem, and concubines in lower esteem than that. To have so ardently wished to be made a concubine, for it to seem like the grandest of all elevations in my social status, spoke to how far I had fallen when I had left home to live as my true self. But I pushed those thoughts away. So what if being a concubine was sneered at by men? I'd been happier as a dancing girl and a thief than I ever was as a prince, and now that I was going to be with Arjun forever, I was happier still.

I took one of Arjun's hands in mine and asked, "May we go inform my guru and my sisters, my prince?"

"Of course," he said. He helped me to my feet and led me away from his father's throne. I was happy for that. Udai had not yet been intentionally cruel to me, but he always made me feel like I was just one slip of the tongue away from some awful punishment. I could breathe easier when it was just Arjun and me. And Padmini. She was pressing up against the wooden gate that led into her pen, her bright eyes focused on Arjun, her short, plumed tail thrashing excitedly.

Zahhaks were funny creatures. While it was possible for a man to ride a zahhak that didn't belong to him, if she was incredibly well trained and well disciplined, zahhaks bonded to one person and one person alone. That person tended to be the first person they saw when they hatched from their eggs. They would respond to that person before any other, no matter the circumstances, like that person's face had been etched inside their hearts at that moment. That was why zahhaks were used so often in poetry to describe the kind of single-minded faithfulness that men reckoned ideal in women.

I felt a twinge of guilt as Arjun led Padmini out of the stables. I had left Sultana behind. I had abandoned her to be ridden by a stranger, or to be left in pens for breeding. But it had been the only way to escape. If I'd tried to get to the stables, I would have been caught for certain. And anyway, if I'd stolen my zahhak, my father would have been able to track me easily, and he'd have killed me when his men caught up to me.

Still, none of that erased the guilt and the hurt. I took some small comfort in stroking Padmini's face and kissing her snout, which she tolerated because she had come to realize that I meant something to her master. I think she probably saw me as a kindred spirit of sorts, another of Arjun's servants and confidants. I was just glad that zahhaks didn't get jealous of human women, or I'd surely have been a well-charred appetizer.

Arjun saddled Padmini and then helped me into my seat. I started strapping myself in as Padmini twisted her long neck to watch. I smiled at her, but she didn't respond. She was mostly just watching Arjun, studying his every move, trying to anticipate his desires.

Once in the saddle, Arjun clucked his tongue, and Padmini bounded forward, following the movements of the reins. She leapt off the ground with her stronger front limbs, and we were soon flying over the palace in gentle circles, letting some of the day's rising air currents lift us up. The view was spectacular, and the sky was so blue on this summer day that its contrast with the reddish desert sands on the horizon was intoxicating.

I leaned back in the saddle, resting myself against Arjun. His arms came around my waist, holding the reins just in front of me. He guided Padmini toward my dera with such practiced ease that I didn't think he was even aware of his own movements, of the subtle shifting of his weight, the pressure of his heels against his zahhak's shoulders, or the slight pull on the reins. It was like he was a part of the animal, the pair of them fused to become the perfect aerial predator.

"I wish I could have seen you fly in the battle," I murmured.

"I wish you could have flown with me," he said.

"Me too. I would give anything to get Sultana back. Do you think if I ever found her again that your father would let me fly with you as one of your retainers?"

He laughed and rested his chin on my head. "I don't know, Razia. I don't know how I would feel about it myself."

"What do you mean?" I asked.

"I mean that I would worry," he said. "Fighting is dangerous."

"You made me worry about you," I reminded him, as I didn't think I'd ever forget the tension in my guts that I'd had while I'd been left to wait and wonder if he would ever come back to me.

I spotted my dera in the distance, and my heart skipped a beat as I remembered what I'd forgotten in the excitement of being named Arjun's concubine. We still had to talk to Ammi about the thefts. We had to tell her that I was moving into the palace. We had to tell her that we were taking Sakshi and Lakshmi with us. God, this was going to be difficult. She was going to be so furious with me.

Oh, well, the time for worrying about it was over. Padmini was circling down, slowing herself gradually as she approached our courtyard. Lakshmi rushed out of one of the rooms and waved her arms, jumping up in the air she was so excited to see me again. I realized then that I'd forgotten to buy her that souvenir I'd been planning, but I supposed if she was going to be my handmaiden, then she could come to the bazaar with me.

Padmini landed, and I wasted no time in unstrapping myself and climbing down from the saddle, but I wasn't quick enough for

Lakshmi, who was wrapping her arms around me almost before my feet hit the ground. "Welcome home, Akka!" she exclaimed, squeezing me tightly.

"Thank you, Lakshmi," I replied, putting my arms around her and holding her close to me. "How are you? Is everything all right?"

"Everything is fine," she said. "But where did you go? We thought you would be home the night before last, but you never came back."

"That was my fault, I'm afraid," Arjun said, bending over so he was at her eye level. "I had to take her with me to Rajkot, the capital of Mahisagar, so she could help me plan a battle against the Firangi fleet."

"Really?" Lakshmi exclaimed, her eyes lighting up as she looked to me for confirmation.

"Really," I said. "I devised a brilliant strategy, and Prince Arjun defeated two ice zahhaks in a great aerial battle over the ocean."

Lakshmi frowned and looked up at me, her eyes getting big. "You weren't in the battle, were you?"

I saw the fear on her face, and I hugged her tightly. "No, sweetheart, I was safe in the palace. But I was very worried for Prince Arjun."

"She didn't have to be," he told Lakshmi. "I've never been defeated in the air before."

"You went all the way to Rajkot?" Sakshi asked, having come up behind us. "What was it like?"

"Beautiful, but Prince Karim was there." That last came out as a kind of grumble.

"Prince Karim?" Lakshmi asked.

"He was the one who . . ." Sakshi held a hand over her mouth, realizing that this wasn't something I'd want my little sister over-

hearing. Instead she came to me and embraced me and said, "I'm
so sorry, Razia."

"It's all right," I said. "I have good news for all of us."

"And what news might that be?" Ammi asked. She was joined
in the courtyard by Jaskaur and Disha.

I took a deep breath, knowing that I had to just come out and
say it. I forced myself to smile brightly, and I wrapped my arms
around one of Arjun's, and I said, "His highness has officially
named me his first concubine."

Sakshi squealed with excitement, but she was the only one.
Jaskaur narrowed her eyes in jealousy, Disha tried to force a smile
that she didn't feel, and Ammi, well, she looked like somebody
who'd had the rug snatched out from under her. She looked from
me to Arjun and back again for a long moment, trying to work out
all the implications for her, for the dera, for her income. She
wasn't happy, that much was clear.

I felt like a traitor. My heart ached, and my stomach was twisting itself in knots. She'd been counting on me to see her through
her declining years, to live off my earnings. But hadn't I provided
enough? Shouldn't she have been able to live comfortably off what
she already had? And I hadn't even told her the rest of it.

I sighed and said, "There's more."

"More?" Ammi asked, her voice carrying a sharp edge.

"I've named Sakshi and Lakshmi as my handmaidens. If they
wish, they will be coming to live in the palace with me and will
have allowances commensurate with their positions."

"I'm going to live in the palace with you, Akka?" Lakshmi
gasped. She hugged me so tightly that it hurt.

"I took you in off the streets!" Ammi growled. "When you had
nothing, when you were sick and starving and afraid, I brought
you into this dera and raised you as one of my own! And now you

repay me by stealing my celas from me? By abandoning me in my old age when I need your income to survive?"

"I will pay you five thousand rupees for each of your celas," Arjun said.

My eyes widened. Fifteen thousand rupees? God, how could he afford such a thing? How could anyone? It was more money than I would ever see at any one time in my whole life. The average laborer would have to work for a thousand years to see that much money. It was more than I ever would have dreamed possible.

Ammi closed her mouth, her eyes flickering as she did the sums in her head. Arjun didn't wait for her response. He said, "And you can consider my not having you executed for theft to be an additional payment. Razia confessed what you made her do to support you, how many things she's stolen from the local havelis. I would be within my rights to take you before the headsman for your crimes, but out of respect for the way you treated the woman I love, I will spare you. I will also keep it a secret so that you and your celas can continue to make money the way you always have. But I expect you to remember this act of charity and to never force any other young girls to do what you made Razia do."

"His highness is most gracious," Ammi said, bowing to him, though the tone of her voice suggested that she thought he was anything but. She scowled at me, and then looked back to Arjun, clearly trying to figure out how best to maneuver this turn of events to her advantage.

"You will have no claims on Razia's earnings or the earnings of her handmaidens," Arjun said. "You will not approach them for money. If you need money, you will come to me directly and make your case to me. As you are my lover's mother, I will listen attentively to whatever requests you make."

I was shocked when Varsha just nodded to that. This was not

how the conversation would have gone had Arjun not been here. She would have chased me around the courtyard with a branch broken from one of the mango trees. She'd have screamed and cried and pounded her breast and pulled at her hair and rent her clothes until I agreed to whatever it was she wanted. But with Arjun standing there, giving orders, she just accepted them.

To us, Arjun said, "Go and collect your belongings, ladies. We'll be leaving immediately, and we won't be returning."

"Yes, my prince," I agreed. I put my arm around Lakshmi and led her away from the courtyard, toward the storeroom where we kept any valuables.

Lakshmi seemed oblivious to Varsha's reaction. She was skipping along beside me, saying, "What's the palace like, Akka? Is it beautiful? Will I have my own room? Will I get to wear pretty clothes too? Do you think Prince Arjun will give me a new zahhak? I miss my Mohini so much."

"I don't know about a zahhak, little sister," I said, stroking her hair as we walked, "but you'll have a beautiful room and pretty clothes and a generous allowance. And you'll get to play with the zahhaks in the stables."

"I can't wait!" she exclaimed, and she hugged me again. "Thank you for taking me with you, Akka!"

"You're welcome," I said. "I would never forget my favorite little sister."

"I'm your only little sister," she pointed out.

"So definitely my favorite, then," I replied, enjoying the way she dramatically rolled her eyes like a young lady so many years older.

In the storeroom, I took the only thing of value I had in the dera—my box with my katars. I opened it up to make sure they were still there, still in perfect condition. They were. I hugged the box to my chest then and asked Lakshmi, "Do you have anything you want to take?"

"Can I take my clothes?" she asked.

"You could," I said, "or I could buy you better ones in the bazaar."

"Really?" she gasped.

"Really," I assured her.

"Okay, let's do that," she said.

"It's settled, then." I took her hand and walked back to the courtyard with her. Sakshi had already returned, cradling the only thing she wanted—her sitar. She too had left her clothes and jewelry in her room. It would spawn fewer arguments with Ammi and make her feel a little less cheated, I thought, though there was nothing about this arrangement that would make her happy.

"What's in the box?" Arjun asked me.

"Take a look, my prince," I replied, and I opened it for him.

His eyes got big as he took in the wootz steel of the blades, the golden zahhak heads, and the koftgari lightning motifs. "Those were yours?"

"Once upon a time, when I was the crown prince of Nizam," I said. I closed the box. Shutting it always felt like shutting that chapter of my life. For a long time, that had been such a bittersweet feeling, but not today. Today, I was hopeful for the future, and not just mine, but Lakshmi's and Sakshi's too.

"Well," he said, taking the box from me and placing it in one of Padmini's saddlebags, "I suppose we should get back to the palace, then."

"Are we all going to fly?" Lakshmi wondered, looking at the two-seat saddle with concern.

"No, Padmini is strong, but she can't carry so many people," said Arjun. "But you can ride her if you promise to keep her on the ground."

"I promise!" Lakshmi exclaimed.

Arjun grinned and picked her up, setting her in the front seat on the saddle. I knew then what I had to do next. I looked to Sakshi and said, "Would you like to ride her too?"

"Could I?" Sakshi gasped, looking to Arjun with eyes that were bigger and more excited even than Lakshmi's. Sometimes I forgot she was just eighteen, not so much older than me, and she'd always been younger in spirit.

"Of course, my lady," Arjun said, and he helped her into the saddle and made sure she was settled comfortably. He wagged a finger at Lakshmi then. "Remember, no flying. Your big sister doesn't know how to strap herself into the saddle, and I don't think she wants to drop her sitar from a hundred feet above the city."

"I'll be good, your highness," Lakshmi promised, her voice as solemn as I'd ever heard it.

"Well," Arjun said, nodding to Varsha. "Say good-bye, ladies."

"Good-bye, Ammi," I said, but I didn't come forward to embrace her, and it was clear from her posture that she didn't want to embrace me either. Still, I said, "Thank you for everything. I know I would be nothing without you."

She snorted at that, but said nothing. Arjun cut in then, saying, "I'll be back with the fifteen thousand rupees."

"Your highness is very kind," she said, though it was plain she didn't believe a word of that.

Personally, I didn't see why she was so bothered. She would be the richest hijra in all Bikampur after receiving that payment. What more did she want? Her plans for the dera had been about making herself rich and comfortable and established, about putting her on equal terms with the best of the tawaifs. She'd done that now. She should have been happy, but some people will never be satisfied.

A week ago, I'd have been so hurt and so scared at the prospect of leaving the dera that I'd have flung myself at Ammi's feet and sworn to do whatever she wanted to prevent it. Today, while I was hurt to be leaving the woman who had cared for me for the last four years, I knew I would survive it. But that courage didn't come from me. It came from Arjun, from Sakshi, and from Lakshmi. Without them, I'd have wondered if anyone in the whole world could ever love me unconditionally. But now, I knew that they could.

So I turned away from her, and away from the dera for what was probably the last time, and I walked beside Arjun as he led Padmini by the reins out into the street. She barely managed to squeeze through our gate, and Lakshmi and Sakshi had to lie flat in the saddle to keep from getting their heads taken off, but they came out the other side safe and sound.

Sakshi was grinning. She kept running her hands over the serpent-like scales on Padmini's back and neck, shaking with excitement each time. To me, she said, "I can't believe I'm really riding a zahhak!"

"Oh, that's nothing," Arjun said. "I'll take you up later after you're settled in the palace. There's nothing like seeing the world from the air."

"I would be so honored, your highness," she said, bowing low to him again.

"Razia is my concubine. She's like a wife to me. That means you're like a sister to me now," he said.

"Am I your sister too?" Lakshmi asked.

"Absolutely," he said, which brought a brilliant smile to her face and melted my heart. I was going to give him quite the reward once we were alone again.

We walked through the streets, and I noticed that the common people stayed well out of our path, staring at us with wonder. They had no idea that we were hijras. They must have thought we were exotic foreign princesses, walking with the great Prince Arjun and riding his magnificent zahhak. I smiled and whispered in his ear, "That's how people used to look at me. I'd forgotten what it felt like."

"Well, you'd better get used to it," he replied. "That's how they will look at you for all the days of your life from now on."

I kissed him on the cheek for that, drawing exclamations from the onlookers. Lakshmi clapped a hand over her mouth and giggled, like kisses were the funniest things in the world. I was so grateful for that. Nobody had forced her to kiss when she didn't want to yet. And now, nobody ever would. If I did nothing else good for the rest of my life, I could die peacefully knowing that I'd spared one little girl that fate. And maybe, just maybe, if she was very lucky, she would experience the pleasure I felt at kissing someone I did love.

# CHAPTER 14

"If you don't hold still, then I'm going to have to start all over, and you'll have to sit here twice as long!" Shiv exclaimed, exasperation tingeing his voice.

"I'll be good!" Lakshmi promised, as the threat of prolonging her hair braiding was just about the only thing that could stop her from fidgeting. Not that I could blame her—I hated sitting in one place for too long too.

I noticed that Shiv was getting worn out, though, so I put my hand on the eunuch's shoulder and said, "Thank you for your patience, Shiv."

"It's my pleasure, my lady, I assure you," he replied, and he even sounded like he meant it. He went back to work and, after a little bit of fiddling, finally got Lakshmi's hair the way he wanted it. "There you are, Lady Lakshmi," he said, with such genuine affection that it brought a smile to my lips.

"I look like a princess . . ." Lakshmi murmured as she admired herself in the mirror. She wasn't wrong. She was wearing the new sari I'd had made for her, as that was what women wore in Virajendra. It wasn't so different from a lehenga, with its short-sleeved blouse that bared her midriff, but its long pallu served as skirt and dupatta both, and I thought it made her look beautiful. The fine silk cloth was a brilliant emerald green, with turquoise feather patterns woven throughout. She wore it with my acid zahhak jewelry, as she'd been desperate to borrow it ever since she'd first laid eyes on it. I'd thought it was only fair, as she was the only acid zahhak rider in the family.

She leapt up from her cushion, spun around, and embraced Shiv as tightly as she could. "Thank you! I've never looked so pretty before!"

Shiv hugged her back and said, "Oh, it was nothing, my lady. The gods did most of my work for me."

"Do you think I look pretty, Akka?" Lakshmi asked me.

I put my hands on her shoulders and studied her intently, like Ammi used to do when she inspected me before I met a client. I was surprised by what I saw. She looked so much more mature, dressed this way. She seemed taller than she was, because she was still so skinny, like most girls her age, but her figure was beginning to change from the treatments she'd started receiving. She'd have her nirvan soon, and then she would change more. But right now, she looked like a Virajendran princess on the cusp of womanhood. I knew from the way she had gazed excitedly into the mirror that she was finally the girl she'd dreamed of becoming when she'd run away from home and given up her old life of comfort for the struggles of the dera.

"You're the prettiest girl in the whole palace," I told her, embracing her without wrinkling her sari or mussing her hair. I took her by the hand then and said, "Now, how about we go to the courtyard and have a little breakfast?"

"Yes, Akka!" Lakshmi agreed.

"I'm famished," said Sakshi.

"You can come eat with us too, Shiv," I told him.

"I'd be honored, my lady," he replied, and he fell in step with us as we left my apartment.

We found breakfast being served beneath a lovely pavilion in the garden. It still amazed me, how pretty the harem was, with its ancient, gnarled mango trees and its innumerable flowers. Channels of water lined with stone created little rivers that fed both the plants and the marble fountains, which had been carved all over in floral motifs. The ladies of the harem were all seated beneath the pavilion, dining on half a dozen dishes, and servant girls were standing by with pitchers of aam panna, waiting to refill empty goblets.

A large group of servants were standing around one woman in particular. She was quite a bit older than I was, though there wasn't a trace of gray in her perfect black hair. She was dressed elegantly, with dozens of golden bangles on her arms and a diamond-encrusted collar around her neck that glittered in the early-morning sunlight. Her dark brown eyes flickered over to me, and she beckoned me to her. "Come here, girl."

I came to stand in front of her, and she asked, "Do you know who I am?"

"The maharani?" I ventured, as I suspected she must have been Arjun's mother and Udai's primary wife. Otherwise, why were the other women gathered around her? Why else would so many servants attend her?

"That's right," she said. "I am Gayatri, maharani of Bikampur, and you are my son's newest infatuation." She made a big show of looking me over from head to toe, and then grumbled, "Well, I can't tell you're a hijra by looking at you, so I suppose your presence here won't be a total humiliation for this family."

She let the barb sink in before gesturing to the cushions beside hers. "Sit down, girl—and your maids too."

"Yes, your majesty." I sat down beside her, showing none of the irritation I felt at being referred to as a potential source of humiliation for her family. I couldn't stop my cheeks from burning, but I was at least able to keep my face impassive.

Once we'd sat, Gayatri continued, "I've heard rumors about you. They say that you were Salim Mirza, the crown prince of Nizam, before you came here and did that to yourself." She gestured to the whole of my body with the back of her hand. "Is it true?"

"It is, your majesty," I said, wondering what I'd done to so infuriate the woman. I knew from experience with Ammi that in such circumstances it was best to keep calm and quiet and wait for things to blow over. And anyway, I knew how precarious a woman's place in the world could be if she didn't come from a fine home, and I knew how easy it would be for the maharani to speak to her husband and have me thrown out on the streets if I angered her. So I wasn't going to anger her any more than my presence already had.

She gave a derisive snort and took a sip of her aam panna, before gesturing to me with her glass, saying, "If you'd been a man, you'd have been the most powerful man in Daryastan. As a woman, you'd have been the most desirable princess in the known world. As you are, you're of no value to anyone."

"Your son seems to value me, your majesty," I replied, biting back all of the more aggressive responses that sprang to mind.

"My son values pert tits and a tight ass," she replied, drawing shocked gasps from the other court ladies. She nodded to me. "You're nothing more to him than a pretty face who can warm his bed at night, and you forget that at your peril."

"I know what I am, and I know my place, your majesty," I replied. It sounded like agreement, but it was anything but. Someday, she would know my place too, but for now I would keep quiet, and I would try to fit into my new role in the harem without causing ripples that might get back to the maharaja himself.

"Why?" she demanded.

"Your majesty?" I ventured, not sure what the question was referring to.

"You could have been the sultan of Nizam!" she exclaimed. "Do you know how many of us palace women dream of what life would have been like if we'd been born boys instead of girls? Instead, we have to spend our whole lives trapped here, like birds in a gilded cage." She gestured to the women around her for emphasis. "But you chose this. What on earth possessed you to do such a stupid thing? Are you insane?"

"I have a woman's soul, your majesty," I said, as it was the only way I knew how to express the path my life had taken.

She snorted derisively. "A woman's soul? You think all women are born to wear pretty clothes and cuddle babies and submit to men, do you?"

"No, of course not, your majesty," I replied.

"Then what are you doing here?" she demanded. "You could have been the sultan of Nizam. If I were you, that's what I would be."

"No, you wouldn't," I snapped. "You have no idea what you're talking about!"

Her eyes widened, and she smiled, and she opened her mouth to speak, but I spoke over her. "You don't know what it feels like to have a body that disgusts you, to have parts that you'd rather not have, to know with an absolute certainty deep inside yourself that you are a girl and not the boy everyone calls you. It has nothing to do with your position in society, or what you want or don't want for your life, it has to do with who you are on the basest, truest, deepest level. You think I want to be here?" I gestured to her and the other harem women. "What I want, what I really want, is my Sultana back. I want to fly my thunder zahhak through the skies again; I want to use her to smite my enemies and to protect my family. But I, like you, am not permitted to do those things. I, like you, am stuck here—in spite of the fact that I'm a better flier than the men here, in spite of the fact that I'm a better tactician than the men here, in spite of the fact that I'm good with a pair of katars. You think I chose this?" I gestured again to the harem surroundings. "I chose to live as my true self, and this is what was done to me by the world as a result.

"And worse," I said, because she was studying me in silence, and I didn't feel like shutting up and playing the meek, mild courtesan any longer. "You have no idea what I've suffered, what men have done to me. You were brought here when? At age fourteen, having seen nothing of the world but your father's palace? And you came here to be a queen, with servants and handmaidens waiting on you hand and foot. You've never bartered your body for bread. You've never been forced to smile at the embrace of every fat, greasy man who ever looked at you, just because he had money and you didn't. So don't you tell me what choices you would have made. I've paid for my choices. What have you paid for yours?"

The whole harem had gone ghostly silent. Even the birds seemed afraid to chirp out their songs in the wake of my tirade. My stomach was tight, and my heart was pounding. What had I done?

If she wanted to make my life difficult, she could, and at this point I had no doubt that she would.

"I'd heard you hijras were famous for your sharp tongues," Gayatri said, "and you don't disappoint." She smiled at me. "What's your interest in my son? A way out of that gutter you put yourself in?"

"I love him." The words tumbled out of my mouth almost unbidden. I hadn't meant to say something so saccharine, but it was true. I did love him. I saw her roll her eyes and open her mouth, but I spoke first. "I don't care what you think. I do love him. I would do anything for him. Of course I like living in a palace better than living where I was living. Of course I like the clothes he gives me and the allowance he gives me. But those things only increase my devotion. I'm not a princess. I don't have a family now. Arjun is everything to me, and I'm not stupid enough to believe that I will ever have anything better so long as I live. So I will care for him better than any wife, protect him better than any bodyguard, and counsel him better than any noble lord. Because without him, I am nothing."

I was shocked when Gayatri smiled at me, more shocked still when she gestured to my sisters and asked, "And these young ladies? Who are they?"

"My sisters from the dera," I said.

Her eyes widened slightly. "They're both hijras?"

I nodded. "Sakshi is my older sister, and the finest sitar player in all of Bikampur—maybe the world."

"Razia!" Sakshi exclaimed, her cheeks turning scarlet at my boast. To Gayatri, she said, "Really, your majesty, I'm not that good."

"I'll be the judge of that," she said. "Go and get your sitar and play for us."

"Yes, your majesty," Sakshi replied, and she rushed off to do it.

While she was gone, Gayatri looked to Lakshmi and said, "And this one?"

"My little sister." I wrapped my arm around her shoulders and held her close to me. "Her name is Lakshmi, and she was once the son of Vidarth, the zamorin of Kolikota, one of the most powerful governors of the great Virajendra empire of the south. She was a zahhak rider like me, but she ran away from home to escape the beatings and the insults, and to live as her true self."

"Gods . . ." Gayatri murmured. "Are all hijras the children of far-off princes, then?"

I caught the skepticism in her voice, and I said, "I've proved myself to your son, and so has Lakshmi. Arjun let her take Padmini's reins and control her in the sky. He knows she's well trained. Not that it matters now." I gestured to our attire, and to the harem, with its tall walls and its eunuchs guarding the gates.

Sakshi came back then with her sitar and sat beside me. She started to play at once, and the sounds that reverberated through the harem then were as heavenly as any I'd heard. I knew the song she'd picked too. It was the one I'd sung for Arjun the night we'd met. She gave me a significant look, and I sang along with her playing, putting my heart into the music because it was this song that had finally changed my life for the better.

When we'd finished, Gayatri nodded to Sakshi and said, "You're right, she's very good. I suppose having the three of you here won't be a total loss, then."

"Your majesty is very kind," I replied, my voice laden with sarcasm.

She smiled back at me. "Go on, girls, eat." She gestured to the food in front of us.

We were all hungry, so we started to eat, dining on halwa poori and fresh mangoes. The other women watched us as we ate, probably waiting for the maharani to continue her sparring match with me. For the moment, however, she seemed content to watch us eat, and I was content to do the eating.

I was just taking a bite of halwa when Lakshmi demanded, "Why are you so mean to my akka?"

I dropped my food back on my plate with a sigh. "Lakshmi . . ." I began, but I got no further than that before Gayatri answered her.

"I am Arjun's mother," she replied. "It's my duty to make certain that the girls he brings home are acceptable, that they will be devoted to him, that they will help him and not hurt him. I had to discover for myself what sort of girl she was."

"She's a nice girl," Lakshmi informed the maharani hotly. "She's always been nice."

My cheeks reddened, and I put my arm around Lakshmi's shoulders and whispered, "Eat your breakfast, Lakshmi." I gave her a pat on the cheek and then glanced back in Gayatri's direction. "Apologies, your majesty."

"Not at all," she said. "It seems that loyalty is something you hijras understand well."

"We have to. Without each other to lean on, we'd have all died in the streets."

She grunted at that but said nothing to it. I went back to eating. The food was delicious and the aam panna was refreshing. There was nothing quite like mango juice and mint to make my whole body feel cool and comforted. It also helped to assuage the anger I'd felt on being questioned so pointedly by the maharani. But I supposed she'd had a right to do it. She ruled this harem, and I was the one sharing a bed with her son.

"Good morning, ladies."

I turned to see that Arjun was walking toward us alongside his father. I wished his father hadn't come; he was likely to join in with his wife in cataloging all my various defects.

"She's not in tears," Udai remarked, nodding to me. "Has my dear wife lost her touch?"

"She's not what I expected," Gayatri admitted.

"And what do you think of her, dear sister?" Arjun asked.

I looked over in surprise at a girl I had ignored. She was perhaps a year or two younger than me, which made her four or five years older than Lakshmi. She was dressed in a very fine red silk lehenga, and she wore ruby-encrusted bangles and earrings. She was quite pretty, with the dark, almond-shaped eyes men found so alluring.

She smiled at me and said, "I like her, brother. Anyone who can leave Mother speechless is a welcome addition to the household.

"But it occurs to me," she added a moment later, "if she can ride a zahhak, and little Lakshmi can ride a zahhak, then there's no reason I can't ride a zahhak."

"Absolutely not," Udai declared.

"But, Father—" she began.

He cut her off. "Don't 'but, Father' me, girl. You are not going to be dragging our family name through the dirt so you can play at being a man. You are going to marry soon, and until that time, you are going to stay here and behave yourself."

"Why do they get to play at being men, then?" she asked, gesturing in my direction.

"They don't," Udai replied. "The girl comes with Arjun because she's a courtesan and has no family name left to disgrace. But when we go to battle, she sits in the palace like a proper young lady—as you should."

The girl scowled. "I'd make a good zahhak rider, Father."

"You would, Anju, but it's not a proper thing for girls to be doing," Arjun said.

"Only because men say so," I muttered. The words were out of my mouth before I realized that I probably shouldn't have been giving Anju any more ammunition for her argument.

Udai seemed to feel the same way because he whirled on me and growled, "You will not foment rebellion within this harem, girl."

"Of course not, your majesty, forgive me," I responded, bowing my head and looking properly submissive. Keeping Arjun happy was easy, but his family was another matter entirely, and frankly the maharaja frightened me. I knew he didn't like me much, and that meant that he was probably looking for any opportunity to cast me out. So, best to placate him, even if I thought his ideas were ridiculous.

"Father, she's hardly 'fomenting rebellion,'" Arjun chided. He came over to me and held out his hand, and I took it and he helped me up. I wondered what that was about, until he said, "Father won't admit it, but he has need of you this morning."

"Need of me?" I asked. I hoped Arjun was talking about strategy, as there was nothing of the angry older man that appealed to me sexually.

"Javed Khorasani has sent us an ambassador," Arjun explained. "He arrived on the back of a thunder zahhak not an hour ago."

"A thunder zahhak?" My eyes lit up. "So we kill him and take it."

Udai surprised me by grinning at that suggestion. He said, "We might have, but the ambassador he sent isn't one of Khorasani's sons, he's one of Sultan Humayun's nephews."

"One of my cousins?" I gasped, not liking the sound of that a bit. My cousins had despised me growing up. They were both older than me, and both had coveted the throne. The last thing I wanted was a family reunion.

"That's right," Udai said. "So we can't just kill him without bringing the whole of Nizam down on our heads. We'll have to hear him out, and I want you there when we do. You know Nizam better than anyone. If he's lying, I want to know it."

"Of course, your majesty. It would be my honor," I replied, though inwardly I was dreading seeing whichever cousin of mine it was. I just hoped he didn't recognize me, otherwise I was going to end up dead. Of course, after four years of daily treatments, and having had my nirvan, I didn't think there was much chance of one of my cousins recognizing me, not unless he'd heard the rumors that were no doubt swirling through the courts of Registan. That thought brought to mind a possibility that chilled my blood. What if my cousin was here for me?

"Come along, then," Udai grumbled.

My feet felt like they'd turned to lead. I suddenly wanted to run as far away from my cousin and this audience as I possibly could, but if I did that, I could kiss my place in Udai's court goodbye. So I turned to my sisters and forced a smile I didn't feel, saying, "Sakshi, look after Lakshmi. Maybe take her to the bazaar?"

"Oh, we'll have such fun!" Sakshi promised, draping her arm across Lakshmi's shoulders, winning a big grin from the smaller girl. But I could tell that Sakshi was alarmed. She knew me well enough that I couldn't fully hide my fear from her.

I wanted nothing more than to pour out my fears to her, but I had to follow behind the maharaja instead, my arm entwined with Arjun's. My mind was spinning. Which of my cousins was waiting for us? That was the question that kept running through my mind. Tariq was the elder of the two, a fierce warrior, but not much of an ambassador. He was too quick-tempered for that, and too important besides. With me out of the picture, he'd be heir apparent these days. Rashid was about my age, the younger of my eldest uncle's two sons, probably too young for something so important, though he'd always been the more silver-tongued of the pair of them. Of course, I had other cousins, from other family members, but not many of them had made much impression on me at court. But I supposed I would find out who it was soon enough.

We left the harem and entered the courtyard where the zahhaks were kept. My heart started to beat a little faster. I stood on my tiptoes, craning my neck to see into the pens.

Arjun chuckled. "Last pen on the right." He knew exactly what I was after.

I let go of his arm and ran then, having to clamp one hand on top of my head to keep from losing my dupatta. I reached the pen, and I looked inside, and my heart stopped.

Thunder zahhaks were, to my eyes, the most beautiful zahhaks in all the world. Their feathers were barred blue on their upper parts, with little hints of white at the tips. Their underparts were bright gold, like the sun itself, and their scales were the color of cobalt tiles crackling with golden koftgari, bright and shining and gorgeous. They were smaller than other zahhaks, not big enough to hold two riders, not even the largest females. But their swept wings made them fast and agile in a way that not even an acid zahhak could match, and their cobra-like hoods could make them look big and menacing on the ground, or help them turn tighter circles in the air.

But it wasn't the beauty of the zahhak in that pen that had made my heart stop. It was her familiarity. I knew every scale on her snout, knew those emerald eyes better than my own. I was the first thing they had ever seen.

"Sultana!" I exclaimed.

Her head shot up from where it had lain on the straw lining the pen's floor. She stared at me for an instant, and then she leapt to her feet and pressed her body against the pen's gate, stretching her neck beyond it, until her snout was touching my nose.

"You've come back to me, girl," I said, my voice trembling with emotion. I wrapped my arms around her neck, embracing her tightly, and she made a groaning noise of contentment. I ran my hands over her snout three, four, five times, trying to convince myself that she was real. There was one sure test. I looked her right in the eyes and said, "Right hand."

She raised her right wing and held its claw out to me for inspection. It was a silly trick I'd taught her while I'd been hiding in her pen from my father one day. She still remembered it all these years later. I stroked her scales again. "Do you remember when you were small enough to ride me?" I asked her, as I recalled those days so fondly, when she had stood on my glove, waiting to fly out after gazelles on our hunts across the plains.

"This is your zahhak?" Arjun asked. He was standing back a little ways, as it was always dangerous to approach a strange zahhak too closely. While they could be tamed down, they only truly obeyed their masters, and their only true masters were the ones they had laid eyes on upon hatching.

"This is Sultana," I said, pressing my cheek against her snout. "Isn't she magnificent?"

"She is, but what's she doing here?" Arjun asked.

"She was the ambassador's mount," Udai replied.

"What is the ambassador's name?" I asked.

"Rashid," the maharaja answered.

"Ah." It all made sense to me then. "Rashid was only a little older than me, and he was the younger of two sons. His father hadn't yet procured a zahhak for him when I left. My father must have given him Sultana when I ran away." I couldn't keep the anger out of my voice at that.

Sultana leaned forward and sniffed at me, trying to figure out what had made me angry. I gave her a few gentle pats and said, "It's all right, it's nothing to do with you. You're perfect."

"Razia . . ." Arjun came forward and put his arms around me, which aroused Sultana's curiosity, but not her protective instincts. She seemed to sense that I liked him. "You can't have her back. She's not yours anymore, and trying to take her would start a war."

I felt like an idiot. Of course I couldn't have her back, but until he'd said it, the thought had never crossed my mind that she wouldn't stay with me forever.

I felt like somebody had torn my guts out. She was going to be taken from me a second time, and there was nothing I could do to stop it. I sucked in a deep breath and fought back tears. I managed to hold them at bay, but only just.

"Come on," he said. "Let's go see what your cousin has to say."

"Yes, my prince," I murmured, but he had to lead me away

from Sultana like a reluctant horse, and she whined in response. It was a sound that pulled at my heartstrings, that made me want to turn around and run back to her, but I knew I couldn't. I had to do what I was told. I had to be helpful to the maharaja and to be a proper little courtesan for Arjun. That was the only way to keep what little status I had garnered for myself.

I tried my best to steel myself for the conversation that was coming. I hadn't seen Rashid since I was twelve years old. I wondered if he would recognize me. He'd always been the kindest of my family members. I hoped that was still the case—for Sultana's sake, if not for my own.

## CHAPTER 15

Five years had turned Rashid from a boy into a man. He'd always been a good-looking youth, but now he had a man's physique to match his bright green eyes and straight teeth. His jaw had squared out quite a bit, and his once slender frame was now rippling with muscle, but there was no question that it was the same Rashid I had known from my childhood.

He had been the kindest of my cousins. He had never beaten me for my effeminacy, though he'd never understood it either. He would take pity on me, protect me sometimes, but more often try to coach me in the proper way to be a man, as if I just needed an umpteenth mentor to finally understand my place in the world. Still, I couldn't complain too strenuously. Compared to what his brother had done to me, Rashid had been a saint.

I didn't think he recognized me. How could he? My treatments and my nirvan had changed my body drastically. And anyway, it had been five years since I'd seen him last. Perhaps if I hadn't known his name in advance, I wouldn't have recognized him either. There certainly wasn't much chance that he would guess that the pretty courtesan doting on the prince of Bikampur was his long-lost cousin.

"Welcome, Lord Rashid," Udai said from his place atop his throne on the pavilion's central dais. "To what do I owe the pleasure of your visit?"

I held my breath as I waited for the answer. Had he come for me? If he had, he certainly wasn't paying me much attention, but just the possibility that he had arrived on the whiff of rumors of my reappearance was enough to make me feel sick to my stomach.

"Word reached my uncle, Sultan Humayun, of the attack that the sultan of Mahisagar carried out on our allies, the Firangis. Our messengers informed us that you participated in this act of aggression against our interests, and I see from the presence of Prince Karim himself that our agents were not mistaken in this."

"Aggression?" Karim growled, putting his hand on the hilt of his firangi. "What do you call the raids that the Firangis carried out on merchant vessels hailing from our ports? What do you call Javed Khorasani's troops making maneuvers along our borders?"

Rashid looked surprised at the allegations. That was interesting. Either he was a very good actor or he was a very bad one. Either way, did my father really intend to convince the maharaja of Bikampur that Javed Khorasani's intentions had been perfectly innocent? Given the history between the two men, that seemed absurd on the face of it. What angle was Rashid playing?

"I know nothing of these accusations, your majesty," Rashid told Udai. "However, what's done is done, and my uncle, in his wisdom and generosity, is willing to forgive the part you played in this unfortunate incident."

"Oh?" Udai asked. To an outsider, the question would have seemed innocuous enough, but I could hear the rumble of anger in it. If Rashid wasn't careful, he wouldn't be leaving this audience with his head.

"If you surrender the fort of Rohiri to Lord Javed Khorasani, his imperial majesty's subahdar, all will be forgiven. If not, the twelve zahhaks my father has dispatched to Zindh will decide the matter on the battlefield."

Cries went up from the assembled noblemen, and murmurs too. All eyes looked to Udai as they wondered what he would do in the face of such a mighty force of zahhaks. But I was suspicious. Twelve zahhaks represented nearly half of my father's personal strength in the animals, and an eighth of the empire's total. With his forces struggling to maintain his enormous empire to the south, to the north, and to the southwest, how could he place so many zahhaks in one place? He would risk an instant counterattack along an undefended border.

Moreover, placing twelve zahhaks under the command of anyone but himself was asking for trouble. Any general with twelve zahhaks in addition to his provincial numbers could make himself an independent warlord, and there were plenty of subahdars waiting to do just that. From what I remembered, Javed Khorasani had four zahhaks of his own—with twelve more under his command, he would hold a larger force than any man in Nizam but my father himself. Why would he not just anoint himself the sultan of his own empire?

Worse, Rashid's father, my uncle Shahrukh, had been coveting the throne for the whole of his life. He'd been smart enough not to make any moves against my father, which was why he was still alive and my late uncle Azam wasn't, but if my father were foolish enough to place twelve of his zahhaks under Rashid's command, that would surely change. No, Rashid didn't have twelve zahhaks, but neither had he gone to Zindh alone.

It was an act. My father wanted to look strong without creating a war that would entice others to attack him while he was distracted in Registan. So he would send Rashid to Khorasani with enough zahhaks to support him, but not enough to entice a rebellion or endanger the empire.

The question was, did I tell anyone that fact, or did I keep it quiet? God help me, there was still a part of me that loved my father, that wanted to please him, even after everything I'd suffered in Nizam. There was a part of me that yearned to return home to Nizam, that would never view Registan as home—not fully. But if I didn't speak up, Bikampur might be fatally weakened, which would endanger Arjun's life. That decided things in my mind.

"Four."

"What?" Arjun asked.

"Four, my prince," I whispered into his ear. "My father wouldn't have sent half of his personal zahhaks to Zindh. He'd have sent four to give Rashid's threats some teeth, and to protect Zindh from the counterattack your father and Ahmed are no doubt planning. This is a bluff."

"Are you sure?" he asked.

"I'm sure, my prince," I replied. I may not have been the ideal son growing up, but I'd come to know my father as well as anyone. However much he'd despised me, he'd still intended to make me his heir, after all.

While Udai was still considering Rashid's threat, Arjun spoke up. "I think you meant four zahhaks, Lord Rashid."

"What?" Rashid demanded, and I saw just a hint of color fly to his cheeks. It wasn't much, but it was enough to tell me that I was right.

Arjun must have seen it too, because he seized on it. "Your uncle sent you with four zahhaks to Zindh, not twelve. I'm sure you simply misspoke."

Rashid was silent for a long moment, and I knew then that the lie had been his idea. My father wouldn't have told him to do anything so stupid, as it would have been easily proved false, but he was trying to win a big victory for Nizam. The reason why came to me a second later. With me out of the picture, the succession was wide open. Tariq was the favorite, as the eldest, and a man my father had doted upon, but any cousin of mine might be named the heir if he caught my father's eye. This was Rashid's first big chance to win territory for the empire, and to force a victory over a tenacious enemy like Udai Agnivansha.

I whispered in Arjun's ear, "Tell him that if he wants to become my father's heir, he has to take things slowly. He doesn't like flashy young princes who overplay their hand."

Arjun chuckled, and it was only then that I realized that the whole audience hall had gone silent. Everyone was staring at us, including Udai, who had a slight smile barely visible behind his bushy beard. I kept my head down and my dupatta wrapped tightly around me to hide my face from my cousin. I didn't think he would be able to guess my identity, but I wasn't going to take any chances.

"Would you like a bit of advice, Lord Rashid? From one young prince to another?" Arjun asked.

Rashid bristled at the reference to his youth, but he gave a sharp nod. At that, Arjun said, "If you want to be Humayun's heir, you have to take things slowly and earn his trust gradually. He doesn't like flashy young princes who overplay their hand."

Karim chortled at that and pounded his thigh. He knew the source of those words, and he must have found it doubly funny that my cousin was being undermined by his own prince. As for Rashid himself, his face turned the color of chili powder. He was silent for so long that I felt a little sympathy for him. I knew what it was like to be humiliated in this palace. Of course, he deserved it far more than I had.

Udai's grin was too big even for his monstrous beard to hide now, and he said, "Well, boy, I trust you've learned your lesson not to lie in my court? My agents are very well informed."

Rashid swallowed hard, and I wondered then if he would resort to bluff and bluster and threats, as most young men might have in his place, or if he would try to negotiate in a more sensible fashion. His brother would have favored the former, but I didn't want to believe that Rashid had become so much like him in just five years. I hoped he chose the latter course.

"The subahdar of Zindh, Javed Khorasani, has my uncle's full support," Rashid said. "Your attacks against our interests must be met with force. If you do not surrender the fort of Rohiri, we will take it. Our zahhaks are more than sufficient to ensure our superiority in the air, and our cavalry on the ground will ride roughshod over your men."

It wasn't quite bluster, but it wasn't far from it. I felt a little sorry for him. If only he'd spent four years as a courtesan, he might have come to understand how to get what he wanted from powerful men. Demanding outright surrender, forcing a man to choose between his reputation and his life, was rarely a sensible choice. Men much preferred their reputations to their lives, in my experience.

As if to prove it, Udai said, "I would welcome a chance to meet Javed Khorasani in the skies once more."

"As would I!" Karim declared. "The people of Mahisagar will not so easily forget the aid that was rendered to us by the illustrious maharaja of Bikampur, and we will rally to his cause!"

"It's a well-known fact that thunder zahhaks are the indisputable masters of the skies," said Rashid. "You would be flying to your deaths."

It wasn't a wholly toothless threat. Eight thunder zahhaks could beat any other eight zahhaks in the world in an aerial duel.

But risking every animal in Zindh on a meaningless battle over a matter of pride was nothing short of idiotic. Battles left too much to chance.

I almost pitied my cousin. He was two years my elder, but still hardly of an age or disposition to serve as an ambassador. I wondered why my father had sent him. He was making a mess of things. He didn't understand that sometimes reasoned conversation made a man seem far more intimidating than demands and threats and promises of victory in battles not yet fought. And anyway, he was overlooking something that would end these negotiations once and for all.

I leaned over to Arjun and whispered in his ear, "The khan of Khuzdar, Mir Nasir."

"You're heartless, you know that?" He kissed me on the forehead, drawing murmurs from the courtiers and the full attention of my cousin, Karim, and the maharaja. Arjun noticed that all eyes were on us, and he said, "Forgive me, Lord Rashid, my concubine was just reminding me that it's been a very long time since I've paid a visit to our old friend Mir Nasir, the khan of Khuzdar."

Rashid's jaw dropped, and after a moment of stunned silence, he growled, "Does your concubine always play the role of your chief strategist?"

"For the most part," Arjun admitted, not lending the insult any weight by simply not acknowledging it for what it was. "She's quite clever."

"The girl is right," Udai said, puffing out his chest and sitting up a little straighter. "It has been quite some time since I have sent an embassy to my dear friend Mir Nasir. I daresay he'll be interested to know how focused Javed Khorasani is on the fort of Rohiri. After all, it would be a terrible shame if the subahdar were to lose control of Shikarpur. Think of the embarrassment it would bring to him in the eyes of the sultan."

"And anyone associated with him," Arjun added, offering Rashid a wicked grin.

"I've had enough of these insults," Rashid growled. "If you think you can flaunt the will of the sultan of Nizam, you are very much mistaken." He stood up and stormed out of the pavilion to laughter from some of the courtiers—though not from Arjun and Udai.

The older man turned to his son and said, "Make sure he doesn't cause any trouble with that thunder zahhak of his."

"Don't worry, your majesty," I said, "Sultana won't hurt anything while I'm here."

"Well, see to it, then," he ordered.

I nodded and stood up alongside Arjun to go chase down my cousin. Karim got to his feet too and rushed over to us. He asked me, "Did you just say that your cousin's zahhak was your old mount?"

"That's right, your highness," I replied, remembering that he liked to be addressed that way. Much as I was tempted to disrespect him while Arjun stood close by to defend me, I knew better. The time would come when I would find myself alone with him, and then he would make me regret it. It was always better to be polite and deferential to those who might one day have power over you—a lesson my cousin would have done well to learn.

"It must be hard for you, seeing her ridden by an imbecile like your cousin," he observed.

"It is, your highness." I forced a smile to keep from grimacing. I was going to have to watch Sultana fly off with Rashid. Just the thought of it made a lump form in my throat. My mind fought to come up with some scheme that would let me keep her, but I knew better. It would be war if I took her back—and not just with Javed Khorasani, but likely with my father and his army. He couldn't let a theft like that stand, not if he wanted anyone to respect him.

No, I had lost Sultana four years ago when I had run away, and there was nothing I could do to change it.

We caught up to my cousin in the courtyard where the zahhaks were kept. He was standing there, fuming, waiting for one of the stableboys to bring Sultana around for him. He saw us coming and crossed his arms over his chest, but said nothing. He must have known that we were there to keep him from devastating the city with his zahhak in his rage. Even the stableboys knew it, and they rushed to get Padmini and Karim's mount, Amira. Though, if you asked me, the fire and acid zahhaks didn't stand much chance against Sultana, not if she got into the air first. She was too swift and too agile, and her lightning bolts could strike down an enemy zahhak at tremendous range. She wasn't quite so effective in laying waste to cities or to ships, but when it came to fighting other zahhaks, there was no animal to match her.

Rashid must have been thinking the same thing, because he said, "Are you sure you boys want to risk getting into the air with me?"

"Any day," Karim replied, squaring up to him, showing off his height to best effect. My cousin was a little shorter, but he was broader through the shoulders and more heavily muscled these days. Still, Karim was older, and he had a tiger's grace about him, a kind of liquid strength that oozed from his pores. He had always struck me as dangerous as a child, and I knew the years had only made him stronger and more skilled. If it came to a fight, much as I despised him, my money was on Karim.

Rashid chose to ignore Karim, instead turning his attention to me and grumbling, "What sort of man parades his concubines around in public?"

"Razia?" Karim asked, and his grin sent cold dread right into the pit of my stomach. Was he going to tell my cousin who I was? It would mean the death of me. Instead, he slapped Rashid on the shoulder before the younger man could react and said, "Don't mind her, she's a hijra."

Rashid's eyes widened. "That's a hijra? God, she must have been cut young."

"Thirteen, wasn't it, dear?" Karim asked me, an insufferable grin plastered across his face. He was enjoying taunting my cousin with the details of my life, knowing I was powerless to stop him.

"Yes, your highness."

"Did it hurt?" Rashid asked.

"It was a relief, my lord," I said, not seeing any point in lying about that. "Whatever discomfort I felt was nothing compared to the tortures I would have suffered had it remained."

He shook his head in disbelief at that response and asked Arjun, "You share a bed with that thing?"

"As often as I can," Arjun said. He put his arm around my waist and pulled me close to him. "She's very talented in all sorts of unexpected ways."

Rashid gave a snort of derision and turned back toward the stables. Sultana was being led by the reins by a stable lad, but Rashid was impatient. He stepped out into the open, gestured to the spot at his feet, and said, "Here, girl!"

Sultana leapt forward, and the stableboy was smart enough to let go of the reins before she dragged him across the courtyard's paving stones. She sprinted toward us, eager to get into the air once more, but she ran straight past Rashid and stopped in front of me instead, raising her snout to sniff at my face, to make sure it was me behind the thin silk fabric of my dupatta.

"Sultana!" Rashid exclaimed, his irritation growing at being made a fool of by his own zahhak. "Here!"

She ignored him completely, instead pressing her snout under my hand, lifting it up so that it fell on top of her head. She liked it when I stroked her scales there. I'd nearly forgotten. But she hadn't, and that made my heart ache. I stroked her scales and whispered, "You have to go to him, girl. You don't belong to me anymore."

"Sultana?" Rashid sounded more concerned than angry. "What in God's name do you think you're doing? Get over here!"

She didn't even glance in his direction. She just pressed herself up against me, twisting her body until she'd boxed out Karim and Arjun both, and she had me standing right beside her saddle so that I could mount with ease. She wanted me to take her for a flight more than anything, but I couldn't risk that, not without giving myself away. My fear for my own safety was clashing with my desire to have her back, and it wasn't clear which meant more to me just then.

"Sultana," I whispered, my voice thick with emotion. "Please go back to Rashid, or you'll get us both in trouble."

She glanced up at me, making it plain that she'd heard me, but she didn't budge. She just stared up at me with those big green eyes, and my heart melted. I wrapped my arms around her neck and stroked her sapphire scales. "I know you don't want to go, sweetheart, but you have to."

"What is the meaning of this?" Rashid demanded, storming over to us, his eyes flashing with fury. "What have you done to my zahhak? Is this some kind of trick?" He reached out to grab me, and there was a roar and a flash of movement, and a scream.

The next thing I knew, Rashid was lying on his back, Sultana's wing claw pinning his chest down, her jaws poised directly above his neck. She was small by the standards of other zahhak species, but she was still big enough to cut a man clean in half with one bite. Her eyes were flickering back to me, looking for orders, waiting for me to tell her to just eat him and get it over with. That was probably the smarter move. If I gave commands to Sultana, he'd figure out my secret eventually, however dumb he'd become over the last five years since we'd seen each other, but I couldn't let her kill him. It would mean war, and it was a war Bikampur couldn't win.

"Stop that!" I shouted. "Let him go!"

Sultana held on to him for a moment, making it clear that she was thinking of eating him just to make a point that men weren't to touch me. It was a point she'd made many times back home in the palace when my father's men, or my cousins, had taken it upon themselves to "cure" me of my femininity. But that was different. She'd been my zhahak then, and I'd been a prince—unassailable by lesser beings. Now I was just a courtesan, and if she killed Rashid, my father would bring a storm down on this place the likes of which had never been seen before.

But then she did release him. She turned back to me and pressed her snout into my hands so that I could give her the reward of my affection as I always had when she'd saved me back home in Nizam, but this time I pulled my hands back. "Absolutely not, you naughty thing! You think I'm going to reward you for menacing him like that?"

She hung her head, looking absolutely devastated that I could think to critique her behavior, and it melted my heart so fast that I wrapped my arms around her neck and said, "Oh, it's all right, darling. I know you were just trying to protect me like you always did." I kissed her on the tip of her snout. "You're a good girl. I've missed you very much."

"Salim?" Rashid gasped. He picked himself up from the cobblestones cautiously, staring at my face, trying to find some trace of my old self in it. "Those eyes . . . I should have seen them before . . ."

My heart sank. Suddenly, letting Sultana kill him seemed like the preferable alternative to whatever fate would befall me once my father found out. I stroked Sultana's scales anxiously, fighting back tears. When I found my voice, I could just barely squeak out, "Please don't tell anyone, Rashid."

He looked confused for all of a single second before the implications dawned on him one after another. I was the heir to the throne, but I'd had my genitals removed and I was a hijra and I was living as a courtesan in Bikampur, as the concubine to Prince Arjun no less. And my father would pay very well to anyone who could tell him my whereabouts. And once he found out where I was, he would stop at nothing to punish me for the insult I had offered my family. To say nothing of the fact that my continued existence endangered the succession, which meant any number of claimants might want me dead.

"He'll kill me," I said, hoping that my cousin still had enough fond memories of me not to wish that on me.

"It's what traitors deserve," he snapped, with more venom in his voice than I was expecting. It was angry enough that it elicited a low growl from Sultana and a baring of her teeth in his direction.

"Traitors?" I asked, wondering what on earth he meant by that. I was many things, but I'd never betrayed my father, not really. I'd just followed my heart.

"You helped humiliate me in front of the maharaja!" he declared.

"Don't flatter her, boy, you were doing that well enough on your own," said Karim, which I supposed was the very nicest thing he'd ever done for me.

Rashid gritted his teeth at that insult and jabbed his finger in Karim's direction. "Careful. If I tell my uncle who she is, she's as good as dead. Or my father, for that matter. Even my brother, Tariq, is rich and powerful now, Salim. Your father gave him the province of Lahanur. He could have his pick of assassins."

"Two very good reasons not to let you leave this place with your life," said Arjun, and he drew his khanda then.

"Wait, my prince." I grabbed his arm to stop him from setting upon Rashid then and there. The boy was scrambling to draw his katars, even as Karim's firangi whisked from its scabbard. "He's my cousin!"

"So?" Karim shrugged. "I've killed one of my cousins. It was quite enjoyable actually. He'd always been a miserable bastard to me growing up."

"Well, when I was growing up, Rashid was kind to me," I said.

"And this is how you repay me," he snapped. "By trying to humiliate me in front of your new masters. And don't think I didn't hear about how you helped strategize the destruction of the Firangi fleet. We have our agents still."

I didn't quite know what to say to all that. It was true, I had worked for my new masters against my old homeland. I wanted to believe that it wasn't my fault, but that didn't change the fact that I'd hurt Nizam to help the likes of Prince Karim of Mahisagar. But I'd only done it to survive—not that I thought I could ever make Rashid understand that fact.

"You deny it, then?" he asked.

I sighed. "You don't understand what it's like to be a woman."

"You're not a woman; you're a freak! Tariq was right about you all along."

The words hurt more than I wanted to admit. Mostly because they shattered whatever good memories I'd had of my cousin, which had been among the only happy memories of my childhood. I sighed. "Please stop threatening me, Rashid. If you keep it up, Arjun is going to kill you, and I don't want your blood on my hands. I was trying to stop you from getting into a war you were going to lose!"

"Yes, and I'm sure you let him fuck you for my benefit too," Rashid replied.

"We should just kill him and take his zahhak," said Karim.

"We'll let Razia ride her. I'll summon my father, and we'll attack Javed Khorasani while we've got him outnumbered."

"He's a member of the royal family," I said, holding up my hands for calm. "If you kill him, my father really will bring a dozen zahhaks down on our heads—and maybe more than that."

"If we let him go, he'll tell your father, and then we'll be facing his armies anyway," said Arjun, his hands squeezing the grips of his katars until his knuckles turned white.

"So we make him swear an oath not to tell," I suggested.

Karim gave a snort of laughter at that. "You've lived four years as a whore and you still trust men to keep their oaths?"

*Arjun has kept all of his.* I didn't say it, but I thought it.

"I trust my cousin to spare my life in return for sparing his," I said, looking Rashid in the eyes as I said it, wondering if I really did trust him to do that. Once he was gone, he would have all the motivation in the world to betray me. "Please put the weapons down, my princes. I don't want his blood on my hands."

"Not until he swears his oath," Arjun replied.

We all looked to Rashid then, to see what he would do. He was holding his own katars in his hands, but I could tell from the grimace on his face that he knew he didn't stand much chance against Arjun and Karim together, and personally I didn't think he'd have done much better against either of them solo. After a moment's consideration, he said, "Fine. I give you my word that I won't tell Uncle that I found you, Salim—or my father or brother, for that matter."

I breathed a huge sigh of relief on hearing that. "Thank you, Rashid. I'm sorry if I hurt you today. I hope you'll find it in your heart to forgive me. I'll always remember our time together as children fondly."

"God, you really are a woman, aren't you?" He rolled his eyes and sheathed his katars. And then he looked to Sultana and said,

"Give me back my zahhak. If you're so desperate to be a lady of the court, you have no need of her."

Trusting Rashid's word had been hard, but it was nothing compared to giving up Sultana for the second time. I cradled her head in my arms and pressed my forehead against hers for a long moment. Tears were spilling down my cheeks when I finally gestured to Rashid and said, "Go. Go obey him."

She knew what I was asking of her, and she didn't look pleased about it, but after a moment, she turned to Rashid and walked toward him. He wasted no time in taking up her reins and climbing into the saddle. He gave them a flick and cried, "Up!" She turned and looked at me one last time, and then she leapt into the sky and beat her wings, and I watched her soar as if through a rainstorm from all the tears that were pouring from my eyes.

# CHAPTER 16

You should have let me kill him," Karim growled, shoving his firangi back into its scabbard with a heavy sigh. He was still looking to the north, the direction in which Rashid had fled on Sultana's back.

"He's my cousin . . ." I said, knowing that Karim would never understand that. He didn't know what it had been like for me at the palace. Everyone had despised me. They'd all made that so plain. I'd suffered beatings at the hands of all my relatives—aunts, uncles, cousins, parents. Rashid was the only person in that palace who hadn't beaten me, hadn't screamed at me, hadn't told me how disgusting I was. And maybe now things were different, but for as long as I lived, I was never going to forget that I had felt safe in his presence, all those years ago.

"Well, he's gone now," said Arjun. He was holding me close to him, hugging me tightly as I cried into the fabric of his kurta. He rubbed my back with strong hands. "You should get some rest,

Razia, and we should get back to my father. He'll want to plan for the war that's coming."

"You'll need me for that," I said, wiping the tears from my eyes with my dupatta.

"You don't have to do that. Not after everything you've been through."

"I want to," I told him, and I really meant it too. If I was going to survive, Arjun had to survive, Bikampur had to survive. That meant beating Javed Khorasani's army. The trouble was, he had as many zahhaks as we did now, and thunder zahhaks had the advantage in aerial duels. If we couldn't find a way to overcome that advantage, we were finished.

"Well, then I suppose we'd better get moving." Arjun was grimacing. He knew what was coming, and he knew as well as I did that we didn't stand a chance. Eight thunder zahhaks would clear the skies over the battlefield in a heartbeat, and then our troops would be helpless—not that it would matter. He and his father would die first, along with their closest retainers. No, facing Javed Khorasani in an open battle was no kind of strategy.

The men were all murmuring to one another in the throne room. Lord Udai was staring into the distance, his beard twitching as he went through the likely scenarios. For all the talk of getting help from Mir Nasir, there was no guarantee that he would agree to join us. Even if he did, he only had fire zahhaks to add to the battle, and I didn't think those would make much difference, not against thunder zahhaks. The grimace on Udai's face told me that he was coming to the same conclusion.

Arjun took his seat, and I sat on the cushion beside him, keeping my arms wrapped around one of his, both to reassure him and to reassure myself. My stomach was tying itself in knots. I'd let my cousin go. If he told my father where I was, then I was as good as dead. It was as simple as that. But even if he didn't tell my father, he would be coming for us with everything he had, and Javed Khorasani would be eager to fight alongside him. They would launch their attack soon, before the Mahisagari army could reach us. It would be a matter of days, a week at the most. How were we going to get the Mahisagari army here in time to help?

"The boy left?" Udai asked.

"He did, Father," Arjun said. He hesitated for a second, and then sighed. "He found out who Razia was. He swore he wouldn't mention it to Sultan Humayun, but . . ."

I was surprised when the maharaja just shrugged. Normally, he took every opportunity to put me down, to remind me what a burden I was, to tell me how worthless I was. This time, all he said was, "Well, if Sultan Humayun comes for her, we'll deal with it when the time comes. Until then, Javed Khorasani's army is the bigger concern."

"I'll inform my father of the danger, your majesty," Karim promised. "We'll gather our forces and march to Rohiri with all speed."

"It won't be fast enough . . ." I murmured.

Karim didn't deny that. He just spread his hands and said, "We'll fight alongside you, your majesty, but the girl is right. If Javed Khorasani chooses to attack swiftly, we may not be able to get there in time to help."

"Khorasani's army doesn't worry me," said Udai. "It's the zahhaks that concern me. We've faced thunder zahhaks before, and it wasn't pretty the last time. We downed two for the loss of five, and still haven't recovered our full strength. And he only had six then. Now he has eight." He glanced to me. "I don't suppose you know how to beat thunder zahhaks in the open air, girl?"

I shook my head and made a careful study of the marble floor. "No, your majesty."

"Anyone?" he asked, looking around to the rest of his courtiers. There was nothing but uncomfortable silence.

"Acid zahhaks can tangle with them," said Karim. "Their lightning is better suited for aerial combat, but we're almost as fast and agile as they are. If we have the altitude advantage, we could make a real fight of it."

"But there are eight of them and just four of you," Arjun reminded him. "And I fought against Javed Khorasani's thunder zahhaks last time. Padmini is fast and agile for a fire zahhak, but every moment was a desperate struggle. I was lucky to down the two I did. If they'd been flown by competent fliers, I wouldn't be here today."

"Girl." Udai nodded to me.

"Your majesty?" I asked.

"How soon before Javed Khorasani attacks?" he asked.

That was the real question. How much time did we have to prepare? It wouldn't take Rashid long to inform Javed Khorasani of the situation. Then, the subahdar would attack. He must have already had his troops in position, or near enough, otherwise he wouldn't have been willing to let Rashid tell us his plans. We knew he wanted Rohiri fortress. Now that we knew, he would strike.

"He'll march tomorrow morning, your majesty," I said. "Setting out from his capital of Shikarpur, it will take him three days to reach Rohiri fortress with his men and his cannons. If we leave in the morning, we'll get there a day ahead of him, not more."

"I don't suppose he'd call it off if we delivered you to him?" Udai asked, nodding to me for emphasis.

My heart skipped a beat. Arjun's arms came around me, holding me tightly. "Father!" he exclaimed. "After all she's done for us, we're not going to abandon her like that!"

"Not that it matters," Karim said. "I may not know Humayun and Javed Khorasani as well as Razia, but I know them well enough.

You deliver her to them, and they'll attack anyway. They'll see it as weakness. The only way to survive this is to fight with everything we've got."

I nodded my agreement and looked up at the maharaja. "Your majesty, if I thought for one second that I could trade my life to keep Arjun safe, I would do it in an instant. But Karim is right, there is no way to avoid this battle."

"Then we make ready," Udai declared. He nodded to Karim. "Go and alert your father, young man. I want all four of your acid zahhaks here by morning."

"I'll see to it, your majesty," Karim promised, and he stood up then.

"I'll see him off," Arjun offered, standing up then too. His father acknowledged him with a nod, but said nothing more than that. He was lost in thought, already playing out the battle in his mind.

I joined Arjun in following Karim out of the throne room. My mind was churning too, and my chest felt tight. We weren't going to win this fight, not by playing Javed Khorasani's game. His zahhaks were too powerful in the air. They were made for killing other zahhaks. They were the reason my father had managed to create such a massive empire. If Arjun went up against them, he was going to die, but I couldn't for the life of me see any alternative.

"No brilliant plan to get us out of this?" In another tone of voice, it would have been a taunt, but Karim's face was deadly serious. I could see the fear in his eyes. He knew as well as I did that if he went up against Javed Khorasani's thunder zahhaks he likely wouldn't come home again.

I shook my head. "No. I'm sorry, your highness."

"Me too," he muttered.

"We'll be all right, Razia." Arjun was trying to sound reassuring, but there was no confidence in his voice. One glance at his face told me that he was as worried as I was. I could feel it too in the tension of his hand against the small of my back.

We were walking through the courtyard, toward the zahhak pens, like a group of condemned criminals on the way to the gallows, when I heard a girl scream. It was coming from the zahhak pens. I exchanged a horrified glance with Arjun, and then we both took off running. Zahhaks could never be truly tamed by any but their true masters. Even the stableboys had to spend months working with the zahhaks before they gave off trying to eat them. If one of the harem girls got in the zahhak pens . . .

I heard growling and thrashing and the desperate screams of a terrified child, and I ran headlong into the stables, knowing that without a weapon I had no chance at all of fending off an angry zahhak. Even with a weapon, it was suicidal, but I wasn't going to let some child die.

I took one look in the stables and screamed. "Lakshmi!"

She was lying on the ground, curled up in a ball, Padmini standing over her, her neck low, the scales behind her head, which normally lay flat, splayed out in a display of supreme aggression, but she wasn't attacking Lakshmi, she was protecting her. A second fire zahhak, Udai's brightly colored animal, was cowering in the face of Padmini's wrath. Padmini was clearly the stronger, more aggressive beast, and she let her smaller cousin know it. With a bull rush, she hit the other zahhak with her snout, physically shoving her back into her pen.

I ignored the zahhaks and ran straight for Lakshmi. I threw myself down beside her, looking her over for any injuries. She still had all her limbs. Her face was okay. There was no blood. No burn marks. She didn't look hurt. She was crying, and clinging to me like a baby, but there wasn't a scratch on her.

"It's okay, sweetheart, I'm here," I whispered into her ear, rocking her back and forth gently. "It's okay. Nothing is going to hurt you. Arjun is here, and Padmini won't let anything hurt you."

"Is she all right?"

I was shocked that it was Karim doing the asking, but his firangi was out in his hand, and he had come to stand between me and the other zahhaks. I noticed then that Amira was out of her pen, standing beside him protectively, her tail of iridescent feathers swishing behind her in her eagerness to fight.

"She's fine," I said, and then I added something I didn't think I would ever say to him. "Thank you, your highness."

He smirked at that and shoved his firangi back in its scabbard. To Amira, he said, "Ready for a flight, girl?"

I glanced then to Arjun, who was calming Padmini down, putting her back in her pen. He'd already dealt with his father's mount, returning the brightly colored zahhak to her place. When he was finished, he turned to me and growled, "What are you doing here?"

It took me a second to realize he meant Lakshmi. She knew right away, and she squeezed me tightly and buried her face in my dupatta, still shaking with fear. I narrowed my eyes at Arjun and said, "She's frightened enough as it is, don't scare her more."

Arjun had caught the tone in my voice, and his face betrayed his irritation at being spoken to that way. I was about to apologize, but he held up a hand to stop me from talking. "It's all right, Razia, I know she's your little sister." He took a deep breath to calm himself down, then asked Lakshmi in a much softer voice, "What happened?"

"I wanted to see the zahhaks," Lakshmi whimpered. "I'm so sorry, Akka, I know I shouldn't have come here, but I missed my Mohini so much that I just wanted to see them and pet them."

"And that one attacked you?" I asked, nodding to the brightly colored one.

She nodded. "It jumped out of its pen. It tried to bite me, but then Padmini saved me." She looked at Arjun's mount with wonder and longing and gratitude. "She jumped in front of the other zahhak and drove it back. That was when you got here."

"You're a very lucky girl," Arjun informed her, kneeling beside her. "Padmini likes you very much. That's why she protected you." He looked to me and said, "It's a good thing she's the dominant one in the stables, otherwise . . ."

He didn't have to tell me what would have happened otherwise. If Padmini hadn't been dominant, she'd never have risked challenging the other zahhak on Lakshmi's behalf, and my little sister would be in bloody pieces in that zahhak's stomach by now. I squeezed her tightly to me as belated fear overwhelmed me. I hadn't been scared just a second before, I'd been too concerned with saving her, but suddenly my eyes were filling with tears and my body was shaking. I'd come so close to losing her. If not for Padmini . . .

"She's okay, Razia," Arjun told me, rubbing my back in gentle circles.

I nodded to show that I understood, but it didn't keep the tears from pouring down my cheeks. I kissed Lakshmi on the top of her head and rocked her gently back and forth, more for my benefit than for hers. I'd raised her ever since she'd come to us. I'd taken care of her. I'd protected her. I'd never have forgiven myself if anything had happened to her.

"I'm sorry, Akka," Lakshmi said. "Please don't cry. I won't do it again, I promise."

"You are never to go in the stables without Arjun, do you understand me?" I demanded.

"Yes, Akka," she agreed, hanging her head. "I'm sorry."

"You're lucky I don't box your ears like Ammi would have," I muttered.

"I'm sorry," she said again.

I took a deep breath and wiped the tears from my face, and then stood up and walked over to Padmini's pen. The big zahhak was watching all of this with interest. As I approached, she leaned her snout closer, and I gave it a vigorous rub. "You're a very good girl," I told her through tears. "We're going to give you so many treats tonight for being such a good girl."

I felt Arjun's hand on my shoulder. "Come on, let's see Karim off and get Lakshmi back to the harem before my father's zahhak decides to test Padmini's dominance again."

"She's the dominant one in the stables, so all the other zahhaks submit to her . . ." I murmured, like it was some great discovery.

Arjun gave me a funny look. "You didn't have any dominant zahhaks in your stables back in Nizam?"

"We did," I said. Then I turned around and threw my arms around his neck and kissed him right on the lips. He seemed taken aback, but I kissed him again, and a third time for good measure, grinning to beat all. I couldn't help myself. It was like a crushing weight had been lifted off my chest. I could breathe again. The whole world seemed brighter.

He brushed the hair back from my face, looking concerned. "Razia? What's gotten into you?"

"I know how to beat Javed Khorasani," I said, and I looked then to Karim, who was still standing beside Amira. "You're not going anywhere, your highness, not tonight. We have work to do."

"All right," he said, returning Amira to her pen. When he'd finished, he asked, "What's this plan of yours, girl?"

"You'll see." I took Lakshmi by the hand and led her out of the stables, back toward the throne room, with Arjun and Karim following close behind me. I knew Arjun wanted to ask me what I was planning, but he would find out soon enough.

When we arrived in the throne room, Udai was still sitting on his throne, mulling over his options. He glanced up at me, at my tear-streaked face, at Lakshmi with her mussed-up sari and the tracks of tears on her own cheeks, and he growled, "I haven't got time for this. Arjun, whatever problem your concubine and her maid have, it belongs in the harem, not here."

"Forgive me, your majesty, but there is no problem, only a solution," I said.

He narrowed his eyes. "This is not the time to speak in riddles, girl. If you have something to say, say it, otherwise leave me in peace. I have a battle to plan."

"I know how to beat Javed Khorasani, your majesty," I replied.

His eyes widened a little, and he gestured to the cushion where I typically sat. "Well, go on, then, girl, don't leave me in suspense."

I sat down, with Lakshmi in my lap and Arjun beside me, his arm draped around my shoulders. "Lakshmi was nearly killed in the stables, your majesty. She wanted to pet the zahhaks, and your mount tried to eat her."

Udai had the good grace to look sorry for it, but he said, "This is why little girls are not permitted in the stables. Zahhaks are dangerous animals. I would think as a former prince, she would have known that."

"You're right, your majesty, but that's not what I came here to talk to you about. You see, Padmini had taken a liking to her, and as the dominant zahhak in the stables, she protected Lakshmi from harm."

He frowned. "Are you nearing a point, girl?"

"The point, your majesty, is that zahhaks will submit to the dominant female. If you control the dominant female, you control the stables." I let that sink in for a second before adding, "And in the stables of Nizam, my Sultana was the dominant female."

He looked intrigued then. "But how does that help us defeat Javed Khorasani?"

"If we could infiltrate the stables in Shikarpur, I could use Sultana to dominate the other zahhaks, and then we could steal them and fly them back here."

"Infiltrate the stables in Shikarpur?" Karim gave a derisive snort. "That's your plan? How do you expect us to do something like that?"

"With fire zahhaks," I said. "If we flew all four of them to Shikarpur tonight, each one carrying two riders, then four of us could infiltrate the stables while the other four flew the fire zahhaks back here. We could snatch four thunder zahhaks and fly them home, leaving Javed Khorasani badly outnumbered, and giving us the strength to oppose him in the open air."

"That could work, Father," Arjun said, his voice betraying his excitement. "Fire zahhaks can see in the night like it's day. They could get us over the walls of Shikarpur's fortress without anyone spotting us. Then we'd just have to get inside the stables and get out before the guards caught us. And we'd have zahhaks to fight back if they did try anything."

"And if we're spotted?" Karim asked.

"Then we set the whole place on fire," I replied, feeling a stab of pain in my heart as I said it. "Starting with the stables. But I think we have a real chance of stealing the thunder zahhaks right out from under Javed Khorasani's nose, your majesty. Sultana will protect me, and she was the dominant zahhak in Nizam. She'll be able to keep the others in line."

"Even if that's true, we haven't got eight zahhak riders. Counting Karim, we have six, including you. If I ask Govind Singh to dust off his old goggles for one last flight, that's seven," Udai said.

"Eight," I corrected, giving Lakshmi a gentle pat on the head. "She's young, but she's well trained. She was the prince of Kolikota before she came here."

"You want me to trust that little girl to steal a thunder zahhak from under Javed Khorasani's nose?" Udai scoffed.

"She can do it. And we haven't got a lot of choice. We haven't got any other trained fliers, and it's going to take a trained flier to get a thunder zahhak back to Bikampur when it's never been ridden by that person before."

I had him there. Trained zahhak riders didn't grow on trees. It was too expensive for any but the highest nobility to engage in. If he didn't let Lakshmi fly, then we'd only be able to bring three zahhaks back, and I could tell that he wanted all four. He saw the advantage in capturing a full flight of them.

"All right, girl. We'll do it." Udai looked to Karim. "You up for it, boy?"

"Wouldn't miss it for the world, your majesty," Karim replied.

"There's one other thing," I said, knowing that I was probably going to be invoking the maharaja's wrath, but not really caring.

"What's that?" he asked me.

"I get to keep Sultana, and Lakshmi gets to keep the zahhak she brings back, and you will permit me to train her as a zahhak rider."

I was surprised that Udai's reaction was just to grin at me. He chuckled. "You're more ambitious than I gave you credit for, girl."

"Do we have an agreement, your majesty?" I asked.

"We do," he replied. "You bring me four thunder zahhaks, and you and your little sister will get your wings back. You have my word."

I bowed to him then, smiling so much that my face hurt. I was going to get Sultana back. I was going to fly through the air again, whenever it pleased me. I was going to be a zahhak rider again. It was all I'd ever wanted in the whole world, and all I had to do was what my ammi had trained me to do for years—steal.

CHAPTER 17

She's eleven years old!" Sakshi hissed into my ear with such force that it made my head twitch.

"I know how old she is," I whispered back as I took my katars from their sandalwood box and thrust them through my black silk sash. "She's also been training to be a warrior since she was old enough to walk."

"A warrior? Are you listening to yourself?" My older sister took me by the shoulders and twisted me so I would be staring right at Lakshmi, who was trying to tie her own black sash around her waist in perfect imitation of mine. She kept messing it up and starting over, trying to get the knot just right. That, more than anything, squeezed at my heart.

"Come here, let me help," I offered, flashing her a smile that hid all the fear and anxiety I was feeling. Sakshi was right, a girl Lakshmi's age had no business flying into the middle of an enemy fortress in the dead of night, but the trouble was, we didn't have much choice. We had to get those zahhaks, or we were all going to die—Lakshmi included.

Lakshmi came to me, and I knelt down and tied her sash for her, and then ruffled her hair, which made her twist away in irritation and squeal "Akka!" as I'd known it would. She immediately went back to the mirror and fussed with it until she'd tamed down the loose strands once more. I watched with a dagger in my heart.

"You can't take her with you." Sakshi's words might have been plucked from my own mind. How could I do this to her? How could I risk her life like this?

"We don't have a choice. We don't have enough zahhak riders as it is. Without her, we won't be able to do enough damage to make Javed Khorasani call off his attack. And anyway"—I turned then and looked Sakshi right in the eyes, certain that she could see the blazing determination in my own—"I'm not going to let anyone hurt a hair on her head."

"I may have been raised in a village, but I'm not stupid, Razia!" Sakshi snapped, and I was shocked by her vehemence. She'd always been the gentle one in the dera, always been the older sister who had cared for me. I'd never seen her angry before, not like this.

"Who said you were stupid?" I asked, my veneer of confidence broken.

She grabbed me by the arm and yanked me into the apartment's adjoining room. She shut the door, locked it, and rounded on me once more. "I don't know anything about zahhaks, but I know that one zahhak among a dozen makes no difference. If you steal three instead of four, you'll still have Javed Khorasani outnumbered. You don't have to take Lakshmi with you!"

"You're right. I don't," I agreed.

"So don't, then." She put her hands on my shoulders, gently this time. "Razia, she's like a daughter to me, and to you too—

how could you put her in so much danger like this? If Ammi had tried to make her steal a zahhak, you'd have died before you let it happen. I know she's the reason you kept agreeing to steal all those things for Ammi, so that you could spare Lakshmi from it."

"And that's what I'm doing tonight—I'm sparing her."

"Sparing her from what?" Sakshi demanded. "A long life?"

"The life that we've had to live!" I growled. "Why do you think I brought her here to the palace to begin with? I brought her so she wouldn't have to sell her body to any man who came along, so she wouldn't have to roam the streets at night stealing, so that she wouldn't have anybody controlling her the way Ammi controlled me. But she's not safe yet. We're not safe yet. Right now, the only thing keeping us off the streets is Arjun's love for me. The only thing protecting Lakshmi is my place in this palace. If I lose Arjun, we'll lose everything, and so will she. But if she has a zahhak, she will be in command of her own destiny. She will never want for anything again so long as she lives. She will have a power and a freedom that people like us have never had."

"Or she'll die," Sakshi replied, and the tears started spilling down her cheeks then, long rivers of them.

I wrapped my arms around her, pulling her head down to my shoulder. "I'm not going to let anything happen to her. I'll die first."

"That's the problem!" She pushed me away. "I don't want you going either! If you die, what are we going to do? Where will we go? Ammi will kill Lakshmi and me for running off with you if she ever catches us. And Arjun is a very kind man, but he has no interest in us. If you die, we lose everything. We'll be thrown out on the streets, and then Ammi will find us and kill us!"

"We'll lose everything if I don't go. This isn't a battle that the maharaja can win, not against eight thunder zahhaks. And if he's defeated, then my cousin will march into this city at the head of an army—and what do you think he will do to us when he gets his hands on us?"

She nodded a few times, wiping her tears on the sheer fabric of her dupatta. "I know that you have to go. I've made my peace with that. But why Lakshmi? If you have a zahhak, you can protect her. She doesn't have to go."

"She does. She needs to have a zahhak of her own. She deserves to have her life back, the life that was stolen from her by everyone because she wanted to be a girl. I'm going to give it back to her tonight."

"Akka is right. I have to go!"

We spun around and saw that Lakshmi had entered the room. Sakshi gasped. "How did you get in here?"

Lakshmi held up a lockpick and flashed me a mischievous grin. "Ammi was teaching me. She thought Razia would leave us, and she wanted me to take over stealing things."

Cold fury welled up within me at the sight of those lockpicks in her little hands. When I got my Sultana back, Ammi and I were going to have words. She'd sworn that so long as I did what I was told, she wasn't going to force Lakshmi into the same life. But after a moment of fury, I realized that it was a convenient set of skills to have, particularly on a night like tonight.

Lakshmi looked to Sakshi. "I want to go with Razia, Akka. I want to have a zahhak again. I can do it. I know I'm not as old as you are, but I'm a good zahhak flier, you can ask Arjun. He says so."

"You're a very good flier, dear," I replied, holding her close to me and kissing her on the top of her head. "But tonight, you're going to have to obey me in everything, all right?"

"I will, Akka," she promised.

"And you're going to have to stay away from the fighting. I know you were trained like I was, but you're still small."

"I'm not so much smaller than you," she retorted, and it was only after she'd said it that I realized she was right. She was grow-ing like a weed, and while she was still a slender little thing, with-out a woman's figure, the top of her head reached my chin now.

"You're right," I agreed. "You're getting to be grown up now. We'll have to find you something to fight with."

"I might be able to assist with that."

I spun around again, annoyed at having been surprised a sec-ond time in as many minutes, and saw Arjun standing in the door-way to my chambers. "My prince! How long have you been here?"

"Well, I could hear you two shouting at each other halfway across the palace," he replied, nodding to Sakshi and then to me. "But I was too frightened to interrupt you."

"Too frightened?" I asked, with a roll of my eyes.

He sidled up to me and put his hands on my upper arms, his palms hot through the thin silk fabric of my kameez. "If there's one thing you learn growing up in the palace harem, it's to never get between a mother and her child. I'm surprised you didn't learn that in Nizam."

"What makes you think I didn't?" I asked, throwing my arms around his neck and pulling his face down a little closer to mine.

"I'll keep her safe," Arjun whispered, his breath tickling my nose. "I promise. No matter what happens, I'll keep her safe. And you too." He hugged me tightly to his chest as if to seal his promise.

As he held me in his arms, I felt the tension melt away. What-ever happened, he wasn't going to let my sisters die in a gutter. He wasn't going to throw them out of the palace. So long as he lived, I knew he would protect them, but then a terrible thought crossed my mind—what if I lost him? What if he was the one who didn't make it home? I didn't think I could bear that, and just the thought of it made me press my face into the fabric of his kurta, taking in deep breaths through my nose, drinking in his scent, knowing that it might be for the very last time.

His thoughts must have been running in the same direction, because he squeezed me so hard that I thought I was going to break. It was only when I let out a little whimper of pain that he realized he was crushing me half to death and let me go. He held me at arm's length then, his cheeks flushing. "Sorry."

"You have nothing to be sorry for, my prince." I placed my hand on his cheek. "We're going to survive this, and Bikampur will survive this. And when we're finished, so will Javed Khorasani be."

He grinned. "I love it when you act like a general."

"Just when I act like a general?" I pretended to pout.

He pressed his forehead up against mine. "Stop it, or I won't be able to think straight when we're in Shikarpur."

"Well, we can't have that," I replied, slipping from his grasp, albeit reluctantly. I turned back to Sakshi and hugged her tightly. "We'll come back to you, sister. I know how much it hurts watching us go, but we'll be home soon."

"I'll be praying for your return," she assured me. And once we were done hugging each other, she enfolded Lakshmi in such a tight embrace that it was a wonder the younger girl's bones didn't break.

"I'll be back soon, Akka, and I'll have a zahhak, and I'll teach you how to ride her," Lakshmi promised.

Now there was an idea. I smiled at the thought of my sisters flying through the skies with me, side by side. I didn't think there was any way I'd be able to convince the maharaja to train a sitar-playing hijra from a farming village to become a zahhak rider, but I made up my mind to try. First things first, though—we had to steal ourselves some zahhaks.

"Come on." I held out my hand, and Lakshmi was quick to take it, smiling with excitement at the prospect of going on a secret mission with her akka. I had to take a deep breath to keep the tears at bay just seeing the way she looked up to me. It was at once the most rewarding feeling in the whole world and the most intimidating. I had a lot to live up to.

"So," Arjun said, draping his arm around my shoulders. "We need to find a weapon for our ferocious Virajendran warrior princess, do we?"

Lakshmi bobbed her head up and down excitedly. "Yes, please!"

"I think I have just the thing," he replied, flashing her a wink that brought color to her cheeks. I couldn't blame her for that, of course; I too was powerless in the face of Arjun's charms.

He led us to a low, squat building in the second courtyard of the palace, not far from the zahhak pens, though I had never visited it before. I realized why a moment later. It was an armory. Spears, swords, and toradars rested on wooden racks, all carefully oiled and polished, ready to be taken out at a moment's notice to defend the palace. Arjun led us past dozens of the heavy flared-tip khandas preferred by the warriors of Registan, past toradars with gold koftgari inlaid on the barrels, until we reached a rack with such strange weapons hanging from its pegs that I scarcely recognized them, though I knew from my father's master-at-arms that these were the weapons preferred by the Virajendrans, our dark-skinned rivals who lived in the jungles of the south.

There were short swords, all beautiful wootz steel, with golden overlays on the first third of the blade, but the blades themselves were curiously bent, rather like the khukuri knives beloved by the Rakhans far to the north. These swords were larger, though, with tips that curved slightly back to aid in the thrust. The swords sat beside rows of strange instruments that looked like chopped-down spears, each with a hook projecting from it. It took me a moment to realize what they were—ankushas—elephant goads repurposed for warfare.

Lakshmi's eyes lit up on seeing the weapons, and I saw in them the same feeling I got whenever I looked at my katars. This was a reminder of her old life, of what it had been like to be someone important, to be a part of a family, a community, a country. All of that had been taken from her, just as it had been taken from me, and I saw the grief of loss flit over her face too, and wished more than anything that I could take it from her. Instead, I put my arm around her as she reached forward and began arming herself.

First, she selected a pair of ferocious-looking daggers, designed in such a way that when they were held a crescent-shaped blade projected from the knuckles, a short blade from the top of the fist, and a long blade from beneath it. However you moved them, they would cut deeply. She tucked the daggers away in her sash and picked up an ankusha next, pairing it with a shield that had a pair of blackbuck horns protruding from it, the tips of the horns replaced with sharpened steel spikes.

To his credit, Arjun didn't ask her if she knew how to use her weapons. He had seen what I had seen: a girl who knew exactly how to hang her elephant goad from her sash, who knew how to place her daggers so they were within easy reach, who handled the shield with the casual ease of someone long accustomed to its presence in her grip. He ruffled her hair and said, "Try to save some Nizamis for us, dear."

Lakshmi flushed with pride and stood a little straighter. I knew from my own experiences in my father's court that it was a rare enough thing for my martial prowess to be recognized. The acclaim had always gone to the boys who had looked the part, the ones who had been taller and stronger—the ones who had looked like men. But as I'd shown Jai on my first day in the palace, looking like a man wasn't everything.

I draped my arm around Lakshmi's shoulders and said, "Come

on, Lakshmi. We have to get to the zahhaks if we're going to get to Shikarpur before dawn."

"Am I flying with you, Akka?" she asked hopefully.

"You'll be flying with my father," Arjun told her.

My heart skipped a beat on hearing that. Udai Agnivansha, carrying my little sister? I shook my head. "No, I'll go with your father, my prince. You take Lakshmi."

It was to Arjun's credit that I didn't have to tell him why I didn't want his father taking her. He just nodded and said to Lakshmi, "Padmini will be excited to see you again."

Lakshmi's smile was so bright on hearing that that it melted my heart. Maybe Sakshi had a point. What was I doing risking her life tonight? And for what? For a zahhak? Was it worth it? The look of joy on her face as we entered the pens gave me that answer. She was like me. She would never be truly happy again unless she was soaring through the air on Mohini's back, and this was the first step toward accomplishing it.

I still wasn't quite sure how I was going to barter a zahhak away from a Virajendran prince, but the idea had been in the back of my mind all along. I would get my Sultana back, Lakshmi would get her Mohini back, and we would return to the skies like I'd always promised her we would on those dark nights in the dera when I'd held her in my lap and told her stories to keep from crying at the memories of some strange man's hands all over my body.

We entered the zahhak pens, and those memories fled my mind, replaced by the here and the now. The maharaja was waiting for us, along with Govind Singh and his son Arvind. Karim was standing beside Ram, the big, burly retainer who followed Udai's orders to the letter. They were all looking at us with undisguised disdain. What were a couple of hijras going to do when the time came to fight in a real battle?

"Are you really the prince of Nizam, girl?" Govind Singh

asked, looking very much amused at the notion that I had been brought to his haveli to dance for his pleasure. I was tired of being on the receiving end of those looks, of that tone.

"The prince of Nizam, and the thief who stole your golden peacock, my lord," I replied, performing a very sardonic bow.

"You what?" he gasped, his face reddening.

"I scaled the walls of your haveli with it strapped to my back. I snatched the bejeweled khanda from under the sleeping nose of Vikram Sharma, and now I am going to steal thunder from Javed Khorasani."

"That's how you were able to get it back?" Govind Singh demanded of Arjun, far more concerned with his stupid peacock than the coming mission. "Your little slut took it to begin with?"

"The peacock was returned to you. The matter is now closed," said Arjun, his voice so imperious then that it resembled his father's more than his own. "And anyway, we should be grateful for Razia's training. Stealing these zahhaks isn't going to be easy, and having a master thief on our side can't hurt."

"If the damnable creature is on our side," Govind grumbled, his eyes still narrowed in my direction, his mustache twitching with irritation.

"Her loyalty is not in doubt." I was shocked to hear those words coming from the maharaja's mouth. It was probably the nicest thing he'd ever said of me. He nodded to me. "You have a plan, girl?"

"Yes, your majesty. I visited Shikarpur twice in my official capacity as heir to the throne of Nizam, and I remember that there is a cliff on the eastern side of the city. Javed Khorasani's palace sits atop it, its easternmost wall forming the easternmost wall of the whole city. That spot is considered to be the strongest point in the city's defenses, so it's usually the least closely watched. However, it is the only place in all of Shikarpur where you can enter the royal palace without first crossing over the city walls. If we can climb the cliff, and scale the palace wall, we will find ourselves in the innermost courtyard of the palace, precisely where the zahhak pens are located."

"I've seen that cliff," said Arvind, shaking his head. "It's two hundred feet tall, totally sheer, and there's a forty-foot wall sitting atop it. You can't just climb that."

"You can't, my lord," I replied. "I can. And I can carry a rope with me for the others."

"And how do we avoid getting spotted by their guards?" Karim asked. Unlike the others, he wasn't phrasing his questions like I was totally incompetent. He knew me well enough now to have realized that being a hijra didn't make me a fool.

"We fly in low over the desert, to the base of the cliffs. They won't be watching for that approach," I said. "Once we land, we get ourselves flush against the cliffs as quickly as we can, and then the zahhaks fly back home, keeping low until they're far enough away that they won't be spotted by the guards on Shikarpur's walls."

"And you really think you can scale a two-hundred-foot cliff?" Udai asked. For once, he didn't sound like he was making some kind of veiled insult. He wanted an honest appraisal of my skills.

"If it means keeping us all alive, I can do it, your majesty," I replied.

"That's not an answer, girl," he growled. "Can you do it, or can you not?"

"I can do it," I replied, meeting his narrowed eyes with a glare of my own. "Get me to the cliffs, and I will scale them, your majesty. I give you my word."

He grunted at that and nodded to Ram. "Go and get the girl three hundred feet of rope."

"Yes, your majesty," Ram said, and he was off to see it done, leaving the seven of us to stand in the zahhak pens, shifting our weight as anxiously as the animals themselves, who were awake and alert, knowing something was up.

"Once you drop us at the cliffs, your majesty, you'll have to send someone to Mahisagar to alert my father," said Karim. "He can have his zahhaks here by tomorrow morning. That should give you the strength you need to fend off whatever force Javed Khorasani has left after we're finished. I give you my word of honor that if we can't get those zahhaks out, we'll set the pen on fire and kill them instead."

I scowled at that, but I didn't argue. It had been part of the plan all along. If we couldn't steal the zahhaks, killing them would be the only way to stop Javed Khorasani from conquering Bikampur. Still, I didn't know if I had it in me to let Sultana die. I'd have rather burned to death myself than see her meet such a terrible fate. She had been my only true friend in Nizam. She alone had accepted me fully, without question. It didn't matter to her whether I wore a kurta or a lehenga, a turban or a dupatta. Even now, four years after I had abandoned her, her loyalty was undiminished. How could I repay that by letting her die?

Ram's return stirred me from my thoughts. He was carrying a huge coil of rope, and he hurled it at me with a grunt of effort. I caught it, but it almost knocked me off my feet it was so heavy.

Karim noticed. "You're sure you can climb a cliff while carrying that?"

"It's lighter than Govind Singh's peacock," I replied, because it was, and because I knew it would annoy the stuffy old man. Sure enough, he rewarded me with a withering glare. I just smiled back at him, knowing that so long as I served well, Govind Singh's petty vendetta wouldn't matter a whit. Once I had my Sultana back, it wouldn't matter what anybody thought. I would have the freedom to choose my own destiny for the first time, and her thunder would keep anyone from taking it from me ever again.

"If we're ready, we should get moving," said Arjun. "The climb is going to take time, and we have to get to those zahhaks before dawn."

"Agreed," said his father. He waved a big hand at Lakshmi. "Come along, girl, you're flying with me."

"Actually, I am, your majesty," I said, stepping forward, putting myself between him and my little sister. "Your zahhak did try to eat her not two hours ago, after all."

The big man didn't argue with me, which surprised me, as I'd thought it was his favorite pastime. Instead, he snatched the rope from my arms and secured it to his zahhak's saddle. Then he held on to the beast's reins, keeping her sharp teeth well away from me, and said, "Mount up."

"Yes, your majesty," I replied, not wanting to call attention to his behavior, lest he go back to his old sour-faced self. Not that he wasn't sour faced. I thought there was still a frown hidden behind that bushy beard of his. No, it was just that he'd found a use for me, and so long as I had a use he seemed willing to overlook the fact that I was a hijra, which I supposed was all I could expect from a man like him.

I clambered up into the saddle and started strapping myself in right away. I made sure the straps were good and tight, as I didn't think the maharaja would care much for me leaning against him the way I always did with Arjun. Once I was settled, he swung up into the seat behind mine and tied himself down with all the care of a veteran zahhak rider.

"Here, you'll want these." He leaned forward and handed me a pair of goggles, of the sort that I had worn once, long ago in Nizam. I rushed to put them on. In Daryastan, goggles were a sign of wealth and power. Only zahhak riders wore them, and so a prince's status could be measured by whether or not he owned a pair.

It was only after I'd lowered the goggles over my eyes that I realized who had given them to me, and I hurried to bow my head and say, "Thank you, your majesty."

He gave an irritated snort by way of reply, rather like a stubborn horse, and then he flicked the reins and got his zahhak moving out of her pen. She was following close behind Padmini. I noted then that Lakshmi had the reins, with Arjun holding her close to him to keep her from getting thrown about too much when they took off. I made a mental note to reward him for that, once we got home. But before I could think too long about the things I was going to do to Arjun when all this was finally over, Udai's zahhak leapt into the air with all the violence of a gunshot, and my thoughts turned to the cliffs of Shikarpur and the mission I had sworn to complete.

# CHAPTER 18

I couldn't remember the last time I'd felt such unbridled joy as I did then, the fire zahhak racing low over the desert sands east of Shikarpur, her wings stirring up dust devils in our wake, her belly practically skimming the tops of the dunes. The wind rushed past me in a great roar, and my body rose and fell in time with her wingbeats. The moonless sky was filled with more stars than there were diamonds in the palace of Nizam, and the cool night air sent chills running over my skin.

It was all clear to me in that moment why I was taking this risk, why I was dragging Lakshmi into it too. This was the feeling that had haunted my dreams in the dera. The remembered exhilaration of flights like this one had brought tears to my eyes day after day. For four long years, I had lived with the certain knowledge that I would never feel this way again. I'd given it up to live as my true self, and while I'd never regretted that decision, it had been a painful one. I had traded the best part of my childhood for a life that was difficult and dangerous, and for a future that was uncertain. But if I could get my Sultana back, then the sky would once more be my playground, and I would want for nothing for the rest of my days. This night wouldn't just decide the fate of Bikampur, it would decide my fate too. Either I would soar through the heavens once more, or I would die. To a girl who had spent four long years pleasing men in exchange for trinkets and baubles, it was an easy wager.

It was only Arjun who had made my life bearable these last weeks. I hadn't realized how profoundly unhappy I had been before meeting him. He had brought meaning to my life in ways I couldn't count. My gaze drifted over to him, silhouetted atop Padmini's lean, slender form. He had the reins now, but he was keeping one arm draped around Lakshmi at all times, and he was leaning forward, talking to her, though his words were lost to me in the roar of the wind. It didn't matter. I didn't need to hear what he was saying, not when his body language spoke to me so much more clearly.

I didn't deserve him. I didn't know what god or angel I had pleased, what act of charity I had performed, that had made me so lucky. I had been desired by dozens of men before him, but he was the first to show me that I could be loved, accepted, cherished even. And to watch him treat my little sister as if she were his own, it made me realize just how special he really was. Whatever happened tonight, I was going to get him home safely to Bikampur, because I could no more imagine being parted from him than from an arm or a leg.

"There it is," the maharaja roared in my ear to be heard above the slipstream. A thick finger shot out beside my face, pointing in front of us, drawing my attention away from Arjun.

It wasn't hard to see what he was pointing at. From this direction, the city of Shikarpur was a marvel. Perched high atop a sheer cliff, the golden sandstone walls of the palace were capped with crenellated battlements. Lanterns hung at regular intervals, giving the appearance of so many twinkling stars against the black backdrop of the city. Huge shadows loomed amid the flickering lights, the minarets of temples, and the hulking forms of the have-lis of the city's well-to-do, their rooftop canopies waving in the desert wind, pierced-brass lanterns providing just enough light to see dancing girls and feasting men—a glimpse of the life I had left behind in Bikampur.

But the palace itself was quiet, as I'd known it would be. Javed Khorasani would be gathering his forces, preparing himself for battle. He would want to wake up early in the morning so that he could steal a march on the maharaja of Bikampur. He would be in bed now, sleeping one last full night before he was to wage war against his longtime rival. He would be confident. With my cous-in's support, and with the four zahhaks my father had sent, the numbers would be in his favor. If I were him, I would have been sleeping like a baby. I hoped he was. I hoped the whole of the pal-ace was resting in self-assured slumber, confident in their coming victory. Otherwise, Bikampur was doomed.

My heart started to beat a little faster as the cliff loomed larger and larger in my vision. Was *that* what a two-hundred-foot wall of solid rock looked like? I'd never climbed anything even half that big before. And scaling buildings was different from scaling natu-ral cliffs. Buildings tended to have handholds placed more or less regularly. It was true, some dressed-stone buildings had such tightly fitted blocks that you could barely fit your fingernails in the space between them, but by and large buildings had decora-tions on them, carvings or windowsills or arches—things to grab on to. You could plan your route and know with reasonable cer-tainty where the next handhold would be. The shadowy cliff in front of me offered no such assurances.

"You sure you can climb that, girl?" Udai's voice rumbled in my ear, his thoughts clearly echoing my own.

"I don't have a choice, your majesty," I replied.

He grunted at that, and I thought he was going to leave things there, but he said, "You're not what I expected when my son brought you to the palace."

"Oh?" I asked, eager for the distraction of conversation to keep my mind off the mountain in front of me.

"When he said he was bringing home a hijra who had once been a zahhak rider, I was expecting a liar, or a man in a dupatta— or maybe both."

I tried not to flinch at those words. How many times had I been called a man in a dupatta? My own family had called me those things growing up—and worse. No matter how many times I heard it, it never stopped hurting. It was like a scab that was constantly being picked at so that the wound could never heal.

"When I saw that you weren't either of those things, I thought you were just a coward," he said, and I did shudder then, because that was the barb that had been flung most often of all. It was the one that had always buried itself in my heart. How many years had I spent believing it? How many countless hours had I lain awake, cursing myself for being so feeble hearted, so effeminate?

"But you're not a coward, are you, girl?" the maharaja asked, the question jarring me from my memories of self-loathing.

"I hope not, your majesty," I replied, my voice guarded. I knew better than to claim courage in the face of battle-hardened men like Udai Agnivansha. I'd had such claims thrown in my face often enough to know that much. Men didn't think much of women, or of the kind of courage most women had occasion to show— the determination to survive day by day in a world not built for them.

"If you succeed tonight, girl, you will always have a place in my service."

The words stunned me, and for a long moment I didn't know how to respond, didn't even know what they meant. But understanding slowly dawned. He knew that a concubine's life span was measured in the wrinkles on her face. He knew that someday I'd be old and unattractive. More than that, he suspected what I feared most—that Arjun's love for me was a passing fancy, that I could be replaced by some fresh-faced girl, or some blushing bride. As a concubine, he wouldn't even need to divorce me if he tired of me; he could just dismiss me, like a common servant.

"I swear that once we reclaim our zahhaks, my sister and I will serve you as faithfully and loyally as I serve your son, your majesty," I replied.

"Make me that promise when you have the zahhaks, girl," he said, the gruff tone returning to his voice.

I nodded but said nothing. My throat was starting to squeeze shut. We had arrived. The cliff was obscuring almost the whole of my vision. Udai was pulling back on the reins to slow his zahhak into a gentle glide. She backbeat her wings once, twice, three times, and we set down at the base of the cliff, its craggy face stretching up until it seemed to become one with the sky.

I hurried to undo the straps tying me to the zahhak. My fear was making my heart beat like a drummer in the fire god's temple. I scampered down from the beast and was met at once by the coil of rope, hurled down at me by the maharaja. I caught the heavy hempen bundle, though the force of it made me stumble.

"Easy there." Arjun steadied me with strong arms, and Lakshmi joined me a second later. I glanced in Padmini's direction and saw Arvind Singh sitting atop her, strapping himself into her saddle. A little farther away, Karim was climbing down from his place atop Ram's zahhak, hurrying to reach us.

"Good luck, boy," Udai told his son.

"See you in a few hours, Father," Arjun replied, with a confidence I wished I possessed. He didn't even sound scared. Didn't he know we were about to run headlong into the heart of his greatest enemy's palace? And that was if we even survived the climb to the top of the walls, which was no certain thing.

There were no long good-byes. The maharaja knew that the longer the zahhaks waited, the greater the odds of our being discovered. He took off, with the other three zahhaks flying after him. They kept low to the desert sands, where the geometric patterns of their sunset-colored scales blended into the ground. They disappeared from view faster than I'd imagined possible, leaving the four of us alone at the base of the cliffs.

"Now we see if you can live up to all your boasting," said Karim, his arms crossed over his chest. He was looking at me with something I didn't often see on his face. I couldn't be sure what it was, but if I didn't know any better, I'd have said it was respect.

"Right . . ." I murmured, and I hefted the coil of rope, draping it across my body so that it wouldn't interfere too much with my climbing. Then I looked up at the cliff, and my stomach did a little flip. It was so much higher than I'd thought it would be. But the rock looked like it was sandstone, with plenty of cracks and crevices to serve as hand- and footholds. And the surface was rough, not slick or smooth, so that was to my advantage.

I knelt down and rubbed my hands in the dirt, getting them as thoroughly covered in the fine dust particles as I possibly could. That would help keep my hands from slipping on the climb. I stood up and turned toward the cliff, only to find Arjun standing in front of me.

He hugged me tightly and spoke directly into my ear, his breath making it tickle. "Be careful, Razia. Take it slow. If you can't make it, it's all right. Better not to chance it."

"If I don't make it, Bikampur will fall, my prince," I replied. I couldn't let that happen. Bikampur was my home, and if it fell, Arjun would be killed in the fighting. Princes in Daryastan never long survived the fall of their palaces.

"Just promise me you'll be careful," he said, knowing that I wasn't going to admit defeat.

"I promise," I replied.

He kissed me then, his lips pressing against mine, their warmth making my whole body tingle with anticipation. He pulled away too soon, his hands still resting on my shoulders, his brow furrowed with worry. "Come back to me—that's an order from your prince."

"You'll be coming to me, my prince," I reminded him, giving the coil of rope a pat. I flashed him one last smile and headed for the cliff. I wasn't going to fall. I wasn't going to fail. We were going to scale the walls of Javed Khorasani's palace and we were going to make him pay for threatening our home.

The first handhold was an easy one—a little ledge sticking out just at my shoulder level. I grasped it, and then put my leg up on another little ledge, and then the climb started. For all the fury and resentment I'd felt at Ammi for forcing me to disgrace myself with a dishonorable profession like thief, I loved climbing. It was the only sport I knew where you were the only competitor, and where your success or failure could be so simply measured. Either you made it to the top or you didn't. But more than that, for me, climbing was like prayer. When I climbed, my whole being was focused on the next handhold, the next foothold, on the pleasant burning in my muscles and the steady sense of progress I felt as I moved one step at a time up the side of a wall.

This climb was no different in that regard from all the others. It was longer, but that scarcely mattered as I tended to lose track of time when I climbed anyway. In a sense, my movements were like the sands of an hourglass. At some moments, I could go from handhold to handhold as if I were climbing a ladder, and in other moments, time seemed to stop as I clung to the wall, searching out the next place to go.

So far, this climb was moving at a frenetic pace. The handholds were everywhere, and there were plenty of little ledges for my feet. I was scampering up the wall faster than some of the other girls from my dera could run down the street. I was brimming with confidence, as each move proved to be the right one. My body felt rock steady. My fingers felt strong. It was almost like a game. It was easy to forget that this was life or death, that the fate of a whole city rested on whether or not I made it to the top.

And then, quite abruptly, I came to a screeching halt. There was a roof above me, or if not a roof, a projecting ledge. It was too far away from the wall for me to reach up and grab hold of it. I'd have fallen trying that. But going around it wasn't going to be easy either. It stretched off to my left for quite a distance, and to my right there was a flat, smooth section of wall that had been eroded by wind and sand.

I stood there, letting my legs take most of the weight so that my hands wouldn't get tired. I was tempted to look down, to see how far I'd come, but it was so hard to tell distance vertically that I didn't bother. All that mattered was how far I had left to go. Going back down wasn't an option. I had to get around this ledge.

My eyes flickered from the ledge, to the easy climbing to the left of me, and to the much harder climbing to the right of me. If I moved left, maybe I'd be able to inch my way around the ledge, but how far would I have to go? To my right, there was a clear gap, but the wall of the cliff looked so smooth there. If I lost my grip . . .

There. My eyes landed on the answer. A jagged fissure snaked its way up the smooth rock wall to my right. If I could jam my hands and feet into it, I could muscle my way around the ledge, and then use it as a resting spot to gather my strength and plan my next move. Of course, the fissure wouldn't be such a perfect platform as the tiny ledges I'd been using thus far on the climb, but it reminded me a bit of the times I'd used the fluting in decorative columns to shimmy my way up them. It was worth a try anyway.

There was one handhold off to the right before things got slick. I reached over and took hold of it, creeping across the wall, putting my left hand where my right had been, and then moving my left foot to the spot formerly occupied by my right. My right foot had nowhere to go. It was hanging in empty space, searching the wall for somewhere it could get a grip, some crack where I could stick my toes. There. It hit something. I couldn't see it, but when I slowly shifted my weight, it held. So far so good.

Now the fissure was in reach. It was narrow; that was good. It would make it easier to keep my feet firmly tucked inside it. I had to move my right hand first, stretching out as far as I could just to reach the crack's edge. It was smooth and round and slick, and I had to fumble with my fingers until I found a spot where they could really hook in. I slowly let that hand take my weight, bracing myself in case I slipped or the rock gave way, but it seemed solid enough.

There was always the temptation when climbing was going well to break the rules, to move a hand or a foot before either was solid, but I remembered the rules my Rakhan instructor had beaten into me in the dera. You always must keep three limbs attached to the wall at any given time. Otherwise, you *will* fall. So I resisted the urge to lunge with my left hand to take the strain out of my shoulder joints, and instead focused on moving my right leg into the fissure.

It was easier than I'd thought it would be. My foot found a

stable spot, and I shifted my weight over as much as I could, though by this time I was stretched out like a spider, my arms and legs about as far apart as they could go. I shifted my left foot to the spot where my right foot had been, feeling out that little ledge, and when I got it, I put my weight on it and lifted my left arm to finally take the strain off my shoulder—and the rocks beneath my left foot gave way.

I was falling. My right foot slipped out of the fissure, and my stomach flew up into my throat as my body started to drop. The sensation of falling ended with a sudden jerk that made me whimper in pain as it felt like my right arm was being torn off my body. I dangled against the side of the cliff, suspended by my hand and wrist, which had somehow gotten wedged so deeply into the fissure that they were totally stuck. I wasn't sure if my arm was broken or not, I just knew that it hurt, and the longer I hung from it, the worse the pain got. If I didn't do something, my bones really were going to snap.

I felt around with my toes, trying to find a stable bit of rock, but the wall of the cliff was so slick that they just kept slipping like they were trying to get a grip on solid ice. Desperate, I tried to find a place to grab on with my left hand, just to take some of the strain off my right. There! There was a spot in the fissure, just above me. I lunged for it, and stuck my left hand into the gap, and pulled. It held.

That took some of the pain out of my right arm, but until I found a place to put my feet, I was totally stuck. There just didn't seem to be anywhere for them to go, and the more I kicked and failed to find a foothold, the more desperate I felt.

Never panic. That was the second rule of climbing, right after keeping three points of contact on the wall. I took a deep breath, in spite of the pain in my arms, and looked around for a foothold, using my eyes to scan the wall rather than trusting my sense of touch. There was nothing there. Just slick rock, well worn from wind and water. Except there. I saw it now, not below me, but almost at the level of my shoulders off to my right. There was a little crack there, about the right size for my foot.

I pulled with both arms, and with a grunt of effort, I was able to stretch my right foot out and shove it into the hole. I got a firm grip with my toes, and when I pushed with my leg muscles, some of the strain came off my arms. Of course, now I was lying practically sideways against the wall, my left leg dangling uselessly beneath me, my right arm twisted like a jalebi beneath my left. My muscles were burning like fire. I needed to find another foothold.

I saw then the old foothold I'd been using for my right foot, before I'd fallen. It was all the way on the other side of the fissure, and it was nearly as high up as the one holding my right foot. I wasn't sure if I was flexible enough to reach it, but I had to try. So I reached out with my left foot, sliding it up along the wall, the muscles between my legs burning as I performed a perfect midair split, but my toes found the crevice, and it held my weight.

Now, with my legs supporting most of my weight, albeit awkwardly, I could try to get my right arm free. It was twisted, and my wrist was burning with pain from the pressure of the rock around it. I tried to pull it free, but it wouldn't budge, not even when I took all the weight off of it. It was trapped in a narrowing of the fissure, and my hand was jammed so deeply into it that there didn't seem to be any way to get it out again.

No matter which way I twisted, no matter how hard I tugged, it wouldn't move, and I was worried that if I pulled too hard, I'd break it. I stood there, legs splayed out to either side, left hand clinging to the crevice, my mind desperately trying to work out how to get my right arm free, when it occurred to me that maybe I could chip the rock. It was sandstone. I reached down with my left arm, drew one of my katars, and slammed the handle hard against the rock encasing my wrist.

It happened so fast that I almost fell again. The rock cracked, my right hand slipped out of the crevice, and I started to go over backward. It was only the very firm grip I had with my toes that saved me. I managed to hang on, to lean my weight forward, and to get a grip in the crevice with my right hand, while my left returned the razor-sharp katar to my sash.

My heart was pounding; my right hand and wrist were aching; my leg muscles were burning. I looked up, wondering how far I had left to go, but my view was mostly blocked by the stupid ledge I was trying to get around. I just needed to get to that ledge, and then I could take a second to take stock of the situation.

I reached my left hand up into the fissure and got a firm grip, and then my right hand joined it. My left foot followed, and it supported me well enough that I could walk my hands up the crevice one at a time. Then my right foot got hooked into the spot where my wrist had nearly been broken. Now I could climb. Like a monkey racing up a tree, I walked up the fissure, hand followed by foot, alternating left and right, until I was up over the ledge.

The ledge was wide and solid, and I wasted no time in scampering onto it. It was big enough to sit on, and I did that, gasping for air, resting my back against the wall of the cliff, my heart racing and my muscles burning. I did look down then, wondering how far I'd gone, and I was shocked to see that Arjun, Lakshmi, and Karim were just tiny specks in the darkness. I glanced up above me, and my spirit soared. I was just ten or fifteen feet from the top! How had that happened? I just had to get up that last little bit, and then I could climb the wall of the fort itself.

I leapt to my feet and attacked the wall, my determination having redoubled at being so near to my prize. I was actually going to succeed. We were really going to break into Javed Khorasani's palace. I realized then, as my sore right hand searched for a hold, that I hadn't really believed we would make it. After all, who had ever heard of stealing zahhaks from someone's palace? It had never been done before, and climb or no climb, if not for Sultana, it would have been impossible still. It was just her dominance in the stables that would keep us from being devoured by the other animals.

But those worries could wait until later. For now, I was cresting the top of the cliff, my heart swelling with pride as I pulled myself over the edge. There was a ledge there, about two feet wide, and I lay on it on my back, my face turned up toward the night sky and the glittering stars. I was nearly there. Now there was just the matter of the forty-foot palace wall to worry over. But we had plenty of time. I could afford to take a moment's rest to get my strength back.

While I lay there, I studied the wall I was about to climb, and I grinned. It looked as if the architect had designed it for climbing on. The mortar in between the yellow sandstone blocks was in want of a little repair, providing cracks for my fingers and toes. And the wall had been built in tiers, with a decorative ridge of stone at the wall's base, with another ten feet above that, and a third band just below the crenellated battlements. They would make perfect ledges for standing on, and the firing slits for the gunners would be good handholds. This was going to be easier than some of the havelis back home in Bikampur.

I took deep breaths in and out through my nose to slow my heart rate, to steady my nerves, and to regain my strength. As I breathed, something tickled my nostrils. It wasn't the usual pristine desert air, nor the stench of a city's sewers. It was something else, something strong and acrid, but distinctive. It was a familiar smell. Where had I smelled it before? I closed my eyes, and I let my memories take me back.

I was ten years old, playing on the battlements with my cousin Rashid, back before he'd turned into a complete monster. I was running from him, because we were playing a hiding game, and I'd had the brilliant idea to hide in one of the watchtowers. Men were on duty in there, standing with their toradars at the ready, the lit matches letting off an acrid smoke that made my nose itch so much that I sneezed, giving my position away.

The smoke from a toradar's fuse? I scowled. Somewhere above me on that wall, there was a musketeer waiting. I didn't think he'd seen me—the ledges would have prevented that, even if he'd been able to lean over the parapets. No, he was likely unaware of my presence, but I couldn't risk him seeing me. If my friends were going to make it up here to join me, they were going to have to climb the rope, and the rope was going to have to be anchored to one of the merlons in the wall. Nothing else would be solid enough to hold the weight of grown men.

I was going to have to kill him. I didn't think there was any way around it. Otherwise, he would alert the other sentries. But what if he wasn't alone? I supposed it didn't matter. All I could do was climb to the top and hope for the best.

So that was what I did. I set my feet against the little ledge of stone molding that the builders had so helpfully provided, and then I stuck my hands in the best cracks I could find and I started up the wall.

It went much faster than the cliff had. It was easy to spot the cracks against the flush, clean surface of the stonework, and the stone molding, meant to give the wall a decorative flourish, provided me with an easy handhold or foothold every ten feet. It didn't take me much more than a minute to scale the wall up to the base of the embrasures, but I stayed low when I reached them, listening for the sounds of footsteps, or breathing, or conversation. I didn't want to throw myself over the battlements, only to find myself in the midst of half a dozen armed soldiers. I hadn't survived the climb up the cliff to be defeated now by a couple of sentries.

The merlons had shooting slits running through the middle of them, and I used those to take peeks at the battlements on the other side. The glow of a toradar's slow-burning match gave away the position of one sentry. I couldn't believe what I was seeing. He was leaning against his gun, his elbow resting over the muzzle, the match burning furiously, sending up little wisps of acrid smoke. Was he an idiot, or just crazy? If the gun accidentally went off, he'd shoot himself right through the armpit!

I looked around to see if he had any friends with him, but the narrow shooting slit didn't give me a wide enough field of vision to really make anything else out. I just knew that there was one guard directly in front of me, and that his weapon was down. He wasn't ready for a fight, and he wasn't wearing any armor, just a turban on his head and a loose white kurta on his body, belted with a broad silk sash that held a talwar. He was a far cry from the cream of Javed Khorasani's army. What was he doing guarding the palace?

The invasion! Of course! It all made sense to me then. The bulk of the professional soldiers had already marched out to the border! Javed Khorasani was stealing a march on us, trying to get his troops in place before we could move ours to mount a defense. I just prayed the zahhaks were still in the stables, waiting for the nobles to fly out in the morning, or all of this was for nothing. Of course, on the bright side, with his army in the field, that meant the city itself, as well as the palace, was defended by peasant levies like this man, who didn't know that the business end of a toradar needed to be pointed away from him. A malicious grin crept across my face. Maybe this wasn't going to be as tough as I'd thought it would be. If the zahhaks were still here, we might still be able to pull one over on Khorasani and make it to Rohiri in time to defend the fortress.

Moving slowly, quietly, with all the grace and stealth of a snow leopard, I climbed into the gap between a pair of merlons, using the shadows to hide me. I crouched low and drew my katars, taking one in each hand. I took one last look to make sure that this sentry was the only one on this stretch of wall, and then I leapt off the wall, straight at him, my katars gleaming in the starlight.

I punched the sentry in the throat, and a blade as long as my forearm tore into his flesh and straight through the spine behind it, nearly decapitating the poor man. He never saw it coming. He had no chance to react. For all I knew, he might have been sleeping. He just tumbled to the ground, his toradar falling with him, clattering to the stones so loudly that I cursed my own stupidity. It hadn't gone off, but it might as well have, it had created such a racket.

I ducked low and froze, waiting for the cries of "Intruders!" and for sentries to rush my position, for the bright flashes of toradars shooting at me from the darkened watchtowers. Nothing happened. Were all the other sentries half-asleep too? I didn't know, and I didn't care. All that mattered was getting my friends up and into the palace. We could worry about what the sentries were doing later.

I slipped the coil of rope off of my body and immediately tied one end off on the nearest merlon. I made sure to use one of the climbing knots my Rakhan mountaineer instructor had taught me, and I tested it with all my strength before I hurled the rope over the wall. It unspooled itself as it fell, dropping over the ledge on the other side of the wall, disappearing from view. I had no way of knowing it if made it all the way down to Arjun and the others or not. I just had to wait and hope for the best.

I crouched down beside the body of the dead sentry. I couldn't help looking at him. He had a scruff of beard on his cheeks, but he was young—no wrinkles on his face. His eyes were wide and staring, the whites gleaming at me. I reached over and shut them, but then I felt the warmth of his face, felt the smoothness of his skin, and I shuddered. I'd never killed anyone before. I'd been training for it my whole life, but training for a thing and doing it weren't the same. I looked away, and huddled against the wall and tried not to think about it, but no matter how I tried, that look of surprise on the young man's face kept flickering across my vision.

I focused on keeping a lookout, just in case another sentry happened to walk past. So far, things looked clear, but we still had to get off the wall and into the courtyard, and then we had to find the zahhak pens in the darkness. I thought they were on this side of the courtyard, somewhere down there in the darkness below me, but it was hard to be certain. It had been so long since I'd visited Shikarpur, and those hadn't been happy times. I'd spent most of my days dreading beatings at the hands of my father or my tutors. It was only on rare occasions that I'd been given the freedom to explore places for myself.

The sound of scuffling jarred me from my thoughts. I glanced around for a sentry, but nobody was on the battlements. So I stood up slowly and looked over the wall, leaning across one of the embrasures, and I was surprised to see Lakshmi's skinny form leading the way up the rope. She was beyond the ledge now, climbing the last twenty feet to the top of the wall, and she was moving with all the speed of a temple monkey. Ammi really had been training her to replace me.

Lakshmi reached the top, and I leaned over and offered her my hand. She took it, and I pulled her over the embrasure, safely onto the parapet. I was startled when she embraced me with both arms, squeezing me tightly and whispering, "I thought you were dead, Akka!"

"Dead? Me?" I asked, keeping my voice low lest we be overheard.

"We saw you fall," she said, and I realized that she was sniffling back tears. "We thought you were going to die."

"I'm fine," I told her, holding her close to me and rubbing her back in gentle circles. "It'll take more than a cliff to kill me."

"Not much more." That was Karim, coming to stand beside us, one hand on the hilt of his firangi. "I was worried I wouldn't have you to torment anymore."

I rolled my eyes, and would have said something suitably clever in response, but at that moment Arjun came over the wall and I rushed over and embraced him instead. I was a little taken aback when he enfolded me in a crushing hug in return, his fingers burrowing into the flesh of my back like earthworms. It was only when I let out a little wince of protest that his grip slackened.

"You're never climbing anything again," he told me, his voice sounding all the more imperious for how low and quiet it was.

I didn't want to argue with him, so I just said, "This isn't the time or place for such discussions, my prince. We have zahhaks to steal."

"Right." He let go of me and drew his khanda, and his buckler, holding them both at the ready, and he nodded to Karim. "We'll take the front. You girls stay behind us where it's safer."

Ignoring the mocking glance Karim sent my way as he drew his firangi, I stepped back to join Lakshmi. She had drawn her ankusha from her sash and had her funny shield with its antler spikes clutched firmly in her right hand. Like me, and many other hijras, she was left-handed.

"Are you ready?" I asked her.

"I'm ready, Akka," she said, and she sounded excited rather than afraid. I decided not to tell her about the dead man who was lying just two or three feet behind her. I didn't think she'd seen him yet, and I didn't want her to. She was too young for that sort of thing. I just hoped we could get to the zahhaks and get out before anybody else had to die.

Karim hadn't failed to notice the dead body. He was glancing from it to me and back again, but he said nothing. That was more tactful than I expected from him, but I supposed he was focused on the job at hand. He and Arjun set off toward one of the watchtowers, where the only stairs leading down from the parapets could be found. There would probably be guards in there, I just didn't have any idea how many.

The tower was a beautiful structure, with an onion-shaped dome, and large arched openings from which the defenders could look out, but there was just enough in the way of walls to hide the occupants from view from where we were standing. So we moved in a low crouch, slowly and quietly, hoping to surprise the sentries, if there were even any of them inside waiting for us.

Crouching behind Arjun's and Karim's much larger bodies, I couldn't even catch a glimpse at what was happening in the tower, I could just see their backs. But we paused at the corner of the wall where it met the tower, and we waited for what seemed like an eternity. Did they see something? Were there sentries? Why were they waiting to attack? My heart was pounding as I waited for the moment to spring into action, but I felt all the more anxious for not being able to see what was in front of me.

Arjun suddenly sprang forward, with Karim right behind him, and I ran after them, more from instinct than from any kind of plan. As I rounded the corner, I saw a pair of sentries looking wide-eyed at the two big princes hurtling toward them, their weapons poised to strike. Karim skewered his man through the throat with his narrow-bladed firangi, killing him before he had a chance to scream. An instant later, Arjun's heavy-bladed khanda separated the other man's head from his shoulders. Blood spurted high, coating the ceiling of the domed pavilion overhead, and the man's body and head tumbled to the ground in front of us.

I grabbed Lakshmi, pulled her close to me, and pressed her face against my chest so that she wouldn't be able to see what was happening. Sakshi was right; what kind of madwoman would bring a little girl to a battle like this? She didn't need to be seeing this—I didn't even want to see it.

"Razia?" Arjun hissed.

I looked up, saw his bloody khanda bobbing in his anxious grip, and then forced myself to look away from it, to focus on his eyes instead. He was nodding toward the stairwell. "Come on, we have to move."

"Right." I had to let go of Lakshmi then, and, being the mischievous eleven-year-old she was, the first thing she did was look at the dead men. Her eyes got really big, and her face paled a little, but she said nothing, and she followed along with me as I chased behind Karim and Arjun, who were running down the tower's spiral stairs.

We emerged on the ground floor, but both men kept back from the doorway that led into the courtyard. They stood in the shadows, watching and waiting. It was Arjun who whispered, "Razia, where do they keep the zahhaks?"

I left Lakshmi's side and crept closer to the doorway, pressing myself up against the golden sandstone of the tower wall. I peered around the corner at the courtyard. It was empty and quiet. There was the pavilion where Javed Khorasani had entertained my father during one of the many interminable wrestling matches I'd been forced to compete in as a child. And over there, all the way across the courtyard, was the palace proper. That was where Javed Khorasani and his sons would be sleeping. That was where my cousin Rashid would be. But the zahhaks, they would be closer to us.

I leaned out of the doorway and spotted the building I was looking for. It was a pretty pavilion in its own right, with big open archways to let in a cooling evening breeze, though the pens themselves had solid walls to keep the zahhaks from getting out and running amok—or eating the palace servants.

"There." I pointed to the spot. It was so close, just forty or fifty paces away. We were almost there. Once we got the zahhaks, we'd be able to fly out unmolested. There was no way a bunch of untrained sentries were going to be able to stand up to four thunder zahhaks.

"All right, let's go," Arjun said, and he didn't wait for acknowledgment. He rushed out of the tower, keeping low but running all the while. I chased after him, but I was slower, and I had to look out for Lakshmi. I wasn't going to lose her, not when everything was going according to plan. In just a few minutes, she'd have a zahhak once again. And then I could take her down to Kolikota and trade her father a thunder zahhak for Mohini. I was going to see that my sister had the childhood I'd never had.

We reached the zahhak pens, flattening ourselves against the warm stone walls to stay out of sight. We were all breathing hard, winded from the climb and the fighting, but most of all I think from the anxiety. Sneaking was a terrifying business. You were always so sure that you were going to be spotted, so sure that someone was going to jump out at you from the shadows, or shout from across the courtyard that they'd spotted you. I'd experienced it when stealing from rich nobles' houses, but here Arjun, Karim, and Lakshmi were experiencing it for the first time, and I could tell by how big their eyes were that it scared them a little.

"I'll go in first, my prince," I told Arjun, as that was just sensible. Sultana would protect me, as the other thunder zahhaks would eat me—or anybody else they didn't recognize. That was why guards weren't posted at zahhak pens—they watched themselves plenty well enough. If not for my connection to Sultana, this mission would have been completely impossible. Even so, I hoped she was the dominant female in this stable that she'd always been back home in Nizam, or we were probably going to die. Then again, it was possible the zahhaks had already left with the army.

I ducked around the corner, and was relieved to see that the zahhaks were present, and asleep, and that there didn't seem to be any guards posted. That last bit didn't surprise me so much, and not just because zahhaks defended themselves well enough. If I'd had peasant levies guarding my palace, I wouldn't have wanted them anywhere near my precious zahhaks either.

Sultana was resting in one of the nearer pens, along with three other zahhaks whose cobalt scales were brighter and shinier than the ones possessed by the zahhaks in the four pens farther along. I suspected these four were the ones my father had sent. They looked like Sultana's siblings. And that meant that she was likely still the dominant female. It also meant that my father's retainers were probably here. That worried me. They were fierce fighters, and if they caught me, they would kill me.

I pushed those thoughts from my mind and instead grabbed Rashid's fancy saddle from the tack room and brought it over to Sultana's stall. She heard me coming and opened one sleepy jade eye. It landed on me, and her head snapped up. She was on her feet in an instant, her tail thrashing with excitement, thudding against the walls of the pen like the beat of a drum.

"I wasn't going to leave you again, girl," I told her, patting her gently on the snout. I opened the pen and rushed inside, fitting the saddle to her and strapping it as tightly as I could. If the saddle fell off in flight, I'd fall with it. With Sultana saddled, I breathed a sigh of relief. Lakshmi would be safe now. Sultana would let her fly her. Come what may, my little sister would get away from all this.

I had just finished setting the last strap when I heard a man scream in the distance. My heart skipped a beat. Then I heard the shout: "Intruders!"

I tried not to panic as I led Sultana out of her pen by the reins. At that moment, Karim, Arjun, and Lakshmi came rushing in, but Sultana paid them no mind. The other zahhaks were a different story. They were awake now, and they started to growl threateningly, their cobra-like hoods flaring outward, making them look twice as big as they really were. The one directly across from Sultana's pen reached its head out and snapped at Lakshmi.

Sultana's response was instantaneous. She lunged forward, punching the other zahhak's neck with her snout. The attack was met with immediate surrender on the part of the other zahhak. I had guessed right—my Sultana was definitely the dominant female.

"Get the saddles. Get them on these three zahhaks." I gestured to the three prettier ones. "We've got to move."

"Right, this one's mine," said Karim, nodding to the one that had nearly bitten Lakshmi. He would want that one. It suited his temperament anyway.

The three of them sheathed their weapons and went to grab their saddles. Already, drums were beating in the distance. Men were shouting. I heard footsteps in the courtyard. We had to get going if we wanted to escape, though I didn't think anybody would check the zahhak pens. What sort of insane assassin would go willingly into a den of thunder-breathing monsters?

My friends came running back into the stables carrying their saddles. Karim went right to work on the mean zahhak, but it didn't resist, not when it was clear that we were made off-limits by Sultana. Arjun picked a big, proud-looking female in the pen beside the one Sultana had lately occupied. It glanced from him to Sultana and back again, but didn't attack. Lakshmi had me the most worried. She was more or less bite-size and wouldn't command a lot of respect from a strange zahhak. The one she had been left with was smaller, but probably the most beautiful of the bunch—Sultana excepted, of course. It didn't attack her, which I supposed was a stroke of luck, given that the shouts of sentries were growing louder in my ears.

"Take your time with your saddle straps," I told Lakshmi, rather than urging her to hurry. If she hurried and made a mistake, she'd fall to her death. Better to do it thoroughly. Now that we had the zahhaks under control, we had powerful weapons to use against anyone who stumbled across us anyway.

Lakshmi had just finished the last strap, when she slammed the heel of her palm into her forehead. "Akka! I forgot the bridle!"

"It's okay," I said. "Run and grab it. Be quick, okay?"

"Okay, Akka." She rushed out of the pen, past Sultana's twitching tail, and disappeared into the tack room. An instant later, I heard her scream.

My katars were in my hands before I knew what I was doing, but before I could so much as take a step in her direction, a man came around the corner, holding her tightly with one hand, his other pressing a dagger to the hollow of her throat. I was so focused on the blade that it took me a second to realize that I recognized the man holding it. "Rashid!"

"You!" Rashid hissed, his face twisted with rage. He pressed the dagger more tightly against Lakshmi's throat, and I held up my hands desperately to stop him, the katars tumbling from my nerveless fingers.

"No! Don't hurt her! Please!"

As Arjun and Karim hefted their swords to cut Rashid down if he hurt Lakshmi, half a dozen toradar-armed men rushed into the stables behind Rashid, their weapons leveled at us, their fuses burning red-hot. I spread my hands out to show that they were empty. "Please, Rashid, let her go. She's just a child."

"She's a thief!" he snarled, and he made sure the edge of the dagger dug into the flesh of her throat enough that it was just on the verge of drawing blood. If he hurt her . . . I didn't have words for the punishments I would inflict on him.

"Please, Rashid, you don't have to kill anyone. We'll surrender. Just don't hurt her, I'm begging you."

"You!" Rashid nodded to Karim. "Away from the zahhaks. Go stand with her. You too, *Prince* Arjun! Drop your sword and go and stand with your hijra slut, or I'll spill this girl's blood all over this room."

Swords clattered to the ground. I was shocked to see Karim drop his. Did he care so much for Lakshmi? Or was it a calculated risk? I didn't know, but he came to stand with me, and so did Arjun. We waited with bated breath for what Rashid would do. Already, more sentries were rushing into the stables behind him, all carrying toradars, more than a dozen of them. There was no way we could fight off so many.

"What's this girl to you, *Razia?*" Rashid demanded, turning my female name into a curse.

"She's my sister," I replied, seeing no sense in lying to him. "Please, Rashid, I'll do anything you ask. Just don't hurt her."

"Oh, I won't hurt her," he said, and the knife fell away from her throat. He gave her a hard shove, sending her sprawling to the ground at my feet, the bridle she'd gone to fetch still clutched tightly in her little hands. I rushed to pick her up, and I held her close to me, trying to protect her with as much of my body as I could from whatever it was Rashid was planning to do.

He stepped back and nodded to his musketeers. "Shoot them."

I stared, wide-eyed, as the men pointed their toradars at us, nearly a dozen of them. And then I remembered that I had a weapon of my own. I pointed at Rashid, and I shouted, "Sultana, thunder!"

I threw myself against Arjun, slamming him to the ground, with Lakshmi sandwiched between us. There was a tremendous crack, like the heavens themselves had been torn asunder, and there was a bright flash of light, and for a moment I thought I had been killed. But there was no pain, just a horrible stuffiness in my head and an interminable ringing in my ears.

I looked around and saw dust and smoke filling the air. Some of the stones from the stable roof had fallen and smashed themselves on the floor. The wooden doors of the stalls had been crushed to splinters from the force of the shock wave. But Sultana was standing proudly, mouth agape, and before her more than two dozen men lay in various stages of consciousness, moaning on the floor, bleeding from their ears.

I scrambled to my feet, shouting, "Get the zahhaks! Now, while we have a chance!" I didn't know if anyone heard me, as I couldn't even hear myself, but I shoved Lakshmi in the direction of the zahhak she had chosen, and then I snatched my katars from the floor and shoved them through my sash. On either side of me, Arjun and Karim were grabbing their weapons and running to their own zahhaks.

I swung into Sultana's saddle, racing to cinch my waist strap, not worrying about the shoulder straps, not when time was of the essence. I took up her reins and gave them a snap, and she took off running through the open doorway, stomping on the prone forms of the dead and the wounded.

In the courtyard, it was total chaos. The sentries must have heard and seen the lightning bolt that Sultana had shot from her mouth, and now a whole battalion of them were running toward us from the direction of the palace. If they got themselves organized, they could shoot us to pieces before we could take off.

I pulled on the reins, twisting Sultana's head in their direction, and I shouted, "Thunder!"

This time, seated behind her head, the blast wasn't quite so blinding or so deafening. The lightning bolt struck the middle of the group of men, and the force of the explosion sent them tumbling to either side like rag dolls. Dirt and cobblestones flew through the air like missiles, wounding more of them.

By then, the other three zahhaks had made it out of the stables, and now they shot their lightning bolts too, nearly disintegrating some of the poor sentries, setting off their muskets and ripping the clothes from their bodies. One man caught fire, and his screams turned my stomach.

I glanced back to make sure that Arjun and Lakshmi were with me, and then I snapped the reins and gave pressure with my knees, and Sultana started her takeoff run. She ran full tilt toward the wall that overlooked the cliff and leapt into the air, beating her wings madly on either side of her. For a terrifying moment, I didn't think we would make it, but then we were over the wall, with nothing but empty air beneath us.

I twisted in my seat and saw Lakshmi off my left wing and Arjun off my right, with Karim bringing up the rear. Bright yellow flashes of light accompanied by white puffs of smoke told me that the sentries were trying to shoot us down with their toradars, but hitting a flying target at night was no easy matter, and these were not Javed Khorasani's best troops. We slipped away into the darkness, my ears still ringing like bells.

# CHAPTER 19

My ears had more or less cleared up as the walls of Bikampur loomed out of the desert. The sun was still tucked safely behind the eastern horizon, but I knew that wouldn't last long. Already, the sky was starting to turn gray and the stars were starting to fade. In an hour, maybe two, the sun would rise, and armies would march. If Javed Khorasani reached Rohiri fortress before we did, then stealing these zahhaks might count for nothing. We needed to get the army moving, and we needed to do it now.

I saw a smudge on the horizon, and as I flew closer, I realized what it was—dust being kicked up by an army on the move. I smiled then. Udai Agnivansha may not have been the most pleasant man I'd ever met in my life, but he was no fool. He'd already gathered his forces and marched them out of the city. He was trying to steal a march on Javed Khorasani. It was clever, but of course he couldn't know that Khorasani had beaten him to the punch.

Still, I suspected the maharaja himself would be waiting in his palace for our return. If we were lucky, then Karim's father and his fellow Mahisagari fliers would have arrived ahead of us. With them, we would be ten in total—eleven if Govind Singh cared to risk flying a foreign thunder zahhak in battle. Still, whether it was ten or eleven didn't much matter, not when our enemies had only four zahhaks left. I wondered if Javed Khorasani wouldn't just cut his losses and sue for peace. That would be the smart move, even if it would humiliate him and anger my father.

Somehow, I didn't think he'd be that smart. To admit the loss of four of the sultan's own zahhaks would be more than a man like him could bear. That kind of blot on his honor would have to be met with courage in battle, or he would likely lose his position as subahdar of Zindh. That meant there would be a battle, and soon, as he was already on the march, and a swift victory would be more important now than ever, given the loss of four of his zahhaks.

I stopped worrying about Javed Khorasani and the coming battle as we reached Bikampur. Sultana was flying at rooftop level, her wings beating a blur on either side of her. It was too early in the morning for any late carousers to catch sight of us, but the exhilaration of racing past the city's havelis was just what I needed to lift my spirits. Whatever came next, we had accomplished our mission. We were all whole and healthy, and I had my Sultana back. I would never have to sell myself for money again. I would never have to live under the thumb of a guru or a male client. For the first time in my life, I could live the kind of life I wanted to live, and I couldn't imagine anything better than that.

I skimmed over the walls of Bikampur's palace fortress and brought Sultana down in the second courtyard, where the zahhak pens were located. I wasn't surprised to see that a crowd of people were waiting for me, Udai Agnivansha most prominent among them. But I saw that standing behind him and the other important men of Bikampur was Sakshi, her hands clasped to her breast as she watched the zahhaks flutter to the ground.

The crowd came racing up to us, and the zahhaks shifted uneasily, but by this time they'd come to obey their riders, and they didn't attack. I saw that the sultan of Mahisagar, Ahmed, was standing beside his Bikampuri counterpart. That meant that the acid zahhaks had arrived ahead of us. I smiled. With them in the air, and as many of our new thunder zahhaks as we could find fliers for, we'd be unstoppable.

I undid my straps and climbed down from Sultana's back, joined an instant later by Arjun, Karim, and Lakshmi, who were all treating their mounts with a good deal more caution. They needn't have bothered, of course, as none of the zahhaks would dare to attack them while Sultana was watching. Had she not been there, it would have been a totally different story, but as it was, she stood straight and tall and let the other zahhaks know precisely what the punishment would be for hurting her humans.

Udai shocked me by rushing forward and hugging his son. He pounded him on the back with his meaty palms, lest the embrace seem too much like that of a frantic mother's, but he couldn't hide the worry that had been eating away at him. I couldn't blame him for that. Arjun was his son and heir, and a worthy one besides, and where that might have led to a rivalry between father and son for control of the crown, it had seemed to only strengthen their love and respect for each other. I only wished my own relationship with my father had ever been so strong.

If Udai had shocked me by embracing his son, what he did next left me speechless. He turned and embraced me too. I was so horrified that I didn't know what to do. I just barely managed to choke out, "Your majesty?" before he let me go.

He flashed me a grin that made it past his bushy beard and

slapped me so hard on the shoulder that he nearly knocked it out of joint. "You're not nearly as dainty and frivolous as you look, girl!"

"She's plenty dainty, Father," Arjun assured him, draping an arm across my shoulders. "You should have seen the way she hid her eyes when we killed the sentries."

"Not that it stopped her from blowing her own cousin to pieces with a lightning bolt," said Karim, and he was grinning at that, like it was the funniest thing he'd ever witnessed.

"Rashid is dead?" Udai asked me.

I frowned. Was he? Maybe? I didn't know. "I didn't see what happened to him, your majesty. There was too much happening all at once. He might have been killed, but he might have survived, but that's not what's important now. I saw something you should know about."

"Well, spit it out, girl," he said, nodding for me to continue.

"Javed Khorasani's palace was guarded by nothing but peasant levies. I think his real army has been on the march for Rohiri for some time. They're probably at least a day ahead of us, maybe more."

"If they beat us to the river and cross it . . ." Arjun murmured.

"Then there'll be hell to pay," Udai growled. He looked to me. "How many zahhaks does Khorasani have left?"

"Four, your majesty," I said.

"And we have twelve . . ." he muttered. "I sent for help to the other maharajas of Registan, but there's no telling if they'll arrive in time or not."

"And we don't even have enough riders for the zahhaks we do have," Karim noted.

"And our army?" Arjun asked. "I saw that it was marching."

"The vanguard set out four hours ago," Udai replied. "But if Javed Khorasani really marched his men out yesterday, they won't reach the river in time."

"If he even chooses to attack now," said Arjun. "It could be that he'll cut his losses and sue for peace."

"He won't," I said.

"And how can you be so sure, girl?" the maharaja asked me.

"I stole my cousin's zahhaks. These are from my father's stables. Javed Khorasani still has his four beasts. I suppose he could give them to my father in exchange for clemency, but I think it's more likely he'll try to fight to win back his honor. Otherwise, he'll lose his post as subahdar within a week, and he'll be lucky if he doesn't lose his head in the bargain. My father doesn't tolerate failure from his provincial governors."

"If he's that desperate, maybe he'll attempt to take Rohiri fortress before his army even gets there," Arjun said. "With his zahhaks, I mean."

"Let him try," said the maharaja. "I've warned the garrison. The watch has been doubled; the men are ready. Their toradars will shoot them to pieces."

"And there's no profit in it," I said. "Taking Rohiri isn't going to do him much good if he can't hold it. He's going to want to win a battle in the field. If he can get his army across the river, he may be able to storm the fortress and take it, and then we'd be the ones buckling down for a long siege to take it back. And if there is a siege, your majesty, my father will rush to his aid, of that you can be certain."

"Well, in that case," said Udai, "we have no option but fly to Rohiri with all haste. We'll have to beat back his zahhaks and use our own beasts to halt his army before it can cross the river. Of course, we only have nine fliers for twelve zahhaks, so that reduces our advantage."

"Ten fliers, your majesty," I replied, nodding to Lakshmi, who was being embraced tightly by Sakshi.

The maharaja frowned, but Arjun said, "She flies well, Father.

She's been trained by some of the finest tutors in the Virajendra empire. She's young, I know, but I flew my first battle at thirteen, and she's only two years younger than that."

"You can't mean to send her into a battle!" Sakshi exclaimed, holding her close. "Razia, hasn't she done enough?"

"Not yet," I said. "And anyway, she wants to go, don't you?" I addressed the last at Lakshmi.

"Yes, Akka!" Lakshmi chirped, standing up straighter and throwing off Sakshi's embrace. "This new zahhak flies almost as beautifully as my Mohini."

"She'll fly my wing, your majesty, and we'll support Sultan Ahmed's acid zahhaks against Khorasani's beasts while you and your fire zahhaks lay waste to his army," I told Udai.

"What do you think, Ahmed?" he asked the Mahisagari sultan.

Karim cut in, before Ahmed could say a word. "You can say what you want about Razia, Father, but she's one of the best zahhak riders I've ever met. When she was Salim Mirza, she put her cousins to shame in the air, and the way she flew tonight was as smooth as anyone."

"I've seen her put Padmini through maneuvers that taught me a thing or two," Arjun agreed. "And as I said before, Lakshmi may be young, but she's been well trained by the finest masters in Virajendra. You'd be a fool to judge either of them by their appearances alone."

"I don't much care for leaving military matters in the hands of hijras," said Ahmed, scowling at me. "But I suppose she has an exemplary record thus far, so I have no objection."

"If I may, your majesty," I said, bowing my head in Udai's direction. "I recommend leaving the other two thunder zahhaks in reserve. They'll be useful bargaining chips for my father, and there's no sense risking them with untrained riders."

He gave a curt nod of his head in response. "We'll have the

stableboys deal with those two"—he gestured to the zahhaks that Arjun and Karim had been riding—"and then we'll take to the skies and make for Rohiri with all haste."

"Very good, your majesty." While the two thunder zahhaks were led away, I went over to Sakshi, who was still hugging our little sister.

"You're as bad as Ammi, you know that?" she snapped, slapping my shoulder the moment I got within arm's reach of her.

"I what?" I gasped.

"Forcing Lakshmi to fly zahhaks in battle, to break into palaces, to see dead bodies!" She shook her head. "You ought to be ashamed of yourself, Razia! I thought you of all people would understand that Lakshmi deserves better."

"She does deserve better," I agreed, my voice thick with a swirl of emotions—guilt and resentment chief among them. I wasn't like Ammi. I wasn't asking anything of Lakshmi that she didn't want to do anyway, and it was for her own good. Once this fight was over, she'd be able to get back everything she'd lost. Why couldn't Sakshi see that?

"You know why she has to fly with me today." My irritation finally showed through in my voice. "With a zahhak of her own, she'll have status and power in her own right. She won't be beholden to men or to gurus like we've been. She'll be able to choose things for herself."

"Except whether or not to ride off into battle!" Sakshi countered.

"I want to go, Akka!" Lakshmi chimed in. "Razia is right, I want to do this! It's all I've ever wanted, ever since I left home. And I'm really good at it—even Prince Karim says so."

"Prince Karim is not a nice man," Sakshi muttered, keeping her voice low enough that the Mahisagari men wouldn't overhear.

"That's not the point, Akka!" Lakshmi exclaimed. "I'm a really good flier! I trained to do it my whole life! This is what I want to do."

Sakshi sighed, but before she could say anything, Lakshmi said, "I'm not a baby anymore, Akka. I know I'm not as old as you or Razia, but I can do this."

"I'll keep her safe, I promise," I said, enfolding the pair of them in a hug.

Sakshi sighed. "Fine, you take her with you, and you keep her safe, but when you come back, you're going to teach me to ride one of those zahhaks, because I'm not going to let you leave me behind like this anymore."

"It's a deal," I promised her. "It'll be just the three of us, soaring through the skies, like my great-grandmother Razia and her squadron of woman fliers. You'll see."

"You always did have a way of spinning stories . . ." Sakshi muttered.

"One of her many talents," said Arjun, coming up behind us with Padmini trailing behind him. He nodded to me. "Ready to go?"

"Just about." I gave Sakshi one last hug. "We'll be back soon."

"You'd better be—or your ghost and I are going to have words." But she hugged me one last time, and Lakshmi after that, holding us for such a long time that Udai had to clear his throat to break us apart.

My cheeks burned as I noticed that the men had been staring at us. I murmured, "Sorry, your majesty," as I hurried to help Lakshmi into the saddle. Once she was seated, I started working on one of her shoulder straps while she worked on the other. "Remember, make it so tight you can hardly stand it."

"I know how to do it, Akka," she replied, with such a lofty air that for the first time I saw the young prince she'd been before her arrival in the dera.

I rolled my eyes. "Fine, you do it, then, but if you fall out, I'm not going to catch you." I stood up on my tiptoes and ruffled her hair, which annoyed her and pleased her in equal measure, and then I went back to Sultana, who was waiting patiently.

"You're a much better little sister than that other one," I told her, giving her a pat on the snout. "She never listens, no matter how hard I try."

"I listen!" Lakshmi protested, as I'd known she would.

I felt well pleased with myself as I climbed into the saddle. I was careful to strap in tightly and to make sure everything was set before turning Sultana so that she was in line with the other zahhaks to take off. I hadn't seen so many in one place since leaving Nizam, and never three different species. The acid zahhaks were in the lead, as they needed the shortest takeoff distance, followed by the fire zahhaks, with Lakshmi and me in the rear on our thunder zahhaks. Our animals were the fastest, so we could have given the others a head start and still caught up without too much difficulty.

I looked over at Lakshmi, who was sitting proudly in her saddle, her reins held with the kind of practiced ease born of long experience, and I smiled. She was made for this, just as I had been. "Remember, you're flying my wing today. I want you to follow my orders, but keep good spacing, and if you see a chance for a kill, take it."

"Yes, Akka!" The thought of shooting down another zahhak in an aerial battle had made a light shine in her eyes. It was the ultimate achievement for a warrior prince. I was sure it had been beaten into her head as often as it had been beaten into mine—a prince who didn't claim an aerial victory was no sort of prince at all. And we, as effeminate hijras, were thought to be incapable of it. That was certainly what my father had believed about me, and none of the stories Lakshmi had told me of her father had led me to believe he was any different.

"Razia."

I looked up and saw that Arjun was twisted backward in his saddle to talk to me.

"Yes, my prince?"

"I don't know what's going to happen today, if we're going to face Khorasani's zahhaks or not, but just promise me you won't do anything too crazy, okay?"

"Crazy?" I frowned at that. "What do you mean?"

"I mean like climbing a two-hundred-foot cliff with your bare hands," he said, and his voice was half admiring, half horrified. "When you slipped . . ." He clenched his jaw and shook his head, like that could drive away the pain of the memory. "Look, we have the upper hand now. We have the advantage in numbers. You don't have to save us single-handedly. You don't have anything to prove to me."

My heart skipped a beat. He understood. He knew why I climbed two-hundred-foot cliffs bare-handed, why I killed a sentry with a katar thrust to the throat, why I shot a lightning bolt in a crowded stable. He understood all of it. He knew that my whole life I'd been told by those closest to me that I was a worthless coward, and that every day I tried to prove them wrong.

"I'll be careful, my prince," I promised him.

"We'll talk more in Rohiri," he said, and then he turned in his saddle and Padmini started her takeoff run.

I glanced over at Lakshmi, swallowed the lump in my throat, and said again, "Remember, keep good spacing off my wing," because I wanted to say something to her, and "I love you" seemed too final, like the words would bring bad luck crashing down on our heads.

All that was lost on Lakshmi. She just said, "Yes, Akka," and she lowered her goggles down over her eyes, and the sight of her brought a pained smile to my lips. She looked like the perfect Virajendran warrior princess just then, the sort of girl who should have made any father proud. I didn't think I'd ever understand our fathers, and why they despised us so much.

I drove those thoughts from my mind, lowered my own goggles over my eyes, took up the reins, and gave them a quick snap. Sultana lunged forward, her talons scratching the cobblestones as her powerful front legs threw us off the ground in a single bound, my whole body shaking from the force of it. An instant later, the trauma of takeoff was over, and I was gliding with perfect smoothness on still wings, a trail of zahhaks in front of me, all heading northeast toward Rohiri and the coming battle.

I wondered just how much of a march Javed Khorasani had on us. If his army had already crossed the river, they'd be in position to assault the fortress and there might not be anything we could do to stop them. With four thunder zahhaks, they could blow the gates open, and their men would be able to do the rest—especially if they had artillery support. It was how my father had captured so many enemy cities over his long career. Once he gained aerial supremacy, it was as easy as raining thunderbolts down on his adversaries.

Whatever promises I had made to Arjun, it would be up to me to stop them. The fire zahhaks would have their hands full with the enemy army, and while the acid zahhaks were fast and agile fliers, they were no match for a thunder zahhak in the open air in a fair fight. It would fall to me, and to Lakshmi, to take out Khorasani's remaining zahhaks so that our other fliers could concentrate on his army. At the very least, we'd have to tie him down to keep him from interrupting the fire zahhaks in their attack runs.

I gave a bemused shake of my head then. I'd never imagined when I'd run away to the dera that I'd ever find myself on Sultana's back again, let alone flying off into battle. I'd given all that up to be a girl. The idea of being able to do both had never occurred to me, and as good as I seemed to be at strategizing, it could never have competed with living as my real self. But now, here I was, living a life with space for both. It was like a dream come true.

That was what I would be fighting for today. Udai was fighting to protect his landholdings and to increase his status as a warlord. Ahmed was fighting to solidify an alliance. Karim was fighting for glory. Arjun was fighting to defend his home. I was fighting to have the life of my dreams, to be able to spend my days showing Lakshmi the finer points of flying zahhaks and my nights showing Arjun the finer points of everything my very expensive tutors had taught me in the dera. What more could a girl have possibly wanted?

As the sun rose over the eastern horizon, casting its golden light over the desert, I felt a sense of peace settle in my heart. I knew that there was still a battle to fight, but now I saw a whole world of opportunity opening up before me, one that I'd never been able to see before. If I survived this fight, I wouldn't just be the concubine of some prince. I would be a noblewoman in my own right, and perhaps the first lady zahhak rider since the days of my great-grandmother Razia and her entourage. She'd been to Zindh too, before ascending the throne of Nizam. Could such a future be in store for me as well? I'd never conceived of myself as an ambitious woman, but now that I had my Sultana back, I could imagine myself following in her footsteps as a powerful, independent noblewoman, fully the equal of any man, and I liked that image a great deal.

"Razia?"

I glanced up, roused from my thoughts by Arjun's voice. He was right beside me, just ten feet off Sultana's right wing. It was terrible formation practice, far too close to be combat effective, but it brought a smile to my face all the same. "Yes, my prince?"

"What were you thinking about?" he asked, amusement twisting his lips into a slight smile.

"The future, my prince," I replied.

"The future?"

"The future," I agreed.

"Well, did it look nice?" he teased.

"It did, my prince," I said. "It looked better than nice. I don't think I've ever seen anything that's made me so happy."

He looked wounded. "Not even me?"

"When did I say that you weren't in my future, my prince?" I asked.

That brought his smile back. "And what was I doing in this future of yours?"

A mischievous impulse rose up in me that I didn't care to suppress. "You don't want to know."

"I don't?" He leaned to the left, bringing Padmini's wing just that much closer to Sultana's.

"No, it's far too improper for a prince," I informed him.

He raised an eyebrow. "I don't think I like you having your zahhak back."

"Oh?" What on earth did he mean by that?

"I like having you in my saddle with me," he said, patting the empty spot.

"In the future, there will be time for that too," I promised him.

"So you think we have a future?" he asked, and I realized then that he was nervous.

"Why wouldn't we?" I asked.

He shrugged. "I don't know. Javed Khorasani has stolen a march on us. He might have sent for help to your father, and we'll be facing four thunder zahhaks with just two of our own to counter them. It's no guarantee of success."

"My father's army won't have any chance of reaching the field in time, even if he does help," I assured him. "And your fire zahhaks are going to obliterate Javed Khorasani's army."

"And the thunder zahhaks?" he asked.

"Leave those to me," I said, a grin creeping across my face as I envisioned the battle to come. I wasn't scared. I was *happy*. "Does that make me crazy?"

"Does what make you crazy?" Arjun asked.

"I'm not scared of Javed Khorasani's zahhaks," I said. "I'm excited. I want to tear into them more than I've ever wanted anything."

"If that's crazy, then you're in good company!" Karim shouted to me, from a little distance off my left wing.

"You want to fight?" Arjun asked, and he sounded more concerned.

I nodded, and struggled to put into words what I was feeling. After a moment, though, I realized it wasn't really that complicated. "I trained for years to do this, my prince, and I never had the chance. I had to give up my whole life to be my true self; I had to endure years of abuse, of insults, of beatings, of men telling me that I never could have been any good at this because I wasn't one of them. Today, I'm going to prove them wrong. Today, I'm going to prove my father wrong."

"You've already proved me wrong," said Karim, which was a more generous gesture than I'd ever expected from him. I still hated him for what he'd done to me, but I supposed maybe he'd done the growing up my cousin Rashid hadn't.

"Razia, you swore that you wouldn't try to win this fight single-handedly," Arjun said, and I realized that I was the reason he was so anxious. He wasn't afraid of the fight to come; he was worried about me. "You don't have anything to prove. I know what kind of person you are. I've known it from the moment we met. You don't have to risk your life because of your father. You don't have to do anything for that miserable old bastard."

"I swear that I won't do any more or less than is needed, my prince," I replied, though I knew that wasn't the promise he was looking for. He wanted me back home in the palace; I could see it in his eyes. He didn't want me risking my life in a battle. Well, now he would know how I'd felt being forced to sit on silk cushions and await his return in Mahisagar.

I glanced forward, to check our progress, and I saw the fortress of Rohiri, perched on a cliff not unlike Shikarpur's, though this one overlooked a river. On the other side of the river was Javed Khorasani's army. The cannons were already belching smoke to keep the fortress's defenders' heads down, and men were starting to move across the river on makeshift rafts. Soaring high above the fight were three thunder zahhaks, their golden underparts gleaming in the morning sunlight.

"Three thunder zahhaks, dead ahead!" I cried. "Fire zahhaks, engage those boats, we'll give the thunder zahhaks something to think about!"

"Why are there only three of them?" Udai asked. "I thought they had four."

It took my mind all of a single second to come up with the answer. "They sent the fourth to my father to beg his help in this fight, your majesty. We have to drop those zahhaks and burn those boats now, before my father answers the call. He could be here in just a few hours if he flies."

"Right." Udai gave a nod of his head that rattled his bushy black beard. "Fire zahhaks, with me!" He pitched his zahhak up before rolling her onto her belly and pulling her into the dive. One by one, the other fire zahhaks followed him down, Arjun last of all.

"Your majesty," I said to Ahmed, who was flying just off my right atop his splendid emerald and turquoise acid zahhak. "Take your fliers up for altitude. Lakshmi and I will tangle with the thunder zahhaks. We'll try to drag them lower. Once we do, you pounce on them and use your altitude advantage to make up for their advantage in speed."

"A good plan if ever I heard one," Karim said, before his father could register a complaint at being ordered around by a hijra. And then he said, "Good luck, Razia—give them a taste of the hell they gave you as a child."

"A good plan if ever I heard one," I replied, flashing him a wink. I glanced over to make sure that Lakshmi was with me. She was in perfect position off my right wing, about a turn circle's diameter away. I couldn't have flown it better myself. "Pick your target. We're going to turn with them and try to get them good and slow for the acid zahhaks."

"Yes, Akka!" Lakshmi answered. She scanned the sky in front of her, and her eyes locked on to one in particular. "I've got the pretty one with the white tips to her tailfeathers."

"I see her," I said. "I've got the big one on the far left. Now, let's get moving and make them pay for attacking our country, all right?"

She nodded her agreement and snapped her reins, and her zahhak raced toward the fight. For my part, I gave Sultana all the urging I could with pressure from my thighs and snaps from my reins. Her wings beat a blur on either side of me, and the force of the wind pressed me flush against the stiff back of my saddle. Oh, how I'd missed this.

The other thunder zahhaks got big in a hurry. They'd spotted us, and they were flying toward us too. They knew that if they dove down to stop the fire zahhaks we'd pounce on them. Their only hope was to kill us, and then deal with Udai's zahhaks in turn. So they came at us with all the speed that they possessed. We'd been miles apart, but now it was just hundreds of yards. I saw one of the zahhaks open her mouth, and I twisted in my saddle just as the lightning bolt exploded out of her throat. It ripped through the air, just off my left wing, narrowly missing me, and the smell of burning wind filled my nostrils.

I rolled back level, put Sultana's nose on the enemy rider who had just shot at me, and shouted, "Thunder!" Her mouth yawned open in response, and there was a mighty crack and a burst of light hotter and brighter than the sun, and the enemy zahhak twisted to escape the bolt of lightning that crossed the distance between us in the blink of an eye.

The enemy flier dodged the lightning bolt, but he was out of position now, leaving me alone with my chosen opponent—the man flying the biggest of Javed Khorasani's zahhaks. I wondered if that was Javed himself, or one of his sons. They were all justifiably famous for their skill in flying. Not that it mattered. I was going to turn these provincials into so much smoldering dust.

The big zahhak shot a bolt at me, but I ducked beneath it with a quick pull of the reins. It was a well-timed shot the rider had taken, so close it was almost impossible to dodge, but his concentration on shooting had given me an advantage. The safest place to be in an aerial battle is right behind your opponent, where his zahhak can't shoot you but you can shoot him. So the whole key was to get behind the other flier and bring him down. With his zahhak having recently shot a bolt, she needed a few precious seconds to recover herself before trying again, and that gave me the chance to cut inside the turn we were both preparing to make.

It was a dangerous maneuver, because it exposed me for a split second to his zahhak's breath, but with her lightning still recovering, he couldn't shoot. So when he turned back into me, our zahhaks passing each other in midair as we started to chase each other's tails, I was already a few precious seconds ahead of him.

With Sultana's wings tucked in, forming sickles of feathers on either side of her body, I tore through the air after my opponent, Sultana's nose inching closer and closer to his zahhak's tail, the blue feathers spread wide as she dug into her turn. Another few seconds and I would have him dead to rights.

Of course, we were fighting two against three, so I couldn't keep my eyes fixed on just one enemy. I twisted my head and looked high inside the turn, which was where I would have been if I'd been the third zahhak rider looking to make an attack. Sure enough, there he was, screaming down at me, pulling hard to get enough lead to take a shot.

I leaned left and jerked the reins hard in the direction of the third rider, tightening Sultana's turn. Then, with a flick of my body weight, I sent her rolling back to the right, pulling back on the reins, forcing her to climb as she rolled, forming a corkscrew in the sky. The sudden climb slowed us down so much that the enemy zahhak shot out beneath us. That was when I pounced. I flicked the reins for speed, and Sultana dropped right in behind him. I shouted, "Thunder!" and she roared.

I'd heard stories growing up, mostly from my father, about what it was like to knock down another zahhak in aerial combat, but I'd never seen it before. So when the lightning bolt hit the enemy zahhak and her rider, and the pair of them smoldered and crumpled and fell, I could scarcely believe my eyes. Was it really so anticlimactic? They'd just gone limp and started to tumble, but I knew from the way they were falling that they'd never recover.

"Akka! Break right!"

I didn't know how I heard Lakshmi's voice over the roar of the slipstream, but I didn't hesitate. I twisted to the right, jerking the reins in that direction, and Sultana broke into a hard right-hand turn. An instant later, a bolt of lightning shot by beneath her belly. I twisted in the saddle to look behind me, and I saw the big zahhak back there. She was powerful, and her wings were taking huge beats, letting her keep up her speed in the turn.

Lakshmi was back there, on the big beast's tail, but she had another one coming down on her. If she didn't move, it was going to kill her. "Lakshmi, break off!" I cried, praying that she would obey me.

Lakshmi's head twisted, she spotted the threat, and she immediately turned against it. I smiled then. Good girl. Whatever else happened, I had total faith in her. Now I just had to teach Javed Khorasani a thing or two about flying a zahhak, as there could be no doubt who the gray-bearded flier behind me was. He was gaining on me in the turn, and it wouldn't be long before he could take another shot. He wouldn't miss a second time.

She was a big beast, that zahhak of his, and that was going to be her undoing. It made her powerful and very fast in level flight, but I knew it would make her accelerate more slowly. So I pulled as tightly into the turn as I possibly could, knowing that it would slow me down, but knowing that it would also let me get closer to Khorasani's tail. I kept up the crushing turn until Khorasani's zahhak stopped moving relative to mine. Then I left off the reins and squeezed my knees and let Sultana fly straight and level away from him for as long as she could.

Javed Khorasani must have thought I was running away from him. He tightened his turn, eager to get on my tail and shoot me down. I waited until Sultana had some speed back, and then I turned as hard as I possibly could against him in our swirling, spiraling fight. Suddenly, I was the one moving toward his tail, not the other way around. In his eagerness to get behind me, he'd slowed himself down, and that big beast wouldn't be able to regain her energy like Sultana could.

His only hope was to pull as hard as he could to try to take a shot, and that was just what he did. He turned tight; I turned tighter. We were about to go head-to-head for one brief second, but I wasn't going to let him win the fight that way. I wasn't going to die here. I waited until the last second, and then I pulled Sultana's head down relative to the turn, ducking beneath the bigger zahhak at the instant before she got the shot she was after.

Once I was past them, I reversed, pulling right into them. He reversed too, but his zahhak was bigger and slower. Still, she was a good beast, very obedient, fierce, and she was going to make a fight of it. She turned toward me more tightly than I would have thought possible, but I had another trick up my sleeve. I pulled back on the reins, climbing as I fought to get behind her. My lighter zahhak easily got above Khorasani's heavier one. Now, as we twisted back and forth, each trying to get behind the other's tail, I steadily climbed higher and higher above him.

There! I had him. I twisted into the dive, coming down right on top of him. "Thunder!"

It all happened so fast that my eyes couldn't track it. There was a blast of heat and light, and then I was diving below the big zahhak, searching the skies for her. I spotted her a second later, tumbling out of control, her feathers smoldering. That was two down—just one left.

I looked all over for Lakshmi, praying that she was still alive, still in the fight. When my eyes finally found her, she was chasing the tail of the pretty enemy zahhak, which was in turn about to bring down an acid zahhak—Amira. Karim was in trouble. It was just a question of who shot first.

Lakshmi's high-pitched voice cried, "Thunder!" and her zahhak responded at once. The sky rumbled and the air shook as a lightning bolt erupted from her zahhak's mouth. It hit the enemy rider squarely in his back, and both rider and zahhak went limp at once and started the long tumble to the ground. As they fell, I looked around for the acid zahhaks, wondering why the rest of them hadn't bothered to help us out, and I saw that they were busy down below, taking out the cannons on the far shore. The

fire zahhaks had their hands full setting fire to the boats still trying to cross the river.

With the skies clear, Karim slid into position on my left wing
with Lakshmi on my right. He shouted, "You fly like the stories
people tell of Razia Sultana."

I preened a little on hearing that, which made him laugh. "It
was good work, Razia." He looked over at Lakshmi on the opposite side of me and shouted, "And thank you for the rescue, my
lady!" He gave her a grandiloquent bow, which made her blush. I
allowed myself a smile, but I wasn't going to let my guard down. I
knew what he did to eleven-year-olds.

"Shall we get down there and help Arjun punish the Nizamis?" Karim asked, nodding to the fire zahhaks, who were now
attacking the infantry columns.

I was about to say yes, when something caught my eye—dark
shapes on the horizon. There were at least a dozen of them, all
thunder zahhaks—my father's aerial army. They had come after all.

There were far too many to oppose in the open air, but if I
could slow them down, then maybe the Nizami army would be so
badly routed that my father wouldn't feel the need to press the
attack. It was our only hope of surviving.

"Yes!" I shouted to Karim. "Let's get down there and take out
the infantry!" I made sure that Lakshmi heard me. I pitched
up, then rolled over like I was going to dive, but I didn't dive; I
hung there for a second, watched Lakshmi and Karim fall away to
help out fighting the infantry, and then I rolled Sultana back level
again. I put the twelve thunder zahhaks on her nose, and I urged
her on with every last ounce of speed she possessed.

## CHAPTER 20

I didn't know what I was thinking, racing headlong toward my death when my life was finally starting to make sense. All those thoughts of the future that had seemed so near on the way to the battle now seemed impossibly distant. Arjun was somewhere far below me, and unless I was a better flier than I thought I was, I would never see him again. Or Lakshmi. Or Sakshi. No. It seemed that my father would have the last laugh.

Twelve zahhaks were coming at me like musket balls fired from toradars. They were getting so big so quickly. In a moment, they'd be in range to shoot me, and I was sure they would know from the way I'd been flying with acid zahhaks a moment before that I was an enemy and attack. I could dodge the first volley— maybe. But after that, it would be hopeless. There were too many of them, and I was totally alone.

Still, I was going to have to put up a fight, going to have to de- lay them. There was no other option. If I failed, Arjun would die, and Lakshmi too, and Rohiri would fall, and then Bikampur, and Sakshi would die then. No, it all rested on my shoulders. I was going to have to find some way to hold them off.

"God, why do you have to make my life so hard?" I asked, as I raced toward certain death. He didn't reply, not that I'd expected him to. I took a deep breath and pressed my knees tighter against Sultana's flanks. She started to move a little faster. We'd need that speed if we were going to survive the first enemy volley.

I was just getting into range when the enemy fliers did a funny thing. They broke off. All of them just suddenly turned and started to move away from me. They were running from me? I knew I'd flown pretty well against Javed Khorasani, but what were they doing running from me?

I looked behind me, wondering if maybe they were seeing something that I wasn't seeing. I couldn't believe my eyes—almost two dozen dark shapes were back there, winging their way toward me. Four of them were acid zahhaks, one was a thunder zahhak, but all the rest were fire zahhaks—twenty in total. Where had they all come from? What were they doing here?

I looked back toward the thunder zahhaks in front of me. They were spiraling down to land in the open desert. Did they want to talk? It certainly looked that way. I turned Sultana away from them and flew back toward the fire zahhaks behind me. I knew I was going to catch an earful from Arjun for doing what I'd done, but I couldn't help it. I wasn't going to let my father kill him.

Already, the fire zahhaks were beginning to spiral toward the ground too, so I followed them, landing in their midst after a rapid descent. I'd barely managed to undo my saddle straps when strong arms jerked me down from Sultana's back.

"You promised me you wouldn't do anything crazy!" Arjun exclaimed.

"I scared them off, didn't I?" I asked.

"Yes, I'm sure they were terrified of you," he agreed, but my joke, and my being alive and healthy, had wrested a smile from his lips. He kissed me on my forehead and pulled me close to him. "I'm just glad you're safe."

"Me too," I replied.

"You flew beautifully," he said. "I saw it from down below. The way you killed Javed Khorasani . . ." He shook his head. "I've never seen anyone outwit him like that before."

"Well, you and your father don't have to worry about him anymore," I said.

"No," Udai agreed. "We just have to worry about your father, it seems."

I felt my cheeks burn, but he wasn't wrong. "If turning me over to him wins you peace, your majesty, I am ready to serve."

"Nonsense." He waved the suggestion away. "You are my retainer, a noble lady of Bikampur, and my finest flier. I am not going to sell you to Humayun Mirza, not if he offers me a crore rupees."

"A noble lady of Bikampur?" I gasped, not sure I'd heard him right. It was one thing to be a concubine, but to be a noble lady, I would need lands, titles, an estate, the money to support it all, to say nothing of military obligations and the hereditary privileges that came with all those things. Giving all that to a hijra, even one who had been a crown prince, was utterly unthinkable.

"We'll work out the details later," he said. "For now, let's get organized and see what your father wants with us."

"Yes, your majesty," I agreed.

He turned then, to address the fire zahhak riders who had joined us in fending off my father's attack. They were all newcomers, but all clearly nobles of Registan, judging by their fine kurtas and the khandas hanging from their sashes. They must have received Udai's message and come with all haste to Rohiri. One particularly tall man with a well-trimmed gray beard seemed to be in charge.

"Udai Agnivansha, it's been too long," the gray-bearded man said.

"Maharaja Rajesh Chauhan of Jaigarh, you couldn't have come at a better time," Udai replied. "And I see you've brought friends. Maharaja Zorawar, you honor me with your aid in my time of need."

"We'd heard that the sultan of Nizam was sticking his nose where it didn't belong," said Rajesh. "I can see that we were not misinformed."

"No, you weren't," Udai agreed. He nodded to the group of Nizami noblemen who had gathered about half a mile in the distance. "Shall we go and see what they want?"

"Yes, I think that would be best," said Rajesh.

I let the maharajas lead the way, preferring to walk with Arjun and Lakshmi—and even Karim. Though the latter was saying, "You ask me, we should have let her take them on. After the way she tore apart Javed Khorasani and his sons, she might have managed to bring down her father in the bargain."

"Don't encourage her," Arjun warned.

"Why not?" Karim asked. "She's not my concubine."

"I'm not sure she's anyone's concubine now," Arjun murmured, looking over at me uncertainly. "Not after what my father said."

"Whatever I am, my prince, I am yours," I told him, taking his hand in both of mine.

Karim snorted laughter. "Is that really how you slept your way to the top? With lines like that?"

"I don't think it was her words so much . . ." Arjun murmured. He laughed when I clapped my hands over Lakshmi's ears.

"She shouldn't be listening to this kind of talk at her age," I said.

"She killed a man," Karim countered. "I think she'll find a way to survive."

He was right. She had killed a man. I'd killed two today. I didn't even feel guilty about them, not like I had with the poor peasant sentry in Shikarpur. The men I'd been flying against had been trying to kill my family and destroy my home. What I'd done was justice. And that went double for Lakshmi, who had saved Karim's life. I lowered my hands from her ears and draped them around her shoulders instead. "You flew beautifully today."

"Not as beautifully as you, Akka," she replied. "If not for Prince Karim helping me, I might have been killed."

"And if not for you helping me, I would have been killed," I told her. I kissed her on top of her head for that. "You're a very fine wingmate."

She flushed with pride and stood up a little straighter as she marched along beside me. I was grateful that she was safe, that nothing had happened to her, that I wasn't going to have to greet Sakshi and give her horrible news about her little sister. For all the money and glory that men won in war, it hardly seemed worth the risk to me.

We were nearing the knot of Nizami men now, getting close enough that I could make out the individuals. There was the perpetually scowling face of Sikander, my father's master-at-arms. He was older now, his beard holding more salt than pepper, but his disposition didn't look like it had changed much. And beside him was Shahrukh, my father's younger brother and the most powerful subahdar in the empire. His sons were standing beside him—Tariq and Rashid. The former had his hand resting on the hilt of his talwar, and the look on his face told me how desperate he was to use it. Beside him, his little brother, Rashid, was smirking at me. Somehow, he'd survived Sultana's lightning bolt in the zahhak stables. I wasn't sure how I felt about that, but then my eyes landed on my father, and I forgot all about Rashid.

My father hadn't changed much either. He still had the same silly mustache that stuck out too far from his cheeks. His hair was still mostly black, though I saw gray there that had once been absent. It was the eyes he shared with me that were most notable— the emerald green of the royal family of Nizam. He wore the same businesslike kurta and trousers he always had, devoid of any flowery embroidery or bright colors, which he reckoned belonged only in the women's quarters. The only decoration he wore on his person was the gold koftgari on the handles of his katars. Otherwise, he was a warrior king, a man of simple tastes and a disciplinarian above all.

I half wished I was wearing one of my beautiful outfits that Arjun had bought for me. I was wearing my bangles, because no proper young lady would be caught dead without them, and they were my pretty fire zahhak bangles, but beyond that I was dressed in little more than a sweat-stained black silk kameez and matching shalwar. It was a shame. If my father was going to have me executed, I'd rather have worn something that really merited the punishment. Still, I had my dupatta, and that would infuriate him well enough.

The two groups stopped about a dozen paces from one another, then stared each other down for a long moment. It was my father who finally broke the silence. He said, "Udai Agnivansha, I did not know you to be a man with so many friends."

The maharaja of Bikampur laughed at that. "It occurs to me, Humayun, that I didn't know it either."

"Well, for my part, I am inclined to add myself to that list," my father told him. "I will ensure that the new subahdar of Zindh does not cross the border or meddle in your trade routes along the coast. I only ask for one thing in exchange."

"And what is that?" Udai asked, though I thought he already knew. I knew.

"My son and the zahhaks he stole," my father replied.

Udai laughed at him, which I thought was pretty courageous, considering people who laughed at my father in Nizam tended to lose their tongues. "Your majesty, forgive me for correcting your arithmetic, but that's five things."

My father just shrugged. "That is the price of my friendship."

"Well, we can discuss the zahhaks," said Udai. "But I know nothing of any son of yours."

"Liar!" Rashid exclaimed. "He's standing right behind you! He's right there!" He jabbed his finger at me for emphasis.

"Razia?" Udai raised an eyebrow. "Razia is my son's concubine. Is your son my son's concubine, your majesty?"

I'd never seen my father's face turn quite the shade that it did then. It was verging on purple as the blood rushed to his cheeks. His pulse was pounding in his temples and the veins in his neck were bulging. He said, through clenched teeth, "The girl will be given to me or I will wipe your city from the face of the earth."

"What are you going to do with her?" Arjun demanded.

"Something I should have done a long time ago," my father replied, and he rested his hand on his katars to make the threat perfectly explicit.

"You'd kill the golden goose?" Karim marveled. "Your majesty, I've known you most of my life, but until today I never thought you a fool."

"I would think very carefully about my words if I were you, boy," my father warned. "I am in no mood for games today."

"Who's playing games?" Karim asked. "You know as well as I do what I thought of your worthless son. But in the last twelve hours, I've seen that girl scale a two-hundred-foot cliff with her bare hands, steal four zahhaks from the palace of Shikarpur, and bring down Javed Khorasani in single combat in the air. If it had been me that had done those things, they'd be singing my praises from the mountains of Rakha to the jungles of Virajendra. And that's not all she's done. It was her strategy that defeated the Firangi fleet. She outwitted your pathetic nephew Rashid. And she devised the plan to steal the zahhaks from under Javed Khorasani's nose to save Bikampur. You've got a blind spot where she's concerned. In your eyes, she's worse than the basest criminal, but if she were my child, I'd buy her all the pretty bangles she wanted and thank the gods for not sticking me with someone as stupid and worthless as that thing." He nodded to Rashid for emphasis.

Nobody dared speak after that. Everyone knew who I really was. Sikander was glaring daggers at me. My father was still furious. The maharajas of Registan looked vaguely amused at the whole situation. Arjun was standing in such a way that nobody could get to me without going through him first, and Lakshmi was clinging to my arm.

"I will speak to the girl alone," my father said, and his tone didn't tell me much. He was angry, but he was always angry. At least he wasn't fondling his katars any longer, so maybe he wasn't planning on murdering me. Though, I had katars too, and I knew how to use them.

"By all means, your majesty," said Udai. "You settle things on that score, and when it's finished, we can discuss the terms of a truce."

My father started walking off to the north, and I followed him, albeit reluctantly. The last thing I needed in my life was another lecture from him. Hadn't I run away from home to avoid them?

He stopped walking about fifty paces from the others and whirled on me at once. "You enjoy humiliating me, don't you?"

"I hate it, Father," I said, gritting my teeth. "I've always hated it. That's why I left, so my presence wouldn't be a constant source of humiliation for you."

"And so you thought you would run away to Registan and fuck the sons of my enemies to—what? Please me?"

"No, that pleased *me*," I replied, for once meeting his glare with one of my own. "I'm a woman. I always have been. Nothing is ever going to change that. I'm never going to be the man you wanted me to be. And if you haven't figured that out yet, then I can't help you."

He scowled but said nothing. He just stared at me for a long moment, his eyes flickering over my face, my figure, the bangles on my wrists. "You've been cut."

"When I was thirteen," I replied. "And I take essential salts every day. I was a hijra courtesan for most of the last four years, until Arjun took me as his concubine."

The word made my father shiver with barely suppressed fury, but he said nothing. He ground his teeth, his mustache twitching. At length, he asked, "And the nonsense Karim was spouting?"

"All true," I replied, and I stood a little straighter then. "When I was made a hijra in Bikampur, my guru trained me to be a thief, to scale the walls of havelis and rob them. Scaling a cliff is not so different from scaling a wall, and stealing thunder is not so much harder than stealing gold."

"You're a thief?" he scoffed.

I shrugged. "I had no choice. When I left home, I had nothing. I've done things I liked a good deal less than stealing to keep from starving, Father, and I would do it all again."

"You didn't really bring down Javed Khorasani in single combat . . ." he murmured.

"I did," I countered. "And one of his sons too. I know you've always despised me, Father, but I was a good flier. Even Sikander would admit that."

When he had no response to that, I added, "Udai Agnivansha has made me a noblewoman of Bikampur, and a flier, and one of his most trusted counselors. Tell me, Father, does he strike you as the sort of man who would elevate a hijra to such lofty posts if she hadn't earned it?"

I thought I saw a chink in his armor, but I couldn't be sure. Not that it mattered. I didn't know why I bothered trying to get through to the man. He'd never listened to me before. He was my father, it was true, but he'd never been a father to me, not really. And he was less a father now than he'd ever been. Now, he was a foreign tyrant who seemed bent on ruining my life.

He gave a terse nod and walked away without another word. I couldn't quite believe it. He was just going to walk off? Not even a good-bye? God, how I hated him. I stalked back to the Registani men, taking my place at Arjun's side, acutely aware of the eyes on me from both sides. I was just grateful that the Registani side was showing me some modicum of respect.

"Here are my terms," my father said, once everyone had gathered to listen. "I offer you peace, and a guarantee of your borders, and that your ships will remain unmolested while at sea. In exchange, you will surrender the four zahhaks you have stolen to the new subahdar of Zindh."

"And the girl?" Udai asked.

"The new subahdar of Zindh," my father replied. "Razia Khanum, princess of Nizam."

I was so shocked that for a long second I couldn't think straight. I was just grateful that I wasn't the only one. Jaws were hanging open all around as the men fought to process what he was saying.

"You're offering the province to me?" I asked, when I could think to ask anything at all.

"Why not?" My father shrugged. "You're my daughter. It couldn't be in safer hands."

I grunted as I saw the genius of it. My father hadn't built an empire on stupidity. With me as the subahdar of Zindh, I would be beholden to him. I would bring my talents and my hard-won zahhaks back into the fold. And I would ensure peace on this frontier, because I was the prince of Bikampur's lover and on good terms with the prince of Mahisagar. And my successes in battle and in politics had shown me capable of doing the job. All my father's problems would be solved in an instant, allowing him to focus his attention on the border tensions with Virajendra.

"Your daughter?" Tariq growled, and his talwar was halfway out of its scabbard before my father stopped him with a gesture.

"Daughters can't inherit the throne." He gave me a significant look to make sure I understood that.

"That was never my intention, Father," I replied.

He glanced to Udai. "What do you say?"

Udai stroked his beard for a second as he mulled it over. At length, he said, "I agree in principle, but your majesty must understand that your daughter has been a great expense to me. Maintaining a princess of Nizam in the lifestyle to which she is accustomed is no small matter."

My father snorted laughter. "Ten lakh rupees. No more."

"Your majesty is most generous," said Udai with a bow of his head. "We have an agreement."

"Good." My father turned to me then. "Razia, I will meet you in Shikarpur no later than two weeks from today, where I will explain to you your duties, and you will carry them out as well as you have carried out your duties in the maharaja of Bikampur's service."

"Yes, Father," I agreed, immediately regretting my decision. Good-bye, freedom. I was back under my father's thumb again, even if it would be hundreds of miles distant. Not that he had even bothered leaving me with a choice. If I'd refused him, he'd have attacked just to make a point.

He left then, walking back toward his zahhaks, and his retinue followed. It was just Sikander who lingered for a moment to stare at me. I was surprised not to see pure loathing on his face, but maybe killing Javed Khorasani in aerial combat had shown him that I wasn't completely worthless.

Arjun's arms came around me, and I forgot all about Sikander. I hugged him tightly, burying my face in the sweaty fabric of his kurta.

"The subahdar of Zindh . . ." he murmured.

"I'm sorry," I replied.

"Sorry?"

I nodded. "I wanted to stay with you."

"This is much better," said Udai. "Now our northern border is secure, I'm saved from having to come up with the money to care for four thunder zahhaks and a princess, and the trade routes are once more open on the western sea. I couldn't think of a more perfect ending."

"I could . . ." I murmured, throwing my arms around Arjun's neck.

"I'm a prince, you know," he told me.

I laughed, wondering why he'd felt the need to tell me that. "Yes, you are, dear."

"A prince," he said, leaning his face closer to mine. "Not a princess. I don't have to sit around the palace in Bikampur. If I want to stay in Shikarpur at the subahdar's invitation, my father isn't going to stop me in the name of honor."

"Mine might," I replied, but I found myself liking where his thoughts were going. Maybe being the ruler of my own province wouldn't be so bad after all.

"Come on." Arjun patted me on the back, moving me in the direction of Sultana and Padmini and the rest of our zahhaks. "Let's get home, get cleaned up, and celebrate."

"Celebrate . . ." I wasn't sure I was in the mood for celebration, but I wanted a bath and a bed and a stiff drink, and I wasn't going to find them out here in the middle of the desert.

# EPILOGUE

I gazed out at the palace gardens, their bubbling fountains reflecting the orange and yellow light streaming from hundreds of bright brass lanterns, and I sighed. I'd only just arrived in the palace, and already I was leaving it behind. It was a bittersweet moment. I'd made something for myself here. After four long years of work, obeying my guru, being berated by my tutors, and dancing for every man in Bikampur with two rupees to rub together, I'd won the heart of the prince of the city, stolen my zahhak back, saved my sisters from Varsha's clutches, and been named a noblewoman by one of the gruffest, most no-nonsense maharajas I'd ever met in my life. And now I was going to be the governor of my own province. Not bad for a hijra.

While it hurt to leave Bikampur behind, I wasn't leaving the things that really mattered. I had Arjun. I had my sisters. I had Sultana back. I'd never imagined I'd see her again, much less ride her into battle like the stories I'd read of my great-grandmother

Razia Sultana. Whatever happened in Zindh, I knew I'd be able to handle it so long as I had my family at my side.

"What are you doing out here?"

I turned, just as Arjun came to stand before me. He wrapped his arms around me and pulled me tightly against him. "This is supposed to be a celebration. Why are you standing out here all alone?"

I shrugged. "I was just thinking . . ."

"Sometimes I think that's all you do," he teased, pinching my chin between thumb and forefinger, with a playful smile on his face. "Don't you ever tire of scheming?"

I rolled my eyes. "I wasn't scheming . . . exactly . . ."

I threw my arms around his neck and rested my cheek on the soft silk of his kurta. "I was just thinking about my family, that's all."

"Oof." He sighed. "Was that all?" His hand was rubbing my back in gentle circles. "Don't worry about your father and your cousins—that can wait for another day."

"Who said anything about my father and my cousins?" I asked, raising an eyebrow, unable to keep my lips from tugging upward in a smirk as I enjoyed the look of confusion on his face.

He wrinkled his forehead and scrunched up his nose. "Have I missed something?"

"I said I was thinking about my family: Lakshmi and Sakshi and Sultana and *you*." I punctuated the sentence with a firm kiss on his lips.

"That sounds like a beautiful family," he whispered, his face poised just an inch from my own.

"It really is," I agreed. "And part of me wishes we could stay here in Bikampur forever, living like a real family."

"You'd get bored," he teased.

"I can promise you I wouldn't," I replied. "Ammi gave me *very* expensive tutors, and I haven't even shown you half of what they taught me."

I stood up on my tiptoes and planted a kiss on his lips that he was quick to return. I was tempted to drag him back to the harem and forget all about this celebration that Udai had thrown in my honor. I had such a lovely bed in my chambers, and it had seen so little use of late . . .

It took me a moment to realize that Arjun was saying something. "What?"

He grinned. "So that's what it takes to stop you scheming?"

"Oh, I was scheming," I replied, fixing him with my most alluring smile, "just not about politics."

"Now, that sounds like a worthy use of your intellect." He kissed me on the neck, working his way up toward my lips. As he went, he said, "Tell me more about this plan."

"Plan?" I whispered, my breath catching in my throat.

"Mm-hmm," he replied, not pausing in his work. "You said you had a plan."

"I forgot," I lied, because this was better. With the cooling breeze floating over the gardens, and his strong arms wrapped around me, I couldn't imagine what more I needed.

Arjun paused in his kisses for a moment, his amber eyes gazing off into the distance. "I can't believe we're leaving this all behind so soon."

"Now you want to talk about that?" I demanded, wishing he would go back to the kissing, as that was doing a far better job of making me forget my worries than anything else could.

"Sorry." His fingertips brushed across my cheek, tucking a loose strand of hair behind my ear. "I just couldn't help thinking about it."

"I've been thinking about it too," I confessed. "Do you think going to Zindh is the wrong move? I could try to beg my father to change his mind . . ." I let that thought trail off, as we both knew how unlikely it was to succeed.

"I think you're going to be a brilliant subahdar," he said. "And I'm going to be right there with you the whole time—I give you my word as a prince."

"I'll hold you to that," I warned him.

"Have I ever broken a promise to you?" he asked me.

I shook my head. "No." He never had. And I knew he never would.

# ACKNOWLEDGMENTS

No book is solely the product of a single person's mind. *Stealing Thunder* began as a private project to amuse myself, my family, and my closest friends, but it has since grown beyond my wildest expectations, and I want to take a moment to thank the people who helped it to get there.

First, I want to thank my family. Thank you for sticking with me at a time when few others did, and when the world's understanding of what I was wasn't where it is today. Mom, thanks for reading every book I've ever written, from silly stories of talking camels, all the way up to *Stealing Thunder*'s sequel. Dad, thanks for considering my writing career an investment that would someday pay off, even in those years when I didn't think it ever would. Greg, thanks for accepting me without question, for being a friend at the darkest time in my life, for bearing the full weight of our parents' expectations for grandchildren, and for your insightful lessons in story structure.

To my best friend and coconspirator in all things trans activism, Shannon Andrews—thank you for demanding that I finish *Stealing Thunder* when I'd given up on it. I can't imagine what my life would be like today if I hadn't listened to you. Thank you for giving me a home when I needed one, and for being such a wonderful beta reader. Without your excitement driving me along at times when I was discouraged, I would not be a published author today.

To Qazi Asad, Syeda Atif, Sneha Bolisetty, Amrita Chowdhury, Ujaan Ghosh, Shahzadi Khan, Aarzu Maknojia, and Zadian, thank you for your support for this project, your enthusiasm, your advice, and your cultural expertise.

To the staff of the American Institute of Indian Studies in Lucknow, and to Sageerun Nisa Hussain, thank you so much for sharing with me your passion for the language of Urdu, and the history, literature, and culture of South Asia.

To Hallie Funk and Omar Gilani, thank you so much for your work on the promotional art for *Stealing Thunder*. It's been incredible working with you both, and I'm so honored to have been able to share my world with you.

To USAF Lieutenant Colonel (Ret.) Bill "Conan" Behymer, thank you so much for taking me under your wing and teaching me the arcane arts of the fighter pilot. If not for you, there's no way Razia would have pulled off that lag roll reversal in the last battle of the book, and her tactic for dealing with the Firangi fleet wouldn't have been nearly as cool. Hope to see you in the skies sometime soon.

I don't know how I'll ever be able to thank my agent, Andrea Somberg, properly. You plucked me from obscurity with a phone call that changed my life. Your help at every step of the labyrinthine process of publication has been absolutely invaluable. Thank you for having so much faith in *Stealing Thunder*, and for helping me to share it with the world.

To my first editor, Rebecca Brewer, you have made me a better writer already. This book wouldn't be as good as it is without you. Thank you so much for all your hard work, for being so incredibly gentle with your critiques, and for being so generous in answering the anxious questions of a first-time author.

To my second editor, Kristine Swartz, thanks so much for taking my book on, and for making the transition a smooth one. I've appreciated your feedback, and I am excited to work with you on the next installment in the series.

Last but not least, thank you to Dr. Kevin Cook for saving the life of a suicidal trans teenager so that she could go on to write this book.

# GLOSSARY

## PEOPLE

**Ahmed Shah** *(Ah-med Shah)* [starting off easy]—sultan of Mahisagar

**Ammi** *(Uh-me)*—name for Varsha, it's a word literally meaning "mom," sometimes used by hijras when addressing their gurus

**Arjun Agnivansha** *(Ahr-joon Ugh-nee-vuhn-shuh)*—devastatingly handsome prince of Bikampur, and Razia's chief love interest

**Arvind Singh** *(Ahr-vind Seeng)*—son of Govind Singh, a noble of Bikampur, and skilled zahhak rider

**Disha** *(Dee-shuh)*—Razia's sister from the dera

**Firangi** *(Fih-rung-ee)*—a foreigner from the west

**Gayatri Agnivansha** *(Gai-ah-tree Ugh-nee-vuhn-shuh)*—Arjun's mother and the maharani of Bikampur

**Govind Singh** *(Go-vihnd Seeng)*—a noble of Bikampur who possesses an overly large golden peacock statue

**Humayun** *(Hoo-mah-yoon)*—Razia's father, and the sultan of Nizam

**Jai** *(Jive without the v)*—a eunuch servitor at the palace in Bikampur

**Jaskaur** *(Jahs-kohr)*—Razia's sister from the dera

**Javed Khorasani** (*Jah-vayd Kor-ah-sah-nee*)—subahdar of Zindh, and an enemy of Udai Agnivansha

**Karim Shah** (*Kuh-reem* [but roll your *r* a bit] *Shah*)—son of Ahmed Shah, prince of Mahisagar, and all-around jerk

**Lakshmi** (*Luck-shmee*)—Razia's little sister in the dera, a former prince of Kolikota, and a brilliant zahhak rider

**Rashid** (*Ruh-sheed*)—the younger of Razia's two cousins, and son of her uncle Shahrukh

**Razia Khan** (*Rah-zee-uh*)—former crown prince of the sultanate of Nizam, who is now living as a courtesan in Bikampur

**Sakshi** (*Sahk-shee*)—Razia's older sister in the dera, and the finest sitar player in the world

**Salim** (*Suh-leem*)—Razia's deadname, used by jerks

**Shahrukh** (*Shah-rookh*)—Razia's uncle, and a powerful subahdar

**Shiv** (*Shihv*)—a eunuch servitor at the palace in Bikampur (the nice one)

**Sikander** (*Sick-under*)—the master-at-arms of Nizam, and one of Razia's least favorite people

**Tariq** (*Tah-rick*)—the older of Razia's two cousins, and the subahdar of Lahanur

**Udai Agnivansha** (*Oo-day Ugh-nee-vuhn-shuh*)—maharaja of Bikampur, and father of Arjun

**Varsha** (*Vahr-shuh*)—Razia's guru, a mother-like figure who runs the Bikampur dera; often called Ammi by her celas

**Vikram Sharma** (*Vih-kruhm Sher-mah*)—Bikampuri noble who possesses a lovely khanda

**Viputeshwar** (*Vih-poo-t(h)esh-wahr*)—grandfatherly courtier in Rajkot fort

## PLACES

**Bikampur** (*Bee-kahm-poor*)—a city in Registan ruled by the Maharaja Udai Agnivansha

**Daryastan** *(Duh-ree-ah-stahn)*—the subcontinent on which the story's principal action takes place

**Kolikota** *(Koh-lee-koh-tah)*—the coastal city where Lakshmi was born, currently part of the Virajendra empire

**Lahanur** *(Lah-huh-noor)*—a Nizami subah to the north of Zindh, ruled by Razia's cousin Tariq

**Mahisagar** *(Muh-hee-sa-grr)*—a sultanate on the west coast of Daryastan, ruled by Ahmed Shah and home to Prince Karim

**Nizam** *(Nih-zahm)*—the capital city that lends its name to the sultanate of Nizam, the greatest empire in northern Daryastan

**Rajkot** *(Rahj-kot)*—a fort in Mahisagar

**Registan** *(Reh-gih-stahn)*—a desert land famous for its warrior kings, its beautiful fortresses, and the wealth that flows through it on its way to or from the sea

**Shikarpur** *(Shee-kahr-poor)*—capital and largest city of Zindh

**Virajendra** *(Veer-uh-jehn-druh)*—a major empire to the south of Nizam

**Zindh** *(Zind)*—a subah of the sultanate of Nizam to the north and west of Bikampur

## TERMS

**cela** *(chay-lah)*—a disciple of a guru living in a hijra dera

**crore** *(kror)*—ten million

**dera** *(day-ruh)*—a hijra house

**dupatta** *(doo-putt-uh)*—a scarf or shawl-like garment worn by women to loosely cover their hair

**haveli** *(hay-vay-lee)*—a mansion or townhouse

**hijra** *(hee-jurd-uh)*—a member of a community of transfeminine individuals who were assigned male at birth

**jalebi** *(juh-lay-bee)*—a dessert made from a sweet batter deep-fried in pretzel-like twists

**kameez** (*kuh-meez*)—a long tunic with slits along the sides

**katar** (*kuh-tahr*)—a punch dagger with an H-shaped grip and a triangular-shaped blade, often used in pairs—if you're still confused, look at this book's cover!

**khanda** (*kuhn-dah*)—a word meaning sword, it normally refers to one with a straight, double-edged blade, usually with a spatulate tip and basket-like hilt

**kurta** (*koor-tuh*)—a long, tunic-like garment, similar to a kameez

**lakh** (*lahk*)—one hundred thousand

**lehenga** (*lehng-uh*)—an outfit consisting of a tight-fitting, midriff-baring blouse, a full A-line skirt, and a very large dupatta wound around the body for modesty

**maharaja** (*muh-hah-rahj-uh*)—the title given to the ruler of a Registani city-state

**mirza** (*meer-zuh*)—an honorary title used as a surname granted to Nizami princes of the royal line

**nirvan** (*nir-vahn*)—a surgical procedure that removes the genitals

**paisa** (pl. paise) (*pay-suh; pl. pay-say*)—a small monetary denomination equal to one one-hundredth of a rupee

**rupee** (*roo-pee*)—a common monetary unit, usually minted in the form of silver coins worth one hundred paise

**samosa** (*suh-mow-suh*)—a savory, deep-fried snack of pastry stuffed with a spicy filling

**sari** (*sah-ree*)—a long piece of cloth wrapped around the body as a garment, usually paired with a petticoat and blouse underneath

**shalwar** (*shuhl-vaar*)—a pair of loose-fitting trousers usually paired with a kameez or kurta

**subah** (*soo-buh*)—a province

**subahdar** (*soo-buh-dahr*)—a provincial governor

**talwar** (*tuhl-vahr*)—a word meaning sword, in the weapons trade it refers to a single-edged, heavily curved sword with a short hilt and disc-shaped pommel made for slashing attacks

**toradar** *(tore-uh-dahr)*—a matchlock musket

**zahhak** *(zuh-hawk)*—one of several different species of large, feathered, flying creatures that are capable of using their breath as a weapon, and which are ridden by Daryastan's nobility

**zamorin** [a corruption of Samoothiri]—the hereditary ruler of Kolikota

© *Spencer Micka Photography*

**Alina Boyden** is a trans rights activist, author, and PhD candidate in cultural anthropology. As an ACLU client, her case secured healthcare rights for transgender employees in the state of Wisconsin. Her work in cultural anthropology centers on the civil rights struggles of transgender women in India and Pakistan, and consequently she divides her time between the United States and South Asia. When she's not writing, traveling, or working on her dissertation, she spends her free time indulging in two of her childhood passions—swordplay and flying airplanes. *Stealing Thunder* is her first novel.